IMAGINARIUM 2013

INCLUDING THE WORKS OF

DON BASSINGTHWAITE

JOCKO BENOIT

TONY BURGESS

PETER CHIYKOWSKI

DAVID LIVINGSTONE CLINK

ROBERT COLMAN

PETER DARBYSHIRE

INDRAPRAMIT DAS

A.M. DELLAMONICA

DAVE DUNCAN

AMAL EL-MOHTAR

M.A.C. FARRANT

GEMMA FILES

GEOFF GANDER

LISA L. HANNETT & ANGELA SLATTER

CLAIRE HUMPHREY

MATTHEW JOHNSON

MICHAEL KELLY

BARRY KING

CATHERINE KNUTSSON

HELEN MARSHALL

SUSIE MOLONEY

MATT MOORE

SILVIA MORENO-GAR

DOMINIK PARISIEN

A.G. PASQUELLA

IAN ROGERS

J.W. SCHNARR

CHRISTOPHER WILLARD

WITH AN INTRODUCTION BY TANYA HUFF

FIRST EDITION

Imaginarium: The Best Canadian Speculative Writing © 2013, edited by Sandra Kasturi & Samantha Beiko
Cover artwork © 2013 by GMB Chomichuk
Cover design © 2013 by Samantha Beiko
Interior design and layout © 2013 by Danny Evarts
All Rights Reserved.

Distributed in Canada by
HarperCollins Canada Ltd.
1995 Markham Road
Scarborough, ON M1B 5M8
Toll Free: 1-800-387-0117
e-mail: hcorder@harpercollins.com

Distributed in the U.S. by
Diamond Book Distributors
1966 Greenspring Drive
Timonium, MD 21093
Phone: 1-410-560-7100 x826
e-mail: books@diamondbookdistributors.com

ISBN 978-1-77148--149-6

CHIZINE PUBLICATIONS
Toronto, Canada
www.chizinepub.com
info@chizinepub.com

Proofread by Michael Matheson

Canada Council   Conseil des arts
for the Arts   du Canada

We acknowledge the support of the Canada Council for the Arts which last year invested $20.1 million in writing and publishing throughout Canada.

ONTARIO ARTS COUNCIL
CONSEIL DES ARTS DE L'ONTARIO
50 YEARS OF ONTARIO GOVERNMENT SUPPORT OF THE ARTS
50 ANS DE SOUTIEN DU GOUVERNEMENT DE L'ONTARIO AUX ARTS

Published with the generous assistance of the Ontario Arts Council.

Printed in Canada

the best canadian speculative writing

IMAGINARIUM
2013

EDITED BY

SANDRA KASTURI
& SAMANTHA BEIKO

WITH AN INTRODUCTION BY TANYA HUFF

ChiZine Publications

To Dr. Runte,
Thanks for the support!
Always good to see you.
Lethbridge ComicCon
2014

table of contents

introduction to imaginarium 2013: in which i speculate

TANYA HUFF

If you're a Canadian writer of speculative literature and if you attend SF&F conventions—the fan run kind, not the for-profit Creation monstrosities—then I guarantee that at some point in your career you'll end up on a panel about the differences between Canadian and American genre fiction (where American refers to those from the United States rather than the inhabitants of either North or South America). I will further guarantee that this panel will take place at a Canadian convention. Because Americans don't care.

But we do.

Why? Why do we continuously try to define what specifically it is about our genre voice that makes it different from the Americans?

I suggest that we are in genre as we are in life.

The search for Canadian identity is so pervasive that it's become a major part of our Canadian identity. Ask any twelve of us what it means to be Canadian and you'll get fifteen different answers; four of them in French. But while we may not be able to agree on what we are, the one thing we can agree on, from coast to coast, from north to south—or as far south as we go—is that we're not Americans.

And we're polite.

Politer than Americans, at least.

Although I have a friend who suggests we're not polite, we're passive aggressive and, in all honesty, I don't think she's wrong. We apologize when someone steps on our feet, for crying out loud. Although you'll notice she's merely making a suggestion; were she American, she'd probably be more definitive. But I digress.

So, what are the differences between Canadians and Americans?

Go as far north as you can go in the US—excluding Alaska—and that's as far south as you can go in Canada. We live in a country where the environment can kill us for six months of the year. A little less in some places, a little more in others. Is it any wonder we're polite? The last thing you want to do is piss off the person who might be the only person available to pull you out of the ditch in a blizzard. On the other hand, I bet they don't want to do that in North Dakota either.

We have more real estate and one tenth the population.

They got the Irish and we got the Scots; which is why they have politicians with personality and our banks don't fail.

Thanks to the presence of the North West Mounted Police, our west was never particularly wild.

Our answer to "Truth, justice, and the American Way!" is "Peace, order, and Good Government." Note the lack of a Canadian exclamation mark.

We were not as overt in our attempts to destroy the culture of our First Nations, but we are just as culpable.

We have two official languages, we're a mosaic not a melting pot, and our head of state is an unelected, soon to be great-grandmother who lives in another country entirely and most of us are okay with that. Enough of us believe that the government has no business in the bedrooms of the nation to allow the government to enforce the belief that they have no business in the bedrooms of the nation. Our government is parliamentary not representational and a sizable number of us have no idea what the hell is up with that whole electoral college thing they've got going on south of the border. Although, in fairness, that last point may be more of a similarity than a difference.

Socialized medicine may be tottering, but most of the time we can judge how sick we actually are by how fast we jump the queue when we need to see a specialist.

Some of us do say eh, although not as often as many Americans think we do.

It's been said that when you flatter an American they accept it as their due, but when you flatter a Canadian, we think you're trying to sell us something.

And how does any of this make our speculative lit different than that written in the USA?

A while ago, I read an article that said Canadian writers use more qualifiers than Americans. We don't tend to make definitive statements. (See what I did there?)

According to Wikipedia, we've been at it since 1896 when Ida May Ferguson from New Brunswick published *The Electrical Kiss*, set in late 20th century Montreal, under the pseudonym of Dyjan Fergus and

I suspect only Canadians would still be working on a definition one hundred and sixteen years later. Wikipedia is a little sparse otherwise, although as I'm mentioned a number of times, I don't want to sound like I'm complaining. In 1992, David Ketterer wrote *Canadian Science Fiction and Fantasy*, 228 pages of what some called an annotated bibliography while others commended the territory travelled. Ketterer's book was published by Indiana University Press which either speaks volumes to the Canadian inability to see value in our own work or could merely indicate that Indiana had extra grant money in 1991.

I think that the paranoia in our national psyche makes it into our writing. I think that we come from a place where "the other" is not only acknowledged, but supported, by law, and that gives us an unique ability to give our antagonist a voice, and to develop the stories we tell in a non-linear manner. I think that our willingness to ensure a certain basic level of security allows us to take risks in our writing that someone who might lose everything to a hospital bill can't. I think the amount of empty space pressing down on the thin line of population hugging our southern border allows us a greater insight into those trembling souls huddled around a hundred metaphorical campfires, their backs to the dark. I think our national awareness of things larger than us, dangerous and completely beyond our control gives us an advantage when it comes time to populate that darkness.

But most importantly, I think our constant questioning ensures that we give all facets of our stories their due.

And I think that this volume of the best in Canadian speculative fiction proves that we're damned good at what we do.

TANYA HUFF
ONTARIO, 2013

the best canadian speculative writing

IMAGINARIUM
2013

blink

MICHAEL KELLY

This story starts here, at this first line. First lines are important. The first draft began with this line:

"I thought you'd be taller," she says.

I blink. "Me too."

She laughs. A good start, I think. Every story needs a good beginning.

"And," I add, "I thought you'd look like your LoveMatch.com profile picture."

"Me too," she echoes, smiling. Then, smile fading, "That's some other me."

I pick up my beer glass, the cardboard coaster stuck to the bottom. "We all have some other version of ourselves," I say. "Other identities. Avatars. It's the new reality."

"Do you write science fiction?" she asks. "Your profile said you were a writer."

I grin, gulp beer. "Yes. That's one version of me."

"Oh," she says, disappointed.

"What?" I ask. "What is it?"

She sips her drink, some fruity concoction. "Nothing really," she says. "I don't read that stuff—science fiction. Never appealed to me." Her lips circle the straw, suck. "I thought we might talk about books. Writers."

I try a joke. "It could be worse. I could write horror."

She stares at me. Still good, I think. Characterization. Every story needs good characters.

We are quiet a while, sipping our drinks, glancing around the bar. Actually, a bar is too cliché. I'll try to keep the clichés to a minimum. It isn't my strong suit.

Instead, we're at the . . . zoo. It's a brisk day. High grey sky knotted with thick dark clouds. A chill breeze. Damp and salty. Autumn, then

We're at the ape house, watching one of the male primates masturbate.

I clear my throat. "We can, you know," I say. "If you like."

She blinks, puzzled.

"Talk about books," I say. "I'm not completely inept. I have read outside my genre." I cough. "On occasion."

She laughs, and I relax. It's a good sign. I thought we were heading for a rough patch, but the story is progressing.

After the ape house is the lion's den. The lions lay still, sleeping or dead. The clouds are thinning; the day brightening.

"What are you working on?" she asks.

"Hmmm," I say, distracted, staring at the dead lions.

"Your writing. What are you working on?"

I turn away from the dead animals. "Why don't we talk about you?"

"I . . . I," she starts, but just shrugs.

Of course, I haven't really constructed her yet. She's mostly me. A facsimile. Another avatar.

"Mabel," I say, and it's an old-fashioned name but she seems pleased with it. "I'm sorry, Mabel, but your profile was a bit sparse. You're a . . . paramedic?"

No reaction. She's as dead as the lions. "An actress?" I say, hopefully.

A weak smile. She says, "A writer."

I stare at her. Then I laugh. She grimaces. A lion yawns. Not dead, then.

"Sorry," I mutter. Too easy, I think. Too cliché, recreating myself. Lazy writing. Yes, write what you know. Still, it's lazy.

She's quiet, wide-eyed, looking around the zoo. She blinks, and something shifts, changes. It's like a television screen winking off.

Salt air and cool wind. Dark wet sand underfoot. We're at the . . . beach? Sky like an Etch-A-Sketch. Still autumn, then. All this scene-jumping isn't good. Revisions are needed.

"You didn't answer my question," Mabel says.

Further up the beach, in the shallow tide, there's a desk with a laptop open on it. There's a dark figure sitting at the desk, hunched over, typing. My eyes are wet. From the sea-wind.

"I . . . I, hmmm," is all I can muster.

She sighs, impatient, a tad angry. "Your writing." She's staring at the figure in the foamy surf, typing, as if addressing them, not me. "What are you working on?"

4

"Short stories," I answer. "My favourite form. Science fiction." I dry my eyes on a rough coat sleeve. "There's no money in it, though," I add quickly, defensively.

"Oh," she says, disappointment or regret tingeing her voice.

"What?" I ask. "What is it?"

She sips her drink, some fruity concoction. "Nothing," she says. "I just don't read that stuff."

It's as if we've already had this conversation. Where'd she get the drink? Was that a previous construct?

"I was thirsty," she says.

"Huh?"

She smiles, takes another sip. "The drink. I was thirsty."

It's quiet. Too quiet. The tide is soundless; the wind suddenly mute. My head hurts. We've reached the figure at the desk, bent to the keyboard, typing. There's nothing on the screen. It's white. Blank save for a large vertical black slash, a cursor, blinking like a judging eye. Then there's a choking, gasping sound and the dark figure slumps, falls into the dark tide and is carried out to sea. My eyes tear up. There's a pain in my chest. The world wavers, ripples, shifts again.

"What's happened?" I ask.

No answer. Mabel doesn't know. How could she?

But why don't I know?

Because you haven't thought it through.

Whose voice? A POV change! I blink. No, damn it, I'm not changing the point-of-view.

"No need," she says. "I will."

"You? You did that?"

Mabel smiles. "I didn't like him. Or you, for that matter. Not that there was any difference between the two."

He's trembling with rage. Another tilt, and there's a thrum in the air, like particles charging. His vision blackens, fades. He's shrinking, becoming less, or something else. "But you're only a character," he says. He blinks, curses her.

Blinking cursor.

She smiles. "Aren't we all?"

Mabel walks into the water, sits at the laptop and begins to type:

This story starts here, at this first line. First lines are important.

One thousand words later she stops and reads the story so far. Not satisfied, Mabel selects all the text and hits delete. She thinks she hears a tiny scream.

The screen is blank except for the infernal, blinking cursor, waiting.
Mabel doesn't know what to do.
She'll have to make something up.

nightfall in the scent garden

CLAIRE HUMPHREY

If you read this, you'll tell me what grew over the arbor was ivy, not wisteria. If you are in a forgiving mood, you'll open the envelope, and you'll remind me how your father's van broke down and we were late back. How we sat drinking iced tea while the radiator steamed.

You might dig out that picture, the one with the two of us sitting on the willow stump, and point out how small we were, how pudgy, how like any other pair of schoolgirls. How our ill-cut hair straggled over the shoulders of our flannel shirts.

You'll remind me of the stories we used to tell each other. We spent hours embroidering them, improving on each other's inventions. We built palaces and peopled them with dynasties, you'll say, and we made ourselves emperors in every one, and every one was false.

If you read this, you'll call your mother, or mine. They'll confirm what you recall.

By then, though, you will begin to disbelieve it yourself.

If you think on it long enough, you'll recall the kiss. I left it there untouched, the single thread you could pull to unravel this whole tapestry.

You'll start to understand none of these things happened the way you remember. If you read this, you'll learn how I betrayed you.

We gave ourselves names of power. We signed them in the guest book at the gallery. I called myself Faustine Fiamma, after a dream. And you: Rosa Mundi. Rose of the world, rose of alchemy. Flame and flower, two girls in flannel and training bras. We made up addresses in Paris, Ontario, because we could not speak enough French to have come from the other Paris.

Your father carried his sculpture, wrapped in brown burlap. One of the ones he'd done of you, as a smaller child, dancing. You whispered to me that now every art-lover in Ontario would know you had an outie.

We slipped away, outdoors: this much, I left you. In the garden was the sundial. A great barbed face streaked with verdigris. It told no time just then; the sun too low behind the curtain of purple blossom, the light pearly. Herbs grew in beds around the plinth. Thyme and rosemary both, probably, and a dozen other things; I don't remember them all. Only the warmed scents of them on the air. We walked counterclockwise about the beds, touching all of the brass plaques, which bore the names of the herbs in Roman capitals and in Braille.

You shut your eyes, and I wrapped my scarf about your head and tied it behind, and led you by both hands.

Here's where I stopped. To be safe. Here's where your father came outside and told us it was time to go. I think I made him realistic, don't you? Fox-bright eyes and hair, and a dozen pockets on his jacket; I think he really had a jacket like that.

You're thinking right now that you don't want to hear what comes next. Stop reading, then. I can make my choice without you, if I must.

Your father didn't enter the garden. He didn't take us out to the van or back to Toronto, not then. He didn't finish up with his friends in the gallery until after midnight.

No. You and I circuited the garden. After a while the sun went down, but the light in the sky lingered, grainy and soft like an old photograph. Bats darted overhead.

"It's nearly time," you said.

"Time?" I plucked a sprig of rosemary; I bit down on one of the leaves, and I placed another at the entrance to your mouth. You opened, tasted it; your breath warm on my fingertips.

"I've had enough of being blind," you said.

I untied my scarf from your eyes.

I saw your pupils blown open. Like those wells the glaciers grind in rock, deep and wide, breathing cold air.

You looked past me.

"Can you hear that?" you said. "A horse. Someone's coming."

And you fell down at my feet.

Grass crushed beneath you. I felt the tender shoots of it smear my hands when I reached under you. I lifted you, by your shoulders; I dragged you against my body but I could not raise you up.

You were awake, though. Your eyes huge and swimming dark, your lips parted, smiling.

"She comes for me," you said.

She came, indeed. I heard her horse stamp and breathe. I heard her stirrup chime. I felt her step on the earth. I kept my face turned down.

"Rosa Mundi," she said.

You always told me such vivid stories. I countered with stories of my own. We pirouetted through hours of fascinating lies. If we'd been a bit younger, or a bit more innocent, it would have been a game of let's-pretend.

Instead it was let's-become. We spun ourselves costumes to wear into the world. Our stories were about ourselves, the people we might be someday, the people we might love. Play was turning into practice.

I gave myself a dozen different fathers better than my own, who was no more than a cigar box full of yellowed Polaroids. You gave yourself a wise-woman to replace your mother, who was often drunk in those days. You related how she taught you to weave a chain of clover for luck in your dance recital, to burn an owl-feather to keep away nightmares. It was too bad she was a fiction.

Or so I thought, until she came for you.

"Queen of Air," you said, which was a phrase you had said before, amidst your tales. Your voice strained, winter-husky.

She laughed, and answered to it. "Rosa," she said. "My Rosa. You are mine, are you not?"

"Yes," you whispered. I pinched your arm, where it was palest and softest, but you twitched away. "Yes," you said again, nearly soundless.

"Not your father's muse. Not your mother's helper."

"No," your mouth shaped. Your lips began to darken.

"Not the one to warm your brother's milk."

"No."

"Not the one to pour your stepfather's wine."

"No." You arched your back. Your arm fell free of my embrace.

"Not your teacher's pet. Not the one to . . . What is it that you are to this one, Rosa Mundi?"

You tried to answer. Froth burst on your lower lip.

"She's my friend," I said to the ground.

Her laughter withered the grass around her feet. I saw it shrivel, spreading out from the toe of her slim brown boot.

I still had not looked at her face.

"What are the rights of a friend, Rosa Mundi?"

9

You were past answering by then. I could feel you shivering in long wracking waves.

All the stories you'd told me were true. Wonders and horrors.

I knew the shape stories took. I was a studious child.

"She's my love," I said.

By claiming it, did I make it true?

The Queen of Air heard me and stood still. No noise of boot on grass, no ring of horse-gear.

Only a moth in the thyme, a bat in the dusk, a gnat caught in the long strands of my hair.

"Faustine," she said.

I still wonder what would have happened if we had named ourselves different names that day.

"Faustine, maker of bargains. Bargain with me. Of what worth is your love?"

My first kiss: Dane Ellison, behind the portable, during the sixth grade Hallowe'en dance.

My second: Dane again, under the willow by the creek behind his subdivision.

My third kiss: you know my third. I left it in your memory just as it was. I know you have not forgotten, although you will never speak of it.

Those earlier kisses were to this one as ice cubes in a glass of tap water are to an iceberg, looming above and beneath the sea.

The Queen of Air, for I still have no other name for her, bargained with me. Even before she finished speaking, I felt the breath shock back into your body, the rigidity leave your spine. You turned against me, coughing and heaving. I found later a spot of blood upon the leg of my jeans.

Maybe we all get such offers, once or twice or thrice in our little lives. Maybe someone takes every one of us up on the mountain, shows us the breadth of the world, and tells us it could be ours.

Maybe, in our wisdom, most of us turn it down.

I took it. The breadth of the world was held in the span of my hands, spitting blood onto my pants.

I took the bargain. I took the choice from you.

The kiss: my grass-stained hands cradling your face, knotting in the wealth of your hair. You tasted of blood and rosemary.

Your lips shut for a moment against mine but your breath still came hard. You pulled away to pant through your mouth.

I watched your pupils narrow down, and the sinews in your wrist draw tight as your hand closed.

It closed on nothing. The Queen had turned away. The fur at the edge of her mantle brushed my elbow; I still have the scar, a pale frostburn.

You gulped air, wiped your mouth on your sleeve. You shook your head dizzily.

When I saw your eyes meet mine again—proper blue now, tear-wet—I touched your hair and smoothed it down and freed a broken stem from the strands.

You slapped my hand away.

"What will I do now?" you said, your voice still scraped raw. "Where else can I go?"

By the time your father had done selling his sculpture, the one of you as a little girl dancing, I had cleaned up everything. You, your mind, your face, my hands. All except for the spot of blood on my jeans, which no one noticed.

Some of the richness went: the royal purple wisteria dulled down to plain greenery, the sunset smeared and pale. Some of it stayed: the taste of herbs, and the brightness of your hair.

I left you the kiss, but you never let me repeat it. You met Jason Krantz not long after that, and you dated him most of the way through high school. I never saw you with another girl.

Jason Krantz used to corner you in the stairwell and rope your hair around his fist and pull your head close to his, seizing the tip of your ear between his teeth. He used to make you sit on his lap in the coffee shop, and he'd pinch your thigh if you moved too much.

I asked the Queen if I could do something about Jason Krantz. She reminded me of the terms of my bargain. I asked her about the clover-chains, the owl-feathers, the little protections she had given you once upon a time. She told me they had not been protections.

You went through a plump phase, and then through a phase where you were thin as a grass-stem, bent under the weight of your sweaters. You and I took to hanging out in one of the restaurants on Spadina where no one asked for ID. You would order Tsingtao while I ate chicken fried rice. If you stumbled on the way out, I would walk you home.

All of this happened just as you recall, and I am to blame.

I said you were my love. I made you stay.

I get to know, each morning, that I'm waking into the same world in which you live. I get to see you, every few months when you're back in the province. Sometimes I even get a stiff little hug, and my hand touches the paintbrush edge of your hair before you pull away.

(Not lately. Not since those things I said after your wedding. I wrote to apologize. You didn't write back.)

I get to hear, from my own mother, that you and your husband are in town over the holidays. I get to imagine you in your old house, sitting on the window seat. For a few days you and I get to share the same weather. I get to leave messages at your mother's house, and wait for your call, which does not come.

For this, I'm promised to a hundred years beneath the hill.

The winter before our graduation, you held the hand of your stepfather as he lingered in a morphine dream. You told me you'd forgiven him, and I watched your fingers go tight and bloodless on his. When he was gone you stopped wearing the gold cross he'd given you for your First Communion.

You said you'd go to prom with me. I bought a suit in the boys' department at Eaton's. A week before the night, you said you were going to get back together with Jason Krantz instead, and wasn't it great that you had found a real date. I went home silently and cancelled the order for your corsage.

You dropped out of Art, and passed History, and aced Chem. On the edges of your notes, you wrote your first name, and a blank line for your last, with hearts and question marks about it. Never Rosa Mundi, nor any other such name. You had stopped telling stories by then.

Sometimes I'd catch that wide dark look in your eyes. In the cafeteria, while you picked the chocolate chips out of your muffin. Outside the locker room, while you waited for Jason Krantz to pack up his football gear. Or in the Annex, as we walked past the dance studio, where you were no longer enrolled.

You still wanted to leave. You couldn't remember how.

I caught the bouquet at your wedding. It crumbled to dust in my hands, not right then, but later, in the hospitality suite, at the end of the night. The Queen and I agree on this: you are my love, and I will have no other.

You, however, have always been free to love as you will. I did not have the foresight to arrange it any other way, and for this I am grateful; I was not a cruel child, but I was a child. I could have made things so much worse.

There is a Faustine in a poem, you see, who I did not know when I chose the name. To love her is to court death.

You seem happy with your love, truly. Eric Farrar: a real person, a person you chose for yourself. He has given you a son. He likes trading stocks and baking cakes, he dislikes motorcycles and fitness enthusiasts, and he does not remind me of either your stepfather or your father. On your wedding day, Eric Farrar wore a lake-blue pocket square to match your eyes. You took his name.

I haven't seen the dark look on you in some years, now that I think of it.

The Queen comes, now and again, to watch you when you are near me. She breathes over my neck, leaving blisters. She reminds me that if I break my bargain, you must go with her. She tells me all I need to do is ask.

If I break my bargain, I will not spend a hundred years under the hill, and I will not have an icy Queen stirring the curtains of my bedroom, driving away any lover who might spend the night. I will not have to pant over the tiny scraps I have of you: a hair ribbon, a sport top you left at my house.

You will not have Eric Farrar. Your son will not have his mother. But you'll have what you wanted, all those years ago, in the garden.

If you read this, you can tell me: do you want it still? Does the Queen's voice ever call to you, out of my hearing, subtle and cold? Do you ever wake troubled, forgetting your dream, with a frost on your lips?

Are you opening my letters? Or will this one, like the last, be thrown away still sealed?

The Queen brought me that one to taunt me, I think; she left it on my bedside table, the envelope cold-parched and wrinkled by her fingertips. Your address was smudged a bit, as if by rain. Through the paper I saw the ghost of my own script, heavy and black.

This choice should not be all mine to make, but how can I compel you to answer me? Shall I stand beneath your sensible vinyl-framed bedroom window and cry out until you rise from your marriage bed?

Rosa Mundi, in which world will you bloom? In which world will I finally catch fire?

the ghosts of birds
HELEN MARSHALL

The ghosts of birds are difficult to banish:
they know no religion, answer no priest
and are so close to their living selves
that they are hard to identify.

Passing noiselessly through backlit windows
thumpless whole bodies
snow-ball heavy
that never break on impact.

The ghosts of birds are thickest in autumn
when blood-red kites sit light
on telephone wires that never
sag beneath their weight.

They howl and shriek at midnight:
no change in pitch for the dead.
The dead and the living mate easily.
It does not matter if they cannot touch.

All birds are dead.
Dinosaur poltergeists,
flashing from earth to heaven
but lingering in the open space.

They are their own echoes:
of noise,
of life,
the shadow passing overhead.

the last love of the infinity age

PETER DARBYSHIRE

I come back to life when the sleeper nuke Doc Apocalypse hid in the subway system goes off and destroys the city. Except I'm not really dead before that. I'm stuck in the Frozen Zone of the city with a few thousand other popsicles who got caught in the crossfire back when the Union of Soviet Super Comrades brought the Cold War home to us.

One minute I was standing there in the flower shop, a bouquet of flowers in my hand for Penny. Then there was the sudden white light as the Comrades' flash freeze hit. And for the next twenty years I was a block of ice in the flower shop, a bouquet of flowers frozen in my hand for Penny.

Then there's another flash of light, this one from Doc Apocalypse's nuke, and the next minute the ice melts away and I'm shaking uncontrollably as I thaw out in the ruins of the flower shop. I'm ankle deep in water. The roof of the shop has collapsed, and the clerk who'd sold me the flowers is scattered around the room in frozen chunks. He doesn't know how lucky he is.

The flowers have shattered in my hand and are just ice shards melting away in the water now. I leave them and crawl out through a narrow passageway left amid the fallen beams and ceiling tiles. I follow the light.

Outside, the city is melting. Waterfalls pour down the sides of buildings that are still standing. Other buildings have crumpled into themselves under the weight of the ice, or parts of them have broken off from the shock wave of the nuke and fallen into the street. The entire side of an office tower a few buildings away has come off completely, crushing all the cars and pedestrians frozen underneath it. People still sit in the offices inside, some of them blocks of dripping ice at their desks and conference tables. Others have been freed from their prisons like me and are stumbling around the skating rinks of their floors.

I watch a man in a suit and tie break his way out of a frozen cubicle a few levels up. He steps forward, into the air, because the rest of the office has fallen away. I don't bother yelling a warning to him. He never listens. He falls, screaming, out of sight behind the jumble of rubble in the street. He hits something metal on the other side and the screaming stops. No heroes come to save him. They're too busy trying to save us all.

Trinity flies overhead just then, ripping a white line through the burning sky. His suit is torn and scorched from the nuke, but he doesn't waver. Nothing can hurt Trinity. The people he loves, though, they're a different story.

Cries go up across the city at the sight of him. He doesn't look down at us. It's a day like any other.

I don't waste time watching him disappear into the clouds still mushrooming up from ground zero. I run down the street, out of the Frozen Zone.

The first time I thawed, I thought maybe the USSC had won the Cold War. Before I was frozen, it was always cities in some other country being turned into snow globes. Never here. When I stumbled out into the ruins of my city that first time, I thought they had detonated the nuke to finish us off. And when I saw Trinity fly across the sky, I thought he had come to save us.

Now I know better, of course. And I wish our fate was something as simple as being oppressed by a bunch of communist supers. You never know how bad things can get until things get that bad.

I hit the border of the Frozen Zone and keep running. I stumble a little, as I always do, when I leave the ice and set foot on the buckled asphalt of the street outside the Frozen Zone. Torn up by the nuke's shock waves. The air is a swirling fog of dust and shards of paper. Most of the buildings have collapsed, but a few stand here and there, skeletal grave markers looming over the remains of the city. Fires burn everywhere and no one comes to put them out. They're all trying to catch up to Trinity.

Everyone but me. I'm just trying to get home to Penny.

There are people on the streets with me. Ashen from the dust cloud, like ghosts. I don't bother talking to any of them. I've learned all I can from them already, in the other times I've thawed. They are the ones who told me I haven't woken up into the Cold War. It's been over for nearly a decade, ever since Trinity found the USSC's secret space station and warped it back in time, flying one of the patterns only he understands around it until it winked out of existence. We found its remains later, when a water probe deep inside the moon drilled into the station. Trinity had sent the station back to a time where the moon had occupied the same point in space. The USSC were just more dust now.

The people on the street are the ones who explained to me that I've woken up into the Infinity Age, a time when everyone has a super power. Well, almost everyone. All those who got a shot of the super serum as children. There are still a few old-timers like me around, whose only power is lack of a power.

I run past them all, and they wave a greeting. They don't bother trying to talk to me anymore. They understand I'm in a race against time.

Cars and buses are scattered around the streets, some on their sides or flipped over, others crushed by pieces of metal debris I can't even recognize. There are a few that are still right side up, still in working order, but I ignore them. I know from past experience they're useless, their electronics knocked out by the nuke.

I run even though I'm out of breath. I'm not in good condition after being frozen for twenty years. And I still feel a little frosty. But I have to run. Such little time.

I met a woman once, one of those ghosts, who was going through all the cars looking for a working phone. She said she just wanted to message her lover in Paris. He was too far away to ever reach again, she said, but if she could only see his face, or even read his words, all this would be bearable. I don't know that she's right, but I don't know that she's wrong either.

And she told me that some people had chosen to be frozen in their homes when the Cold War started, to wait for their partners trapped in the Frozen Zone. I don't know what Penny chose to do. Maybe she's in our house now, frozen in a cryogenic chamber in our bedroom, waiting for me. I have to get home to find out what happened to her.

I've never seen that woman again. I wonder if she ever found a phone that worked.

I reach the parking garage in record time. Trinity makes his second pass overhead as I hurry inside, trying to keep those extra few seconds. He rips the sky open in a line that intersects with the other one. He's too far away to see his face. I wonder, as I always do, what he thinks when he looks down at us.

The top floors of the garage have collapsed and are a jumble of wreckage, but the entrance and exit are still relatively clear of debris.

There are only a few hubcaps and a single side mirror that catches my reflection. I ignore what I see there. I pick up the mirror and go down to the lower levels, passing the cars I know I can't use. I find the one that still works two floors down. I use the side mirror to shatter the driver's side window and then toss it aside. The car's alarm goes off. I get in the car and hit the start button. I don't bother with the seat belt. I take the levels of the parking garage as fast as I can and drive out into the ruined street above. I want to make as much ground as I can before Cyborg stops me.

I smash through the debris on the street and knock the dead cars out of the way. I ignore the airbag that goes off and punches me in the face. I get maybe a block more than any other time before Cyborg leaps from the remains of a building that's been torn in two and lands on the street in front of me. His feet dig up more asphalt at the impact.

"Stop and produce identification for the vehicle emitting the alarm," he says.

Cyborg was one of the first supers, back before I was frozen. A self-made hero, not serum-made. He'd once been part man, part machine. Now he is part machine, part corpse. The metal parts of him are rusty where they're fused with his flesh, but most of that flesh is gone. He's half metal, half bone rattling around inside the metal. A skull is all that's left of his head, the implants from the power suit holding it in place atop the lifeless but still operating body. A metal chip dangling from his spine by some wires talks for the dead hero.

"Produce identification or I will be forced to make a citizen's arrest," he says.

I stop the car and get out. Trinity crosses the sky overhead once more, adding a new line. The light that shines forth cuts through the smoke and haze, but not in any way anyone wants to see.

Cyborg ignores him. "The car alarm indicates a crime in progress," he says. He lifts an arm with a gun mounted on it. The gun is the kind you normally see mounted on attack helicopters. But the end of it is splintered away, like something has exploded in the barrel. "Are you a criminal?" he asks, those empty eye sockets staring at nothing at all.

The hero is dead, but his cyborg circuitry survives. It's trying to follow its logic routines as best it can. There's no reasoning with it. I've tried too many times.

"I left my ID in my office," I say. "I'll just go get it."

And I run past Cyborg and continue down the street. He keeps the gun pointed at the car, which continues to sound its alarm.

In the air above me, a scattering of men and women, some in colourful suits, others sporting wings, chase after Trinity. Too late. Always too late.

I climb over a scorched refrigerator that's fallen into the street from somewhere, then dodge around a burning office chair. I jump over a tricycle with melted wheels, kick aside a mess of photo frames all fused together. I remember shopping with Penny in a department store for things for the house. My heart pounds in my chest so hard I think I may have a heart attack. Not for the first time, I wish I had joined the lineups for the super serum shots all those years ago.

But we weren't sure what it would do back then. The researchers who developed it said it was just a shot to help our bodies fight the new generation of superbugs. It was supposed to accelerate our defences, to help them adapt and evolve quicker than the bugs evolved. But even the scientists admitted they didn't know what the side effects would be. I don't think anyone could have predicted the mutations it caused in youth when they hit puberty, mutations that we came to call super powers.

Maybe if I'd been injected with the super serum too I wouldn't be staggering with exhaustion as I run home. Maybe I wouldn't be worrying about dropping dead in the street from a heart attack. Maybe I'd be leaping what was left of the buildings in a single bound. But it's too late for all that now.

The next time Trinity crosses the sky, the air around him explodes with blasts of all different sizes and colours as heroes and villains alike open fire on him with their weapons and powers. Trinity just absorbs them as usual. He's the most powerful hero of all, the recipient of a secret government variation of the super serum. So powerful he destroyed the lab and the scientists and the formula itself after he evolved, for fear it would fall into the hands of a villain. If he'd only known he would become the greatest villain the world had ever known, maybe he would have destroyed himself as well. Maybe.

I hit the intersection a few seconds before the bus. I pause and use the time to catch my breath as it drives up the street to me. The Human Cannon and Pulsar are on the roof, blazing away at Trinity overhead. The other heroes watch from their seats inside, unable to do anything from this distance.

The bus doesn't slow but I've learned to grab on to the side and pull myself in the open passenger door. Rally is behind the wheel as always, and he nods at me.

"You're early," he says, steering the bus around a couple of crashed taxis without losing any speed.

"I've been working on my route," I gasp.

It doesn't save me any time to reach the intersection a few seconds early, because I have to wait for the bus anyway. But hopefully the few seconds of rest will give me more energy when I need it later.

The inside of the bus is full of the heroes who can't fly or hover, who can't leap into the air, who can't join the fight against Trinity. Not unless someone can get a lucky shot in somewhere and bring him down for a few seconds. Then this batch and all the other buses and trucks and cars full of heroes and villains chasing Trinity across the city can pile on. Maybe they can stop him from rising up into the air again through the force of sheer numbers. Maybe they can finally stop him from ending the world again.

I sit in the front seat closest to the door, beside Siren, as always. She smiles at me, as always, and says, "Maybe this time."

I nod at her but don't say anything, just like usual. I work on taking as deep breaths as I can. I'm trying to supercharge all my cells with oxygen.

Siren was the one who'd first explained to me that Doc Apocalypse had set off the nuke to try to kill Trinity, not wreck the city. She said Doc Apocalypse had sworn to destroy all the major supers before one of them destroyed the world. Everyone had once thought him a typical mad genius, but now we all saw he'd been right about the future. For all the good it did us.

The nuke hadn't killed Trinity. It had done something far worse, Siren explained to me on one of our many bus rides. It had killed tens of thousands of people, among them Trinity's secret lover. Secret because a hero like Trinity couldn't reveal too many details of his personal life. It would make everyone he knew a target for villains. But there were rumors. Siren said she'd heard it was Electron Girl. The Leprechaun, who sat in a different spot in the bus each time, said he had it on good authority it was Shiva, but he wouldn't tell us what that authority was. Legion swore one of his ghosts had seen Trinity kissing the Manhattan Effect up in the sky one night.

It didn't matter. Doc Apocalypse had killed her with his bomb, whoever she was, and Trinity was going to bring her back to life. He always brought her back to life. And he always ended our lives in the process.

We drive for a few minutes in silence, except for the artillery sounds The Human Cannon makes and the sizzling in the air from Pulsar's blasts. And Rally's humming to himself as he steers around wreckage in the street. I've lost count of how many times I've done this with them, and I've never once seen him brake for anything in the road.

The next time I look at Siren, she's turned into Penny. She smiles at me, and I can't help but smile back, even though I know she's not really there. She takes my hand and puts it on her belly, and I feel the baby kick against my palm. So strong.

"Thank you," I say. Penny just nods and puts her hand on the back of my head. We rest out foreheads against each other for a moment.

Then there's the bang of displaced air as Masterminds teleports in overhead in the quantum sailer, just behind Trinity. Masterminds is getting closer and quicker each time. Maybe someday he'll figure out how to get here from his secret dimension before Trinity rises into the sky and starts his pattern, perhaps even before Doc Apocalypse sets off the nuke that's condemned us all. And maybe he can stop this all from happening.

But not this time.

The Masterminds clones all open fire at once with the guns mounted on the sailer. Purple beams lance out and strike Trinity, shells burst all around him with green flashes, a net that seems to be the opposite of colour hurtles through the air and wraps itself around him. The net is a new one. Masterminds is always experimenting.

And Trinity shrugs them all off. As he always does. He continues to fly along, ripping the sky open behind him and letting more of that white light through. He stares straight ahead, like he can't see any of us. Or won't.

Rally shakes his head and eases off the gas a little. "Checkered flag time," he tells me. Penny gives my hand a squeeze and then lets me go, and now she's Siren again.

"You'll make it one of these times," she says. "Maybe even this one."

I can see in their eyes that they all hope I can find Penny. Their loved ones are too far away for them to reach. The only way they have to see them again is to stop Trinity. But I have a chance at seeing Penny again, even as the war rages on. Maybe this *will* be the time.

The Masterminds clone flying the quantum sailer turns it in the air and accelerates after Trinity. The other clones all begin shouting instructions through loudspeakers.

"All flying heroes set up a screen between the Frozen Zone and 32nd Street," one of them says, fluid leaking from the helmet protecting his massive brain. Teleportation is hard on the Masterminds. "Those of you with projectile or plasma powers, concentrate them into a force wall. The others form a human wall behind them. Swarm him like a bee and try to bring him down to ground level. In the Trinity Museum Park if you can."

"Flying villains form a high-altitude blanket between the Trinity Museum Park and the point of our last teleportation," another of the Masterminds says, sparks flying from his helmet. "Force him down with everything you have. Ground-based units spread out throughout the same area. Grab him and hang on."

They're not orders for this time. It's too late. We've already lost again. We can't stop Trinity. They're orders for the next time. Trinity can hear them, of course, but there's nothing anyone can do about that.

Then Masterminds crashes the sailer into Trinity, and there's a purple flare from the new force field, but it doesn't matter. The sailer spins down into a residential neighborhood a few blocks away. Trinity weaves in the air a little, shaking his head, and then continues ripping the sky open.

Rally slams the button that opens the door and takes his foot off the gas completely. This bus full of heroes isn't going to make a difference in the fight now.

"Don't slow down until you're over the line," he says, and the others shout encouragement as I jump out the door and hit the street rolling. I know they want to come with me as I race back into the past, back to my wife and home in the suburbs and an era where there were no supers like Trinity. But it's too late for all of that now. It's too late for them.

I'm up and away instantly. I've done this so many times I know how to roll perfectly and come up running. I cross the street as the bus continues on past me. The Human Cannon and Pulsar keep on firing at Trinity, even though there's no point now. I guess that's what makes them heroes.

The sky is on fire from everyone trying to stop Trinity. It's actually burning in places. The flames suck away the oxygen, and I have to take deeper and deeper breaths as I run, but it seems like I'm filling my lungs with nothing at all.

I sprint down a couple of alleys that I've learned shave off a few seconds from my travel time, and I emerge in a neighborhood of houses. The doors hang open, the windows are shattered. No one has lived in these places for a long time. I don't know what's happened here while I've been frozen, and I've never taken the time to learn. Not when I'm this close.

Trinity rips overhead in a different direction as I turn at the next corner. A howling sound I've never been able to identify follows in his wake. I think sometimes that it's the sound of his grief, but I don't know.

Then there's the quantum sailer lying wrecked in the ruins of a couple more houses, flickering in and out of existence. Some of the Masterminds clones lie in the street, their helmets shattered from the impact. Purple fluid is everywhere.

One of the gunners is still hanging off his gun, waiting. He seems me coming and fires the gun at the burned-out minivan in my path. The minivan vanishes with a whoosh of air sucking into the space where it had been. I run through the area without breaking stride. The Masterminds clone waves at me and then slumps behind the gun.

I don't stop to talk to him. I've already done that. He's the one who explained to me that Trinity can't do everything. Trinity can't raise the dead. Trinity can't stop time. But Trinity can turn time back. So every time Doc Apocalypse sets off the nuke that kills his love, Trinity rips open the heavens and resets the clock, taking us all back to the months before the nuke. Back to the time when his love was still alive. None of us knows what he does with her. Does he tell her what's going to happen? Do they look for a way to escape? Or do they just live each day like it's their last?

Then the nuke goes off, and Trinity throws himself up into the sky to rewind it all again. To rewind us again.

We're all trapped in his dream.

I can't blame him, really. I understand. I hope to hell all the heroes and villains manage to stop him someday. But I understand.

I turn again at the next intersection, where four cars have somehow managed to crash into each other, and there it is. My home. The house I shared with Penny before I was entombed in the Frozen Zone. I run across the neighbours' lawns to get at it, jumping over the fences and hedges. A house is burning now because of the debris that's fallen from the sky. Smoke alarms are going off inside all the other houses, and people stagger out of their homes. Neighbours I don't recognize. More ghosts. They point up and scream as Trinity passes overhead one final time.

I hit our lawn and cross it in a couple of steps. I have no air left in my lungs at all now. I won't be able to speak if I find Penny inside. But I still might be able to hold her. It's been my best time yet. I've never made it past the burning house before.

I touch the door handle with my fingertips—

—and then there's a flash of white light, and the whole world screams.

too much is never enough

DON BASSINGTHWAITE

The bullets hit before Marco even heard the sound of the guns that fired them. The first ones slammed into the back of his shoulder as he ran, burning like hot wires, only heavier. The impact almost knocked him down. He managed—in his mind at least—to take a couple more long, terrified steps before more wires lanced through him. His legs went numb and stopped working. Marco did a face plant onto the hard tile floor. The fall knocked the wind out of him. Adrenaline and terror kept him going, dragging him along on hands and elbows and a slick trail of his own blood. His tie, caught under his chest, pulled at his neck with every movement.

You got greedy, Marco. They were waiting for you.

Footsteps echoed through his dying. He saw their boots. Corporate security on either side of him. They didn't fire again or try to stop his slow escape. Marco kept crawling. He'd shit himself. The smell of it mingled with lingering traces of floor cleaner.

"He's down, sir." One of the security guards on his comm. "Yes, sir. No, sir. Bleeding heavily. Lower spinal damage, I think. Still fighting, though. Definitely a fighter." Pause. "He probably will." Pause again. "I understand." A click as the guard changed comm channels. "Clean-up, standby."

That was it, then. At least you're making a big mess for them.

Marco slid a little farther.

Along the hall, a door opened. New footsteps came down the floor. The guards fell back.

Marco crawled.

A man in a blue suit crouched down beside him. Marco twisted his head against the noose of his tie to look at him. The man had a plastic smile.

"Marco Cole," he said, "how would you like to live?"

Music, fast and hard, woke him up—fast and hard. The leap to waking left his head pounding. "Off!" he groaned. "Off!"

His cell, nestled in the induction cradle of the console on the side of the hotel room, winked obediently into standby. The music left behind the heavy silence of soundproof walls. Marco rubbed his eyes with both hands, bringing specks of coloured light to the darkness behind his lids. Then he threw back the sheets. And stood up.

That still felt so good.

"Lights."

Illumination flicked on, left him blinking. The corporation hadn't touched his eyes. Even if they had touched almost everything else.

A mirror filled the place of what would have been the window in another hotel. Or in a more expensive room in this one. Not that there was that much out there to see. He'd had the view on the flight in two weeks before. Qingaut was a corrugated steel pucker of a place, warehouses and secure compounds squeezed between the bulk of the complex that housed the hotel—among other businesses—and the bustle of the only deep water port on Canada's northern coast. The warming Earth had made deserts out of prairies but it had also made mining and drilling the resources of the Arctic profitable, and what came up from the ground needed to be shipped out to a world eager for it. The airport outside town and the rail lines that converged on the port were like skid marks smeared out across the marshy tundra. Nobody came to Qingaut for the sights.

Marco preferred the mirror anyway. It seemed almost sick, but he hadn't been able to stop looking at himself since . . .

Since.

He dropped into a crouch, brought his hands up, and made a few quick jabs at the air. Muscles he'd never had before bunched and slid. It didn't take much to get them warmed up, to get blood flowing through them again after an evening's nap. Marco spun, shifted his weight, leaned back, and snapped a leg up in a sharp kick. Stopped his motion at the imagined strike point and held the pose. He'd never been so fast. So flexible. He clenched his jaw and a face that was his but stronger, more sculpted, tensed.

So damn *hot*.

Marco lowered his leg, stood straight, and turned for himself. Every little imperfection was gone. Every mole and scar. The barbed stripe of a tattoo that had crawled up his left side from hip to armpit, product of an adolescent need to rebel. He missed it less than he thought he would.

His cell went off again, the snooze function of the alarm bringing it back to life to make certain he'd gotten out of bed. He hadn't actually needed it since the corporation had done its work on him, but it was force of habit to set it. A reminder that he had work to do. He pulled his gaze away from his naked reflection and went to get dressed.

"Time?" he asked.

"8:50 P.M.," answered the cell. "You have one hour and forty minutes before the scheduled start of your next bout."

There was a picture stuck up inside the door of the room's shallow closet, a man with a perfect smile and intense eyes. His shirt collar was open and his tie hung loose. The picture had been enlarged and cropped out of another photo, but there were hints of a good time going on in the background.

"Perfect," said Marco.

"The essential specifications from corporate were simple, yeah?" said Dr. Ting. "Better. Faster. Stronger." She smiled, full lips stretching wide to show her teeth. "Sexier."

Marco stared into the mirror and touched a face that was less familiar than Dr. Ting's. "What—?"

She didn't let him finish the question, but just rolled on, a mild Caribbean accent softening the clinical descriptions. "Oh, the basics are nothing out of the ordinary for a high-en' military op." That smile again. "Enhanced strength. Wired reflexes. Protection for organs an' vulnerable parts. Extensible tendons for flexibility. You'll find soldiers an' veterans around the world with comparable enhancements. Not the same quality, of course. You get what you pay for and corporate did not want a Frankenstein. You were approved for some additional procedures, as well. Accelerated cellular repair. Improved muscle memory—"

Marco glanced away from the mirror long enough to look at her blankly. She rolled her eyes and took the mirror away from him. "You'll learn how to use your strength an' speed more quickly. You'll heal faster. Oh, an' this—this I am proud of."

She pulled out a tablet and brought up a video. Marco looked at his unconscious face—his new face, not his old one—and watched Dr. Ting's hand smash a surgical hammer into his nose. He flinched instinctively. She snorted. "Don' be a baby. Watch." She drew a finger across the tablet surface, accelerating the frame rate.

Marco watched his broken nose rebound, reshaping itself, bruises draining away.

"Smart fibres integrated into your facial structure," said Dr. Ting. "Coupled with your accelerated healing factor, it means someone could hit you across the face with a cricket bat half a dozen times an' within a few hours you'll look fine." She patted his cheek. "Nothing is going to spoil that mug, my pretty boy! You can take a punch, shake your head, an' walk away."

He looked back at her. "Is that going to happen?"

Her face tightened as if she'd said too much. Her gaze darted away to focus on something—someone—behind him.

"Don't bait the doctor, Marco," said a voice he'd heard in his dreams for the last three months. "She did her job very well. We expect you to do the same."

Shoes clipped on the floor and the man in the blue suit moved into the room. He nodded at Dr. Ting and she turned away, disappearing as he had appeared. The man in the blue suit looked down at Marco, smiled his plastic smile, and said, "You can call me Jameson." He held up a picture of another man with an open collar, loose tie, and intense eyes. "This is Eric Roy. You're going to help us make sure he dies."

Three months ago, Marco's reaction would have been shock or fear or disgust. Now he just felt numb. "Tell me more about him."

"There's nothing more you need to know."

"How, then."

Jameson patted his cheek just as Dr. Ting had, but with none of the warmth. Marco twitched his head away. That didn't seem to bother Jameson. His hand followed Marco's face and patted him again, harder this time. "We chose you because you're a fighter, Marco. That's all we want you to do. Fight and win." He stood back. "How much do you know about Stomp Brawl?"

It all came together. The body mods. Dr. Ting's comments. His gut should have dropped out from sheer fear. It didn't. Instead fear brought a rush of unexpected pleasure. It must have showed. Jameson's smile became a little more genuine. "The doctor didn't mention that particular modification, did she? Dopamine switch. I think you'll learn to enjoy it. Now . . . Stomp Brawl?"

Marco sucked breath. "I've seen it."

"Good. Because you're going to be a star."

Tej jumped to his feet when Marco opened the door into the hall. The shiny candy bar of his camera, clutched in his fist like a stainless steel ticket to fame, shot up even faster. Coloured light danced on the inside of Tej's glasses. If Marco looked closely he could see himself there, reflected in the heads-up display that linked to the camera.

"Take a break, Tej," he said. "There's nothing to see here."

"The fans want to see it all, Marco. Your ratings are on the rise." Tej had the always-bright voice of a natural entrepreneur. As Marco walked along the hall, he followed without seeming to watch where he was going, all of his attention on the shot from his camera. "How are you feeling tonight? Rested up?"

Play it up, came Jameson's voice like an echo. There had been trainers to teach him how to fight—he'd found out what Dr. Ting meant by improved muscle memory when he'd absorbed a master's knowledge of Brazilian Jiu-Jitsu in just a couple of days—but the man in the blue suit had taken a personal interest in teaching him how to use his new appearance.

Marco turned his head and looked into the camera. "I'm rested. The only one going to sleep tonight is my opponent. As to how I feel—" He slid an open hand across his chest, pulling the fabric of his shirt against his pecs, flexing as he moved. "I feel damn good."

Make them want you. Get them hooked. Everyone watches. We just need to make sure the right person sees.

He caught the movement of Tej's throat as he swallowed. "Yeah. Yeah, that's good. You know who you're fighting yet?"

Marco shrugged. "Does it matter?" He strode on along the hallway. Tej scrambled to keep up, all the time murmuring commentary to accompany his vid-stream.

The hall spit them out into a grubby lobby, gateway to the seething chaos and permanent twilight of the Big Alley that ran through the heart of Qingaut's main complex. Every roughneck rig worker, dirt-grubbing miner, and drill-monkey soldier stationed in the North with time off rode the resource trains or hopped a flight to blow his pay and a load at the biggest non-stop party between the Bering Strait and Greenland. The corporate suits assigned to this part of the world came, too; the junior execs sometimes mixed it up in the Alley, the more senior execs sticking to the higher floors of the central complex and ordering their pleasures by cell. The whole town smelled of oil and hot metal, fried meat, booze, and man-stink.

Perfect place for a Stomp Brawl. In the two weeks that Marco had been here, the population had doubled. Qingaut was a 24-hour riot. There'd been reports that some of the smaller mines were operating on skeleton crews. Everyone else had gone to watch the fights.

It wasn't just the usual roughnecks crowding the town either. Luxury jets were crowding the airstrip and private ships were locking up port space. Stomp Brawl might have started with videos of schoolyard fights in America, club brawls in Asia, and backroom bare-knuckle matches in Africa, but it had come a long way. Everybody watched Stomp Brawl, more people around the world than had ever watched professional wrestling or mixed martial arts back in the day. The model was different. There were none of the in-ring dramatics of wrestling. None of the rules that burdened MMA. None of the corporate control. No one owned Stomp Brawl. No one sponsored the games; they sponsored the cameras and the vid-streams that fed the spectacle to the world. Marco Cole, broadcast by Tej Majumder, brought to you by Toprail Fine Molecular Spirits: "Like angels grinding on your tongue."

It was a big step up for Tej. When Marco first met him, the vid jockey had been sponsored by Toprail's down market brand, Loose Gringo tequila.

The night's roster of fights had already started. Every shop, every grease joint, every bar, every rub and tug, every whorehouse along the Big Alley had a monitor showing some vid stream or another, all of them running banners for products or services alongside bare-chested men beating the crap out of each other. Or standing in the wings psyching and medicating themselves up to beat the crap out of someone. Or pissing themselves in advance of getting the crap beaten out of them. And these were still the bantam and lightweights, no-names ready to jump into the ring for notoriety and the hell of it.

Marco felt a flutter of empathy for them, just enough for the dopamine switch Dr. Ting had installed to kick over. His heartbeat picked up and his breath quickened, unease feeding pleasure. An eagerness for the fight flooded through him. The lightweights were no challenge. His body craved a challenge, the rush of real danger. He wanted the fight. He *needed* the fight.

Damn you, Jameson.

"Pick it up, Tej." Marco opened up his stride, forcing his way through the jostling crowd.

The shuttle from the airport pulled right into a bay underneath Qingaut's central complex. Marco felt a vague sense of disappointment. The freedom of Qingaut counted for something, but after months in the corporation's facilities he craved fresh air, even what little he could have caught beneath the mingled exhausts of the port. The atmosphere in the bay was stale.

And he felt like a lost freshman as he followed signs and arrows through the complex to the Stomp Brawl staging area. "Class?" asked the fat man working the sign-in desk.

Just because there were no rules didn't mean there was no organization to Stomp Brawl. Fans still wanted to see a fight that lasted past first contact. "Augmented super-heavy," said Marco.

The fat man lifted his head and looked him up and down. Marco knew what he was thinking. Most of the fighters who put themselves in the augmented super category carried the scars of brutal military service and the surgeries that had transformed them. Frankensteins.

"I had a good doc," he added.

Maybe he shouldn't have. The fat man snorted and bent back to his tablet. "Light heavy."

Annoyance burned Marco's face. "Augmented super—"

"Listen." The fat man raised his head again, slow like it was a burden. "Do you know how many guys try to prove themselves by fighting above their class? They end up kissing canvas. You want to show the world how hard you are? Don't get into a fight you can't win." He pointed, dismissing him. "Pick up your schedule over there."

Marco's ears thundered. He straightened up and turned around to face the next would-be fighter in line. "Hey, you—what class?"

The man wore a fringed leather jacket and a high and tight haircut; he had a gut but there was nothing soft about it. "Heavy," he grunted.

"Yeah?" Marco's fist pistoned into the man's jaw so fast he didn't even have a chance to flinch. Fringes flew as he reeled back into the next guy behind him. To his credit, he came back with a roar, charging at Marco with arms wide, going for a pin.

Marco stepped aside easily and tagged him with another punch over his kidneys as he passed. The other man groaned, his charge turning into a lurch that left him sprawled briefly across the sign-in table before he slid to the ground. The guy who had been standing behind him— easily as big or bigger—yelled something and started forward. Maybe they were friends. Marco dropped him with a high kick to the chest.

"Security!" yelped the fat man behind the desk. Across the room, three men in T-shirts tight enough to cut off circulation were already watching. Dopamine-induced ecstasy warming his body, Marco balanced on the balls of his feet, ready to take them on. His pulse was a hammer. The bigger, the better.

But the biggest of the three just studied him, then looked at his friends, twitched his head, and returned to leaning on the big barrel that served as a stand-up table. Marco took a deep breath, forced himself to relax, and stood straight. He turned back to the sign-in desk. "Augmented super-heavy," he said.

"Augmented super-heavy," the fat man repeated. His voice had risen a bit. He made the change on his tablet. "Blades, spurs, claws, or razor nails?" Marco shook his head and the fat man pointed again, a new direction this time. "Augmented super-heavy has a separate roster. That way."

"Thanks." Marco stepped over the fighter in the fringed jacket and went where the fat man indicated. He was in. So far, so good. Jameson was going to be happy with that.

Rapid footsteps behind him brought a new surge of fear and pleasure. He spun around to face a lanky, brown-skinned young man with a cam, flickering HUD glasses, and a shirt carrying a Loose Gringo logo. "Easy!" the newcomer said. "I just want to talk to you."

He hesitated as if waiting for permission, dark eyes still fixed on Marco's face. It was going to take a while to get used to that from strangers. Marco jerked his chin. The young man swallowed. "Thanks. My name is Tej Majumder. You're new, right? You got a vid jockey yet?"

Get acquainted with a cameraman, Jameson had said. *Someone eager. Someone who'll follow you like a puppy. Someone to catch every fight you win and every dump you take. You need to be on screen to get noticed.*

"Aren't you shooting me already?" Marco asked.

Tej hesitated, then lowered the camera. "I mean a dedicated vid jockey. If you do in the ring what you did back there, people are going to watch. They're going to want to watch anyway once they get a look at you."

That was the plan.

He named a price, a lowball percentage of what Tej would be able to get from sponsors and followers. Tej jumped all over it. "Deal," he said. "Anything you want while you're in Qingaut, you just say. I know people. I can hook you up. Booze, drugs, better food than most places sell—I know a guy who can get you *real* meat, hunts it out on the tundra. Companionship? Women? Men?"

Marco grabbed his arm before he could bring his camera back up. "How about information? Strictly off the record. No cameras involved. I want to know about a guy named Eric Roy."

"Why?" Tej asked, then backtracked at the look Marco gave him. "Yeah, sure. Who is he?"

"That's what I want to know." He turned Tej loose. "Find out for me."

A fist the size of a child's skull and studded under the wrappings with big bony warts slammed into Marco's belly. The pads of thick gel Dr. Ting had inserted beneath his skin and muscle absorbed the impact but the punishing force of the blow still doubled him over. The fist came in again. Marco sucked in a hot breath and writhed aside, then slid lower to avoid an elbow strike aimed at his head. Three quarters of the way to the mat. A vulnerable position and his opponent—the Junk Pile he called himself—knew it. Marco sensed movement as he hunched forward, ready to wrap arms twice as big as they should be and corded with misshapen muscle around his exposed torso, lift him off his feet, and slam him down hard.

Marco dropped even lower and those arms closed on empty air. For a moment his sweat-slicked stomach touched cold canvas then he slithered out from under Junk Pile's shadow. He twisted as he moved, sweeping both legs hard against the other man's shins.

Off-balance after his missed grab, pulled further off-balance by his massive arms and shoulders, Junk bellowed and pitched forward. Marco got his feet under him and rose, then darted forward to stamp hard at one of Junk's exposed calves.

Outside the ring, the crowd roared its approval at the reversal. Bodies crashed against the barriers that kept them back from the cage of the ring. More bodies leaned forward over the railings of the open floors above, nothing more than vague shapes beyond the brilliance of hanging lights. Whoever had designed Qingaut's main complex had probably intended this part of the Big Alley to be a tranquil atrium. They certainly hadn't designed it with Stomp Brawl in mind, but no one seemed to care.

Marco got in one good stomp, then Junk Pile kicked out like a mule, forcing him back. Junk took the opportunity to scramble upright. For a moment they circled each other, curled hands swaying in front of their faces, ready to take advantage of an opening, ready to block an attack. Marco could feel blood on his face, trickling over a cheekbone and from his lip, but Dr. Ting's smart fibres were doing their job. It was hard to tell how much damage Junk Pile had really suffered; like the muscles of his arms, the man's face was already lumpy and discoloured with bilious blotches and streaks. There was swelling along his left jaw line where Marco had landed a series of punches, though, and the pupil of one eye was noticeably larger than the other. Marco bounced forward a couple of steps and threw a light jab. Junk flinched away, earning a round of disdain from the crowd.

The bell rang—still an actual heavy, old-fashioned bell, not digital playback—and the round ended. Junk Pile retreated to his corner, lumbering like a damaged tank. Marco could feel the bout in the ache of his body, but he made a point of throwing one fist in the air, saluting the audience as if he'd already won. The crowd rewarded him with a wave of deafening enthusiasm. He could imagine people around the world watching on monitors and cells, at home, in bars, sneaking in the fight at work, all screaming along. He jogged back to his corner with a grin on his face.

Tej handed him a water bottle with one hand while the other kept the camera high. "Looking good, looking good!" he said. "The ratings— you're a hero, man. The ratings are through the roof! Other jockeys are starting to watch us."

"Yeah." Marco sipped from the bottle, then splashed water over his face. Medics stood by to look at his cut—most Stomp Brawl fighters didn't travel with support crew—but he waved them off. He knew the itch of a closing wound. By the time the next round started, all that would be left on his skin was a smear of blood.

"Mr. Cole?"

Marco glanced over and found a young man with slicked hair and a tailored suit waiting for his attention. Someone's assistant—someone important or security would never have let him near the ring. The young man held out a folded paper. "My employer invites you to join a party in his suite after your bout."

No question of whether he'd win or not. Marco could guess the invitation had been extended only after victory was clearly locked up. He took the folded paper and glanced at it.

It was what he'd been waiting for. *Qingaut Bathurst Exclusive Hotel, Suite 402. Hope you can join us. —Eric Roy*

He folded the paper and passed it to Tej. "I'll be there. Can I bring the camera?"

"Of course." Roy's assistant nodded and left.

The instant his back was turned, Tej stared at Marco with startled eyes and flicked a button on his camera. Just below the lens, a red light flashed beside the word "mute." "Eric Roy?" he said. "You're kidding me. That's no coincidence."

"Hey, Tej, you think your followers would like to see inside a Stomp Brawl after-party?" Marco asked. The vid jockey looked at him like he was crazy for even doubting it. Marco showed his teeth. "Then don't ask."

It hadn't been difficult for Tej to turn up information on Eric Roy: he was the CEO of Zinmar-MacKenzie, one of the major players in Arctic resource extraction. He wasn't one of the tightly buttoned, all-work type corporate executives, either. Young and energetic, he ran with a rich crowd and enjoyed a party. He hit his targets and spent his bonus appropriately—work hard, play hard, just like the roughnecks farther down the corporate ladder of the North. He wasn't shy about it.

He wasn't shy about his love of Stomp Brawl either. Word was that Roy had even gone a few rounds in a couple of local fights. More often, though, he was among the wealthy fans who travelled the world to see a tournament in person. The photo Jameson had given Marco turned out to be a frame capture from video of a Stomp Brawl after-party in Mumbai.

With a tournament in his own backyard, how could he not be in Qingaut?

How could he not invite the rising star of the tournament, a man with Hollywood looks and the attention of half the net, to his own after-party?

Marco tipped his head back and looked up the height of the atrium at the crowded balconies overhead. The Qingaut Bathurst Exclusive was up there. Posh suites. No mirrored window substitutes there. They would have real windows looking outside, plus a balcony overlooking the open space of the atrium. The figures that leaned over the railings were indistinct, blurred by the bright lights that illuminated the ring, made silhouettes by the midnight sun that lit up Qingaut's night and glowed through the atrium's glass roof, but somewhere up there was Eric Roy. Waiting for his killer.

The bell rang once, calling the fighters back. Marco dropped his gaze, sipped again from the water bottle, tossed it away. "Let's end this," he growled and stepped out into the ring.

Tej screamed encouragement at him, but his shouts were lost in the roar of the crowd and even that was only background noise in Marco's ears. Junk Pile came out cautiously, a little unsteady on his feet. Marco dogged around him like a surfer on the waves of the crowd. Junk tried to track him, lurching around in a circle, heavy muscles bunched, hands raised in defence.

Marco struck fast and hard. He lunged under Junk Pile's big, slow hands, yanked at his legs, and threw a shoulder right into his gut. Junk slammed onto his back hard enough to send tremors through the canvas. He tried to kick as he went down in an attempt to ward off his opponent but Marco kept hold of his legs and threw them back, pressing Junk's massive shoulders against the mat. A fist jabbed up. It would have been a weak blow from anyone else, but from Junk it could have been enough to daze him. Marco wove to the side. Someone else might have been afraid. Marco rode the rush of his fear.

He ground down on Junk Pile, forcing his hips even further back and trapping the outthrust arm between his side and Junk's own thigh. There was nothing the muscle-bound Frankenstein could do but try to batter at Marco's lower back. Not even his strength could give him the leverage to do any damage. Junk struggled against the compression, fighting to draw breath as much as he fought to break free. Bloodshot eyes suddenly filled with panic.

Marco drove his fist hard against the side of Junk Pile's skull, hammering at it until those frightened eyes rolled back and Junk's body went limp under his. It happened so suddenly Marco almost fell over. For a moment he was face to unconscious face with his opponent.

Blood trickled out Junk Pile's ear.

Marco heaved himself upright and thrust both arms high as the roar of the crowd filled Qingaut.

"When you've won enough fights, he's going to want to meet you," said Jameson. "He likes meeting the top Brawl fighters. He likes having them around him and he's got the money to make it happen." He shrugged. "Not that it takes much from what I've seen."

Marco's arms protested in silent agony as he curled a weight that was almost more than he had been able to press before. Dr. Ting might have given him muscles but they needed to be maintained. "So then what?" he asked through clenched teeth. "Roy meets me, I get him alone, and then I . . . do the job?"

He couldn't make himself say the words even though the fear behind them brought a warm trickle of satisfaction with it. His breath caught a little on his exhale as he lowered the weight. Jameson gave a smug smile, maybe at his squeamishness, maybe at the effect of the dopamine switch. "What exactly do you think I want you to do, Marco?"

A few crazy ideas had run through Marco's head. "Go ninja on him. Break his neck. Shoot him. Strangle him." He pumped the weight hard, trying to focus on the strain of exertion and not the artificial pleasure of his fear. He looked Jameson in the eye. "You could have stuck a bomb inside me."

Jameson actually laughed. The laugh was like his smile, all show and no substance. "You think I'm some kind of monster?" The grin stretched wide, showed teeth. "I just want you to shake Eric Roy's hand."

Marco dropped the weight, letting it crash into the floor. The impact made his feet tingle. Jameson didn't even blink.

"Well, not just shake his hand." The man in the blue suit—always the same blue suit—held out his right hand, spreading it wide, and motioned for him to do the same. Marco's palm was red and hot from the workout, ringed with yellowed calluses at the base of the fingers. Jameson traced a circle on his own palm. "You've got one more mod, single-use. Trigger it—we'll show you how—and you'll secrete a strong contact neurotoxin. It becomes inactive very quickly when exposed to air, five seconds or so, but it has excellent transdermal absorption properties."

A chill ran up Marco's spine. "I'm going to poison Roy with a handshake."

"Or any other way you can get your hand on his skin," Jameson said. "Whatever flicks your switch. It will work better in public, though, because it takes about fifteen minutes for the toxin to do its work and by the time Roy's kicking on the floor, I want you gone. Just walk away and no one will even think you were involved. How many times do people shake hands at a party or in a crowd?"

The chill didn't leave him. "I won't poison myself?"

"Do poison dart frogs worry about licking each other? Relax. We made sure you're resistant to the toxin. You'll be fine. You can't trigger it by accident and because the neurotoxin decays so rapidly, you're not going to accidentally poison anyone else. It's idiot-proof."

Marco's gut kicked over. "Someone's going to figure it out."

"That's where your cover comes in again. Make sure your camera man is with you. You'll have a video record of your alibi and the world's largest pool of witnesses."

Marco looked at Jameson with narrowed eyes. Jameson's plastic smile didn't falter. "You think I want you getting caught?" he asked. "I look after my people. You just worry about winning fights, getting famous, and making that one handshake. That's not too much for you, is it?"

Roy's employer was the key and the answer turned out to be no farther away than Marco's Stomp Brawl registration pack, tucked inside a slick little display about the history of Qingaut. Once a village so small its official population was zero because no one lived there year round, the whole port complex had been developed early in the century by a consortium of seven resource companies looking for a cheaper way to get their goods out of the Arctic. Over the years, companies merged, were bought, sold, and traded between corporations like hockey cards, until the seven members of the consortium had been consolidated into two: Dutta Geological and Zinmar-MacKenzie.

And if Eric Roy was CEO of Zinmar-MacKenzie, Marco had a pretty good idea that Jameson worked for Dutta. Maybe at a distance, through a twisting maze of corporate entities, but he worked for them. Canada's largest Arctic port was under the thumb of just two corporations and Marco would bet that soon it would be in the hands of just one. People had been killed for a lot less. Exactly how Roy's death would help consolidate power for Dutta Geological he didn't know, but Jameson probably had a plan for that, too.

Marco took a deep breath as the elevator—two big bouncers who could have stepped right out of Stomp Brawl super-heavy turned it into a private lift—stopped at the fourth floor of the Qingaut Bathurst Exclusive. Fear and excitement tore around in him like weasels on acid.

"Easy," said Tej. "It's just a party. You kicked ass in the ring. What do you have to worry about?"

"Just stay close."

"Hero, this camera is not leaving you all night!"

The doors of the elevator opened onto a party that had spilled out of suite 402 and colonized the hall. Marco recognized other victors of Stomp Brawl bouts, their faces more bruised and swollen than his. A couple gave him a nod of recognition; others didn't look up from earnest conversations with well-dressed, but not-so-well-connected fans. Another bouncer at the door made sure they kept to their place on the fringe. He glanced over Marco and Tej, though, and ushered them right on through.

Walking into the party proper was like walking into a warm embrace that was only a lingering touch away from turning into something more. Smells unlike anything the Big Alley had to offer enveloped Marco. Good food. Fresh meat that smelled of herbs and spices instead of stale fry oil. Wine and liquor—a pretty, young server slipped past with a tray of cocktails that looked hand-mixed rather than pre-poured, leaving a lingering scent of lemon and orange in her wake. None of the sweat, exhaust, and industrial grease that pervaded the rest of Qingaut.

Not that the atmosphere was refined. The music was as loud and driving as a nightclub and nearly as varied. Marco found he couldn't tell who in the crowd was corporate, who was just extremely rich, and who was simply there as a companion or entertainment. The mods they wore were subtle, the cosmetic enhancements less so. Brazilian Portuguese, Russian, Mandarin, and Hindi crossed the room as frequently as English.

The lights of the Stomp Brawl ring flooded through the windows that formed one wall of the suite. The balcony on the other side was crowded with cheering guests. A roar signalled a solid hit from the fight going on below—a roar echoed inside the suite as the scene was repeated on the dozens of vid-screens mounted on every available surface.

"Why come all the way to Qingaut if you're not going to bother watching the tournament live?" he asked Tej. The vid-jockey just laughed.

"You think it's too much? Sometimes just being close is enough."

Not all the screens were set to streams of the fight. Marco caught sight of his own image on one of the biggest screens. Someone had set it to follow Tej's feed. A little murmur spread through the crowd as they recognized their own party in the background of the shot, and turned around to look for him. Scattered shouts and applause broke out when they spotted him. Marco's wave of acknowledgement came more out of numb reflex than any conscious thought.

Tej groaned and flicked his camera onto mute for a moment. "What the hell is wrong with you, Marco? Put a little life into it. Get something to drink. Get out there and mingle."

Marco's stomach tightened with mixed fear and pleasure so intense it made his head swim. He tried to push past it. "I need to find Roy first," he muttered.

"Say hi to the host, sure. Someone raised you right."

"Yeah. That's it." Marco stretched his neck, peering over the crowd—and found Roy like the sun at the centre of his own little solar system as people paused to greet him, then moved on. A trio of Bollywood starlets clustered around him while their own vid-jockey worked the angles. Roy grinned for the camera, teeth flashing as bright as the intense eyes that had looked out from Marco's photo for so many weeks.

The CEO of Zinmar-MacKenzie stood so close under the screen set to Tej's feed that he probably hadn't noticed Marco's arrival yet. Marco clenched his hand into a fist, then forced it open again. "This way," he said.

He didn't bother to check to see if Tej followed him, but just pushed into the crowd. Manicured hands reached out to slap his arms and back as he passed. Praise and congratulations for his victory swelled around them. He barely felt or heard either. Only the most utterly oblivious fans tried to cling to him or failed to get out of his way.

Roy was facing away when he emerged from the crowd, still occupied with the trio of actresses. Marco hesitated for a moment. How did you greet the man you'd been sent to kill?

"Mr. Roy?" he said. "Eric?"

Roy swung around, opening up a good view of the starlets—and of the man who stood on his other side. Shock drove a spike of dopamine through Marco.

Cool as chrome, Jameson gave him a plastic smile.

Marco froze. Roy didn't seem to notice. "Marco Cole!" Teeth and eyes flashed in a grin that was everything Jameson's wasn't. "I am enjoying your fights, sir!" He stuck out his hand.

Jameson's face twitched in anticipation. His chin rose just slightly in almost imperceptible encouragement. *Do it.*

Marco reached for the offered hand—

—and missed it as Roy spread his arms and stepped in close to give him a back-slapping hug. "You're going to be huge, damn it! Huge!"

Marco's deadly palm stuck out uselessly in the air behind him. The man wore a jacket. Skin-to-skin contact, Jameson had said. Marco bent this arm, thumping Roy's back in return. Over his shoulder, Jameson's mouth had tightened into a thin, cold line.

The starlets laughed as if nothing at all was amiss. Roy turned at the sound, one arm staying around Marco's shoulders as he pulled him forward. "Marco, the Alahan sisters. I think you'll recognize them from their movies. More proof that everyone loves Stomp Brawl."

"Not just for the fighting, Eric," said the tallest of the three. Her eyes roamed over Marco as hungrily as Tej's camera. One of her sisters laughed again and poked an elbow into her ribs.

"Careful of that one, Marco," Roy said. "If you think some of your opponents in the ring have been tough . . ." He turned Marco, bringing him face to face with Jameson, the hard set of his mouth once more plastic and mild. "And now the exception to the rule. VP of Arctic

Operations for Zinmar-MacKenzie, Evan Cameron. First time I've ever managed to drag him to a Stomp Brawl tournament and I still don't know why he agreed to come."

Because, Marco thought, he wanted to watch his boss die. He wanted to step up and take control in the chaos afterward. Dutta Geological had nothing to do with this.

The man he knew as Jameson just smiled and self-consciously slid his hand into his pocket.

"Hey, none of that." Eric Roy pulled away from Marco and grabbed Jameson's arm. "He's not going to bite. Shake hands with him."

Jameson's eyes flicked to Marco.

We chose you because you're a fighter, Marco. That's all we want you to do. Fight and win.

Shock and fear ebbed before a cleansing certainty. Marco smiled. "That's right, Evan. Come on." He stuck out his hand and watched Jameson swallow—then stand straight and give in to Roy's urging.

His eyes didn't leave Marco's as he returned the handshake. His grip was clammy, but it was solid.

"There you go," said Roy, slapping them both on the back. "You boys get to know each other. Marco, tell Evan something about Stomp Brawl. Evan—well, whatever. I'll be back." He turned away, offering his arms to the Alahan sisters. "Ladies . . ."

As soon as Roy's back was to them, Marco squeezed. Not hard, but enough to keep Jameson from pulling away. The man who had turned him into a killer stiffened. "Don't do it," he said under his breath.

"Give me a reason not to," Marco growled.

Jameson's mouth opened and closed, then he asked, "How much do you want?"

In the background, Marco heard Tej clear his throat. "Uh, Marco—we're losing ratings here. People want to see the party, not you shaking hands."

"Just a second, Tej." He met Jameson's eyes and named a price. "Too much?"

Jameson hesitated for a moment, then shook his head. "No such thing. You'll get it."

"We go our separate ways. I never see you, you never see me."

The smile crept back onto Jameson's face. "Of course."

"And him?" Marco jerked his head at Roy as he talked with the Alahan sisters and a pair of fighters fresh from the Stomp Brawl ring.

"Don't give him a second thought," said Zinmar-MacKenzie's VP of Arctic Operations.

Marco looked back at Jameson—then let him go. Jameson took back his hand, wriggling his fingers cautiously, and bent his head. "Good luck with the rest of your fights, Marco," he said. He turned and walked into the crowd.

The last Marco saw of him, he was reaching for his cell. Marco turned as well, grabbed a drink from a passing server, and slammed it back without seeing what it was. The alcohol burned down his throat.

"Marco," said Tej.

He looked up. Tej's eyes were sharp behind the images that flickered over his glasses. He tapped his camera. The red mute light was on again, but so was a blinking green light. "Did you know these things have audio enhancement?"

"Doesn't matter." He grabbed a second drink. "How much did you stream?"

"I cut away."

"Good. How much did you hear?"

"Enough."

The vid-jockey practically had dollar signs rolling across his eyes like an old cartoon. "Forget the money, Tej," Marco told him. He took another drink, this time for Tej, and passed it to him. "I can't give you a cut of something I'm never going to get."

"You don't think he's going to follow through? What did you have against him anyway?" The greed vanished from Tej's face, replaced by fear. "Is he going to put a hit on you?"

"He's going to try, but I don't think he's that fast. Forget him. He's a piece of crap." He clinked his glass against Tej's. "Unmute your camera and let's show the fans around the party before we leave. We've got about fifteen minutes."

bigfoot cured my arthritis

ROBERT COLMAN

I was no different from the rest,
only beyond weak as he walked the clearing.
Crippled up, cut from fear, I said,
"Alright, I'm all yours to gut or throw,
I'm all tapped out."

And that's when he rested
the weight of his arms on mine,
a warmth wriggling free
of the cold threat of air.

I wondered at the root of his magic,
those imposing, slab-like hands,
the matted fur, the smell of him
working through my joints.

Just placing my palm in his
was monumental, another idea—
not really a hand at all.
A form of mythology that heals
by proving itself true.

wing

AMAL EL-MOHTAR

In a café lit by morning, a girl with a book around her neck sits quietly at a table.

She reads—not the book around her neck, which is small, only as long and as wide as her thumb, black cord threaded through a sewn leather spine, knotted shut. She reads a book of maps and women, turns every page as if it were a lock of hair, gently. Every so often, her fingers stray to the book that sits above her sternum, twist it one way, then the other; every so often, she sips her tea.

"What is written in your book?" asks the man who brought her the tea. She looks up.

It is said, she reads, *that a map drawn on a virgin's skin creates a land on the other side of the moon. Whole civilisations rise, whole empires are built in the time it takes for bath water and scented soap to tear its minarets down, smash its aqueducts, strike its flying machines from the star-sewn sky. This is likely nonsense, but as no one has been to the other side of the moon, it remains entirely possible.*

The man blushes, then frowns. "That's nice," he says, "but I meant in *your* book. The one you wear. What is written there?"

The girl's lashes touch her cheeks. "A secret."

He opens his mouth to ask another question, then shuts it. He walks away.

The girl with the book around her neck sits quietly beneath a chestnut tree.

She reads a book with a halved pomegranate on the cover, a wasp stamping its black feet in the juice. She turns every page as if she were lifting a veil, delicately. The sun is bright against the paper, makes the words swim green against her eyes.

Another girl comes by, her hair curly, her step light. She wears a bag over one shoulder, and sits down near the girl with the book around her neck. She smiles. The girl with the book around her neck smiles back. The girl with the bag pulls out a loaf of bread, a wedge of cheese, a small jar of amber honey, and a knife; she begins to slice, to pair, to drizzle honey on the lot.

"What are you reading?" she asks, curious.

Once, reads the girl, *only once, for never has this happened since, nor is it likely to, a bird lit down on the head of a young man seated beneath a peach tree. The bird's plumage was most fine, smooth as linen, bright as the afternoon sun drinking garden petals. The man could not gaze at it, but sat very still, so as not to disturb it; he closed his eyes, for even the barest flash of tail or pinion as it shifted about his scalp was painful to him, was too beautiful for his gaze. The bird whispered in his ear the secret to immortality, which involved the consumption of nectar, the building of a fire, and the bathing of his limbs in a sacred pool. So deep was the young man's gratitude, so fierce was his love for the beautiful creature perched on his head, that his heart burst in his chest and he died on the spot.*

The girl with the bag, who had begun to chew her honeyed cheese and bread, coughs a little as she laughs. She wipes her mouth modestly and offers the girl with the book around her neck a morsel of her own. She accepts it, and they munch together in silence. Then, as they are rubbing their fingers together to clean the honey from them, the girl with the bag asks, "What is written in the book around your neck?"

She blushes. "A secret."

"Oh," says the other girl. They spend a few more moments together, before the girl with the bag gathers up her effects, bids the girl with the book around her neck a kind farewell, and goes on her way.

The girl with the book around her neck sits quietly on a jutting rock by the sea.

The sea is not quiet; the sea is an angry choir of dissonant voices, all taking turns striking their rage against the shore. The waves curl foamy fingers towards the rocks, smash their delicate salt bones to glass. Everywhere is a fine damp mist.

The girl has no book to hand. She pulls back the left sleeve of her raincoat, dips her fingers into a tidal pool, lifts a mixture of sand and clay from it, and tries to draw a map on her skin.

It is not thick enough; the wet sand will not make lines, only prickle her as it winds its way along her forearm. She pulls her sleeve back down. She looks out at the sea, at the gulls mewling, the crows cawing, and tries to think of a song.

A boy approaches the rock on which she sits. He looks up at her. She looks down at him.

He wears a raincoat too, grey as the sea, and a dark blue scarf around his neck to keep the damp from his throat. It is sensible; she does the same. They look at each other a long moment.

Then he says, "Would you like to hear a story?"

She nods.

"It is said that once every five hundred and sixty-three days, two people will walk on the beach with matching raincoats. It is further said that every one thousand one hundred and twenty-six days, these people will have matching shoes. But it is rare as a bird with feathers linen-smooth, rare as a city on the dark side of the moon, that they will both wear books around their necks, and rarer still that those books will hold secrets."

"Come up," whispers the girl to the boy with a book around his neck. "Come up here."

He does, with his hands to the rock, his shoes like hers, his coat like hers. He unbuttons the collar, unwinds the scarf from his neck. There is a book there, the same length and width as hers, black cord threaded through its sewn leather spine, knotted shut. He reaches for the knot with slender fingers.

"Wait," she says, "wait." She unbuttons her collar, unwinds her scarf, bares her own book for the opening, bites her lip as she looks at him. "Are you sure?"

"I want to tell you a secret," he says, firm.

They open their books. They turn every page as if touching each other's cheeks. They read the same word, the only word, buried in each book's deepest heart, nestled up against its sewn leather spine, behind its knotted ribs.

When the tide comes in, it finds a clutch of soft grey feathers sticking to the rocks, spilling from the pages of two tiny books with no words in them. The tide yawns; it licks them like a cat; it tangles the black cord that threads them, knots them together, and swallows them into the sea.

arrow

BARRY KING

The day I was chosen by Fletcher, I had killed Civet. Sango and Chelo and I were playing with our *barbañas*—the small bows given to boys to play at hunting. Papa had been unhappy with me for killing the small sparrows that cluster like mice on thin branches. Like mice, they have no wisdom, no breath-spirit, he told me.

That day, I was leader of our little hunting-party. I wanted to take away the shame I felt, so I called the hunt in the early hours, and we went, barefoot in the cool damp of early morning. I remember us being very serious, as only boys can be when they play at being men.

Civet was coming home to sleep. We smelled him first. We trod the path lightly, the swish and crackle of leaves under our feet quieter than Leopard-Cat's wake. Pulsing choruses of shrieking birds and hissing beetles masked our breathing. We were dark and invisible in the canopy-gloom, where dawn comes late in broken blue fragments from above. I took care to keep the clearing behind me, and well that I did, because when Civet returned to his home, dawn light filled his eyes with a blue-green glow and I saw him.

I think it was because of that meeting that Fletcher chose me. There, beneath the slender bone-arms of the *Batam*-bush, Civet and I met for the first time as equals. I could see his shape against the broken sky above. One hand was raised, poised to take another step along the branch, and that's when our eyes met, and he knew me and I knew him. He stopped for me and offered his breath-spirit to me like a mother gives her child nutmeats she has chewed herself. The spindly shaft, iron-tipped, sped true from the rickety little *barbaña* and caught him just below his chin, but he was already dead, having given his spirit to me with his eyes.

I picked up the shaft, and Civet hung from the end. That is how I carried him back to our longhouse, holding him by the arrow buried in his neck, an ugly gap of red around the wound marring the pattern of his coat. His smell was strong like smoke, but animal and potent, and it surrounded us like the morning chorus, giving us the strength of his blessing. I was thrilled at my first real kill, and was looking forward to Papa's praise, mother's stew, and basking in the respectful gaze of Sango and Chelo, who were already looking to me as if I was Headman.

Fletcher was waiting. We did not see him until he was right there in front of us. He was sitting on a rock in the clearing, his knees up under his chin, his old, creased face the skull of Death himself. Like Death, he watched me with cold, dark, patient eyes, and for a space of a few breaths, I felt apart in the world from the others. Only Civet, myself, and the arrow that joined us were real beneath the gaze of Fletcher. He stood slowly, unfolding from his seated position until he stood above us, looking down from the rock. He stepped down lightly and made a brief gesture to the others. Sango and Chelo ran back to the longhouse without a word.

Fletcher looked at me, his head bent down, studying me and Civet. He paced around me, and I felt his eyes all over. I didn't dare move. Then he squatted down before us and examined the arrow, running his finger along the shaft and touching Civet where the arrow pierced his coat. He ran his finger through the blood. Then he looked up and asked me, "Did you make this?"

I nodded, unable to speak.

He touched me, then, right at the breastbone, where Civet had been pierced, making a small circle. I had never seen Fletcher this close. I looked into his headdress, which swept up over his head. His hair had been woven with feathers from the Red Macaw and the Orange Pangpang. His brow was bound by a bright cloth into which thin wires of gold had been woven. They shone in the pale light coming through the mist above the canopy.

He led me back, behind the thick stilts of the longhouse, to the small hut outside where he lived apart from the clan. His two wives were outside the hut, coaxing the fire back to life from the embers. He waved them away and then told me to take the arrow out of Civet while holding him over the fire. I did. The arrow was barbed and did not come out cleanly. A trickle of blood fell from the wound and hissed on the hot coals. The smell of cooking mixed with the musky smell of the animal, mixed with the smoke from the fire. He took Civet from my hands and gave him to his older wife, a woman almost as ancient as himself, telling her to prepare a feast with her own hands and her hands alone.

Then he broke my arrow. He did it quickly, snapping it like a twig and throwing it into the fire. I wanted to stop him, but I knew I should not. Fletcher is the master of arrows, and all arrows are his, even the ones I make for myself.

I wake up in darkness. The low hum of the air conditioner dampens any sound from outside. My nose is dry, cracking inside, and my head hurts. I spin in the darkness and remember that I have drunk too much of the black rum. I feel the sadness and sickness that comes from the liquor. I listen, as I always do in the night. Maybe the liquor hides the Little-Men from me. Maybe there are no Little-Men. But I am still afraid in this mill-house. I feel them, I think, sometimes. I feel they are angry with me. Or maybe they are just angry.

Someone is crying. It is Chelo. He cries because his mother is dying. The missionary said it is because she lived a bad life, and she must accept it. He must accept it. But it is the old logger that is to blame, I think. He put his death into her before it killed him. A woman should not outlive two husbands.

It only takes a day, now, to reach the village. With five days off from work, we decided to stay two days. Now I wish we had not gone. Yalai was there, still, with her shop. She will not speak to me anymore. But she will sell me rum. She is still cold in her eyes, as before. Cold and strong like the river. She will outlive me. She will outlive all of us.

I don't remember coming in last night. Chelo and I started drinking before we reached the logging-camp. He is mourning his mother. I can't say what I'm mourning. But it was I who bought the rum.

I raise myself on my elbows. "Chelo," I tell him in our own tongue, "be strong. She will live. You'll see. You'll be paid again next month, and then we can buy her more medicine."

"The medicine doesn't work. The Murphy said so."

The Murphy—the missionary in the village—would know. He is a healer, one of theirs they call "Doctor." He knows about their illnesses.

I roll over, facing away from him. He still follows me, like he did years ago. Maybe there is a Little-Man in him that wants to remind me how I have failed. Maybe it is Fletcher's death that waits in Chelo. Waiting for his time to strike me from behind, like the arrow you never see, never hear.

Fletcher never taught me to make arrows. But he showed me how to make the hunter's bow. While his wife was preparing Civet for the feast, he took me to the longhouse. Mama was weaving on the boards of the high room where the morning sun came in. She was sitting in the sunlight, the weaving stick between her feet, humming a weaving-song. She did not see me enter with Fletcher, but kept pulling the cords and knotting them back and forth. Fletcher touched my shoulder and nodded his head at her, so I went to her to show her I had come back from the forest. First she touched the spot on my neck.

"Did you cut yourself?" she asked me.

"No."

"It looks like blood."

"He put it on me," I said, and pointed to Fletcher.

She squinted at the shadow behind me. Fletcher was quiet. Mama was quiet, too. She stood up and rolled her unfinished cloth around the weaving stick. She did not look at Fletcher.

"Where is your Husband, Ayani?" Fletcher asked.

She would not speak to him. Instead, she thrust an arm towards the hills.

"Tell him I will take the boy to the mountain. He will go to the tree now."

She looked down at her feet and said nothing. Then she turned away from us and disappeared into the gloom of the rear.

"Mama?" I called for her, but she did not answer. I went to follow, but he stopped me with a touch on my shoulder.

"Come. You must come with me now. We have a thing we must do before you can return."

I was too scared of him to say no. We walked a long way, along the ridge towards the high *lauan* trees. I watched his feet as he led the way. This I learned about Fletcher from walking with him that first time: when he walked, he moved with perfect precision. His feet thought for themselves, like the feet of Leopard-Cat. His legs placed every footfall exactly where it was best to step, like the legs of Mouse-Deer. His arms swam through the underbrush, gliding smoothly through the thicket like long-tailed Macaque goes through the branches above. His head scanned the forest, taking in all sights and sounds like wide-eyed Tarsier. But his body he held like a man, his torso and his chest never rising or falling, never tilting this way or that, always in balance. He must have been older than any man of the village, but he moved like a man half his age and twice as strong. I began to understand the honour I was receiving.

He took me to the highest *lauan* tree that stood on the top of the hill above the longhouse, and had me sit. He gave me water from a gourd at his belt, and he gave me a leaf to chew. He called it *kampar*. It was strong-tasting and made me gag, but he had me swallow it all with small sips from his gourd. I coughed many times, and my nose began to run and my lungs hurt like I had breathed in smoke. My eyes burned and I squeezed them shut to stop the burning.

Then he showed me how to make the Little-Man. He began to tap me on the chest where the blood was. He was singing, and my ears were ringing from the coughing. I thought I was coughing up a bit of stuff from my lungs, trying to clear them, but it fluttered in my chest like a live thing. Like a butterfly.

When his song ended, he whispered in my ear. "Let the Little-Man out. The Little-Man that you trapped today."

I tried to cough it up, but it wasn't in my lungs. It was in my chest somewhere, and just as I felt I couldn't gasp another breath, something came out of me. It seemed to come out of my chest, not out of my mouth, but in my mouth there was a taste like blood.

"Good, good," he said, and massaged my back until I could breathe again. My eyes stopped stinging, and I felt a calm come with the end of my coughing, like falling into your hammock after you have walked all day, toe-to-heel, on the forest-tracks. He made me sit on a root of the tree and rest.

Sitting with him there up on the hill in the sunlight, the biting flies were at my hands and feet, and I swatted at them while we talked. He said that before he could teach me to hunt properly, I had to have the Little-Man taken from me.

"Today, you think you killed Civet. You did not. He gave you his life. So you took his death as well."

I told him I didn't understand. The flies were distracting me, though they didn't bother Fletcher.

"When a thing, whether fish, or bird, or beast, gives his life, he also gives his death. The death must be spoken for, or it will always look for a chance for vengeance."

I slapped a biting fly. "Even flies?"

"No. You do not understand. Listen to me. When a thing *gives* its life. Chooses to give it. In sacrifice. Civet gave you his death. You are a man, so his death is a man for you. A Little-Man that waits for you, waits for a chance to pierce you like he was pierced by your arrow."

"Where did it go?"

"I put him in the tree. You will learn to do this."

"Why?"

He looked at me with those eyes. I stopped slapping the flies. Under those eyes I felt like a fly myself. He could just swat me down, and my death would take me away just like that. It would mean nothing to either of us.

"I understand," I said slowly, because I did. This pleased him.

We talked for a while. He spoke slowly, in a gravelly voice. I asked him about the tree. He smiled and touched it, both of his dry dark hands clasped around the rough grey bole before him.

"Many deaths live in this tree. Fletcher before me filled it with deaths. And Fletcher before him. It is full of deaths, this *lauan*. You will fill it with your deaths when you return from the hunt. And one day, if it is your fate, you will know a Little-Man has come to a youngster, and you will teach that one to put his deaths into this tree."

"Do all the hunters do this?"

"No, only the Fletcher."

"Why?"

"Why should flies matter? Come. Before the day is over, we must plant a *panaka*-vine."

Everyone knew what the *panaka*-vine was for. "To make a bow?"

"Yes."

"For who?"

"Who do you think? Your mother?"

"But it will take years to grow!"

"Of course. And when you are ready, it will be ready."

The air is better outside the dormitory. You can hear the forest awaken, before the sawmill begins. Out on the edge of the forest where the yellow earth is carved deep by the rain, the air is moist, and rich with the smell of soil. They are building again. This means they are first tearing down. Clearing.

Soon the yellow-cap men will come out of the mess-hall and start up the great yellow machines, but for now the rhythm of the birds and the hissing of the crickets and the cicadas and tree-frogs weaves around me. The music swells and fades like a vast pair of lungs, breathing in sleep. My heart stirs with their song, and I feel the spirit of Leopard-Cat still there, crouched in the darkness of my chest.

I breathe deep the musty scent, and catch a whiff of pig, reminding me of why I'm out here.

Balthazar the cook gives me a two-handled stock pot, deep and heavy, filled with tailings and mash for the pigs. His back hurts him as he leans out of the back door and lowers it down to me. He complains, grinding his golden teeth as I take the pot off his hands. The dogs under the kitchen floor get up and follow me, but not all the way to the fence. I don't think they like the smell of pig. I don't, either, but it is better than diesel-smoke, which robs the body of its strength.

I look around, but nobody is watching. Behind a board by the sty I have a cracker-tin. Inside I keep some money and my cigarillos. I can't keep them in the dormitory, they get stolen, so I keep them here with some dried meat and a fire-piston. Only I feed the pigs, so my secret is safe, even the other tin, the new one. Before I dump out the pig-swill I light a cigarillo from the piston's burning punk and blow the smoke into the roof of the sty so it doesn't show in the mill-windows.

The smell of tobacco wakes the pigs. They come running up, tails and ears bobbing, their little black eyes hungry. They remind me of someone, but before I can think who, Chelo calls me. He is calling me up the hill. I point to the stock pot with my chin. He shakes his head. He looks angry. No. He looks worried. He hunches forward and begins to run down the hill to me with little quick steps, his hands out, jiggling in the early light. He has grown fat here, in the mill camp. His chin wobbles. I know who I was thinking of, now. But that thought makes me worried, and I do not laugh. I stub out the cigarillo and pick up the pot as he reaches me.

"Did you hear about Raul, big-brother?"

"The foreman?"

"He is in the infirmary, getting bandaged up."

I chuckle. "Did he cut off his pee-pee?"

"No, big-brother, I am serious. He has been beaten."

The pigs are pushing each other aside to get at the peelings. "Who by?"

"Villagers, he thinks. It was dark. He was locking up and saw people in the shed."

"Does he know who?"

"No, big-brother. It was dark."

He calls me big-brother now and sometimes I call him little-brother, just like the villagers do. But it upsets me. More than Raul being hit would upset me, I know. Raul is a liar and a thief. I tell Chelo I suspect he has been selling the yellow-caps' things to the villagers and maybe this time he was cheating them.

53

"Is he hurt?" I ask.

"Not much. They hit him on the face. But they took everything."

"Everything in the shed?"

"Yes."

"We're lucky, then."

"Big-brother?"

"No work today. Not until they replace what was stolen."

Chelo grins and snorts with laughter. More than ever, he looks like a pig. I am afraid for him. *Run, little-brother. Run away.* But he does not.

I never took a wife. I don't regret it. Not now. But for a long time, I did.

Seven years it took to make my bow. Fletcher and I tended the vine and made it grow into the right shape. When he and I hunted together, we would always go check on my vine before going to the hill to fill the spirit-tree. I had learned to make the Little-Man without *kampar*-leaf. I could feel each death in me. I had learned how to keep them in place so they would do me no more harm than the biting flies and I learned how to put them into the tree.

But the days became harder. We had to walk further, then, to hunt. There were more villagers coming, and they often went into the forest, chasing away game with their boots and their rifles and their stupidity.

Sometimes the villagers would come to the longhouse. Not often, but often enough that they learned the trade words: one, two, three, rice, knife, salt fish, yam, pork, cassava, taro, gold, glass, venison. Words like that. At first they had little to trade except gold coins and gold teeth. They were a poor people, and their hair was red and brittle because they were hungry and had nothing but millet.

Later on, they had meat again because they brought their black buffalo from the down-lands. But before, during the hungry time, during those first years while I was waiting for the vine to grow, the down-landers were at war. The warriors of the other country, the big country in the north had killed them with great machines like dragonflies, and the villagers were afraid to go down to their old lands or to clear fields to raise cattle on.

Chelo learned their tongue. He told me they were poor because there were too many of them to live in the village, and not enough for everyone to eat. They were poor hunters. We traded meat with them, because they were so bad at getting it themselves. That way, I gained a good steel knife that I used to make my bow. They said it was "steel from the legs of the sledge that moves itself." Now I know they mean "steel from the springs of a truck," but then I did not understand.

When I cut the vine and made my bow, I made it alone in the woods. I made several bows in the seven years before that. Each was better than the last, Fletcher said, but only the last one mattered. This bow was made from only one piece. It was cut with only one knife, and Fletcher warned me that if I should break it, or break the knife in making it, that I should never make another. That is how the Little-Men tell us our fate. Fate is for only one man at a time.

That year, I almost took a wife. Or I should say she almost took me. Living with Fletcher, I did not go with the girls like the other boys did. So when it came time for me to take up my new bow, I had no woman to make the *patum*, the wrist-guard, from her hair. Yalai made mine and she came to me when I was alone with the knife and the bow was almost finished. Her footfalls were quiet, but not timid, and she kept her eyes high. I put down the bow and she knelt in front of me, tied on the *patum* to see if it fit. It did, and she laughed at her cleverness. "You must keep it now," she said and went away smiling. The strength of her spirit warmed my heart.

Yalai was always the only one for me, and I courted her with gold, but I did not win her over. We ran out of time for that.

Chelo and I do not want to be drawn into some other kind of work, so when Foreman tells us we are not working today, we go up onto the hill to watch the yellow-caps bring down a big *lauan* tree. When the charges go off, there is a flash of fire that fades before a huge crack like thunder shakes the air around us. Every bird for as far as the eye can see rises up into the air at once. It looks as if leaves from every tree are falling up into the sky. For a second, the whole forest holds its breath.

Fletcher used to say that Death comes with every breath. Every time we breathe out, the breath-spirit waits for a sign from Death. If we do not die, we breathe again. And again. And again. But one day, Death nods, and the breath-spirit leaves forever. I waited for the forest to breathe again.

"Was that one of them?"

I know what he means. "A spirit-tree? No. No Little-Men in that one."

The tree starts to fall. Its shaft is perfectly straight, shattered on one side from the dynamite. I think of a feather, drifting softly down to the forest floor. But when it strikes a lesser tree, there is the shimmer of splinters flying, then the sound of smashing and screaming of wood. The sound makes me shudder.

The cracking and shifting dies at last and the drone of chainsaws begins, great flies buzzing in the woods. We turn away.

"Hey you. You guys. Hey!" says a voice from behind. It is Tommy Dos Santos, from our work-gang. He is the only down-lander in the camp, tall and yellow-skinned. We watch him approach and say nothing.

"Raul told me to find you," he says, out of breath, when he comes close. I'll never get used to how the villagers smell. Sour and bitter. Fletcher used to think it was from eating beef and palm-oil. But we all eat the same now, out of cans. Tommy still smells like a villager.

"There's going to be some company-men," he says.

"You mean more yellow-caps?"

"No, big men. VEE EYE PEAS. Foreigners. From the head office."

"Why are they coming here?" said Chelo. I was worried, too.

"I don't know. Maybe they want to see what's going on."

Chelo wrinkles his brow, but I am curious. "Why did Raul send you to tell us this, Tommy?"

He has the goodness to look embarrassed. "He wanted me to say that you are not to talk about what happened last night."

"You mean we are not to let them know he let the shed get robbed."

"He didn't let it. They beat him."

I say nothing.

"Besides," says Tommy, "it's Boss who says don't tell. He doesn't want the Company Men to be worried."

They must be important, then, if Boss is also afraid of them.

"You've told us, then," I say. I suspect something. I say, "You want to stay? I have smokes."

He looks tempted. I think it might be him who had been stealing my cigarillos, but he doesn't give away enough in his face for me to be sure.

"No, I need to get back. You should get back, too. They need people to help with the visit."

"Not me," said Chelo, and looks up to me for confirmation.

I don't give it. "I think I will come. I would like to see these VEE EYE PEAS," I say.

Chelo puts a sulking face on, like the boy he will always be. "You can stay, Chelo," I say to him. *Stay, little-brother. Please stay.*

"No, I want to see, too," he says, lying.

I shrug.

Fletcher only hunted with arrows, and he forbade I should use my knife. I was not allowed spear or club or any weapon. Only arrows, and only those arrows that were made by Fletcher.

Hunting became very bad after I had my bow. The villagers had taken far too much game and we had to make a long trek every day. There was trouble, then, among our tribe. Some wanted to move the longhouse up past the Spirit-Tree Hill, closer to where the game was. Some wanted to hunt the villagers, and to chase them from the forest.

Fletcher would not say one way or another. I did as he did, and remained silent.

One day, as we rested in his hut, Fletcher said "If the tribe goes upland, we will find other tribes, other villages, and we will soon have to go upland again. And again. Then we will reach the green mountains where game is sparse. In your life, maybe your child's life, we will be gone. We need to stay where we are. But if we fight the villagers, they will soon hunt us with rifles." A long time he thought about this. All night and into morning.

The next evening he announced to all the people in the longhouse that he and myself would hunt Pig together, just the two of us, and there would be a feast for everyone afterwards, because we would bring back the game that had gone away.

Every night, for seven days, he told his wives to cook yams on the embers so they became sweet to taste and sweet to smell. We went over Spirit-Tree Hill to the plateau and found a run where a great old boar had been rooting. He put the yams on a banana leaf on the ground and every day we checked that they had been eaten and placed them much closer to the longhouse.

"When hunting Pig, you must draw your prey to the place where you will kill him," he said, "because the Little-Man of Pig is different, and will help us. They are closer to men than other prey."

On the seventh night, Fletcher's wives led the dancing, and they asked the bush-spirits to guide us. On the eighth day, we kept the yams with us and we dug a pit down near the village, where the villagers hunted. He showed me how to knot the bark of the *panaka*-vine into rope and from rope into a net strong enough to hold Pig. He told me this was an up-lander net. Down-landers only made nets for catching fish.

"The up-landers are good hunters, but they are foolhardy. When they hunt Pig with the arrow, too often the hunter is killed. Pig will hold on to his life until he has put his death into you. Then he will tear you open and take his death back. Unless you hit him just right, an arrow will not kill him, and he will not give you time for a second."

I looked down into the pit. It was muddy, and it looked like any pig that fell in would get out easily. "So how shall we kill him when he comes? With a stone?"

"No, you must use the arrow."

"So we will shoot him from here? That does not seem right. It will make him angry."

"Only with the arrow. But here is how it will be done: without a bow. The bow will bring the death only to you. You must not use a bow with Pig."

He did not explain more. Instead, he sat me down on the other side of the track with the yams between us.

We waited for Pig. Quietly, so quietly I could barely hear him, he spoke while we waited. "Today's hunt is different. We will not take a Little-Man to the tree. Instead, we will make him work for us."

We waited, listening for the racket Pig makes when he come through the thicket. Nobody is bigger than Pig, and he moves without fear and, so, without caution.

"Pig's death is great," he continued after a while, "almost as great as a man's. It is greater than any of the Little-Men who now frighten game."

"But it is the villagers that frighten the game," I said to Fletcher.

He smiled. "But the game *stays away* because the Little-Men crowd the air around here. They swarm like biting-flies, without purpose, chasing away others of their kind or driving them mad, and drawing their enemies. Pig will clear the Little-Men away. That is how Pig dies. Then the game will come back."

"Pig too?"

"No, Pig will never come again to where he was killed. He is too wise for that. Kill him, and you drive him away forever."

When Pig did come, the ropes bound his legs, and the netting wrapped him tight. It took all our strength to drag him out. Fletcher showed me how to kneel on his shoulder and to push the arrow into the vessel in his neck. All the while, Pig screamed like a child being burned alive. It was the loudest scream I have ever heard in my life. My ears hurt with the screaming, even after Pig's last blood drained out, taking his death with him. Fletcher told me this is why you must bleed a pig. To let the death out, or it will stay there and try to get into you. It is the way of Pig, to always try to put his death in you before it takes him.

THE BEST CANADIAN SPECULATIVE WRITING

"He is so loud. I wish he would stop."

"No you don't!" he said, grinning, "The screaming chases the Little-Men. Nothing is stronger against them!"

And for a while, the game did return and the villagers stayed away. But I never saw Pig again this side of Spirit-Tree Hill.

Emmanuel the houseboy is missing, ever since last night. Balthazar swears he was in on the robbery, but I can't believe it. Emmanuel is a calm man, young, and slight of build. When we left the longhouse he was half my height and he grew taller but not strong. There is no strength in him to swing a club, no fire in his heart to want to.

"So why is he gone, then?" Balthazar asks me and, truly, I cannot say. I try to imagine Emmanuel striking Raul with a club and I can't. Emmanuel always apologizes, even when he has done nothing wrong. I remember being harsh with him when I was drunk. He just looked down, said no word. I told him to go away, to get out of my sight. He kept his head down and ran, like a little boy, away from me. We have neither seen nor spoken since then. I wish we had. I want to tell him I'm sorry for making him run. He is a good boy. I don't know why I made him run away. I think of what Yalai told me, and I think I am becoming a wicked man.

One of Boss's helpers catches me in the hallway as I am headed for the kitchen.

"You have good clothes you can change into?" he asks.

I say "yes, I do," which is true. I bought them before I came to the camp, although I never wear them. I have a fine shirt and some good pants and shiny good shoes. I don't want to say how I got them.

"You need to wash up, though," he says to me. This is also true. I smell of rum and sweat from the hillside. I ask where I am to go. He says, "Kitchen duty. Go to Balthazar. He'll tell you what you need to do."

"No, you tell me."

He tells me. I laugh. "They can't serve themselves coffee?" I ask.

Boss's man looks at me sternly. "They are too important!"

I am about to say that he can find someone else. But I don't. I want to see these Company Men. I want to hear them talk.

The last hunt with Fletcher was for Leopard-Cat. I did not know it was the last hunt. Maybe he did.

It was a night hunt. There are no dances when one hunts Leopard-Cat. Leopard-Cat is wise, and he listens at the edge of the firelight and listens to people talking. When Fletcher told me what we were going to do, he whispered it in my ear through his cupped hands. Then we made loud talk about how tired we were and how we were going right to sleep. That is how you fool Leopard-Cat.

We met him by the stream that runs down from a seep on Spirit-Tree Hill. The moon was half-full, which is the right time to be hunting Leopard-Cat. When the moon is full, he can see everything in the forest and will stay away from you. When the moon is dark, you will never see him, even if he walks beside you on the track. But at half-moon, you can see him in the water and that is the only time you can kill him, because his Death is blinded by the sight of the moon on the water. It is like looking into the sun is to us, but when Leopard-Cat is thirsty, he will risk blindness for water.

Fletcher and I had hunted so many years together that we no longer spoke. He knew what I was going to do before I did it, and I could feel him move before he moved. When we moved together through the forest, our thoughts were mingled like breath, and like breath, we felt the other's movements without seeing them.

So when Leopard-Cat came to the water, I knew it was I who would be taking him. And then it happened the second time. I saw right into Leopard-Cat's eyes and he knew me, and he gave me his life with his eyes. The shaft struck him between the ears, and like Civet ten years earlier, he was dead before the arrow pierced him.

Fletcher saw what had happened, and the cold light of the moon on his face was terrible to see. And I understood something, then, that he never had to explain. Death was in Fletcher, like a Little-Man that had not been purged. Death had grown steady and patient and fat in Fletcher, and his time had come.

Right there, he skinned Leopard-Cat with my good steel blade and put the bloody skin over my head, the fore-claws knotted under my chin, the tail and back claws on my back.

"Now you will carry the Little-Man of Leopard-Cat in you. Like Leopard-Cat, you will walk unseen and silent. No one will see or hear you, and you will deliver them their death."

"Am I to be Fletcher now?" I asked, but he said nothing.

I know the answer. The last arrow I will ever make had already been broken and burned.

Balthazar shows me how to hold the tray.

"Remember," he says, "always come from their right. Let them fill their cup on the tray and put in sugar or milk. Let them do it for themselves. That is what they prefer."

I nod. I almost want to laugh at how serious he is treating this. He sees my face, and he is troubled, more frightened than angry.

"Don't laugh. Please don't laugh. It will go badly for us if you laugh."

"I won't laugh. Don't worry. But why so serious?"

"These are big men. Very powerful men."

"I know. VEE EYE PEAS. You said."

"Listen to me. Without these men, there would be no camp. There would be no logging at all. These are the men that began this camp. More than that. Many camps. I have children, brother. I need these men. They feed my family, and without them, we would starve."

"You could hunt," I say.

He looks at me like my father catching me killing sparrows, and I feel the shame I felt then. It was unworthy to show him his weakness.

"There are a hundred camps like this," he says in a whisper, "a hundred Balthazars. If they decide that they don't like this camp, they could close it. Like that," he says and snaps his fingers under my nose. "Don't get me in trouble. Not me or any other Balthazars."

"Don't worry, Balthazar. They will not hear or see me."

This much, I know, is true.

The first time I heard an "iron dragonfly," or so we called them, was the morning that Fletcher died. I heard the noise coming from below and I thought it was a night-spirit coming to take me to the dream-place where they live. I had heard that noise once, in a dream. A Little-Man grabbed me once while I was sleeping and the noise was everywhere around me, like I was caught in a drum being played. I was terrified, and he shook me a long time before he let me go. Fletcher told me it was just a mischievous ghost and I should ignore it.

But after that, I was frightened of the night-spirits, so when I heard the noise again, I got up quickly so he could not catch me. Then I noticed the noise was coming from outside the longhouse, not from a dream. I had just made it down to the ground by the light of daybreak when the first rockets hit.

I am a logger. I have grown used to the sound of wood being torn apart by dynamite, but this was the first time I had heard that noise.

I believed the world was over. The world was over, in a way. I could not tell the difference between the scream of wood and the scream of the dying.

Again and again the rockets came. Each one a burst of flame and a noise so loud I thought my bones would shatter. After the first two, my ears couldn't hear anymore except for the thump of new rockets. The longhouse was ripped apart behind me. I saw everyone screaming silently in the firelight. Mama was screaming. Papa was screaming. Fletcher's wives were screaming. Only Fletcher was not screaming. He stood at the mouth of his hut and looked up at the helicopter. He raised his arms to it and I think he was asking it to come. The hut around him burst into a ball of flame and I saw the old man fly from the door like a broken sheaf of branches.

I ran to him. To *him*. Not to my mother and father. Not to the longhouse. I did not try to save anyone but *him*. I ran to the broken body of Fletcher and knelt by him while the helicopter flew off, happy and fat with our deaths.

He was burned on one side and one arm was a broken tree-stump. But one eye was clear and one hand reached out to touch me where Civet's lifeblood had been put on me. I leaned in and he whispered in my ear to tell me what I am. That's when I learned I was never to be Fletcher. There would be no more Fletchers for my clan.

Yalai found me there, long after sunrise. She had been calling for help, but no one came. She cursed me. She told me I was worse than an old woman. While I sat there, her little brothers had burned alive, and I had done nothing. Her shouting brought me to motion, but not to life. I helped her to get whoever was left out of the collapsed longhouse. Her mother was alive in there, but her father was not. I found my mother and father as well, but they had died. Sango was gone, too. Half of his face was smiling, the rest was cut away as if with a fine steel knife. I fainted to see this. Yalai kicked me awake again. Then we got everyone together and walked to the village. It took all day.

Coffee is over. I am waiting in the bar, pretending to wash glasses in the small sink there. Boss is with Chelo, speaking the yellow-caps' language to a Company Man. The Company Man smiles. He looks satisfied and kind, but his eyes are small, black and shiny like Pig's, and they watch. He says something to them and walks across the room to another Company Man. Chelo and Boss step aside and start to talk quietly.

Without looking at anyone, I step out of the room. But only partway. There is a small dark space near the door where I can stand out of sight at the edge of the room and listen. I listen to Boss.

Boss is speaking the villager's tongue, because he does not want the Company Men to know what he is saying. I understand most of it. He is happy I served coffee so well. He thanks Chelo for bringing me. Chelo does not say anything.

Boss then says something I never heard before. He says that maybe all the logging camps will soon shut down, and the company men are here to decide if this will be so. They came here today because this mill is better than the others and they want to know why. Boss knows why. He says the Company Men think we are the same tribe as the down-landers, and they don't understand we are very different.

So he asks Chelo to have dinner with them. He needs Chelo to tell the Company Men that people from our tribe are happy the mill is here. Boss says it's important that Chelo and I show that we are better than down-landers. Maybe Chelo will go back with the Company-men to their country, where he can tell everyone how happy our tribe is to have logging jobs. Then, when their countrymen all see we want the logging jobs, they will decide to keep the camps going.

Boss then talks quietly and says maybe Chelo will be boss himself someday, with a mill of his own. But first he must show how happy we are that the Company Men are here. One tree at a time, Boss says. One tree at a time clears the forest, he says.

Chelo says he will help. And he says he will get me to serve at dinner to show we are good workers and how happy we are that the camp is here for us.

He will not run. I will not ask him to.

I walk back into the room and Chelo and Boss stop talking. But they look at me. They are the only ones. I walk through the room and pick up the empty cups and put them on my tray. Nobody sees me, nobody notices I am there. Even in my white shirt and my shiny shoes, I am invisible.

When we got to the village, everyone came out to see us. They stood in their doorways and watched us, eyes wide. There were only twelve of us left, and three were only children. Of these, I carried one, and Yalai carried another and Chelo led the third by the hand.

The big man of the village came out and met us. When we explained what had happened, he did a strange thing. He opened his mouth as big as it could go and bent over like he was going to be sick. Then he wiped tears from his eyes and welcomed us. He went to the main square and told everyone there to make us welcome and to spare us what they could spare, and to take us in if they could.

Then he went back to his house and did not come out for some time. I wondered at that, but by nightfall, I understood from what I heard from the women talking with Yalai. The helicopter had made a mistake and thought the longhouse was the village. They had been spared, and now they owed us a debt that they did not want to pay, but they also could not refuse. For a while, we were given food and we were given shelter, but not happily and not for long, except for the Murphy, who took in the children and made them his own.

Yalai sold her gold bracelets, even the two I gave her, and bought a house for her and her mother to live in. Chelo's mother left and married a logger only two days after we arrived. She told Chelo not to come. Not to the wedding, not to the logger's house. Chelo was not to be her son anymore. The logger was jealous and did not want a stepson.

We lived on the street in the village for a while, me and Chelo and the other men, until the winter rains came. Yalai invited Chelo to live in her house for a while. She had heard how he tried to see his mother, but his stepfather beat him and his mother did nothing. Yalai did not want me there, but Chelo did, so she let me sleep on the floor in the main room and let the other men stay, too. Chelo slept by my side. He clung to me close like a child for the first few days, and then he stopped talking for a while. None of us spoke much, together, anymore.

A lot of people came through the village that winter. The war was ending, they said. They said that everyone was now "Citizens of the Prosperity Zone." They meant that the warriors from the north had made this land part of their country. So, when the New Year Moon was new, the villagers lit firecrackers and made the beast they call Dragon, which is their way to chase away the Little-Men that the war had made.

Yalai gave the dragon-men money to do this in her house. Also, she only cooked beef now. No pork. No civet. No bush-meat of any kind. I understood. She was telling us that she did not need us anymore. But I know she really meant me, and the same for anyone who was with me. She wouldn't tell me to my face. She would only talk to me if I was with Chelo or someone else, and then she would talk to all of us at once. She never spoke to me as a person. Bile sat in my throat when she talked without looking at me.

I left. We all did, but only Chelo stayed with me afterwards. After that, Yalai turned the house into a shop with rooms to rent. She bought and sold with the boat-men and she made a place for people to eat and sleep, but only if they had money. The war was over, and people were travelling again.

Then there was talk of yellow-capped men in the forest. Even when people began to talk about the new logging-camp they were building, I never saw one of the yellow-caps until I went to their camp. They flew in with their helicopters and began logging. I sold my bow and I sold the skin of Leopard-Cat, and I sold my good knife. I bought good down-lander clothes and I hired a truck to take Chelo and I to the new camp. Fletcher was dead. Yalai wished I was dead. The man I thought I would be had never really been.

But *I* still lived, or so I thought, so I became a logger like the rest of the men from the longhouse. Chelo followed me, like he always did. Even when we walked into the camp for the first time and we saw that they had built it right on top of Spirit-Tree Hill.

It was the hardest thing I ever did, walking into that terrible mill. That mill made of white planks of the *lauan* tree cut from the tallest tree on the hill. From Fletcher's tree.

Walking through the doorway, Chelo behind me, I could hear the Little-Men buzzing like biting-flies. All those deaths, all those vengeful spirits. They filled the air. They filled me. But I was dead; just as dead as they were, and it no longer mattered. They did not see me and they did not hear me. I had become nothing more than an arrow, flying blindly in the dark.

"Keep the cover down until you're ready to serve it. I don't want any flies getting on the chicken," says Balthazar as he hands me the tray. I nod. He trusts me now, and doesn't watch me as I go out the door.

Between the dining-room and the kitchen is the pantry. There is a door there to the outside, to the garbage-hut and the path down the hill to the sties. Instead of walking past it to the dining-room, I turn into it with my shoulder. The latch is undone by my hip and it opens out, the long spring chiming against the frame. Flies are so thick they darken the air. They swirl around me in the hot afternoon sun like Little-Men in the darkened dormitory. I run, holding the cover on the tray with my thumbs.

Halfway down, my polished leather shoes skid on slick roots in the track. I fall, but catch the ground with one hand. Sauce slops out of the side of the tray and the lid nearly comes off. I stop, catch myself with my breath and remember who I am. I rise, balancing against the weight of the tray. My next footfalls are clean, precise, quick as Mouse-Deer's, stepping from root to root until the track flattens out and I am again by the sty.

I empty the tray over the fence. The pigs come running, crowding together, jostling as they wolf down the chicken-parts whole. I hear the little bones crack as they try to fill their mouths, trying to keep one another from getting any. Their squealing is the squealing of beasts proud of themselves, glad to be taking their fill.

From behind the board, I get out the other tin, the one I put there last night. Everything is in it and ready. All I need is the lighter, the one Raul dropped when I hit him. I try it out. It is small, but the flame is high, and I feel the flame bite at the callus on my thumb. I grin. I am ready.

By the time I make it back, Balthazar is looking for me. He is coming out the door, wiping his hands on the towel in his belt. When he speaks, his voice is a whisper so loud it might as well be a shout. His eyes are wide with anger and fear. His open hand quivers in the air like the head of a snake about to strike. I know he wants to strike me, but he is afraid to.

My grin is fixed. I say "Sorry, brother. I must go. I will explain later." Cursing, he lets me by. He does not see the flies swarming around me, blacking out the edge of my vision. I go in. I push the tray through the double doors into the cool air of the dining room. I turn the bolt and pull out the key, letting it fall to the carpet. I turn and almost lose my nerve when I see Chelo. He is there, saying something to a Company Man. He looks like a boy at missionary-school, talking sweet to the Missus Murphy. There is a smile on his face that falls when he sees me watching. But it is too late to save him.

I let the lid fall as the lighter flares in my hand. I rake the flame across the detonators and throw the tray onto the table, laughing with relief as Leopard-Cat springs into the room. Sparks fly from short fuses. Dynamite scatters, rolling on the table, falling into the company-men's laps. They rise, but they are caught here in my net.

I close my eyes and I breathe out for the last time. Around me, Pig is screaming as Fletcher's last arrow strikes its prey. They will work for us, now.

penny
DOMINIK PARISIEN

For Sophie

There is no magic in the world
but this: her, sowing copper-plated dreams on concrete and gravel.

She divines by a flick of her wrist, by the ring of coin on ground
when none watch, thinking, *Investments in folklore*
profit everyone.

At night she dreams of rusted coins melting
into grasping hands, of bloodstreams thick
with wishes.

thought and memory

CATHERINE KNUTSSON

Every morning, the two ravens Huginn and Muninn are loosed and fly over Midgard; I always fear that Thought may not wing his way home, but my fear for Memory is greater.

—the Sayings of Grímnir

And, for our odd news item of the day:

Reports have been coming in from all over the city of a pair of ravens dive-bombing unsuspecting pedestrians. The birds appear out of nowhere to attack the heads of people walking by, only to vanish again, taking hair from those attacked with them. Wildlife officials have been called and are currently investigating.

Now, for the weather . . .

The ravens return at noon, Odin's hour, bearing several strands of hair. They drop them at the feet of the crones and wait, their black eyes glittering as the old women rub the strands between their gnarled fingers, breathe in the scent, put the hair in their mouths, chew.

The first spits the hair into the fire. "Not good. Not good," she mutters as her sisters do the same. She turns to the ravens. "You must go back. It is not him."

The ravens cackle and shuffle. They don't want to go back into the middle world.

"You must," the second woman says as she turns her moon-stained eyes to them. "You must find him."

The ravens whisper to each other and nod before taking wing.

The three women watch as the ravens disappear into the mist.

"They will not find him," the third woman says.

"You have seen this?" the first asks.

"No." The third woman crouches by the fire and tries to warm her hands in vain. The ice is coming. She can smell it. Its chill cuts what little warmth is left in the fire. "I have not seen it, but I can feel it."

"Perhaps you will be wrong," the second woman says, turning to the loom behind her. She sits, taking a moment to settle her ragged dress around her, before reaching into her basket for the last skein of thread. "They must find him soon, or we will have no thread to weave."

"And then," the first woman whispers.

"And then."

"And then."

Celia sits by the old man. She should be doing her rounds, but she's tired. She's been working double-shifts as often as she can because she needs the money. This old man who's forgotten himself, he needs little attention—one of the few—so she takes a moment to sit by his side and maybe, in the process, warm up a little bit. The winter is cold this year, colder than any on record. What happened to global warming, she wonders. Maybe the scientists were wrong after all.

The old man stirs from his sleep and smiles at her. "Hello, my dear. You've come back."

She jumps. This is the most lucid thing he's said since he arrived ten days ago with no identification, only a tag in the back of his worn coat that read "Woidan." The hospital assumed it was his surname, but no one's been able to locate his family. There's only one Woidan in the phone book, and they don't know who the old man is.

"Do you know where you are?" she asks the old man.

He smiles. "In the middle, of course. I must go up, you know." He takes her hand. "Up." His startlingly blue eyes glance towards the ceiling. "Up."

Celia smiles. "No, no. You don't want to go up. That's where the really sick people are." She stands, stretching her tired back, and turns to leave. She must get back to work. If she's found here, sitting down, she'll receive another reprimand, and she can't afford for her hours to be cut back.

The old man catches her hand. "Have you seen my birds? I always have them with me."

"No," she says. His hands are cold, and she shivers. He smells odd, like fallen leaves. "No, I haven't seen your birds."

She brings the old man dinner. She shouldn't; it's an orderly's job, but it's getting cold, and besides, he has no one else.

He's sitting up, brushing his long, white hair which flows into his thick grey beard. If he was wearing red, he'd look just like Santa Claus. Snow is falling outside in soft, thick flakes, and Celia can almost imagine a sleigh pulled by reindeer arriving at the window, with the old man bundling in to disappear into the snow-thick night.

Pea soup, minute-steak, mashed potatoes. The same fare, day after day. The man doesn't seem to care. He wolfs down his dinner and pushes the plate away. Celia takes a napkin and dabs beads of gravy from his beard.

"Thank you, my dear," he says. "Did you know I once had a tree?"

"A tree?" Celia says. "What kind of tree?"

"I don't know," the old man says. "I seem to have thoughts, but I don't remember what they are. If I had my birds, I'm sure I would know what that means."

"Birds?" Celia says as she sets the man's medication in his leathery palm. "There are parrots in the patient lounge—did you mean those birds?"

"No, no," the man says, shaking his head. "Those are silly creatures. My birds were . . ." His voice breaks off as he abruptly turns his gaze to the window.

Celia pours him a glass of water. "Your medication, Mr. Woidan. Time to take it."

He blinks at her. "What, my dear?"

"Your medication."

"Oh." He pops the pills in his mouth and chases them down with a swallow of water. "What were you saying?"

. . . *the longest cold snap in recent years continues, plunging temperatures to below-normal levels and breaking records all over the country.*

In other news, the bird attacks have continued. A representative from the Department of Wildlife suggests that pedestrians in the downtown core wear hats, for it seems that the birds are attracted to hair, particularly that of older men. There have been no serious injuries, but anyone attacked is asked to contact the Department of Wildlife after visiting their family physician.

The ravens return, landing on the branches of the tree that should not be covered with ice. The deer cluster at the base of the tree, pawing at the frozen ground in vain as they try to reach the tree's roots. The old women watch the deer and feel sorrow in their hearts, for the ribs of the deer are visible under their mangy coats.

The ravens descend from the tree and drop hair at the feet of the women.

The first woman holds the strands up. "These look promising." She hands them to the second, who sniffs them and shakes her head.

"No good," the third says. "You must try something else."

The ravens nod and take to wing. They will try something else.

The snow has stopped. Celia pulls her cardigan tight around her and steps into the old man's room. He's singing.

She pauses by the door to listen.

Parsley, sage, rosemary and thyme
Remember me . . .
Remember me . . .
Remember me . . .

He looks puzzled as he repeats the line, then goes back to the beginning of the chorus and starts again, only to falter at the same spot.

"What comes next?" he says as he looks at Celia. Tears fill his eyes. "Do you know?" he says. "Do you know what comes next?"

Celia takes a seat on the edge of his bed. "Remember me to the one who lives there, for she once was a true love of mine."

"Ah yes," the old man says, letting his eyes drift closed. "That is the version here. I know another one, but that will do for now." He hums under his breath as Celia leaves, her footsteps falling in rhythm to the old man's tune.

I'd like to welcome Mike Salinger, a representative from the Department of Wildlife. So, Mike, what can you tell us about these bird attacks?

Well, Dee, we're still compiling information. It's not unusual for ravens to attack people at this time of year, but the continued attacks from this pair—we're pretty sure they're a mating pair—are highly unusual.

In what way?

Well, they seem to be targeted attacks. Ninety percent of the victims are men over the age of sixty-five, and of those men, all of them have long beards.

So, bearded men are the targets. And what's the Department of Wildlife's plan to deal with these marauding ravens?

In normal cases, we wouldn't do anything, but in this instance, clearly there's something else going on. We're hoping to capture one, or both, of the birds so we can do testing to see if there's another issue involved.

Another issue—such as disease?

Well, we're not quite at that stage yet. It could simply be a learned behaviour.

So there's no need for the public to worry?

No, none at all.

Thanks very much, Mike. Now, on to other matters—the weather. Deaths among the homeless population have skyrocketed thanks to this arctic winter snap, and there's no end in sight. . . .

The old women watch the grey sky above the dying tree. No ravens.

"What shall we do now?" the third woman asks as she turns from the loom. "I am almost without thread."

"We shall cut our hair," the second woman says. "That will do for some time."

"But not forever," the first woman says. "The tree is dying. The world is freezing. Perhaps the end is near. Perhaps we should just let it come."

"But we must weave wyrd," the third woman says. "Even through the end to the other side."

"What if there is no other side?" the first woman says.

"Hold still, sister," the second woman says as she stands and presses her shears to the first woman's hair. "We will make another side if this one comes to an end, even if we have to create it with the last of our hair. It, at least, will grow again, if nothing else will." The scissors creak and the first woman's hair falls free, spiralling to the ground in a shimmer of silver. "And now, mine," says the second woman.

"Wait," the first woman says as she claps a hand to her bare neck and stares at the sky. "There—don't you see them? The ravens return."

The other two women turn to watch.

"No," says the second woman. "Only one has come back."

"Which one?" the third woman says, clutching her heart. "Which one?"

The raven alights on the dying tree and bobs to the old woman.

"Thought," it croaks. "Thought has returned."

"That means memory is lost," murmurs the first woman. "He was always certain memory would leave him first."

The three women bow their heads and do not issue a charge to the remaining raven.

Celia stands in the snow. The whole world is thick with grey mist. Snowflakes land on her cheeks, stinging her skin. The world's coming to an end. She can feel it.

Above her, birds turn lazy spirals in the grey. She can barely make them out between the falling snowflakes, but they're there. She can hear them calling to each other.

She should go home, but she can't seem to make her legs move. The cold has frozen her in place. There's nothing to go home to now. The bank has claimed the house; her husband left with the children. So she stands in the snow and hopes it gives her courage to either walk, or remain here, staring at the sky all night. Others in the city have died; why shouldn't she? They say it's a painless way to die. You just go to sleep, though she wonders how anyone could ever really know that. It's not like the dead have memory, or could talk about it, even if they did.

The call of the birds becomes louder, and between the snowflakes, she can just make out a black form, spiralling towards the earth, wings stretched out like desperate hands trying to grab at the sky. She knows she should move. The bird might hit her, but she just stares at it, transfixed. The blank fascination of such a morbid moment, knowing that in three more, two more seconds, the creature will impact with the snow-covered ground in an explosion of black feathers, blood red confetti . . .

It strikes her in the shoulder. Pain ricochets through her entire body. Black feathers scatter across the ground. Celia falls to her knees; she can't breathe, can't see through the pain.

Slowly, as her breath returns in short, ragged snatches, she forces her eyes open and finds the bird staring at her, bleating like a newborn lamb. It tries to rise, and when it can't, it falls back into the snow and mewls.

Celia reaches out, lifts the broken bird in her hands, and takes it home.

If she had looked back, she would have seen a perfect snow angel in the exact spot where the bird landed.

Wildlife specialists now believe the single raven, separated from its mate, is heart-broken and attempting to find a surrogate from another of the city's bird population, regardless of species. . . .

Fallen, fallen, fallen . . .

The words ring the dying tree, shatter the icicles that hang from its branches, sending a shower of nails to the earth. The women scatter, shrieking. The ice impales the earth, the hart, the loom. . . .

"All is lost," the women wail. "Ice walks the earth. We will perish."

A single raven sits among the broken branches, bobbing, sobbing.

Fallen, fallen, fallen, memory has fallen . . .

Celia walks the ward. She's wrapped her shoulder where the bird hit her. Every step she takes jars it, but she can't afford to take time off work. She's being watched.

It's nearing Christmas, the worst time of the year. A few patients are visited by family, but most aren't. These are the forgotten people, the elderly who stare out the windows with vacant eyes. It's the most depressing fate she can imagine.

She visits the old man right before her shift is over. He's pulled a chair up to the window and has his fingers pressed to the glass.

"What are you doing, sir?" Celia asks. "Plotting your escape?"

"Naming snowflakes," he says without turning his gaze away from the night. "Did you know each one has a name?"

"No, I can't say I did," Celia says. "Time to check your blood pressure. Would you mind sitting on your bed?"

The old man shuffles over and huffs as he sits down. "Uncomfortable mattress," he says as Celia leans close and fastens the cuff around his arm. He sniffs her shoulder. "That bird, the one that hit you. I saw you with it. I had a bird like that once . . . it had a name. I can't remember what it was . . ." His face screws up as he tries to recall the name.

"Sir, I need you to breathe while I'm taking your blood pressure. Holding your breath will give an elevated reading."

But the old man doesn't release his breath. His lips move as he tries to form words. Celia unfastens the cuff and sighs. He opens his mouth, his tongue waggling about like that of a newly hatched chick, as he makes a lisping noise.

"Sir," Celia says as she pats his arm. "Sir, can you hear me?"

He nods, and slowly, as Celia holds his hand, he calms down. "I should like to see your bird," he says. "Does it have a name?"

"No," Celia says slowly. "I'm not sure it's going to live."

"Bring it to me," the old man says. "I'm good with birds. I'll make it better."

On her way out of work, Celia is handed an envelope. Inside is a pink slip, and a card that reads *Happy Holidays*.

The next day, her last day on the ward, she brings the bird with her, tucked into her parka. What will it hurt? It's survived two nights; maybe, if it brings the old man just a little joy, its life won't have been lived in vain. Celia wishes she could say the same for her own. She just doesn't care anymore. Doesn't care about anything. She doesn't have the energy.

The old man is sitting in the chair, nose pressed to the window.

"Have you named all the snowflakes?" Celia asks.

"Not yet," he says, "but I will."

Celia closes the door to the room and draws the curtain around the old man's bed. "I brought something for you," she says.

The old man's eyes lights up when she pulls the bird from under her coat.

"My bird," he sighs. "Oh, my poor, poor bird." He stretches out his hands, bird claws themselves. Celia places the broken raven in his palms.

"You'll have to keep it here while I'm on shift," she says. "And keep it quiet."

"Yes, yes," the old man says. "Keep quiet. Ssh," he says, putting a finger to the bird's beak.

Celia blinks. Did the bird just nod?

The old man turns his gaze to her. "We will be very quiet, for we remember now."

"What have you remembered, sir?"

"My bird's name," he says as he strokes the raven's feathers. "It was there all along, in my memory."

Celia shakes her head as she leaves the room. Crazy old man.

The women have ceased weeping. They wait for the cold to seep into their lungs, bite their blood, turn them to stone. All is lost without memory. Thought no longer matters. This is not how they envisioned the end of the world.

They sit beside their pool, waiting, waiting. . . .

The raven in the tree above is waiting too. If they looked, they would see it cock its head from side to side and flutter to the ice that covers the pool. It taps the ice, tap tap, and hops forward. Tap and hop, tap and hop, until it reaches the centre of the pool.

"What is that crazed bird doing?" the first woman asks. "It's lost its mind."

"Without memory, thought is nothing," says the second woman, pressing her palms to her eyes.

"No," says the third. "Look."

The raven has fixated on a single point in the ice, tapping its beak with an increasing cadence until . . . the ice cracks, sending a spider's web of veins racing across the pool. In the distance, the women hear a sharp, distant echo.

"What was that?" the third asks.

"Winter's spine," the first says, "breaking in two."

Celia returns to claim the bird at the end of her shift.

The old man's chair is empty. His bed is empty.

She dashes to the window. He's outside, walking across the snow-covered field in front of the hospital. The bird is on his shoulder. The snow dances past them, fleeing the old man and his path, for behind trails a path of thaw, of green grass, of newly sprung daffodils, a bridal train of spring in the cold, winter night.

She wraps her coat around her and runs down the hall, down the stairs, outside. She will follow the thawed path, follow it until she can't follow anymore.

The old man stops, picks a daffodil, and waits for her to approach. "This is for you," he says. "You cannot come with me. I'm going up." His eyes rise to the clouds and the falling snowflakes.

"I don't want to stay," she gasps. "There's nothing for me here now."

The old man smiles at her as the raven whispers in his ear. "Well," he says, "my memory tells me you haven't heard my stories before." He looks to the sky, and when his gaze falls on Celia again, something about him has changed. His hair isn't quite so grey. His face, softer, less creased. "It's been a long time since I've told my stories to new ears." He holds out his hand. "Why don't you come along then?"

She takes his hand, a sudden warmth against all the cold.

They walk side by side into the snow. "Let me tell you the names of the snowflakes," he says. "They all have names. I remember them now. . . ."

gaudifingers

TONY BURGESS

It was 1946 and the beaches looked like leather. The shells were chairs and the shells were parasols. Everything that started blue became pink. Dads and moms posed to hide the white cubes of exposed winter thighs. This was the thing I was in. A picture like that. Towels and tufts of singing scrub. Pointy-titted ladies with wide crispy eggs for hats. Beefcakes. And the wind that is only invented ten feet from shore but it's a bawling baby shredding the pages of magazines and raising lipstick bubbles on the backs of children. And I am bent in a corner of sky in the sand reading a comic. I deny that I am here. I am turned away. Turned inside. My sister is somewhere pretending to swim in four inches of water. My brothers are building bowls out of the droppings of seabirds. It is a joyful place, I suppose, but in my ten-year-old mind it is the bright sunshine of depression. The gold water and rose warmth of permanent intractable despair. I can't say why it is, but I feel it. Like I'm living in a deep knot.

The sand on my knees covers scudded wounds and each grain is as kind as a diamond. Earlier this week I teased a black kid at school. Not for being black, but for having the last name White. On Friday, yesterday, he tackled me on the sidewalk and brought me down under him. There was nothing for me to do but go home and lie. Maybe it's that. The lying. Maybe that's why I want to die today.

"Why don't you go in?" My mom points out to the sea. She wears sunglasses as big as wheelbarrows. My God, this is an awful place. I bring my knees up under me and look at the back page.

"OK. Well, we're going to walk down to the pier and see the fishermen."

She pauses, adjusts the mad white ribs in her suit. She wants me to think. And yes, I really, really want to see the fishermen, but I'm suicidal today. She doesn't sense this at all and pivots on her heels.

The back page. Sea Monkeys. X-Ray Specs. A six-dollar submarine that can submerge to great depths. If I had about 12 dollars to spare I could watch naked ladies in the cabana. If they caught me I could escape out to sea and drown. I would let my monkeys free to swing in the coral.

I despise this kind of thing. It is such obvious fantasy. The truth is I would be caught. I'd be standing by the cabana peering in through the side of a curtain. An old woman would scream and slap her hands to her bum. Everyone would hear her and everyone would see me. I can feel my knees blush, knowing that one day this will happen. I am changing, though, as the day goes on.

It was wanting to be dead. To be burned alive. Now it's different. After seeing myself at the cabana and being taken that way, I have decided I will be alive. I will kill the old woman in her nakedness. I will pull parasols up like weeds and drive down them into sockets and mouths and bums. The whole beach will be crying and dirty and ashamed. Blood will be pumped into hollow poles and plumes of it will rise and spatter us all. This is where I get to at four in the afternoon. X-Ray Specs. Monkey submarines. Flies leaving the assholes of dogs and wiping their feet on the corner of my mouth.

I close the comic book. On the back is a picture I've never seen before. It's a public warning. BEWARE GAUDIFINGERS! There is a drawing of a young boy and overlapping that an older boy. Then a man. And after that an old man. Then a dead man and then a skeleton. It's not a very good drawing and the lines are wobbly and broken. Beneath the drawing is an important public announcement.

"This is a public warning that needs to be heeded by all. The Gaudifingers contagion is no longer contained. Be advised that contact with Gaudifingers results in rapid aging and painful terrifying death within minutes. In many cases the horror of this rapid transformation kills the victim seconds before their final physical deterioration. Gaudifingers then takes the form of the victim and moves on. The only way to know who Gaudifingers is is to witness this transformation. The authorities are asking the public for assistance in tracking and eliminating this demon once and for all. If you witness the sudden aging of someone please call the police immediately. There is no one above suspicion. Anyone you know could at any time be Gaudifingers."

I scan down the page looking for what they are trying to sell. Is this an ad for a new comic?

A movie? There is nothing on the page to suggest it's anything other than a very serious public warning. I stare at the drawing. The lines are wobbly on purpose. This is what happens: Your skin wobbles and your lines break. It must be so bad. The Gaudifingers touches you and you feel your skin shatter and your heart age 100 years in minutes. I feel that this is something not everyone knows. The news is just getting out now. The threat of Gaudifingers. I picture Rexdale for some reason. Maybe because it's an ugly place. Yellow factories and stubby strip malls. If Gaudifingers was working its way through there, no one would know. Or maybe some do. A woman closes her dry-cleaning shop early and hides in a rack of film-covered gowns. The man at the Sunoco wipes his hands on his pants and runs across the street and down an alley. Oh my God! A baby, just born, is suddenly tumbling in fat and loose sacks of skin, then long yellow teeth punch up through its nose and eyes and cheeks. There is no way to age a baby that fast. The process is confusing. Grey hair clogs its throat. Its arms hunch like crooked backs and skin tags pop across its feet. A momentary monster. Its eyes have heart attacks. Who can say what it is? I have to help somehow.

But how? If I tell people they'll think I'm crazy. I'll just get in trouble. If I show them the page they'll say, "That's interesting. Not now." I know exactly how the world works. How things don't get passed on. How messages die. People get used to bad news. They have things that they say when they hear it, but they don't really hear it, do they? It's as if everyone's under a spell and they can only can only think about getting home, cleaning up, going to bed. And that's exactly how Gaudifingers survives. It may be why Gaudifingers exists.

"Hey you! They caught a baby hammerhead! Come on! You gotta see this!"

I jump to my feet and brush my knees.

"Like a shark? How big?"

I am running backward ahead of my mom. She is excited.

"Well, it's only a baby. But yeah, it's pretty big."

I can't believe I'm going to see a hammerhead shark in just a few seconds.

"Wow, Mom. C'mon! Let's run!'

I run ahead toward the pier. If you think that nearby there is a baby hammerhead shark it's all you can think about. They live for millions of years and now, as a baby, they bounce at our feet and they are seconds away.

I stand at the base of the pier. It is very wide and long. All afternoon there have only been three things: sky then sea then sand. Now as I step up onto the planks I feel as if I'm entering a room that's been hiding in folds. I don't run because I can't gauge the room I have. There is more salt in the air here. I run.

You can always tell when it'll take you. I say that because it may be true and if it is then we are in an amazing world. There is no hammerhead. There are no fishermen. I turn to my mother and one of her arms is 40 feet long and is in the sea. She has thrown a leg, just as long, around and ahead of me. She is screaming; teeth spring though her lips and cut her face. This is one of my final moments. She says it, "Gaudifingers," to scare me more. Her forehead makes a sudden oblong fob against the sun. The fingers come at me. She wails again, "Gaudifingers!" The fact that she's trying to scare me is so hard to understand. The fingers telescope in sloppy curls. I can feel my heart ask to stop beating.

a sea monster tells his story

DAVID LIVINGSTONE CLINK

For Alexa

I have been hatd and huntd my hole life
the seas boyancy holdin my skeletun aloft
holdin this oshun enclosd by skin
in this sea that no longer has anythin for me.

You are on the beech
and you say do not give me things unbrokun
and being a creeture of the sea I have no possessiuns
I can only give you everythin
so at hi tide I come ashore and lie beside you.

The moon has come out.
The wind brings natures fragrance
trees and blossoms
the salt of the sea.

You say lo tide is comin.
I say I know but I dont want to go.
You say you dont want me to go but lo tide is comin.
I say let it come.

In the mornin the water is gone. I can hear
the ancient creek of my bones
my skin gettin crispy.

People from all around are comin to help.
But I tell them with my eyes
that I don't need there help
but they come anyways.

They are pourin water on me.
They have startd a bucket brigade.
They are tryin to save me.

And I tell them with my eyes I dont want to be savd
but they are not listnin
the sun is bakin my skin
I feel week I cant think strait.

When it is clear there is nothin to be dun
you look into my eyes and ask why I didn't leave befour lo tide
why I couldnt be happy visiting for a few hours each nite.

I tell you I have been hatd and huntd my whole life
and the sea held me until I found you
and I will not return to the sea.

I can see it from the beech and I can taste it in the air
along with the scent of flowers and you
but the sea has nothing for me.

My eyes tell you
I am where I have always wantd to be.

son of abish

DAVE DUNCAN

"Louse-infested spawn of a ditch-breeding whore!"

"Spavined cross-eyed dung-eating cockroach!"

A fight was brewing. The old man dozing with his back against a pillar opened his eyes.

"You are a foul-smelling, child-molesting, brigand rapist!"

"From you, that is a compliment."

"Your own mother pukes at the sound of your name."

"Vultures won't eat your fungoid carcase if we spread jam on it."

The setting was the courtyard of the Caravanserai Almukus, a lonely desert station on the Skag Road. The sun had just set behind the smoky Ramparts of Heaven Range, and the camel drivers were seeing to their stock, squabbling over stalls, eyeing one another's wares and women, and preparing for another night of lying, drinking, trading, thieving, and general enjoyment. The two men stoking the fires of fury were both young, both armed with swords, both clearly intent on spilling lifeblood.

One of them was a giant in billowing red robes and a black turban shaped like a puffball. He bore a shiny curved scimitar hung at his belt and a dagger almost as big tucked in the other side of it.

His opponent was younger and clean-shaven, carrying a massive two-handed broadsword on his back. He was not as large as Turban, although quite large enough, and wore very little, so as to display his remarkable muscle definition; he sported a mane of brilliant red hair on his head and a mat of orange moss on his chest.

The old man sighed at having to witness a contest so unequal, so unfair. The conclusion was foregone. In such encounters the gods would invariably award the verdict to the one with red hair.

The caravanserai was a rectangular stone structure, open to the sky. Livestock, slaves, and beggars were bedded on ground level, real people in their own tents on a balcony that went all around. Guards patrolled the battlements above. Brigands lurked in the hills, except when they took temporary work as guards.

"When I have done with you, boy," Turban declaimed, "the dogs will feast on the scraps."

"You are all wind," Redhead retorted. "When I cut off that beard there will be nothing left of you." He not only looked the hero, he had one of those sepulchral voices that vibrate through the soles of listeners' feet.

The cause of the dispute could only be the silk-clad beauty sitting cross-legged under a canopy on the balcony, watching the contest below with glittering black eyes. Her hair was draped with a golden net and her lower face with a silver veil. Enough of her shape showed through her robes to justify several murders in such a place as Almukus. She had ridden in on a westbound caravan, a private parade of just her and her intimidating escort. Had she somehow indicated to Redhead that an opening could be created for a new chief guard by creating an opening in her present one?

The moment had almost come. The audience had ceased work and settled down to watch. The caravanserai was unusually full that evening, sheltering a large host of traders who had entered by the west gate and would leave on the morrow by the east one.

". . . pox-ridden son of a . . ."

". . . yellow-livered, tea-drinking, gelded . . ."

Tea drinking? Either that was a bad translation or they were running out of epithets. Action must follow.

"I will cut off your privates and feed them to the ravens."

"Yours would not make snacks for sparrows." Better. Redhead was still standing with fists on hips, smirking, seemingly dangerously open until he drew that massive pig-sticker hung on his back.

Wisely deciding not to give him the chance to do so, Turban whipped out scimitar and dagger and charged. He very nearly impaled himself on the broadsword, which had appeared as if by magic, extended between them. He stumbled to a halt and tried to slam it aside with his scimitar. It barely wavered. Redhead lunged forward and kept coming, blade outstretched before him like a lance.

With his advantage in reach cancelled out by the absurd length of his opponent's blade, Turban retreated furiously, vainly trying to turn that deadly point aside. He backed into a kneeling camel, thus ending both himself and the camel. Truly the gods are merciless. Could the idiot not tell a budding hero from a brash-mouthed kid?

Redhead wiped his sword on the camel. Its owner was already whimpering and weeping, but not about to make a fuss.

"Take his weapons and clothes and throw his corpse in the midden pit," Redhead boomed. "You will come out ahead unless you catch plague from his vermin." Turning on his heel he headed for the nearest stair and the black-eyed beauty above, who had already withdrawn into the depths of her tent. He followed her in and the flap closed.

In less than two minutes he emerged, his face a startling white under the red mane. He advanced to the parapet, seized it in an ivory-knuckled grip, and scanned the audience with a ferocious gaze, seeking the least trace of amusement at his rejection.

The old man against the pillar beckoned.

The raging swordsman ignored him as beneath contempt and continued to hunt for someone worthy of his bloodlust. No one was looking remotely near him. He did not exist. The naked body of his first victim was being dragged away and there were no volunteers to be his second.

The old man beckoned again.

With a snarl, the swordsman vaulted over the parapet, landed as lightly as a bird, and strode across the sand with murder in his eye.

"What do you want, prune?" he demanded.

"Want?" said the old man wistfully. "To be an indomitable swordsman of less than twenty winters, brave as a lion, handsome as a young god, and nigh irresistible to women."

The swordsman hesitated over that "nigh" word and decided to ignore it. "Quite understandable. It is very nice."

"But you could have so much more. . . . Know that I am Dextrus of Speel, famous in my day."

"Which is long past, since I never heard of you. I am Ahdogon son of Abish, the world's greatest swordsman. What were you famous for, ugly old man?"

"For innumerable great sorceries."

"It is my swordsman duty to slay a sorcerer on sight."

"And mine to turn you into a reptile, but I don't feel up to it today."

The son of Abish raised his hand to his sword hilt. "I do."

"Not so hasty!" Dextrus of Speel said quickly. "Consider what a swordsman and a sorcerer could achieve if they cooperated!"

"An obscene suggestion," Ahdogon said, but he lowered his hand. "Such as?"

"Why I could make you ruler of a great empire, master of innumerable servants, owner of countless vast palaces, commander of the world's greatest army, and lord of the world's greatest harem, with thousands of gorgeous maidens eager to satisfy your slightest whim."

Ahdogon considered the prospect narrowly. "How do I know that you are a sorcerer?"

"I shall offer a complimentary sample of my wares." The sorcerer reached in his tattered robes, took the opportunity to scratch a couple of fleabites, and produced a small box of ivory carved with images of demons and reptiles. "I could not help but observe that your encounter with your lady lasted only a few moments. No man could—or would want to—complete his business as fast as that, so she clearly rejected your advances. Kindly control that sword arm of yours; I have no wish to die because of some scatterbrained female's fickle moods. This tiny casket contains a priceless unguent, which I guarantee will fire her ardour and cause her to clasp you fervently to her bosom."

The young swordsman took the box, opened it and sniffed. He gasped and blinked.

"It is powerful!"

"It has to be."

"What's in it?"

"Mostly musk, with a dash of lye."

"What do I do with it?"

"Simply smear a small amount in your left armpit and another in the right."

Once again the old man's life hung by a slender thread as the swordsman decided whether he detected mockery. "If this does not work, magician, I shall seek you out and stamp you so flat that they will use you as a prayer mat."

"I shall be here. The gates were closed at sunset."

Ahdogon strode off to try his fortune a second time. Dextrus looked around to see who might be persuaded to provide his evening meal.

He was kicked awake at dawn.

A sonorous bass voice said, "I have used up all the unguent. Give me more."

The sorcerer blinked up at the menace looming over him. "Gods preserve me! A single application should have sufficed for the entire night."

"Far from it. Now give!"

"Alas I have none and the ingredients are not available here."

Ahdogon knelt down on the sand beside him. "Then tell me of this kingdom you mentioned."

"Ah!" Dextrus levered himself up to a sitting posture with much effort and creaking of joints. "I referred to the fabled Empire of the East, the greatest and richest of all domains, ruled since the dawn of time by the tyrannical Son of the Sun on the Golden Throne."

"Who is defended by an army of millions."

"But not guarded from dragons."

"Dragons?" the swordsman repeated warily.

"Indeed. Know that when the Son of the Sun's line withers and grows feeble, then the Dragon of the Moon descends upon the Empire and the Son of the Sun must go forth with a sword and slay it in single combat. This is no small feat, which only he can perform. A dragon arrived some three years ago, and the Son of the Sun was wheeled out to meet it. He was over ninety at the time, but the dragon was a small one and appeared satisfied with the meagre nourishment he provided, for it departed."

"And his successor?"

"A grandson succeeded as twentieth emperor of the thirty-first dynasty. But of course at the next full moon the dragon returned, slightly larger and no less ferocious. It ate Number Twenty as well."

"The imperial family was large?" The swordsman was obviously managing to follow the storyline.

"Sons, brothers, uncles, cousins . . . But at every full moon since, the dragon has returned, ever larger and stronger and fiercer. In the meantime, it wastes the land. Armies sent against it are wiped out, but only an imperial sword arm can slay it, and on the evening of the full moon. Now the empire has ran out of princes."

"Wait!" Ahdogon said. "You spoke of a harem of thousands. Sons of the Sun must breed princes uncountable."

"A shrewd observation, valiant sir. But you overlook the rivalry among their honoured mothers, which is expressed in a widespread use of poison and silken cords. Even without dragon difficulties, very few princes survive to manhood, and these days many candidates prefer to end their own lives with some soporific potion than challenge the lizard and die so horribly."

"Um. So what happens now?"

"Now any man may apply to try his luck. The dragon's evil little mind assumes that any single challenger must be the emperor. The first one to slay it will be the next Son of the Sun and found the thirty-second dynasty."

Ahdogon son of Abish sat down and crossed his legs. The bulging money purse now hung on his belt clinked suggestively. That had not been there last night.

"This sounds like a proposition where I do all the work and you only talk. What do you expect to get out of it?"

"What can I hope for at my age but peace and comfort: good food, a soft bed, and the care of a couple of comely body servants? Little enough for an emperor to bestow."

Yet still the world's greatest swordsman demurred. "And you can show me how to slay the dragon?"

"I can. The answer is written in ancient lore I have studied. It has been done thirty times before, remember! Dragon wastings come centuries apart, so the secret gets forgotten. I am sure you can contrive some arrangement such that I do not survive you for more than a few minutes if my counsel proves wanting."

"Very well. It will be a worthy feat. We shall leave as soon as the eastern gate is opened."

"Only if you can provide me with transportation. My aged limbs will not carry me far."

The son of Abish patted his money pouch. "I shall make a reasonable offer on two strong camels." If it had been employment he had applied for in the night, he must be prepared to renege on the deal and abscond with his salary advance. Or else his rewards had been for other services.

Many months of travel and many great perils lay before the two adventurers. The innumerable feats of swordsmanship performed by Ahdogon son of Abish and the incredible supernatural efforts of Dextrus of Speel are best forgotten, but eventually the noble pair did reach the Eastern Empire. And the closer they came to the Forbidding City, the more evident were the misery and devastation created by the dragon: houses and crops wasted, the people homeless, hopeless, and hungry.

"I was informed of this problem only just in time," Ahdogon announced. "Had my arrival been delayed much longer, there would be no empire left for me to inherit." All successful swordsmen lack the wit to question their own abilities.

He was far from the only candidate to step forward that month. On the night of the next full moon, almost a dozen aspiring heroes were admitted to a high balcony overlooking the famous Encircled Square at the heart of the palace, where the dragon would be challenged by the next up, a northerner known as Glutius the Great. Each swordsman was allowed to bring no more than two attendants, whether pupils, trainers, or sorcerers. The entire crowd was surrounded by a sizable company of watchful imperial guards under the command of the Chief Eunuch, who was running the empire until a new dynasty could begin.

As dusk descended and the great golden globe arose, the baleful shadow of the dragon swooped overhead, come for its monthly snack of wannabe-imperial flesh. Trumpets shrilled, and the doughty man from the north strode forth. He was of impressive size, clad in the minimal costume that tradition demanded. Reached the centre of the vast plaza, he brandished his sword and bellowed his defiance to the worm

The dragon saw him, circled down, and landed. It was of enormous size now, and fearsome of aspect: "The body of a snake, the scales of a fish, the antlers of a deer, the talons of an eagle, and the eyes of a demon." It extended its long neck and roared.

It did not breathe fire at the hero. Contrary to common belief, dragons prefer their challengers raw, and reserve fire power for use against armies, property, and commoners. Yet something about that roar seemed to unman Glutius. He dropped his sword, spun around, and fled. The dragon lunged after him.

Dextrus of Speel closed his eyes. He opened them again when the noise stopped, just in time to see the monster launch itself upward, and fly away in search of more sustenance.

"He died quickly," the sorcerer muttered to Ahdogon's muscular back.

"His lower half did. Did you not hear all that fuss his upper half made?"

"My lords!" proclaimed the Chief Eunuch. "If you will kindly move indoors, to the Hall of Lanterns, we shall proceed at once with the elimination bouts that will determine next month's lucky challenger."

Shepherded by the guards, and thus having little option, the candidates and their companions moved as directed. The Hall of Lanterns seemed very bright after the dark balcony, being ablaze with bright tiles and golden tracery. Its magnificence offered a small hint of the uncountable wealth that awaited the successful dragon slayer.

A crowd of courtiers assembled to cheer the would-be heroes. Chief Eunuch stepped up on a dais, where his eyes were closer to level with the swordsmen's. "My lords, you may, if you so wish, now withdraw from the contest, the palace, and the Forbidding City. Your names will be booed at a public gathering scheduled for noon, and you must never return. Those who remain will now fight it out until only one survives to face the monster next full moon. Candidates, please step forward."

Ahdogon strolled forward, idly twirling his broadsword like a balsa wood baton.

The other swordsmen conferred with their advisors. There was much muttering. One by one, they slunk away.

Chief Eunuch bowed to the winner. "Your Temporary Majesty, you may now take the oath as Heir Presumptuous and Die Facto ruler for the next month. Your attendance at the next dragon visitation will be compulsory, though."

"I would not dream of missing it," the son of Abish announced cheerily. "I will take up my duties immediately. Show me the way to the harem."

"Wait!" Dextrus bleated.

The courtiers hissed in disapproval of this disrespect to the Heir Presumptuous, but Ahdogon took no offense.

"Ah, yes. This decrepit old relic will require a place to attend to his studies. Supply his needs."

Chief Eunuch guessed at once what sort of studies were involved. "As Your Imperial Majesty commands, so it is. The Magi's Tower is available. Does Your Majesty wish him chained in there?"

"No, but do not let him escape. Now—the harem?"

Dextrus spent the next month pottering around in the best-equipped sorcerers' tower he had ever encountered. The library alone could have kept him occupied for years, had he been able to read the local script. In the laboratory he found everything he needed, once he had obtained the services of a scribe to translate the labels for him, and he had all his preparations made before the turn of the moon.

His only concern was that Ahdogon might not hold to his side of the bargain, but he need not have worried. A couple of hours before sunset, the door was unlocked and the swordsman wandered it, yawning.

"Came to say farewell, old man," he announced. "I am grateful for your company. More than anyone else I have ever met, you have always made me appreciate my own superiority."

"You do not intend to slay the dragon?"

"I certainly intend to try, but its scales are known to be totally impervious to steel, no matter how strong the wielder. I shall not flee from it like Glutius, and I certainly hope I will not make such a fuss as he did while it eats me, but winning? Not a hope. No matter," he continued around another yawn. "The last month has been worth it. Had I lived to be as ancient as you, old fossil, I could not have—"

"Have you been getting enough sleep?" Dextrus inquired, frowning at the swordsman's blurred and bloodshot eyes.

"At times your naivete amazes me."

"Well, to work then. We can't have much time. First these."

The son of Abish peered at the two white objects being offered on the sorcerer's wrinkled palm.

"Silk worm cocoons?"

"Nose plugs. Insert them now. When the dragon roars at you, you must remember to keep your mouth shut. Its breath contains a poisonous vapor that will instantly turn you into a gibbering ninny. That is what happened to Glutius. Do not inhale its breath!"

Ahdogon seemed to understand and looked interested. "For that advice I thank you."

"And now give me your sword. I shall coat it with this venom, which is utterly deadly to dragons."

"But its scales—"

"Forget its scales, you muscle-bound moron! When it roars at you, you must *throw* your sword into its mouth."

"Throw . . .?"

It took a few repetitions, but eventually Ahdogon got it. "Then I won't die?"

"Of course not. You're going to be emperor and founder of a dynasty!"

"A large one. Well, this is exciting news. Coat the blade by all means. I really came to tell you that I have just signed your death warrant, postdated until midnight. But if your plan works, I shall hasten back and grant you an imperial pardon, I promise."

"You are gracious, lord," the sorcerer murmured, confident that swordsmen were as impervious to irony as dragons to steel. So much brawn, so little brain!

The son of Abish departed, and the door to the tower was locked behind him, leaving Dextrus to watch the proceedings through a small, barred window. Although it did provide an excellent view over intervening rooftops, it was so far removed from the centre of action that he would be unable to participate in the excitement. That might not be altogether bad, he reflected. It would be a shame if his century-old heart were to give out before the climax.

All happened as it should. The dark dragon shape passed in front of the rising moon; the tiny figure of the challenger was just visible, although not audible. The dragon landed, baleful as ever. It extended its neck and, one must assume, roared. But Ahdogon son of Abish did not flee as all the others had. Instead he ran *forward*, closing with the worm. The dragon was seriously nonplused: prey should not behave like that! Its eyes could not bulge any more than they normally did without falling right out, but it forgot to close its jaw as it watched the swordsman approach, and thus he was able to give the coup de grace by hurling his poisoned broadsword right into its gaping maw.

You could see that the dragon didn't like it. It chomped, reared, writhed, and roared so loud that even Dextrus, far away in the magi's tower, could hear its agony. Every effort it made to eject the blade now lodged in its palate only sliced up its mouth and tongue even more. Raising its head to Heaven, it ejected a mighty jet of fire and pink steam, and then slowly collapsed into a heap.

The Forbidding City exploded in a triumph of drums, cymbals, fireworks, and trumpets. So Dextrus's interpretation of the ancient texts had been correct. He had been quite confident, but never certain. He sat down in the middle of his laboratory to wait and see if the swordsman would keep his word and waive the planned execution.

Time passed very slowly for him that night as the rest of the city—with the obvious exception of Chief Eunuch—celebrated the dawn of the thirty-second dynasty. Indeed, it was only minutes before midnight when he heard voices outside, and the lock being turned.

The new emperor strode in alone and carefully shut the door behind himself.

The sorcerer rose and bowed. "Well done, Your Imperial Majesty. You were magnificent!"

"I was, wasn't I?" Ahdogon preened in his new robe of golden silk. "I am grateful for your advice, old man of Speel, but I have decided to let the death sentence stand. You might—purely by accident, I mean, for I do not doubt your loyalty in any way—might let slip some embarrassing remark not in accordance with my noble, but heart-rending, life story, which I am currently planning for the biographers. At your age you have so little to lose, that I am sure you will understand."

"Absolutely, Great Son of the Sun, Lord of the High and the Low, et cetera. My whole otherwise insignificant existence has been justified by this opportunity to serve your greatness . . ."

"That's all right, then." The emperor started to turn, then paused. "What are you staring at?"

"The transformation, sire! Oh, not the robe. Any barbarian bandit could be decked up in that. But already your brow is ennobled by the aura of majesty and historical significance."

"It is?" the former swordsman asked suspiciously.

"Oh, indeed! Here, sire, see for yourself!" The sorcerer handed the emperor a mirror.

It was a large mirror in a golden frame, and Ahdogon took it in both hands. He turned so the moonlight illuminated him, then gazed in satisfaction at that handsome, ruthless, youthful face under its coronet. For a moment. And then, before his horrified gaze, the flesh melted into sags and folds, the skin wrinkled, the russet mane shrank to wisps of white, the teeth grew long, yellow, and loose.

"What is happening to me?" he cried in a timorous wail.

"Justice," retorted a bass voice on the other side of the mirror.

With a shrill croak of despair, the ancient dropped the glass. He was hardly aware of the golden robe being lifted from his spindly shoulders or the circlet from his hairless brow

The glorious son of Abish strode out of the laboratory and again closed the door carefully behind him. This time he even turned the key. Guards and courtiers bowed.

"Quite hopeless!" he announced. "The old man in there has completely lost his head. Cut it off right away."

"We hear and obey," declaimed the head of his bodyguard.

"Now, sire," Chief Eunuch said, "the coronation—"

"Can wait until tomorrow. Everything can wait until tomorrow. I am weary after the battle and wish to retire. Um . . . Remind me: which way to the harem?"

Sorcerers usually get what they want in the end.

opt-in

J.W. SCHNARR

There's a dirty wad of spit on the glass inside a bus stop. It's green and yellow in places, and it curls your stomach to look at it. Maybe there's a bit of brown in there because it was left by a smoker. Maybe there's blood. It has a stink to it too, doesn't it? Everything does. You're holding your breath hoping not to puke and waiting for the bus and for some reason you just don't have the will to turn around and look at something else. You don't dare take your eye off it because it's going to do something terrible the second you look away. Only when that bus comes, it's you that does the terrible thing.

An old Chinese woman struggles to get by you with her perfectly waxed hair and her fold-down walker that she uses to get around because she can't afford new legs on her pension. You pretend like you lose your footing and bump her. It was an accident. Your feet slipped on another gob of slime, one you didn't notice under your feet coming at you like a green hunting snail. Maybe the snot crunches under your feet and you lurch out of that old bus stop, bumping the woman into the glass. She takes the wad of snot with her as she struggles by, oblivious to the corruption you've caused. She clucks like a chicken. And you taste bile in the back of your throat.

The joke's on you though. When she sits down near the spot you've staked out for yourself on the bus, you have to look at that goddamned thing for the next half hour until some kind soul leans down and whispers in her ear. She looks around, shocked, like she just woke up and doesn't know where she is.

Then she pulls out a rag and clucks again. Says something Chinese. Maybe she looks at you and knows you did it on purpose. Maybe she sees something on your face she doesn't like and doesn't push the subject. Maybe she sees the black eye of a moss auto-pump shotgun peeking out from under your coat. But maybe not.

Later you'll remember that look on the old Chinese and wonder if you made a similar face the first time the phone rang.

Let's say you're sitting in your apartment and it's 42 degrees and you're sweating your balls off. You're still wearing the suit Ajax lent you the money to rent, refusing no for an answer and insisting. Shoving fistfuls of dirty paper money into your hand.

"You're not going to her funeral dressed like that, he says, his face twitching from a bad implant. He's got a silver eye that was supposed to let him see in the dark but he's allergic to the metal and it gives him seizures sometimes because there's an optic pin rubbing against something important in the frontal lobe of his brain. He cries out in gibberish sometimes, but you think it's funny. He doesn't. "Don't be an asshole."

So you dressed up nice because Angela's parents were going to be there and they hate you anyway, only now they hate you more. You see her father's ugly glare across the hall the entire time the J.P. is going on about what a sweet girl Angela was and how the Gods have taken her somewhere better. They never found Angela's body so in place of a casket they have a little wooden box and the latest photo taken of her. She's smiling and waving at the camera, and her left arm is out of the picture.

Only it isn't, really, because you have this photo at home and you're in it. Her arm is around your face, and you're both smiling.

Afterward you walk up to her parents and say you're sorry it happened and her father has to be held back by two of his brothers trying to knock your head off and the whole time he's screaming IT HAPPENED ON YOUR WATCH, and IT SHOULD HAVE BEEN YOU and you can't say you blame them and you can't say you disagree with them.

Sitting on your couch in that suit holding the same photo from her funeral you put your hand over your smiling face and think how your happiness would have been a small price to pay for her life if you'd ever been given a chance to give it.

You should take that suit off before your ball sweat costs you an extra hundred bucks in cleaning fees but all you can think about is how you wish you could hear her voice one last time and that's when the phone rings and you pick it up and you hear her breathy voice on the other end of the line.

"Hey Patrick Terran, it's Angela. I wanted to talk to you about the weight you've put on. I know a couple ways to slim that figure down just in time for beach season. . . ."

Maybe you stopped dreaming then, because your dreams all went black and turned into nightmares.

It's called behavioural targeting, and while it may be as old as advertising itself it really got its wheels turning in the post dot-com social media boom at the dawn of the techno age. The goal is simple: by mining your life for information about you as a person, marketing firms can hook you up with advertising you are most likely to be interested in. They call it a service to both consumers and corporate. You don't even think about your shopping habits anymore. Like Coke? Love New Diet Coke Light. Love blue? Check out aquamarine. Targeted advertising works not because they give you what you want, but because Corporate knows what makes you feel bad about yourself and are perfectly happy reminding you how much you suck and how they have a cure to make you the talk of cyber-town.

You'll have 7 million Facebook friends in no time if you just lose twenty pounds. Or change your eye colour. Or get rid of your natural teeth in favour of something with lights. Re-grow lost hair and lost limbs. Stop shitting and farting like a monkey and use subtle liquid waste removal like a civilized person. Design your baby's DNA so they'll grow up smarter, faster, and stronger than you ever could. Buy mechanical pets or household replicants to help with the chores because you're a filthy pig who can't keep house. And why should you? Put your card in the slot and we'll take care of everything.

The new craze in targeted advertising is for simulations of your actual friends and family members to call your line and talk you into losing weight or fixing your acne or getting rid of gross body hair, smells, needs. It's been incredibly effective. Daughters that hear their moms tell them to buy douche are 48 percent more likely to do so. Sons who hear about how their extra body fat is a shame on the family are 55 percent more likely to buy workout pills and diet aids. Corporate is scrambling to cover all the action on this, and they're making enough money to drown any cries that it's immoral to use people's loved ones against them. After all, they've been doing it for hundreds of years.

Angela knew you better than anyone. At some point, she must have told them everything.

You're standing outside the coffee shop where you first met and the rain is lashing your face. Just like that day you met. You might have worked in that place once, covering the bills but not much else. Maybe you had enough money for some drug of choice on the weekend. It wasn't a life, but it was living. And then your job was gone. Shit-canned because you showed up at work one night high off your skull with puke on your shirt and made inappropriate comments to your co-workers on duty about how they were slaves to the Corporate teat and they were all gonna get theirs in the end. Thing is, you didn't even remember doing it until Corporate pulled you into the office and showed you the video screens. You threw a sucra-sweet bowl at an old lady and then ran around trying to kiss the customers' asses.

Maybe you laughed when Corporate said ass-kissing was figurative, and not meant to be taken as a literal action. It left them open to sexual harassment lawsuits. Yeah, you laughed. Corporate didn't laugh though. They handed you your paycheque and told you to get off the premises in the next five minutes or you'd be charged with trespassing.

And don't come back or you'd be charged with trespassing.

And don't call us, or you'd be charged with harassment.

And don't blog about us on your site or you'd be charged with libel.

And don't mention us in passing to anyone or you'd be charged with slander.

And if you're not off the property in 4 minutes and 18 seconds, you'd be charged with trespassing.

So you left. And maybe you stewed on how they treated you after working there for eight years, and maybe you were a little sorry but felt you could hardly be blamed for something that was obviously done under the influence of drugs. You couldn't even remember doing it, for Christ's sake. Maybe the bills were due and you were getting tossed out on your ass and then Corporate sent you a V-mail explaining that they had decided to sue you for damages from that night in the coffee house and don't worry about sliding your card in the phone, because they'd already emptied your bank account and you still owed them another thirty-five hundred bucks and you needed to have that to them by the end of the month to prevent further action.

So you skipped the bus and went for a walk instead, and then there you were in the rain, across the street from your former place of employment fantasizing about going in there and really kicking up some shit, ready to pump your quarters and start the game of your life, when a breathy blonde with a Hello Kitty umbrella kicks water at you and your sour face and then laughs. She leans in close and you smell mangoes and wax lipstick and flowers and other entrancing girl-smells and she whispers, *Come on, this place sucks. I know somewhere.*

You ask her where she came from, thinking Heaven, thinking Miami, and she points to a dirty old city bus winding away from you. The #1, a cross-town bus that literally goes *everywhere*. The sign on the back says VISIT R'LYEH, and there's a happy family having the time of their lives in some distant tropical paradise. The emerald water is black, but you think it's just grime from driving the city streets. Later, you'll realize you were mistaken.

Sometimes your life changes in predictable ways. You see the change coming and there are lots of signs pointing like a curve in the road. Warning you the path to take is changing ahead and if you don't change with it you'll soon find yourself sailing off a cliff into black space. But sometimes the biggest changes in your life come on little, spur-of-the-moment decisions you wouldn't think would affect you in a million years. This was both. You turned your head away from your former place of employment because you wanted to smell that girl again, and she was already dancing down the street. It was a small choice. The curve came when your body moved with your head and took that first step toward her. You never saw it coming.

She was right, the place was better. The coffee sucked, the service was terrible, and they were playing some early century industrial to suit the mood. Nouveau post-something or other she called it. You took it to mean they could forgo expensive light tables and wall aquariums in favour of cinder blocks and rust panelling. Warehouse incandescent bulbs spit dirty yellow light on everything and it hurts your eyes. Everyone wears black and you can't tell the girls from the boys.

But Angela is there, and it makes this place paradise.

She talks about how great the world must have been before simfarming and climate change. She talks about the goldfish they sell in a vending machine on campus that glow in the dark, and how everyone has them for pets and how someone has been putting them in the toilets in the girls' bathrooms. You counter with corruption and greed, your same old shtick. She talks about flowers that smell like candy and simpuppies that always stay small and cute. You hit her with your big guns, you vent about Corporate and how they've turned the world into cancer. She asks if you know cancers are immortal growth and if we can tame them we can live forever. That doesn't sound so bad.

She's an art student and she knows your friend Celina and she saw you a couple weeks ago when you were strobing on a weekend high and ranting about Corporate. You looked so crazy. She found out where you work from Celina and had already been by there a few times but hadn't seen you. She asks if it's stalking and you say yes but you aren't creeped out. You're flattered. Your heart is hammering in your chest and it stutters when she smiles and helps you put sugar in your coffee and your hands touch.

She did it on purpose. It burns you when she smiles and you know you never want to be away from this girl again. It's too early to tell her you love her but you say it as a joke after she names off some bands you like. She just looks at you like she knows it wasn't a joke but it's alright.

You're eating noodles and shrimp for dinner and the phone rings. Your stomach does a quick double flip and threatens to come up on you. You know you shouldn't answer the phone but you will. You have to. Because Angela is calling.

"Hey Patrick Terran, it's Angela." It's funny because in the three years you were together she never once said that to you. She called you Patty-cake. It was cute when she said it.

"Hi Angel," you say, and every letter feels like it's cut from razor blades.

"I wanted to talk to you today about your disgusting foot odour."

"It's good to hear your voice." Your palms are hot and slick and the viewfinder is showing you a composite of Angela's face made up from a lot of different images. It isn't exactly her, but it's damn near her.

"Did you know that you're offending friends and family with disgusting foot odour?" she says. "In fact, one in two people will suffer with this uncomfortable and embarrassing condition. It's caused by a build-up of bacteria feeding off the sweat your feet make in your socks and shoes. Bacteria are disgusting little creatures that live off your old, dead foot flesh and drink the salt out of your sweat. Smelling them on you is both offensive and hurtful to those you love most."

"I knew that because you told me last week," you say. Your words are muted with snot in your throat and in your nose, which can be embarrassing and painful for your loved ones.

"Luckily there's a product designed just for people like you and your stinky feet."

"I'm sorry."

"*Happy Feet* is a Johnson and Simmons product designed to cure unnecessary foot odour and save you from being embarrassed in public."

"I miss you, Angel. I just wanted you to know that."

"Please pick up some *Happy Feet* by Johnson and Smith, Patrick Terran? For me?"

The video face puckers in a playful pout that stabs the air from your lungs. Today it's your bad feet. Other days it's about the weight you're putting on. Other days it's about how you should get rid of your unsightly oily skin with a graft. She calls to tell you all the things she would never say when she was alive. She tells you these things to shame you and hurt you into buying products. And you listen to the whole thing hoping that the end of the conversation will be different this time, because it always hurts so bad at the end, and the way things are going you know it isn't going to be any different.

"Take care, Patrick Terran. I'll see you soon!"

And you listen to those razor words bite into your flesh and if you cry every single time, well, who can blame you.

"That's fucking *horrible*," Ajax says, scratching at his eye. Today it's red and swollen and there is a rime of dried blood around the lid.

"You should have that looked at," you say, pointing to your own eye.

"Yeah, I did," Ajax says. "They say they want to take it out. Say it's going to cause more seizures and eventually I'll be a drooling organ donor. From the optic pins." He makes a funny exploding-head motion with his hands and a popping noise with his lips.

"That sounds pretty horrible too."

Ajax shrugs. "Black market, baby. What are you gonna do?"

"I guess," you reply, watching as he picks at his bloody eye and wipes his fingers on a plastic towel.

"No," he says. "I mean, what are you gonna do? About the phone calls."

"Nothing," you say, but that's a lie. You are definitely going to be doing something.

Later when you leave Ajax to his bleeding eye you walk for a long time sucking in dirty yellow air and scratching your head when the rain makes you itch. You decide Angela was wrong. There's nothing beautiful in the world. The things that made the world beautiful have all been sliced up and zip wrapped or canned. They've been packaged for individual consumption. Give them credits; they give you your life. It's the perfect economy, the way man was meant to live. Everything is fair because money doesn't care what colour you are, or if you're fat or crippled or blond. It doesn't care if you came from unfiltered DNA or from the mining colonies of Io or from Detroit. You either opt-in to the system or you opt-out.

Your feet are sore and you're tired of walking and the rain is giving you a rash. You step into a bus station and there are two girls smoking and one of them hurls a choking cough from her lungs like tuberculosis and spits a wad of bloody phlegm on the glass. Her brown eyes match yours from the corner of your vision and she turns her head slightly to let you know she's waiting for you to say something. You want to tell her she's boring; you've been there and done that. But you don't.

You're too busy looking at the wad of grease on the glass, the way the blood sits in the centre like a red yoke from a counterfeit egg, and you think about how the world is circular. You wonder again if you made the same face as that old Chinese with the slime on her coat the first time you picked up the phone after Angela died and listened to her list off your faults and you realize it doesn't matter. Nothing ends. Opting out of one thing is opting in to another.

The bus comes, and it's the wrong one but you take it. You sit as far away from the girl as you can.

The bus route is one of those long circle jobs that go all the way around the city. It meanders in and out of a dozen neighbourhoods. People get off. A few get on. More leave. Eventually the girl with the brown eyes and bleeding lungs gets off, swishing past you without a glance. You're already forgotten. Some guy who gave her a weird look once upon a time when she spit blood and slime on a window. You wonder if she'll still remember the sight of that red and brown slug long after you've disappeared from her memory.

The bus trundles off and you fall asleep. You dream of that tropical paradise with the black water and happy, screaming families raping and torturing each other. You dream of endless fields filled with some kind of strange fleshy plants with huge, jutting organs sticking straight in the air. There are bloody sheets spewing out of the organs like flags, dancing softly in the wind.

Angela is with you, but her face is long and canine. She's got huge red eyes. She's never been more beautiful. The air is thick with the sound of grinding gears and slapping meat. Some small animal is wailing in terror. And before you, standing like rows like some brutal harvest of flesh are rows upon rows of pink human torsos with tentacles for limbs like starfish. Gorged, erect penises jut straight up from their bellies, and silky red tissue ejects from the piss holes like lung filters in a sea anemone. You see thousands of them, stretching out forever, spewing their red tissue and then sucking it back in again with a flex of their rock-hard bellies. The tissue floats in the air, collecting pain like dust, collecting screams like food.

"They're tireless workers," Angela says. She takes your hand and leads you toward the fields. "Omni-matrix software upgrades have linked their brains together so they function as a collective, sending out millions of calls a day, asking their loved ones to buy their goods. Corporate is our biggest customer."

"Those are *people?*" you ask. The marvel of it all. "How do they survive?"

"They don't. They're dead. But dreaming. It's a very powerful tool. Just think about all those souls linked together. You need never be bored. You need never be lonely. Your every sick wish and desire granted."

"But by who?" you say, thinking of R'lyeh and those torturous family excursions. "If this isn't Corporate, who is this?"

She smiles, her teeth porcelain and perfect.

Hours later the bus driver is shaking you awake.

"You can't sleep here," he says, rubbing his hand on the side of your face. You pull back when you see it covered with burns and warts. It's ridged along the knife of his hand, like a crab's claw, bumpy and red. Like something is trying to scrape through his flesh and get out at the world. His more interesting inner self, maybe, the one he never shows anybody. The one he won't show you. His words are deformed because his teeth are crooked and broken. He's a wreck and you wonder why you never noticed it before.

You check your phone and it says the time is 11:43 P.M. It says you have 32 messages that you didn't hear because the ringer was shut off. You didn't feel it because the buzzer doesn't work. The phone is hopelessly outdated and you should have had it replaced years ago.

"Hey," you say to the bus driver. "Where are we?"

He answers with a word you can't quite get your head around, like he said it with marbles in his mouth. You ask him to repeat it and he does, and you can't understand it still. You ask him to repeat it one more time and he points at a small red sign beside his seat that says END OF LINE. He pops the door and waits for you to get your lazy ass off his bus.

It's cold and you see your breath falls off your face in plumes of grey and the air is thick with the smell of sewage from the river and exhaust from the bus. It's dark and you've never seen this street before. You turn and ask the bus driver for directions and he simply points down the road and says, "Start walkin'," then he slams the door shut. The bus hisses at you and farts propane exhaust as it drives into the night. There are red lights on the back of the bus and green light spilling from within. There's someone sitting at the back and as the bus wanders away the person turns and looks at you and the face is familiar but you can't be sure. Maybe you've seen him before. Maybe you used to work with him or you went to school together. Maybe he's someone your sister brought home once. A moment later he's gone and there you are in the cold and the dark with your phone in your hand and the 32 messages you haven't listened to yet, so you start walking and put the phone to your ear.

"Hey Patrick Terran, it's Angela," she says.

"Hey baby," you say.

"I'm just calling because I wanted to tell you that your genital odour is embarrassing your family."

"I'm sorry," you say.

You listen to her talk and tell you she'll see you soon. The message ends and she tells you about your bad haircut. Then she tells you about how your siblings are worried your hemorrhoids are getting out of hand. She goes through 14 separate things that are wrong about you, things she hates or is embarrassed by or is ashamed of, and then the message changes.

"Patty-cake," she says, her voice breathless. Your heart lurches. "Get off the bus. Now."

You stop walking and look down at your phone. The message is from two hours ago.

Your friend Ajax answers the phone on the third ring. He's holding a towel to his face and there's blood on it. His silver eye is bulging like the orb of a frog; the flesh is waxy and seething heat from infection. He holds the phone carefully with his off hand against the side of his face not crusted and swollen. Your name and face are on the screen, giving him the finger and then breaking into a grin. The scene repeats itself again and again until he answers the phone.

"Hey, buddy!" Ajax says. "What the fuck is up?"

"What?" you say. "No, nothing." The line hisses and pops with static.

"You alright?" he says. "You sound high. And this connection is for shit. Where are you?"

"*I . . . (STATIC) . . . hurt my nose*," you say.

"You what? Hang on." Ajax says. The static is getting to him, and he swears loudly. He shakes his phone. The video-screen you flips him off and laughs again, like you're doing it on purpose.

"*. . . she looks like worms, man. I missed the point . . .*"

"What the fuck are you talking about?" Ajax shouts. "I can't hear you!"

"*. . . Not . . . like . . . this . . .*"

"Pete!" Ajax yells. "I can't hear you!"

"*I'm . . . (STATIC) . . . through a spider's ass*," you say, and laugh.

Ajax hears the cogs in some great machine desperately in need of oil, and he hears you panting and laughing in alternating breaths. You're praying gibberish, a language that can only be spoken with broken teeth and blood in your mouth. And then another voice, which turns his blood cold and he throws his phone against the wall when he hears it, cracking the touch screen and causing a rip in your smiling face.

"COME WITH US," the voice says.

You have no idea how long you've been walking, but you do it because the next message you listened to was Angie telling you it wasn't much farther. You move from the glare of one sodium arc-light to the next, marvelling at how the rain seems to subtly shift direction with every light you pass under. The effect is disorienting, causing the shadows to warble in your peripheral vision. Sometimes they angle away from you, and other times they almost seem to be reaching for you, grasping for your clothes with tiny broken-twig fingers, and when a shadow actually manages to grab and tear a small hole in your shirt, you scream at it and flail away, slamming your back against a light pole and huffing shallow, panicked breaths.

The pole is a cold wet shock along your spine, with a touch like smooth vinyl where it touches your skin. Something buzzes in your hand and you throw your phone in a panic. It bounces across the pavement and comes to a rest in the dark a few feet away. There's a crack on the screen and chipped plastic on the corner where it hit the ground. The lit screen is flashing red and blue, blue and green, green and red. Your next message and it's another one from Angie. You can barely hear her through the tinny little speakers.

"It's alright," she's saying. "Don't be afraid of them, Patty-cake. They're harmless. It's all in your mind. It's all in your mind."

And of course it is. This entire thing is in your head. You don't jump at shadows because shadows aren't real. They're dark copies of real things. They have no substance. You're not afraid. Just like you're not afraid that your phone with the broken buzzer suddenly buzzed in your hand to get your attention.

You step into the gloom, praying that whatever grabbed your shirt won't grab you now, and you swoop in and pluck the phone off the ground. And if the shadows seem to take a little longer than normal before they retreat back away from the light, well, that's probably just something you're dreaming up because you're not scared.

The area is growing more decrepit from street to street. When the lights over the sidewalk begin to flicker it makes your throat burn with bile and you taste burnt oil and smoke in the air. Even the graffiti is corrupt. Gone are the delicate, beautiful works enhanced with Light Tape and AniPaint you're used to seeing. These are crude, offensive scrawls scraped out of the sides of the buildings, in languages you don't recognize. On one wall you pass, a massive dead city has been painted, full of corpses and black shadows that seem to be feasting on the meat. VISIT R'LYEH, it says. The caption is in Filipino or Latin maybe, you can't tell. It seems to be gibberish. It looks like *ph'nglui mglw'nafh Cthulhu R'lyeh wgah'nagl fhtagn.*

Maybe it's Arabic.

"It's not Arabic," Angie's message says. There are only three left.

The pavement here is cracked and chipped and there are dark stains that should maybe be best left unexplained. You avoid them as best you can, and wonder how they can remain even though the rain is a steady cold sheet of plastic against your skin. There are fire barrels here and there with dark, brooding shapes huddled around them; you must be somewhere near Forest Lawn but you've never been here before. There are bus routes here, but every small glass shed you pass says *the number 1 is out of order, please continuing down the line.* They blink in digital clarity like an alarm clock, on and off, conserving power by only being active half the time The other half they are somewhere dark, and you shake your head because that's a weird thought to have about a bus stop light screen. At the next bus stop it's exactly the same, except your belly sinks when you read it because for just a moment it might have read something different, it might have read something like *I want you to eat a live cat.*

You stagger and trip in a puddle, coming to your knees, the bright lancets of pain shooting up your thighs. You shake the water from your eyes and see that you're standing in front of an old subway entrance. PICKMAN TRAM a cracked sign says, and rust flows like blood in the rain from the letters.

The phone in your hand has one more message. You stagger to your feet, and press your hand against the old steel claptrap door to the subway. It grinds on joints that haven't been opened in years. It opens to a gaping black chasm that welcomes you with a rush of gas air, like the stink of propane additive and sour compost. You can't see more than three or four feet past the doorway, but you sense a huge, cavernous space before you, like the mouth of the world if it were to suddenly open before you and swallow you from the face of existence.

There's a small blue light deep in the throat of the black, some tiny spark bug or firefly. It dances back and forth, swaying in some unfelt breeze before you, and your last sane instinct tells you to run for your life, run like you've never run before, blind and brutal, clawing at your eyes like a lunatic and screaming your lungs bloody. But you don't, because it's all so glorious. It's all bigger than you are. God doesn't hate you. He doesn't know you.

As the firefly comes closer to the door, you see it is no life form at all but the backlit screen of a cell phone, and when it floats up to Angie's face you see her features elongated and canine from the shadows, her eyes large and red. Her blonde hair is matted and tacky from some dark fluid; she smells like motor oil and blood. She smiles at you, and her teeth are porcelain-perfect. Her grin stretches unnaturally large, piercing her cheeks and stretching toward her ears, like her smile is a gash threatening to sever the top of her head completely.

And God, how she looks is beautiful.

"Patty-cake," she says, and her voice has taken on a strange duotone quality, or perhaps it's three voices, you can't be sure. You try to focus on the voice you remember and find you can't. Something tickles your face as she speaks. You feel across your lips with scrabbling, panicked fingers and when you pull your hand away you see your nose has been bleeding. For how low long, you can't say.

She's beckoning you to listen to that last message now. A line of drool runs down her chin, pink and sticky. Her own phone is dancing with colour, flashing images of things you've never seen, never imagined: dead cities; tentacled horrors of eyes and teeth; great, mindless things in the deepest parts of space devouring stars and ripping solar systems apart. Between these photos you see images from her life with you, photos of your face; pictures of the two of you, young and free and happy, cheeks touching, comfortable and familiar. In some of them she's the blonde beauty who rescued you. In some she's this fleshy dog-creature with overly large eyes and a smile meant for rending and tearing.

And she's urging you to put the phone to your ear and listen to that last message.

You hit a button and put the phone to your ear.

It's ringing.

"Hey, buddy!" Ajax says. "What the fuck is up?"

"What?" you say. "No, nothing." You're confused. Is this the message you were supposed to hear? The line hisses and pops with static, and Ajax is talking but you can't hear it. "I think Angie hurt my nose," you say.

It's hard to focus when Angie's face is moving like that. Rippling, like her flesh is a sheet covering a pit of fleshy snakes. They rope around each other, and her skin draws back from her stretching teeth.

"... *the fuck are you talking about?*"

You've made a mistake, you can see that now. You've made a simple, terrible mistake. You weren't looking at the touch screen on your phone when your greasy fingers were looking for Angie's last message, and you hit a speed dial option instead. You're missing the point. There was some vital bit of information on that message and you've lost it. You've lost things before, but not like this.

"Not like this," you say to Ajax and to Angie.

The phone is hissing at you. The blood on your hands makes it feel soft and spongy, like you've been holding a spider to the side of your head and trying to talk through its ass.

Angie takes you by the hand. In a moment of total clarity you see the fields again, with those strange plant-like torsos, those flesh anemones spurting their lung-wads into the air and sucking them back in like red flags. You can almost feel the bones in your limbs cracking and the sockets popping as they reform into large bruised tentacles. You can feel your gorge rise and the heat in your midsection, burning ache for your Angel, your loins swelling with blood and tissue and bulging against the seams of your jeans. You feel beautiful. You feel powerful.

"Come with us," she whispers, her teeth clattering as she speaks. It sounds like she's smashing coffee mugs together. She draws you into the dark, her large red eyes never leaving your face.

You shuffle after her, your half-formed feet and arms making you clumsy and unbalanced. You stumble, and she picks you up. She's as beautiful as ever, a true angel. You look up into her dog face and smile. She would never hurt you, and you trust her completely. Everything is forgiven and forgotten, but you're not sure if it's because of love or because the cracking and popping in your skull as your head reshapes itself is wiping out delicate memory networks. You flip a coin and decide on love.

Later, when the screaming begins, you try to hold on to that thought.

There's a phone ringing, and for a long time Ajax doesn't know where it is so it rings and rings. Finally he digs it up from under a couch cushion and sees your cracked, smiling face giving him the finger. His thumb hovers over the answer button. He feels he should answer but he doesn't. There's a small beep and the call goes through to voicemail.

A lone, bloody tear tickles his cheek as he thumbs through to his voicemail options. The phone tells him he has one message from Patty-cake. It asks him if he would like to listen to the message.

He wipes the tear with his hand, and then fingers the eye patch where his silver eye used to be.

The phone asks again if he would like to listen to the message from Patty-cake.

After a long time, Ajax pushes a button.

last amphibian flees

M.A.C. FARRANT

CHICKENS AND US

They sing in a foreign language like opera I'm told. A squawk is a kind of aria fugata.

Mostly they're like old men gathering at the meal replacement shelves at Safeway. That's why Emily Dickinson crossed the road, to speak with them about death.

Kurt Vonnegut thought the chicken's chemical makeup was hilarious. It reacts as if it was some kind of puritanical harbinger of death, he said, and that's why it keeps crossing the road. Kurt Vonnegut did a drawing of a chicken's asshole which has since delighted many.

Chickens will peck each other to death. They can't help themselves once there's a wound. They're like us that way. They love the smell of blood.

Although shaped differently the chicken's beak works similar to a human's mouth, ingesting one small truth at a time.

Chicken Little Syndrome is the condition of hysteria that results in paralysis. This happens when the sky falls on a chicken, another way in which chickens are like us.

At a chicken funeral sad music is played while a chicken relative carries the dead chicken wrapped in tinfoil towards a brightly lit fast food restaurant where a rotisserie awaits.

A chicken brain is about the size of a man's thumb nail. Like ours, it's not big but sufficient for their needs.

Unlike us, a chicken is without a love interest or a dog.

In my day, my father said, we didn't ask why the chicken crossed the road. Someone told us the chicken crossed the road, and that was good enough for us.

Ernest Hemingway said the chicken crossed the road to die. In the rain, he added, and wrote several novels about this.

I cross the road because even though I am a boiling fowl I am still able to cross the road.

There are twenty-four billion chickens in the world and only one billion roads. What will happen next?

I found this question in a magazine: How do you know if you're a birder? The answer: You are a birder if you have ever faked your own death to attract vultures.

Someone must know about Hugh and me.

LAST AMPHIBIAN FLEES CALGARY AIRPORT

Mother died of pneumonia one week after her spare oxygen tank was taken away during our flight to Toronto. An attendant said it didn't have a regulator. Mother was sixty-seven years old, had emphysema and cardiopulmonary disease and had been on oxygen for ten years.

Our boy Alvin who is huge got nasty. There's a hole in Alvin's nature big enough for a truck to pass through. He got convulsed by a violent aversion to the flight attendant. You just don't just take away a person's spare oxygen tank! They put us off the flight in Calgary.

So we were all worked up about that. It took everything out of us and we were just about dying from hunting down hope, and trust, and gleaming promise, not to mention another oxygen tank. So there was failure.

Then Charlie took off after the Last Amphibian which is what he calls Alvin on account of his turning from a sweet baby into a twelve-year-old canister of woe. Alvin was heading for god knows where. My step-father Jimmy went with them.

I could not go on. I could not continue these explorations. A local man gave Mother and me cherries and a few roasted almonds while we waited for them to return which they eventually did, Alvin with two double cheeseburgers, his usual reward for compliance.

I could not know then that I would contribute to Mother's death. I should have known about the airline's regulator rule but didn't. Mother's tank ran out and we had no spare. I was too worried about Alvin to worry about Mother. She seemed happy enough sucking on cherry pits.

It was next day in Emergency when I got another tank. By then Mother had pneumonia.

SMOOTH

During the night I burst out of my fur. Before this I'd been covered head to foot in it. It came off in an explosion; chunks of brown fur lay on the sheets, the bedroom floor, the dog's crate in the corner of the room. The force of the explosion woke me up. I was sweating but quickly realized the significance of what had occurred. Losing the fur was an enormous thrill. It was beyond a thrill; I have never known such happiness. I had to tell someone. It was three-fifteen in the morning. I woke up my husband.

"Feel my arm!" I cried. He didn't stir. "Wake up! Feel my arm! It's smooth!"

He rolled over. "What the hell?"

"Feel my arm! Feel my skin!" I was hysterical with joy. "There's no fur. I'm free of it at last!"

He threw an arm my way and mumbled, "Yes, yes."

"Now feel my neck!" I urged. "There's no fur there either!" This was so amazing!

He pawed my neck. "Do you realize what this means?" I cried. "I am now a completely smooth woman!"

He touched my head. "Your head is bald, Olivia," he said. "Bald as an egg. Better check your pubes."

"This is just like you to spoil my happiness," I cried. "I finally achieve something of real importance in life and you don't even congratulate me."

"Congratulations," he said. "But you're still bald."

"Do you realize how long I've waited to lose my fur? How important it's been to me? How hard I've worked? All the books I've read? All the visualizations I've done?"

"Was that what you were doing Saturday mornings?" he said.

"You know what I was doing Saturday mornings! I was attending my Shedding Your Fur Workshop. Susan down the road lost her fur ages ago. And Lorna, and Mary, and Lynette, none of them have fur anymore. How do you think it's been for me, the only one of my friends still walking around fully furred? Can you even begin to imagine the pitying that's been going on behind my back? Can you?"

He was completely awake now, as was the dog who'd come out of her crate and was sniffing the fur on the floor. "I've always liked you covered in fur," he said, raising himself on one elbow to look at me. "That's the woman I married. I'm too old for change. Did you check your pubes?"

"Raymond!"

"Well, did you?" he said.

"Here, on the most profound night of my life, when I have at last reached the furless state of being, all you can think about is my pubes?"

"I'm going to miss your fur," he said.

"You'll get used to it."

He got out of bed, picked up several patches of fur and together with those lying on the sheets, arranged them on his pillow. "I think I'll go back to sleep now, Olivia," he said, nuzzling the fur sadly.

Too excited for sleep I lie in bed for the rest of the night thinking about tomorrow. Oh, the world was mine now!

white teeth
DAVID LIVINGSTONE CLINK

She lives in a house surrounded by white teeth. The sound on the roof could be rain. A dragonfly nearing a gas station where the attendant smokes while pumping gas is an omen, an assurance that dragons will return, their scales a rattling subway train, their wings a flapping carnival tent. They will strike, as lightning once did, at the earth's mantle, breaking it to reveal a molten core, waking bears from hibernation. No one will be able to sleep, but we'll survive, she tells us, the skulls of newborns will still fuse, people will find themselves on volcanic land masses surrounded by unopened boxes. And the rain's hard knuckles will beat us down. The signs are all around us.

the sweet spot

A.M. DELLAMONICA

"I'm gonna visit Dad." Matt is curled in the passenger seat of their antique minivan, scowling as offworlders tromp and slither past their front bumper. Shooting a glance at Ruthie through long, pretty eyelashes, he flips down the visor to check the mirror.

"Dad's dead, Matt. He can't see your haircut."

"Want to come?" Falsely casual.

"Can't." She throws the word through the driver's-side door; she's outside, waving merchandise: soda, water bottles, scented strips of leather and fur. "I have to pay off Security."

"You could trust Romano with that. You do it for him often enough."

"I could get a job in a feeler bar too," she snaps . . . then regrets it. So much for vowing to be more patient.

Matt gives up on finger-combing his curls. Coaxing a battery out of their aging solar charger, he checks the readout. "Did you use this?"

Ruthie winces. "An old lady paid me forty for half a charge. Her son just died."

A flat glare.

"Forty, Matt."

"So you get forty, I get half a visit with the old man."

"With an answering machine." He can dress it up all he likes, but the battery is just juice for an interactive video of their father. "Waste of credit, waste of time."

"You suck, Ruth." He edges out of the van, stomping off to the cemetery.

Ruthie reins in an urge to beg forgiveness. It's done; she'll grovel later. Instead, she climbs into the van, thumbing the air conditioning and leaning into the vent.

Since they came to Kauai, her fantasies have been about winter. Deep breath, in through the nose, out through the teeth. As cool air chills her sinuses, she imagines snow melting through her mittens.

She mimes packing a snowball, rolling it across an unbroken plain of white. She barely has the bottom ring of a snow fort built when someone raps on the window.

It's Sam, a.k.a. Security, leering down her shirt through the tinted glass.

Ruthie shuts off the air conditioning, grabs the weekly payoff, and slides out into the balmy fist of the Hawaiian afternoon.

Sam is a spotty-faced redhead whose scarred right eye socket bulges with a cut-rate offworld prosthetic. Blue gel shot through with veins pulses at her, fronted by a lens that has the fluted edges of a poker chip.

"Morning, Ruth." Onion breath ruffles her hair.

"Hi." She holds out the weekly bribe.

He pockets it without counting. "We gotta talk. Inside?"

She shakes her head. "Graveyard. I'll have Romano watch the van."

"Please. You think I want a piece of your skinny ass?"

She shrugs. Not all the women on Vender's Row pay their bribes in cash. Besides, she doesn't want that onion smell in the car. "Gotta stretch my legs."

He's not thrilled, she can tell, but he follows her through the converted golf course to the high point of the cliff.

It's a scenic viewpoint, postcard perfect: ocean glittering silver-blue under swirled, fragile clouds. An anti-aircraft platform, purple-black in colour and shaped like a rosebud, drifts lazily among the cirrus wisps, guarding the Kauai channel and the offworlders' undersea military base there.

A hundred feet down, the aliens are splashing around the beach at the foot of the cliff, exuberant as children. They are kids, pretty much—barely grown, they were yanked from the seas of their homeworld to help the Democratic Army in its war against the Fiends.

"I never see anyone but you up here," Sam says. "Gawking at squid makes it hard to forget the war."

Ruthie leans on a sand-coloured boulder. Below, the offworlder soldiers wrestle, dunking each other, spitting water and tootling, churning up the Pacific as they tangle themselves into knots and then slip free. "Is that possible, forgetting the war?"

"Who the fuck knows. Hey, want an apple?"

"In exchange for what?"

"My treat." He holds out the gleaming red fruit and Ruthie can't help but snatch it. It's tart enough to make her pucker, and she nearly moans at the first bite.

"So . . ." Sam glances around. "Army's decided to put in another databank for the graveyard."

Ruthie catches a dribble of apple juice on her chin, licking it off her thumb. "More storage . . . the Democratic Army expects more casualties?"

"Lot more. Fiends have been cleaning their clocks."

"What's that to do with me and Matt?"

"They're not digging up the green for no mausoleum."

"They're putting it in the parking lot?" The fruit in her mouth becomes rubber; she fights to swallow. "How big?"

"Arches, plaques, statues, flowers—the whole nine."

"The entire parking lot?"

"Half," he says. "I'm giving twenty vendors their walking papers."

Yet another crypt. She can already see it, a square, depressing monument to the endless grind of this war. The Fiends—Friends of Liberation, they call themselves—have been making headway in their drive to secure the whole planet.

"Kabuva's gonna have to send even more of them," she says, indicating the squid on the beach.

"Yeah. That'll happen," Sam grunts.

"We're never gonna beat them at this rate."

"It's cute, Ruthie, your belief in the great Demo cause. But I ain't here to debate strategy."

"You're right. Matt and I can pay more, if you give us a chance. There'll be fewer vendors, less competition, more mourners. Can we stay?"

"Well . . ." Sam drawls, fake eye pulsing, snaggled teeth peeping out from under the skirt of his loose upper lip. "That depends."

The graveyard greens are lined with mosaic paths made of slate tiles. Each tile is inscribed with the name and signature of a Demo soldier, along with their mourning catalogue code. Twining over the immaculate fairways, the paths lead to curls of hedge and stone walled alcoves, nooks constructed to offer privacy to visitors.

Near an erstwhile sandtrap is a bench and an interactive obelisk. Ruthie pulls up its menu and lets it eat five of their hard-earned bank credit to pay for power. There's a jack for a battery—it's cheaper to bring your own juice—but she only needs a minute.

Fog machines belch out mist and a micro-projector starts up, projecting an image of Daddy within the fog. He's young, the invincible father she remembers from childhood, and Matt has apparently set his defaults so he's proportionately big. She has to look up, way up, because she only comes to his thigh.

The giant face brightens as Daddy looks down. "You're starting to look like your mother," it says. "How old—"

"I'm looking for Matthew," she interrupts. "I thought this was your spot."

Dad scratches his non-existent beard, buying time as, elsewhere, computers process her statement. "Your brother's not on the system, Ruth."

"Since when?"

"Twelve days, ten hours, six minutes."

She sinks to the edge of the sand trap and buries her face in her hands. Okay, don't be stupid, don't be a baby. Where you been going, Matt? Little lying bastard . . .

The ghost shifts, sitting. "Shits day, kid?"

She remembers the phone call when he asked her that. She was in school . . . she'd failed an art exam. Through a teary haze she sees him flicker, resetting. He resolves on a chair near the obelisk, older now, normal sized. He's playing his guitar.

That does it . . . she melts down completely. Dad plays rock songs under the tree, burning cash she can't afford while Ruthie cries and cries.

When she's stopped carrying on like a diva, he tilts his head: "Want to talk about it?"

"You're an answering machine," she says. "Cobbled-together phone conversations, vidblog entries . . ."

"If you prefer, I'll direct you to my physical remains."

Remains. A Dust-proof tube containing a DNA sample, buried under the slate tile that bears his name. "I'd prefer to talk to Matt."

"Sorry, hon. I don't know where your brother is."

She glares at the illusion. "We're losing our parking spot. No spot, no money. No money, no food. You get that? Matt told you how we live?"

"Yes."

It hurts to look at him, but the tears have carried her back to a hot, achy place where she can function.

"Sam will let us stay, but there's strings."

She can't go on. Demo Intelligence has to be monitoring these conversations, combing transcripts for damaging admissions. Exploiting people's grief. She can't tell him Sam's joined the Fiends. "Anyway, bribe's going up."

"Can you pay more?" Daddy asks.

"That's the question, isn't it?"

Matt turns up after midnight, slipping through the side door and delicately arranging his skin and bones onto their mattress. She doesn't bother pretending to be asleep. He wouldn't be fooled; they've lived this way too long.

"Where were you? I went to the sandtrap."

"It's a big boneyard, Ruth."

She pinches him. "You haven't been online all week."

He lights up. "You talked to Dad?"

"Where were you?"

He bites his lip. "I'm seeing someone."

"Oh." A flare of unease, somewhere in her marrow.

"Yeah, 'oh.' You want to know who?"

"Someone I won't like, I guess, or you'd have told me. But human."

"Yeah, human. I don't do squid, Ruth. It's Holly Scott."

"Oh." Holly's a Democratic war veteran, like Sam. She's royalty here on the Row—lives in a real camper, sells water and battery charges. She runs a good patter on the human and offworlder marks alike; her wares sell well.

She's old—thirty at least, twice Matt's age.

"That's all you have to say? No lecture on fucking the competition?"

He's spoiling for a fight, but Ruthie doesn't have one in her. "If I was that much of a bitch last time you had a girlfriend, I'm sorry."

"If?" He morphs from mad to scared. "No. You've been drafted, haven't you?"

"Worse." She laughs weakly. "Sam's with the Fiends."

"So? We knew there had to be a few on the Row."

"They want us to sing, Mattie."

That gets his attention—his eyes widen, and he lets out a peep.

"He called it a project," she tells him. "We sing, it draws the squid off Fry Beach. Fiends want to plant a bomb there."

"We're a diversion?"

"I guess."

He sits, toppling a stack of soda cans. "No way."

"Half the parking lot's getting demolished. Sam says we can keep our spot—"

"I am not helping those bastards commit murder."

"You think I want to?"

"You're considering it, aren't you?"

"Where we gonna go? We got a good thing here . . ."

"I remember what a good thing is, Ruthie, and this isn't it."

"You ungrateful shit. We're eating, aren't we?"

"You'd rather kill people than go hungry?"

"Hungrier?" But now Ruthie's ashamed of herself. She fumbles for his hand. "We'll offer more money."

With that, the resistance vanishes. Matt presses his forehead against hers, and they don't say any more.

Next morning they pull out all the stops, hustle-hustle, sell-sell-sell. Ruthie does a tune-up on the van, fills the fuel tank, changes the oil. Matt trades their heavy goods for lightweight stuff: touchables, music files, things they can hawk at any roadside. By dinner the van is ready to move. They have a few weeks of water and protein mallows laid by, just in case.

They're discreet, but the Row talks. Sam shows, a disappointed expression on his narrow face. "You pissing on my offer, then?"

Ruthie lets him into the van. Steady voice, she thinks, don't quaver. "We'll pay more to keep our spot—"

"Did I ask for more money?"

"We can't sing," Matt says.

"Can't?" Sam's gelatinous eye rolls in his direction, its false iris cycling wide.

"Take the payment, Sam, okay?" Ruthie pleads.

"No." Sam holds up both hands, making an "L" with his left finger and thumb, mirroring the gesture with his right hand so that his prosthetic leers at them through a rectangular space the size of a photoprint.

"What's that?" Ruthie says.

"Making sure I'm in the now," he says. "Kids, this is the moment when we become Friendly."

Matt puts up a hand. "There's no attitude here."

"No scam," Ruthie agrees. "We'll pay more, or go."

"It's just singing's impossible."

"And I'm—*we're* sorry."

"Gee," says Sam. "Can't I change your mind?"

The back of her hand tingles. Itches. Pinches. A tiny silver dot pimples up from under the skin behind her thumb.

She looks up, horrified, locking on Sam's flinty, half-alien gaze. Her flesh, around the metallic pinprick, is heating up. There are other itches now, too, a scattering of discomfort across her body.

"The apple you gave me . . ."

Sam smirks.

"What's happening?" Matt asks.

The dot behind her thumb begins to smoke. The burn's a candleflame at first—and that's bad enough—but the fiery seed is getting bigger, glowing like the cherry of a lit cigarette, frying more skin by the second.

"Ruthie?"

Another of the itches, above her navel, goes hot.

Matt catches her as she doubles over. She can't squelch a growl of pain. Wasp-heat in her temple, the stink of scorching hair, makes her gag.

Matt is screaming now.

No, she thinks, he's hurting Mattie too. She tries to lift herself off the van floor, to fight back.

Sam is laughing.

And Matt's not hurt, she realizes. It's worse—he's begging. "Stop, you win, we'll do it, don't hurt her."

Tears stream down Ruthie's face—crying again, second time in two days, she thinks—as Sam grabs her hair. "That true, Ruth? You'll sing for us?"

"Yeah," she manages.

The seeds cool off, forming blisters.

"Saturday, dinnertime, at the Atlanta monument." Sam nudges her with a toe; she has his pants leg fisted in her hands. "Sing for at least an hour. Don't try running off—we're listening, we'll know."

He steps over her to the door, patting a furious Matt on the head.

"Sam . . ."

He turns, and she finds herself wanting to cringe, like a whipped dog. "We'll need our stuff."

"That so?"

"She's right." Matt says. "It was in storage in Koloa. Masks, instruments, sound system. Can you find it?"

"We can find anything." With that, Sam steps back out onto the parking lot.

120

Matt slams the door, throws the locks, and flicks the A/C on full. He yanks out their first aid kit, rummaging. "What do we do?" he asks, sounding like a little boy.

Shakily, Ruthie knots her fingers together in an approximation of a Kabuva tentacle knot. "Practice," she says, but the sign she makes is different; it's the squid word for deception.

"Isshy taught us the Kabuva folk songs back when he and Dad were living together," Matt says. He's standing beyond the bedroom door of Holly's camper. Ruthie is stretched out on the bed.

"Your dad had a sugar squiddy?" Holly pokes Ruth's shoulder with a stubby finger; she's using bootlegged med equipment to locate the fireseeds.

Ruthie nods. "By the time I was ten, we were a bona fide novelty act."

"Human kids who sing squid. I can see it." Holly's apparent lack of judgment annoys her. She wonders if this is playacting, if Matt already told Holly their secrets.

"Dancing monkeys, they called us," he says.

"Found another one." Holly eases the point of her knife into Ruthie's shoulder. "Over soon. Just breathe."

Matt keeps talking. "Isshy got on the wrong side of his superiors and got reassigned to The Sponge." He means the massive undersea installation the squid built in the middle of the Kauai channel. "Dad got drafted into the Demo Army. We moved here to live with a cousin, who got Dusted."

"Okay, doll, I got all the seeds. You doing okay?"

"Thanks, Holly." Ruthie reaches for her clothes.

"And now the Fiends want you to sing so they can crisp some calamari?"

"That's their plan, yeah."

"You want my opinion?"

"What, for free?" Ruthie says.

"Do as they tell you."

"Don't joke, Holly," Matt says.

"So not joking."

"But—you fought with the squid against them."

Holly steps out into her kitchenette, where she can see them both. "Democrats are losing the war. The squid'll give up on us."

"Holly, come on! What the Fiends want—it's terrorism."

"I don't want to cross the playground, Matt, I don't. But in another few years, Fiends'll invade the U.S. After that . . ."

"After that, what?"

"It'll take years. But Earth's gonna be all Fiend, all the time. They're gonna crawl over the whole map and eject every offworlder they find."

"There's gotta be some chance."

She shook her head. "Make some Friends, Matt. They're psycho, but they'll be running things."

"Switch sides? You wouldn't do that." He runs a finger down her face, stunned. Ruthie wonders: does he love her?

"This whole war's going in the squatter—"

"We aren't murderers, Holly."

"It's not like they're asking you to kill *people*."

"It is like that. Isshy was a mother to us."

"Squid momma left you here, grafting," Holly says. "For that you defy the Fiends?"

"We're not doing it," Ruthie says. "We just haven't figured out how to screw them yet."

Her brother's fingers come together, unconsciously expressing relief. Ruthie immediately feels better. Mattie's on board, she's still in charge. How hard can fooling Sam be? Being a Fiend doesn't make him smart.

"Thanks for patching me up, Holly," she says, then forces herself to add: "You two should get in some time together while you can. We may have to run for it."

Matt catches her arm. "You won't decide anything without me?"

"I figure something out, I'll text you."

With that, she heads for the beach path, vying with other scrabblers to sell touchables to the squid heading down to the water. She sells fake fur, fruit leather, perfumed gel, acting like everything's okay.

Squid are blind, their senses based in taste, smell, and touch—preferably all three at once. They'll stick a tentacle into any stinky moist thing they can find. Even the poorest scrabblers out here are wearing protective masks over their eyes and mouths.

Of course they'll pay you to take the masks off, to let them ramble their tentacles over your mouth and eyes, better yet into your pants. Every so often, a fry goes into the bushes with one of the vendors, bringing 'em back well-paid and covered in suckermarks.

Ruthie's not up for that, but she leaves her burned hand unbandaged, offering a taste of her blood.

It's over an hour before she gets what she's hoping for—a squid whose mantle veins go green with compassion when it tastes her wound. A bleeding heart.

Ruthie's fingers form the sign for help as the stranger's tentacle slithers over her . . . and before it can pull away, she passes it a KabuBraille note she's been coding, surreptitiously, this whole time.

It recoils, vanishing into the crowd. Ruthie starts coding another strip, hoping for another chance.

At sundown, she goes back to the sand trap. Dad is older when she boots him up: older, uniformed, hollow-eyed. "You look more like your mother every day."

"I need to get Matt somewhere safe," she says. "If Isshy boots you, will you tell him?"

"Isshy rarely—"

"I'm trying to get him a message."

More beard-scratching: it's processing again. "I know you're unhappy about Isshy and me. . . ."

She winces. "Stop. Play guitar—"

"It was love, you know—" He freezes.

Like Matt and Holly? Her face burns. "I'm over it, Dad. I'm sorry they broke you up."

The personality simulator is so good sometimes—he looked surprised, even grateful.

Steel up. Squash that rush of emotion. Ruthie's about to walk off when Dad starts strumming. She sinks to the grass, fixing her eyes on the anti-aircraft platform over the Sponge, the glimpse of ocean through the trees.

That evening Sam turns up with their old music trunk.

"You owe me back rent on that locker," he says. "Fifty, due after the concert."

"Yeah, yeah." They shut themselves in the van and Ruthie restrings her minicello. Matt warms up, warbling soprano Kabuva laments.

As they sing, they flash squid signs back and forth, piecing together a conversation the Fiend listening devices won't pick up. Ruthie tells him she's trying to contact Isshy.

Matt digs in his pocket for a balled-up sheet of seapaper. Ruthie runs a hand over the KabuBraille quickly; it is an advertisement for their concert.

Where? she signs.

All over the Island. Throwing back his head, Matt lets out a string of notes, all too high and atonal to sound musical to human ears. It is one of the squids' favourites, a howl of despair about leaving Mother Sea for faraway, violent shores. Disaffected soldiers went nuts over it.

Ruthie joins in, again fighting tears. She never liked this piece; what's wrong with her?

When the song ends, she turns away, hiding her brimming eyes. "Let's take a break—do some planning."

"You're the planner." Sour. Talk about disaffected . . . ·

"I meant . . . wanna talk song order?"

"Up to you."

She fumbles the mini-cello, which feels small. Her hands have grown. "Matt, you're the one told Sam we'd do the dancing monkey on Saturday."

"I should've let him burn you to a crisp?"

Ruthie's stomach burns. She was stupid; she took candy from a stranger. "Fine, everything's my fault."

"Any song order is okay," he sighs. "Shits, I'm already tired of this."

"We ended up getting drafted after all, Matt."

"Just not by the side we thought?"

"At least our so-called friends are winning," she says, for the benefit of the listening Fiends.

"Now there's a silver lining." He smiles weakly, signing: *Are we gonna be okay?*

In response, Ruthie plucks through the opening notes of a Kabuva folk song. Its first line translates, roughly, to: "All we can do is hope."

Next day she is emptying out the minivan's squatter when two goons whisk her off to the cemetery. It's just as she imagined in her wildest paranoid dreams: there's a secret door within the mausoleum, then a long elevator ride down to dull, fluorescent-lit Demo offices.

The air is stale but cold—air-conditioned. Heavenly.

Matt is already there. "I told them everything," he blurts.

"It's okay—"

"Hurry up." Her abductor, a lanky blond Amazon in a Democratic Army uniform, cuts them off. "We can't have the Fiends noticing you're gone."

They're marched to a squalid concrete box that smells of body fluids. An interrogation room? Ruth tenses. . . .

Then Matt cries out like a baby. Isshy is here.

Her brother hurls himself across the room, burying his face in the slime of Isshy's mantle, keening in Kabuva. Ruthie feels herself glancing askance at their captor. The woman's disgust is obvious.

That makes it easier. When Isshy extends a tentacle, Ruthie takes it without hesitation, pressing her knuckles into the gelatinous flesh of her father's one-time lover, then transferring a tentacle to her armpit so he can taste her.

"You're here to get us away?" she asks, hating that she sounds like a little kid.

Isshy's cap tightens, puckering.

Matt pulls his face out of the slimy hug. "Isshy?"

"I am getting immigration permits for you."

"Immigrate to where? Canada?" Her legs quake with almost sexual longing. Snow, she thinks. Cold.

"You've betrayed the Fiends, child. There's nowhere on Earth we can hide you."

"The Sponge, then?" Matt asks. "With you?"

The soldier grunts. "To a refugee city on Kabuva."

"Offworld?" Living away from Earth, on a wholly squid planet . . . Ruthie tries to imagine it.

"With you?" Matt repeats.

Isshy signs regret. "My term of service was extended. But Earthtown is a good place. It's on Blighted Sea."

Extended service: Isshy is buying their freedom with another tour. Ruthie shoves guilt aside: he got them into this, after all. "Can we leave right away?"

Matt startles. His face darkens.

"Or what, Mattie? Stay and die?"

"Can't we go to the Sponge?"

The alien caresses Matt's neck. "It's not allowed, spawn. We've been infiltrated, twice—humans have been banned from the base."

"I never heard that."

"It's classified," snarls the Demo officer. "Don't leak it. And before you go thinking there's some choice in this for you, let me lay this out. You do the concert for the Fiends, then you go to Kabuva. That's the deal."

Ruthie's jaw drops. "You *want* us to sing?"

"You're bait, child." Isshy is white now—angry. "They hope to catch the Fiends booby-trapping Fry Beach."

"Pardon me for trying to save some of your people, Sir. Fry Beach has state-of-the-art defences, kids. If we find out how the Fiends plan to crack its security . . ."

"We can't go back out there." Ruthie says. "If they realize we've reported them, Mattie and I are dust."

"Life's a gamble. You sing, we bag 'em, you go to Kabuva."

"Or we stay and the Fiends kill us?" Ruthie says.

"Pretty much. We done here?" the woman asks.

She looks at Matt. "What do you think?"

"I think if there was any real choice, you wouldn't ask my opinion."

"Matthew," Isshy says, reproachful. "Your sister is doing her best."

Her brother turns red.

"Say your goodbyes." The woman mimes scrubbing her hands, as if they're dirty. "I gotta get the boy out of here."

"Leave Matt," says Ruthie. "I'll go first."

"He's been missing longer." She takes obvious pleasure in peeling Matt out of Isshy's grip. "We're taking you out near your favourite obelisk, son; far as the Fiends know, you've been visiting Daddy."

Matt clings to the outstretched tentacle until she has bundled him out of reach. Then he's gone, and Ruthie's alone with Isshy.

"Thanks for helping us."

"Child. There was never any question."

"We have to run all the way to your homeworld?"

Tentacles spiral in distress. "Our attempt to help your government is falling into disgrace at home; the number of casualties is catastrophic."

"You never lose. When you show up, the Fiends always retreat."

"Ruth, it may be years yet before we leave. But leave we will. In defeat, I fear. You, Matthew—anyone close to us—you won't be safe. Everyone with sense is getting their loved ones to Earthtown."

"Your pets?"

"I hoped you weren't angry with me anymore, spawn."

"Isshy, we're in the shits now because of you and Dad."

"I can't change the past," he says. "But this could be a better life. Do you want to spend your days jammed in a car, starving?"

"I want my goddamn father back," she says sulkily.

He fluffs his cap. "I wish that, too."

She spends the evening atop her cliff, watching the fry gambol in the tide. Dozing with her back against a tree, she dreams of being on the run with Matt. Her brother is a baby again, easily transported, too young to balk or argue. They hide in a blizzard, amid curtains of freezing snow. Ruthie feels safe, invisible, in control.

When she wakes, Matt is beside her, watching the sunrise. Light spills gold over the water; peach and magenta clouds unfurl, like streamers, across the sky.

His eye falls on one of her burns.

"Don't worry about me," she says, irked.

"Cast iron maiden." It is something Dad called her, before he went away.

"It wouldn't hurt you to steel up a little."

"Get cold," he says.

"Life hasn't been getting easier."

"Cut off human contact. Dump my lover without so much as a 'do you mind, dear?' Yeah, that's an answer."

Tears springs to her eyes. Her fingers twist, of their own accord, into a Kabuva sign: *hurtful, unfair.*

"Sorry. I didn't mean—" He reaches out.

She slaps his hand away. *One of us has to have a hard shell*, she thinks. You can't be an open wound all the time.

"I screw up, Mattie," she says instead. "I don't ask your opinion enough. But this mess—I didn't make it."

He forms a clumsy chain of signs. *We should run.*

Which is ridiculous. Instead of saying so, she signs: *How?*

Matt opens a bottle of water and takes a long, slow gulp. "Something terrible's going to happen," he says, in his clear, light voice and Ruthie feels her stomach dropping into a pit.

Detonate a Dust bomb on a windless day, and it will expand in a sphere before falling downward. The nanotech weapon disassembles everything it touches. If it falls straight down, touching bare ground, the crater it makes will form a hemisphere.

The Atlanta monument, like so many from this war, reflects this reality. Its focus is a copper-lined crater, big enough to stand in and half-filled with offerings: flowers, stuffed animals, photos of the dead. Carved into its rim are images of the city in various eras, artists' renderings of famous citizens and heroes from the Democratic Army. The Fiends reduced Atlanta to atoms.

It is a creepy place to stage a concert.

Ruthie and Matt set up their backstage in a nearby grove of magnolia trees, pitching a small tent and unpacking their gear: the electronic synthmasks that play their backup music, the minicello, and two mesh sheaths woven from strips of seaweed. It has been years since they performed, and Ruthie's sheath is a bit short. But they still fit; neither of them has gained much weight since the so-called good days.

Squid start arriving before they are set up, flowing up from the beach, arriving in flitters, in buses from the barracks in Koloa. First there's a half a dozen of them, then thirty, then fifty.

Sam breezes into the tent, leering. "Ready for the big day, kiddies? Where's your donation bowl? You're supposed to be singing for money."

"We are singing for money," she says. "How long do you need to do your thing? An hour?"

"That should do. I expect a cut, you know."

She goes through the motions of haggling. Finally she says, "I need to dress."

His plastic eye pulses. "Go ahead."

"Get out, pervert," Matt says, and to her relief he does. "You okay, Ruth?"

"No. I'm a big bag of emotion."

"It's not a bad thing."

"Bad timing," she says.

"It's always a bad time," her little brother says.

Wrestling with grief and fear, she peers outside.

In the time it has taken to play out the little farce with Sam, the audience has swelled. Hundreds of squid are out there, setting up seawater sprinklers, lying on kelp mats and each other. They smell of overripe seafood, and they are passing things around—touchables, food, scent packs, drugs. Vendors from the Row hawk goods avidly from the sidelines.

Disturbed, Ruthie wrings out the brine in her dress, slithering into the mummy-wrap of seaweed strips. She swallows a pill called *Hot Flash* that will send her sweat glands into overdrive, then tests the microphone and display screen within her singing mask. Her hair goes into a ponytail; then she slicks it against her neck with gel.

The waiting squid are hooting a tune, their flute-like voices tootling in the meadow. It is a song about death—that's all the fry seem to sing anymore—and it brings up the gooseflesh on her burned arms.

"Lament to Blighted Sea," says Matt. He is in his sheath, ready but for his mask. "You think we'll get to Kabuva?"

"Don't see why not," she lies, then surprises herself by hugging him. "If anything happens, we meet on the cliff."

"The high spot." With a half-smile, he pulls his mask over his face. She does likewise, adjusting her mic.

Tech check. The words appear just above her eyes.

A-OK, she texts back.

"Let's do this," Mattie says aloud.

They emerge from the tent, hand in hand, and the cacophony of singing toots turns into a one-pitch whistle. Matt steps up to the lip of the Atlanta monument. The weeds on his legs and arms whutter in the breeze, carrying scents to their audience.

Ruthie is almost too stunned to move. There must be a thousand of them. How did the Fiends do it? She sees officers here and there, trying to disperse the crowd, only to get slapped down by a dozen hostile fry.

Bad morale, she thinks.

Mattie is letting go with a piercing high note. She activates the synthesized accompaniment coded into her mask, and the air fills with a clatter of shells and stones in surf.

Don't let your mind wander onstage. Daddy's voice, so deeply internalized it feels real. She boots the minicello, playing tones and chirps as her brother works his way into the song. It is a bloody-minded kid's chant about newborn squid drifting below the skin of the sea, yanking birds down from the surface, devouring them.

The listeners are mottling, their caps turning beige and coral as they relax. Ruthie remembers opening with this same piece in dozens of clubs across America. Daddy intertwined with Isshy at the water's edge, Scotch and soda in his hand. A sick and twisted family, sure, but a happy one. Isshy believed they'd win the war. Matt loved it all so much. . . .

They finish singing the birdhunter piece and warble through a transition. Maybe we can do this in Earthtown, Ruthie muses, be dancing monkeys on Kabuva.

Concentrate, her dead father's voice admonishes.

Another platoon of squid wriggles over Vendor's Row as Matt begins a piece about pressure hallucinations—squid hear ghosts when they swim at too great a depth. Ruthie opens her throat, pouring out accompaniment. The words are grim, but the alien harmonies ring true.

They segue into "Mad Moon," a more patriotic piece, and the audience pales.

Ruthie brings the song order up on her mask display, deleting several numbers. She switches the rah-rah stuff with bleaker material, and texts the revised list to her brother. Matt nods without breaking a beat. He cuts the last chorus of "Mad Moon" and starts an awful ballad about two doomed lovers who get poached out on a rock in the sun, because the tide refuses to come ashore and save them.

Yeah, they *love* that one. Morbid fucking aliens.

The crowd gets ever more dense. A few officers go through the motions of trying to curb their wayward troops while clearly enjoying the show. The stick-in-the-muds have been dragged to the middle of the mosh, entrapped, their protests drowned out. The crowd is singing along, so loudly that Ruthie's mask vibrates against her cheekbones.

A thousand squid, she thinks. Why sabotage Fry Beach when they could just drop a dust bomb right here. . . .

Her skin crawls. She misses a note. Matt, lost in song, doesn't notice.

We have time, Ruthie thinks. Sam's only ten feet away . . . if a bomb's going off, he'll get clear.

We have to get them away, she texts. **THIS is the trap.**

Matt doesn't answer; his eyes must be shut.

Dropping notes left and right, Ruthie calls up a menu of folk songs coded into the synthesizer. There used to be some old "Follow the Leader" things, pieces they rarely played in clubs but . . . here. Matt knows this one.

First, they'll need to get these soldiers up. Watching Sam fearfully, she waits for the end of their current number, then wrenches her cello through the opening of a jig called "Jump and Fly."

Matt jerks in surprise . . . then he starts in on the intro as smoothly as if they'd planned it.

We're the trap? He finally responds. **U think?**

Yes. Lead them to the beach.

A creeping chill on her neck makes Ruthie glance back.

It's too late. The fog generators in the graveyard are all running, pouring out an opaque, rolling cloud. Behind them, the ground is crawling with shadows.

So much for finesse. Ruthie stops playing. The crowd, which was beginning to dance, devolves into confusion.

"Run!" Ruthie screams, even as she hears the 'phut' of the first grenade launcher.

Hundreds of the fry react, surging away from each other at shocking speed. Unarmed, out of armor, they can only flee as the first grenades pop overhead, coffee-coloured Dust spreading in the air like bursts of fireworks before smearing into a deadly, downward-drifting haze. Squid who are fully enveloped by the brown wind vanish in a puff. Others lose body parts: caps, heads, tentacles.

The shrieking starts.

Grabbing Matt's hand, Ruthie runs crossways between the approaching Fiends and the roiling, panicked offworlders. She drags her brother toward the cliff. A mumble, an undertone, follows: she is praying. In Kabuva.

Fry surge onto the beach path, fleeing for the ocean and safety. Others charge unarmed into a row of flamethrowers at the front of the Fiend line—with predictable results. One cluster hurls fry over the wall of fire, up and into the oncoming wave of human guerillas. It is an acrobatic trick Ruthie saw performed in the same clubs where she sang as a child. The flying squid vanish into the graveyard, disappearing into the cloud of smoke and artificial fog. Human screams spread where they land.

One freaked-out squid slides toward them, whistling, and Ruth's idiot brother tries to jump in front of her. She yanks him to ground, shouting the word for "Ally" in Kabuva. A line of old-fashioned bullets chops through the alien before she finds out if it heard her.

"Stop!" Matt yells. But Ruthie scrambles up, mulishly using her greater strength to force him to the high ground. If they can get around the Fiends, they might escape before the Sponge orders a strike on the whole cemetery.

"Ruthie!"

"All we can do now is get away!" The words run in her head, getaway, get away, git way. But Mattie breaks free, leaving her with a handful of seaweed rags as he pounces on half of a dead Fiend holding a grenade launcher.

Phut! He fires at the edge of the cliff. A Dust grenade digs out the edge, excavating a crater ten feet deep. He promptly fires two more, creating a scalloped incline within the rock, a crude slide, a new escape route to the beach.

Squid start pouring through the gap, making for the ocean. They don't wait for the Dust to settle, and so they bleed and lose tentacles as they flee.

Ruthie makes a grab for the launcher. "Someone's gonna mistake you for a target."

"Let 'em." His face is wet. Stupid, over-sensitive . . .

He still needs her.

"You've done your good deed; now come on!" A grenade detonates nearby and they flee uphill. The high point of the cliff is in sight; they're clearing the Fiend line . . . almost at the rear. No chance to get to the van from here, the van's gone. She must write it off as she has written off her parents, an education, an ordinary life.

All Ruthie has left is her brother.

A Fiend comes up the path, methodically firing into the crowd of squid escaping down Matt's improvised slide.

It's Holly. Ruthie feels it before she truly recognizes the other woman. Holly has decided that she needs a Friend or two.

Their eyes meet, and Holly's lips move. Shouting Matt's name, but he can't hear it over the battle noise.

Stay quiet. He'll never know who was behind them. Damned cougar—Matt doesn't need her. Run for it, force the squid to send them to Kabuva. He'll never know.

It is an easy choice, the kind she's been making on his behalf for years.

Instead, Ruthie tugs his arm. Points.

Matt turns. Looks. Sees that his supposed girlfriend is in on the squid slaughter.

Ducking a flying piece of monolith, Matt sprints back. He and Holly converge, crouch with their heads close. She reaches for Matt's hand....

Ruthie clutches her chest. Will he take it? If Mattie leaves her, who is she supposed to be?

The ground turns to jelly underfoot.

There's an awful, impossible light, a glow on the horizon. A torch thrusts up from the ocean, burning white-hot to the clouds. It bulges, grows fat, frying the anti-aircraft platform to ash. And now the sound is coming too, a clatter and shriek, something tearing that was never meant to be torn, louder, louder. The sound bites like a saw into her skull.

On the battlefield, everyone—human and offworlder—freezes, staring in the direction of Oahu.

It's the Sponge, it has to be the Sponge, and how could the Fiends touch that? How could there ever be the slightest possibility of them being powerful enough to destroy an undersea squid—

Suddenly everything on the battlefield is after Ruthie.

No, she realizes, they aren't running toward me. They're fleeing to the high ground, like mice. That's right, there'll be a shockwave, won't there?

"Matthew," Ruthie shouts, before a scorching wind lifts her off her feet, ripping her mask off, flipping her ass over tea kettle through the air.

When she awakes, she is soaked, sore, and draped on a delicate arch of rock formed by the cliff's edge and the lip of a dust crater. She raises herself to hands and knees, pulling her seaweed mini-skirt over her ass and staring around.

Water has battered the graveyard, making pools of its many Dust craters. Seawater, she guesses, thrown by the explosion. The rush of water doused the Fiends' flamethrowers, giving the squid an edge in the battle—the offworlders seem to be winning now. Drowned and strangled humans litter the ground, along with Dust-proof tubes containing human DNA samples—coffin tubes—that jut up from the murk of the one-time golf course.

There is no sign of Matt or Holly.

Everything's quiet, Ruthie realizes. The battle is continuing in total silence.

"Actually, spawn, I think you've gone deaf." The words are Kabuva. Dad and Isshy are with her, flickering in the fog.

Isshy is right. She cannot hear a thing.

Her eyes find a column of black smoke rising in the east, where the Sponge was. "Isshy's dead then," she says and it is a surprise how much that hurts.

"Is he?" Dad says.

"I must be," the squid says. "Child's right. Nothing could survive that."

"You're hallucinations," she says slowly. "The baby . . . I would know if Matt was dead, wouldn't I?"

"Oh yes," Dad says. "You would know. He's alive—oh, wait, there's his body."

She screams, curling up in the crater.

"That's not him, Ruth," Isshy says, in that annoyingly gentle voice. "Jacob, you're upsetting her."

Is it or isn't it? She crawls to the gristle lying face down in the bloody sand.

"What did I tell you, child?"

It is a stranger. He is lying atop an old machine gun. An extra cartridge of bullets is taped to his fist.

Ruthie crouches by the body, takes a breath, makes a snowball. She can see it, just as she sees Dad and Isshy loitering beside her. She tosses it into the pond, but there is no splash, no ripples.

Write it off, she thinks. The van, Isshy, escape, even my sanity. But not Matt. Never Mattie.

All around her, the skirmish continues, a disorderly cut and thrust. Down the cliff path, her intended route of escape, is a squad of Demo soldiers and armed squid, trotting up to join the fight. A trio of Fiends has set up an ambush for them. They've hidden behind a toppled cenotaph and are making ready to Dust the upcoming squad.

"What now?" Dad asks. "Dive into the fray looking for your brother?"

"What chance would she have?" Isshy replies. "One side or the other is bound to shoot her."

"He's right. Hon, you can't start looking until the dust settles. Pardon the pun."

"And you can't help your brother if you're dead."

"Shut up!" She covers her deaf ears.

"She should go to ground. Wait this out."

"Sure," Dad says, "And end up a prisoner of whichever side wins?"

"You've been drafted after all, Ruth," Isshy tells her. "Pick a side and go with it."

"The Fiends killed us," Dad reminds her. "They made you do the concert. Sam fed you fireseeds. Isn't that him over there, directing that ambush team?"

"The Fiends are winning the war," Isshy disagrees. "Her best chance for finding Matt might be to get Friendly. Holly thought so."

Is it that simple? Take up the gun, join the ambush? Start killing the Demos, or start killing squid?

"Hon," Dad says.

"Shut up," she says. "You're a hallucination." She looks from one parent to the other, Dad with his guitar and reproachful eyes, Isshy pale-blue with understanding. Who would Matt pick?

Impossible to say. His mom's a squid, his lover's a Fiend.

But she does know who she'd most like to kill.

"Ruth," argues Isshy. "The Fiends are winning. Your best chance to get offworld died with me. Forget the Democratic cause and join that ambush. Pick the winning team."

"They're not winning this battle, are they?" Dad counters. "She doesn't get off the cliff, today, she doesn't get to look for anyone."

Daddy's right. And the squid might be grateful if she pitches in; the Fiends just regard it as their due.

She pries the clip of ammo off the corpse and slithers up to the lip of the dust crater. She takes careful aim at the centre of Sam's back, the sweet spot, as he prepares to slaughter the contingent of Demos and squid coming up from below.

"Ashes to ashes," she murmurs—and it is so weird not to be able to hear her voice, or even the pop pop pop of the gun as she signs up for the Demo cause, pulling the trigger and sending her alleged brethren to oblivion.

verse found scratched inside the lid of a sarcophagus (dynasty unknown)

GEMMA FILES

Never think to hide yourself in death from me.
Before you are even half-digested
my body's adze will pry open your flesh-eating box—
I will bake myself into a clay doll for your tomb
and slip thus beneath the portico, with its net of spells.
I will pursue you through every division of the night
even unto the realm of the fourth and fifth hour,
that howling wasteland where serpents coil
and crocodiles sharpen their teeth on bones.
Knowing well Lord Seker has no care for his own worshippers,
I will pass both him and his eight gods by, move unnoticed
through fields of chopping blocks, pits of vomited fire;
I will fear neither the black rustle of his wings (knit from
resinous wrappings), his two heads on two necks,
that his tail terminates in a human skull.
As the oils of your press turn rancid, curing you in cedar,
I will burn kyphri 'til the air itself hangs heavy
with myrrh, broom and saxifrage,
'til ba and ka alike fall slumbrous as smoked bees.
I will work an Execration Text on you
and sever each part of your soul in turn—
your heart, your name, black shadow of your vital spark—
shape you in wax, in mud, bound and dismembered.
I will crush you flat and scribe my will upon you,
threaten you with the Second Death,
murder your name, erase you, make it so that none
now living remember you ever lived (but me).

As Hathor's blood-drunkenness overcomes me, I too
will collect the dribbled bile of Re, our senile God-king—
like Isis, I will reduce you to torn-up parts, then string
(all I can find of them) back together with my father's spit.
Like Nut, unending sky, I will stretch myself upon you
at last, open your mouth with mine and murmur:
There, it is done, you are Beautified. Rise up now,
and join me. Rise up. Wake to my word, to me.
Rise up, wake, to me, and now. Or never.

I will not be denied.

collect call

SILVIA MORENO-GARCIA

I read a photocopied copy of the *Necronomicon* in Mexico City when I was in junior high and living on the fourth floor of a building which smelled like garbage.

The neighbours used to dump their trash bags outside their doors and there was always a broken light bulb dangling from the ceiling. Which was not so bad. The other apartment buildings around us were even shittier. La Bola's elevator, for example, had a big hole in the floor that nobody fixed. One night, one of the hobos that used to sneak into the building got his leg stuck in it, then made a bloody mess trying to pull himself out and they had to call the cops.

Some kids said they had to amputate the man's leg when he got tetanus from the cuts. La Bola got a good laugh out of it.

He was the one who found the *Necronomicon*.

I knew nothing about Lovecraft until this fat dude who liked to smoke a lot of dope and watch foreign movies lent me a copy of *At the Mountains of Madness*. I was in my Poe phase back then and the dude—his name was Leonardo but we called him La Bola—had seen me thumbing through it.

He circled my desk, shark-like, as I read *The Fall of the House of Usher* and told me that if I liked Poe, I would really like Lovecraft.

Now this dude, he wasn't friendly. The other kids teased him with some creative nicknames. The nicest one of them was La Bola, because he was so big, but he got called much worse.

La Bola had a pierced ear, which was a no-no at our school, and he carried magazines of girls with big boobs and heavy metal music tapes inside his knapsack. In short, he wasn't my sort of friend.

I was the nerd with the glasses and the baggy uniform. My mom had bought it two sizes bigger because she thought she'd save some money if I could grow into the clothes. I never did grow and remained short and skinny, rolling up my sleeves all year long so I could see my fingers.

Anyhow, he gave me the Lovecraft one Friday and on Monday he asked me what I thought.

"It was cool," I said.

"Wasn't it," he said as he sat next to me, giddy with excitement. "You want to read another one?"

That's how we became friends. It was a good friendship. La Bola lent me books and I fed him. His mom, just like mine, worked until late at night and there was rarely anything to eat in his house, so I kept inviting him to have supper with me and my sister. Then we'd rush to my room and listen to some of his music while we chatted about horror stories.

On our way back from school La Bola purchased copies of *La Alarma,* which was a thin, yellow newspaper with graphic crime stories and a naked chick on page five. "Followed Murdered Raped!" screamed the front page.

My sister Marilu loathed the crime rag and she did not like the fact that La Bola ate huge portions of the chicken she cooked for us. However, she was willing to keep her mouth shut about him as long as I did not tattle to mom about Marilu's boyfriend.

Marilu's boyfriend had gone off to the States a few months before and was working in Texas. He phoned her once a week, collect call, and they chatted for a good hour. Mother had forbidden her from accepting his calls and told me to hang up if anyone called collect, but I always passed the receiver to my sister and feigned stupidity when the bill arrived in the mail.

I did not bother Marilu and she did not bug me, and La Bola continued to come over to eat my sister's food and talk about horror stories.

And then there was the whole mess about the book and La Bola stopped visiting.

One morning, when were on our way to school, La Bola stopped to talk to a hobo. We were following our usual path, zipping next to rundown 19th century buildings, art deco apartments with tiles falling off the facade and modern monstrosities shaped like boxes built in the seventies. Some neighbourhoods had turned their old buildings into fashionable nightclubs. There was a colonial church now transformed into a spiffy bar. But not ours. Factories jutted next to vecindades, buildings that had gone up during Iturbide's empire served as a backdrop for prostitutes, and a sad park with more concrete than trees stood as the heart of this grey collage.

The hobo stumbled through a garbage-littered corner just as we left behind the park. I knew him—or knew of him—he sold all kinds of trinkets: old magazines of girls with big titties and drugs were the most crucial items for kids my age, but rumour was he could get any merchandise you wanted.

I stepped aside, pressed myself against the wall to let the stinky fellow go by. But the man recognized La Bola and started cooing, talking to him like they were old friends.

"Hey, long time no see," said the man. "I got some new stuff, some nice stuff for you. You want to take a look?"

He probably meant drugs. I didn't do drugs and there was a strict no pot rule at my house for fear that my mother would belt my ass red if she smelled it. But La Bola bought drugs, smoked cigarettes. He liked to demonstrate his superior sophistication with his knowledge of stimulants.

"Can't right now," La Bola said.

"But this is big stuff. Good stuff. It's that book you wanted. The N."

"Maybe a peek."

"We're going to be late," I reminded La Bola.

He ignored me and started following the panhandler, and I in turn followed La Bola until they crawled inside the abandoned pantyhose factory where some of the kids liked to have sex. The old building had tons of shattered milky-white glass panes and it was easy to sneak inside, but I did not like to go in there, and when La Bola insisted he didn't want to go alone, I said I'd keep watch from outside.

I didn't dare to crawl in.

Through the glass plane I made out two murky figures, shadows, Bola and the man talking. There was a noise, a cry. Not a scream. A cry. Might have been a "no." Might have been nothing at all.

Stuff happens at the old factory and you've got to be careful. Just look away. That morning I put my hands in my pockets and rushed to class, left Bola alone. Left him behind.

I saw nothing.

La Bola was late to school.

A few weeks later, La Bola talked about the invocation and showed me the grease-stained photocopies then man had given him.

It was October and the Day of the Dead was right around the corner.

The streets were filled with sugar skulls and pictures of death in a long Porfirian dress. We were walking next to the offices of Telmex when La Bola suddenly stopped in the middle of the street—it was the same street where the whores gathered at night to ply their trade, causing my mom to pull my arm very quickly whenever we were out late—and said we should try to put the *Necronomicon* to good use.

"Like seriously," he said. "We should call Cthulhu."

I had no idea what he was talking about. We went to sit in the park and I opened my math book so I could do a bit of studying while La Bola went to get some sodas and chips from the corner grocery store. The daughter of the store owner was a plump, gap-toothed fifteen year-old who had a crush on La Bola on account of his "dangerous" earring and the inverted-star drawn on his backpack with red marker. La Bola would spend some ten minutes sweet-talking her and she would give us the junk food for free.

But instead of lining up behind the construction workers who were buying beer and *tortas*, La Bola sat down. He pulled out some photocopies from a yellow envelope and gushed about how he had purchased an authentic facsimile of the *Necronomicon* from the man we had met on our way to school.

"It's the real deal," he told me, very seriously.

"Bullshit," I said. "Lovecraft made that book up."

"That's what some people say. But other people claim he merely used a coded name for a real book. This book. The true *Necronomicon*."

"Yeah, so even if it's true what the hell is a copy of the *Necronomicon* doing in the hands of a panhandler in Mexico City? Shouldn't it be in Boston or New York or some shit like that?"

"Olaus Wormius made a Latin translation and somebody wrote a translation of that into Spanish. This is a copy of the Spanish manuscript, written in Zaragoza and carried by a Spanish scribe to Veracruz. Somebody sold it to Porfirio Diaz and then during the Revolution it got lost, but it was in the library of the UNAM back in the seventies when this dude photocopied it and then someone else made more photocopies."

I shrugged an answer. We had a math test the next day and I was more worried about getting a bad mark in Calderon's class than whatever weird shenanigan La Bola had cooked up.

"It looks like gibberish to me."

He plucked four pages, placed them smack on top of the math book I was trying to read.

"These are authentic aetheric keys. They can be used to invoke all sorts of stuff like Cthulhu and shit. We can call him."

I shoved the pages inside the book and rolled my eyes.

"Why would we want to do that?"

"Because it's neat," La Bola concluded. "Come on, you've got to help me."

"We've got that test."

"So?"

"So I can't play Lovecraft right now."

"Who's talking about playing?"

"Are you going back to the factory?"

"I can't invoke nothing in my place," La Bola said.

"Will that dude be there?"

"Who?" he asked.

"You know," I said, but I didn't say the hobo's name and La Bola pressed his lips together and shook his head.

"I'm not talking to him anymore," he muttered.

"Why?"

"Because, he's a damn cultist that adores Dagon and he wants to sacrifice me to the Elder Gods. Who cares?" He grabbed his envelope, zipped it into his backpack and huffed at me.

"You're always saying stupid shit like that. There's no monsters hanging 'round the park."

"There's monsters," he assured me.

Stupid La Bola. Still dicking around with horror books wrapped in garish covers and little-kid ideas about things from the stars.

I was conscious of the realities and hardships of everyday life. La Bola took photocopies from drunkards, like a modern Jack waiting for his beanstalk to grow.

"Whatever, asshole," I muttered. "You're nuts."

"I am not! You'll see! I'll show you!"

"Nuts."

"Aren't you coming?" he asked, plaintive eyes, voice quivering. "I don't want to go alone."

"No."

I went home, concentrated on my studying. Tried not to think about the *Necronomicon*, La Bola going to the factory by himself.

Cultists.

What if the hobo was hanging around the factory?

Monsters.

A strangled cry.

And I had seen something through the greasy, milk glass window panes, that one time.

Two figures . . .

And then I had rushed to class. Don't be, don't be late.

But back there, in the factory.

Back there . . .

I saw nothing. I saw nothing. I saw . . .

My mother arrived from her late shift a little before midnight. I was still up, reading my textbook in the kitchen.

"Big test tomorrow, huh?" she said.

"Yep."

"Did you finish the spaghetti?"

"Yeah, Marilu warmed it up for me."

My mother took off her shoes and rummaged through the refrigerator. The phone rang. I picked it up at the first ring thinking it was La Bola. I was feeling kind of lousy about our fight and I wanted to apologize.

I held the receiver next to my ear. It was one of those yellow Western Electronic Princess Telephones that my mom had owned forever and sometimes the damn thing did not work right.

"Hello," I said very loudly. "Hello."

There was no answer. Just a crackling, which was not unusual. What was unusual was the other sound I heard. Only it was not really a sound. More like a vibration which went up and down my arm.

"Bola?" I whispered.

I didn't think it was him. Or it was not *only* Bola.

There was something else trying to get through the line.

The receiver, as I held it between my fingers, felt rubbery and pulsated.

I dropped it. It dangled from the cord, brushing the linoleum floor.

"Is that Marilu's boyfriend again?" my mother asked. She picked up the receiver quick as lightning and yelled into it with a loud, stern voice. "You stop calling here! You hear me?!"

She slammed the receiver down, grumbled about Marilu and made herself a sandwich.

I went to bed.

I did well in my exam the next day. La Bola missed it, but that was his tactic. He tried to miss as many exams as he could so I could tell him what the test had been all about, and he could get a decent grade when he took it the next week.

I was not too concerned about his absence. And I was not too worried when he did not go to school the day after that. He was probably still sore at me, nursing his wounds by staying in bed and watching videos all day long.

But he did not go back to class. We heard he had been expelled for drug use. Someone had found him dealing pot or coke or some shit inside the pantyhose factory and he was kicked out of school. Other folks said he went nuts and killed his whole family, then microwaved the cat. I did not think that was very likely because it would have made the front page of *La Alarma* and I did not see La Bola's wide eyes staring at me from the newspaper stand.

One lady who was a friend of my mom said it was a mental break-down and she mentioned the pantyhose factory, and the guy there and there was . . . maybe she said pederast. Maybe she said nothing. I like to believe she said nothing.

And then my mom, she asked me pointed questions about La Bola and I didn't have the answers, so I shook my head no.

No.

Somebody called a few days later. Heavy metal music played in the background. But the caller didn't say anything and I hung up.

Nine years later. Enough to misremember.

I had long finished my bachelor's degree and moved out of my mom's place and into a little apartment. Overall, things were going fine and I was considering applying for another scholarship, this one for a master's degree.

Marilu was married and living in Monterrey. She had just had a second baby. My mom was going to go live with her and watch over the grandchildren. Mom told me that she was getting rid of everything in my room and I better go help her throw out my old crap.

I put a few precious things aside, then piled my old books into a box, including the horror paperbacks La Bola had given me in junior high. I took them to one of the used stores where they buy books and newspaper by the kilo, and got a couple of pesos out of the whole effort.

When I was handing the guys who bought the books and newsprint my stuff, I discovered that at the bottom of one of the boxes there were a few photocopies of La Bola's *Necronomicon*. I folded them and took them with me. Out of a sense of nostalgia I walked through the old neighbourhood, patting the wrinkled photocopies.

The area was still shitty but they were starting to build nice condos here and there. Gentrification was creeping in.

I stopped at the street with the pantyhose factory. That block had not been touched by the cranes and construction crews. The old buildings remained stubbornly in their place, peeling paint and all. The factory itself was even more ruined, dirty and with more shattered glass panes.

I glanced at the photocopies I was carrying, at the building and then back at the squiggly lines that passed for writing.

I heard the tinkering of glass bottles and a panhandler sleeping nearby shuffled to his feet.

"Hey," said the man and I raised my hand to tell him that no, I didn't have any cash to spare but I stopped.

The man was very, very skinny. Bone thin and he looked at least a decade older than me, so he couldn't possibly be La Bola. But he looked like him, only hungrier, his dark eyes very large and fixed on me.

"Hey, long time no see," said the man. "I got some nice stuff for you. You want to take a look?"

I was born and raised in a neighbourhood with its fair share of drunkards, hobos and hookers, and none of them ever scared me, but this man who looked a bit like La Bola sent me shivering like a five year old; and I swear I could feel a cold, cold rubbery *thing* slipping around my neck when La Bola stared at me.

I tossed the papers in the air and ran away, only pausing once to see if the man was following me. He was too busy picking up the pages that I had dropped, fiercely clutching them against his chest and mumbling something I could not make out.

Three blocks from there I hailed a cab. When I was boarding it, my cell phone rang. I answered it, but the line was quiet. I thought I could hear someone breathing on the other end. There was expectation in the air, like the pause after you say "I accept" during a collect call. Then there's a little click and you are connected.

I threw the cell phone out the window and told the driver to go, just go. Where? Not downtown, to buildings and streets three centuries old, not through the old colonias like la Roma. To the outskirts of the city, past Santa Fe, past the DF and into the places where condos and houses are barely going up.

Sometimes the phone rings in the middle of the night and I wake up, and I think I'm a kid again back in the apartment with the hallways smelling of urine and if I look out the window I might see the shadow of the old factory.

Strange things happen there and there are monsters.

I think then, still wrapped in the haze of dreams, that somewhere, Bola's dialing my number, trying to connect. And I'm never taking that call. And I never did.

And I shouldn't have run away.

And I didn't see anything.

And I cry sometimes, but I don't remember why.

bella beaufort goes to war
LISA L. HANNETT & ANGELA SLATTER

Volume Twelfth, 2nd Series, No. 312. July 19, 1873
QUERIES, *cont'd*: ——

MAKING FATE & THE INFLUENCE OF NORNS IN THE NEW WORLD
In pursing research for my book, IN THE FASHION OF WOLVES, *I come, time and again, to the same pressing questions: Does the Norns' power stop when certitude does? When the idea that they decree* FATE *and tend to* YGGDRASIL *weakens, can such myths continue to exist? When faith in them ceases, to what thread might they cling? Without the lifeline of credulity are these things no more than the smoke of memory dispersed on the wind? Or are they weaving still, out of sight and mind, but not out of the world? Opinions and responses are most heartily desired.*

—Valdís Brynjólfsdóttir
South Carolina, United States of America

"What do you see?"

Black things flap and snap on the wire fence running around the vacant land adjacent to the Laveau place. The sun is harsh, reflecting on the hard-packed dirt street, glaring off the two-storey house's peeling white paint; yet the old woman insists upon sitting out on the verandah with the heat and light bouncing up at her, hitting the great diamond hanging like a monocle on a silver chain around her neck.

Sweat creeps down Bella's skin, soaking the armpits and back of her green gingham work dress, trickling from her temples, making her scalp itch worse than the lice she'd been afflicted with last summer. What she wouldn't give to scratch like a dog right about now, or to lift the thick russet hair off her crown like an unwanted hat. But she ignores the urge and concentrates on the widow's question. She squints, stares across overgrown cotton fields, and focuses on the shreds of—*what?*—writhing in the distance. While she gathers her thoughts, Eugenia, as usual, leaps in.

"Dead birds. Ravens. Big ones." This last was added in an uncertain tone, as though she realises she's wrong once again. The old lady's lip curls—she doesn't even bother to conceal it from her great-granddaughter nowadays—and then she slides her eyes to Bella, who senses the expectation in that look, just as keenly as she feels Eugenia's resentment seething off her. Within the first few days of their apprenticeship, she'd overheard the other girl moaning to her *mémé*, saying it wasn't right, her teaching the two of them together. Her own rightful heir and Bella No-Blood. Bella Know-it-all. Bella Who-wasn't-even-family.

Such a waste of effort, staring so hard at someone else's flaws, the Widow Paris had said. *Take a close look at yourself, Eugenia Laveau, and tell me—what do you see?*

"It's skins," says Bella, who wasn't even family, as she smoothes the white pin-tucks of her apron. "Skins taken so they can't fly anymore."

"They?" Eugenia sneers, white-blonde hair a striking contrast against her bronze skin. She props her elbows on the porch railing next to Bella, leans down to take another look from that vantage. Her sharp nose crinkling like there's a bad smell.

"They. Witches. Witches with their wings clipped, with their soul suits taken."

As if in answer, the feathered things wave in agreement, agitating like house-rugs left out for beating clean. The old woman nods brusquely, the closest she ever gets to showing approval. But Bella knows her mentor is pleased, though she covers a smile with her fan, a handsome thing of lace and mahogany. A gift, perhaps, from a grateful follower. The woman's fluttering hands are smooth, ageless. Unlike her face which, in recent months, has sagged dramatically, its rich brown becoming greyish. Against doctor's orders, the widow won't slow down. Knocking on eighty, and still she insists on sitting out in the heat, teaching them, trying to make sure they're receptacles of the knowledge only she can pass on. *Truth be told*, Bella thinks, *Miz Marie feels her time running away.*

"There you have it, child," the old woman says, peering over accordion folds at Eugenia, barely keeping the disappointment from her tone. "Focus. Pay attention. This isn't hairdressing school, no matter what folks been told. Make a mistake with *this* craft and you'll suffer much worse than burnt curls. You need to concentrate: be *certain* before you speak. Words are weapons, girl—you can't just fling them around, willy-nilly. Wield them carefully, accurately, else you'll unleash a world of hurt—on others, sure enough, but first and foremost, on yourself. Stop and *think*."

Eugenia's mouth tightens like she's fit to spit nails. A few seconds pass as she wrangles her temper. Splotches crawl up her neck, blooms of anger and shame. She straightens, pushes away from the bannister, away from Bella, and turns to stand with hands folded, white-knuckled, before the Widow Paris.

"Yes'm," she says through gritted teeth. "I'll bear that in mind."

"You do that. For now, go on in. Tidy up the brushes and arrange the curling rods by size—largest to smallest, handles out, on a tray near the fire—then scrub the combs and scissors. Miss Whats-her-name from Olafsson House is coming 'round in an hour, and I haven't yet sussed if her appointment is for plaits or potions."

Eugenia, thus dismissed, bobs a curtsey, and flounces inside. Soon they hear utensils rattling into jars, iron tools clattering against tin, water splashing, the occasional grumble and mutter. When the screen door finally swings shut on its slow hinges, Bella looks over at the widow, whose rheumy brown eyes are fixed on her. Reduced to slits. Assessing.

She freezes like a hare, resists the desire to gulp. *Be* certain *before you speak.* . . . The Widow Paris had been chastising Eugie, but Bella has a feeling the old herbwoman was talking double. Directing the dressing-down at her great-grandchild, but expecting them both to listen. Telling Bella that she's onto her. That she more than suspects, she *knows*.

That even though Bella's answer was right, it was obvious, to the widow at least, she had *guessed*.

She did it a lot, actually. Guessing. It wasn't laziness, not really. It's just, she can pick ideas out of the air. Sometimes. Most of the time. Very broad hints. And more often than not, they are precisely right. They are enough. Enough to ensure her instinct wins out over Eugenia's increasingly desperate shots in the dark.

Bella tries to distract the Widow Paris with a smile. It withers on her cheeks half-formed.

What if Eugenia finds out, that Bella guesses? Oh, rage, rage, such a rage. And lightning, no doubt. Whirlwinds. Hail. What Eugenia lacks in reading vibrations, ripples in water, tremors in the earth, the story of human expression, she more than makes up for with dark-limned magic. Spells of destruction, thunderous conjuration, explosions of fire and lava. These were her forté. *These* came to her easy as living.

Eugie would make a powerful ally, if she wasn't such a pain in the backside.

"Lemonade?" Bella asks, getting up from the white wicker chair. The old lady holds her gaze another instant, then shakes her head.

"That's enough for today. Better get home, young Isabella, before your uncle starts a-wondering what can possibly be taking so long."

As Bella collects her satchel and packs away the book in which she writes recipes, for hair tonics and potions alike, two men stroll down St Ann Street. Both pretend they don't know they're being watched, but they stand a little straighter, puff their chests a bit as they walk. One's a local parish boy, spends Sundays ushering people into church. The other's a regular jack-of-all trades—does everything from working the cotton gin to digging graves. The sight of him sets Bella's heart to pounding, as it no doubt does to most girls in town. Tall with blue eyes and bone china skin, a spill of Black Irish hair and a smile that makes the day brighter. Bella averts her eyes, but not soon enough.

"Careful, girl," says the old widow. "The worst thing in the world is getting what we desire. Help me inside before you go."

As she bends close to assist her teacher, their faces almost touching, Bella can smell the decay on the woman's sigh, the gust of death soughing up from inside. She squeezes the old lady's hand.

The trellis on the exterior wall is rickety, so Bella chooses the oak tree instead. Its branches are strong and thick and spread *everywhere*; one in convenient reach of her bedroom window, another trailing like a truncated staircase, with just a foot-long drop to the ground at the end. She's standing on the sill, ready to make the leap, when a single loud knock shudders the door behind her. Arms windmilling, she manages to hop back down and carefully arrange her face, a mix of umbrage and respect, before the knob slams into the wall. Only one person barges into her *chambre* so abruptly, trying to catch her out.

"Uncle Augustin."

"Evening, Bella. Have I disturbed you?" Her uncle's expression is hopeful, slightly lecherous. A distant cousin of her father's—not a *true* uncle, *not* a Beaufort—Augustin Fabron was willing to adopt poor, orphaned little Bella, after the accident. To take her in, not as a full family member, of course, but as a high level domestic in his plantation house. Daughter and servant and something else altogether. Something in between, not quite pure, existing in the social limbo dictated by her colouring. Hair red and irises green enough to say "white," but skin a shade too dark, features a tad too Creole, to let her pass without question. Without the protection of papers and a wealthy not-uncle to vouch for her. To provide a room of her own. A safe enough space for now. She's got house duties and other . . . duties . . . Augustin hasn't commanded her to perform. At least, not yet. Not with Aunt Claudette around, and Uncle Augustin's tenure as lord of the manor secure only so long as she is—the property deeds being written in *her* name, after all, not his.

He blinks with eyes like a winter sky, close-set in a long cadaverous face framed with lank hair that greases down to his collar. They are of a height; Bella statuesque, Augustin spindly. It's been a few years since he's been able to look down at her, so he tilts his head slightly back whenever he speaks. Lines her up in his sight, and *peers*.

"Did you do your chores today?"

"Yes, Uncle," Bella says, hoping she remembered them all.

"Only, your Aunt said Evangeline couldn't find you when she wanted her hair done before dinner," he says smoothly. Bella doubts that Claudette's maid reported anything of the sort to him. "It's not that we mind you learning a trade—indeed we think it a sensible idea. After all, we won't be around to support you forever. But we are, however, here now. You must not forget your first duty."

"How could I," she says, thinking, *with you constantly reminding me*, "when you and Aunt Claudette have been so . . . kind."

"We wouldn't want to have to discontinue your apprenticeship, dear niece." Augustin's reply sounds as empty to Bella as hers must have to him. They both know he won't follow through. Claudette has been *delicate* as long as Bella has known her—as long, she suspects, as the woman has been wed. And Augustin is more than aware of what his ward has been learning at the Widow Paris's knee. He relies too heavily on the witch's remedies to keep his wife in reasonable health; when the old lady passes, he'll need Bella to continue administering Claudette's *treatments*.

To keep her sedate, she thinks. *Sedated*.

"No, Uncle. We wouldn't want that," she says, lowering her chin, feigning humility though it makes her pride squirm.

Mollified, Augustin gives unnecessary orders for the morning—her routine hasn't changed in seven years—and takes his leave. The door clicks shut behind him. She listens for a minute, then two, waiting for him to move off the landing. The floorboards creak; he is still on the other side, listening for her too. She sits on her bed, wincing as the springs squeak loudly. Another moment passes and she blows out the lamp on her bedside table, knowing he has watched for the snuffing of the line of light under the door. At last, footsteps. Self-congratulatory and solid along the hallway. He thinks his point is made, that Bella remains under the thumb.

She doesn't move, even after she hears his tread on the stairs, wending their way down to the sitting room, where he will smoke cigars, drink whiskey and read those books he imports from France, the ones with the dirty pictures he thinks his wife knows nothing about. He'll be there for hours and now his *job* is done, Uncle Augustin will not stir. To be safe, Bella waits an extra five minutes before setting off. More than enough time to do a cats-eye spell, to help her find her way under the slivered new moon.

The leap from sill to tree branch feels further, more exciting, more liberating than it actually is—a delusion she's happy to enjoy. Half a mile to the Widow Paris's, which Bella covers so quickly and quietly she seems to fly the distance. All the lights in the place are extinguished. A candle flickers to life, briefly, in the round porthole staring out from an attic gable. *Eugie's room.* It winks in and out of sight two or three times before being extinguished. *The fool never can settle, can she? Fidgeting even when she's alone.* Bella grabs a handful of wild sage from the roadside, some flax and a few black-eyed-susans and crushes them between her palms, scattering the bruised leaves and seeds on her toes, whispering ancient words to make her footfalls petal-soft.

The path between the house and the fairy hill beyond the wire fence is overrun with weeds and old cotton. Few dare tread across the Widow Paris's land in broad daylight, much less after dark, but Bella has no such fears. If pressed, she can identify the marks of everyone who's passed this way. The widow's stunted shuffle hasn't flattened the dirt here for years; but a set of Eugenia's prints, small and wide-spread and deep as a running deer's, head off to the bushes on her right. Wild blackberries grow there by the bucket-load, Bella remembers, and thinks she might follow the other girl's path next time. On her left, another series of tracks. Narrow and heavy-heeled, blurred with urgency. With excitement.

These Bella pursues.

Her boots make a *shhhhhhing* sound as she crosses to the field, barely raising a puff of dust. Mist winds through the shrubs, coalescing into sinuous smoke-women that slip around pecan trees along the field's borders. It seems they smile at her as she hurries to the fence and ducks under, careful not to catch her skirts. The witch-skins applaud her arrival. They shoo her toward the man leaning comfortably against the gentle slope of the fairy hill, as if he belongs there.

Tancred Carew sits with his long legs outstretched, crossed casually at the ankle. The hessian sack he always carries, with a flute he made and god-knows what else, is propped like a pillow behind his broad back. With her cats-eyes, Bella can see him perfectly—a bewitching sight that enthralls her. Cotton boles glowing white, little stars of the earth, surrounding his rumpled brown curls. Glints of moonlight winking in his blue eyes, glancing off his teeth as he chews his nails, beaming off them as he smiles.

"Evening, Miz Beaufort," he says, then wastes no more time talking. When they come up for air, Bella's lips are tingling. She bites them, savouring, and inhales the salty scent of Tancred's skin, sweaty underneath his open-collared shirt. He rests his chin on Bella's head and she can feel his Adam's apple bob against her temple as he talks.

"We should bury them," he says, gesturing at the black scraps caught on the fence. For a second, Bella hears a rustle of wings, loud as a dozen ravens taking flight at once. "It's not right, having them exposed like that."

Bella cranes her neck to look up at him. "We haven't any shovels."

"We've got hands, haven't we?"

She smirks. "Why, Mr. Carew. I can't possibly go fossicking in the earth wearing this, my Sunday best." She pulls away to give him a better view of her faded, ill-fitting gingham. "If I didn't know better, I'd say you had a mind to see me *digging* out of my petticoat."

"Wouldn't be the first time," Tancred grins.

Bella plays coy only so long, and no longer. Soon her dress, apron, smock and bloomers are tossed like offerings to the fairies. Tancred's buttons seem to melt beneath her fingers; the drawstring on his pants loosens of its own accord. Together they work up a sweat and when they're done, they lie on Bella's clothes like they're the finest bed in New Orleans. She traces patterns into his chest hair with her nails, resting her cheek on his lean bicep, and watches him soften. When he's recovered, Tancred looks down the slope to the rusty fence running along its base.

"We really should give them whatever peace the earth can offer."

"All right," says Bella, loving him for his passion, determination, caring. For keeping a noble thought in his head both before *and after* he's spent. Wearing nothing but their unders, they hoist the ragged skins off the wires. Two of them, a leathery jumble of feather and beaks, strands of long hair, boneless faces, and places that shouldn't have bones. Bella's stomach clenches—not with sick, with certainty. Her guess, as usual, had been right.

Witch skins.

Collapsed, they're incredibly compact; the pair of them could easily fit inside Tancred's bag. Instead, he folds them in on themselves, ties each bundle off with its own hair, then passes it to Bella while he gets started on the digging. She stands there a moment, just watching. Admiring the way his muscles strain, the way dirt sticks to his chest, his ribs, his thighs. Almost unconsciously, she plucks at the witch-feathers, tearing at the desiccated flesh, at the matted tresses. . . . And as they strike cartilage, she feels a warmth in her belly, a heat of *knowing*. Ingredients potent as these can't go to waste.

Before she hands Tancred the neatly-tied parcels, she tucks a chunk of salvaged flesh up under her arm, unsure why she takes it, but determined to smuggle it home in the pocket of her apron.

A lamp, turned low, is burning in her room when Bella returns, stepping lightly over the sill. She doesn't really pay attention, happy as she is, reeking of Tancred's sweat, with tender parts tingling as if a charge has been sent through them. She puts her hands to the strings of her apron, the buttons at the back of her dress, doesn't notice the movement in the shadows, her cats-eye spell now thoroughly worn off. It's not until a bony hand closes around the hair at the nape of her neck, fingers gouging into the thick locks, that the magic of the night shatters and she realises she's not alone.

"Insolent little whore!" Spittle froths from Uncle Augustin's mouth, spatters her ear. Waves of malt fumes roll off him as he yells. He shakes her, bolstered by a rage that's simmered since she was a child; unheeded or outright defied by servants who check his orders with a mistress too frail to fulfil her marital duties, maids who lock their doors at night. Augustin fumbles with his trousers, trying to get them undone while keeping a grip on her. "I won't be ignored!"

He hooks a foot around her ankles, jerks hard. There's a jolt, hair ripping, as she tumbles free of his grasp—just for a second. Her head hits the floor. The blow is cushioned by the thick rug, but it's hard enough to make stars and suns pinwheel across her vision. Stunned, she scrambles for purchase, goes nowhere. It gives Augustin time to drop down beside her, shrug out of his suspenders. With one hand, he urgently shoves his pants down, while the other is busy loosening his narrow neck-tie, looping the noose over her head—as if he cannot decide which punishment will come first.

Bella tries to claw forward, but Augustin tightens the garrotte, pins her petticoat with his knees. Fabric tears. He yanks the ribbon tie, tighter, tighter. Bella tries to get words out, but the only sound she can produce is an animal whimper. Augustin's breath, hot, rank, slides across her cheek. Gagging, she tries to scream, tries to cry. And she flails, she flails, but his fingers jab, her skirts are lifted—

Her not-uncle, her un-uncle, grunts, then his grip relaxes enough to let her draw in great gusts of air. His hipbones dig into her rear, his ribs slam into her spine before he pushes himself upright again. Bella takes advantage, tries to shove him off, but he holds on. She realises there's been another noise, a new sound, unexpected. It's followed by a second, a loud, solid *thud*. Augustin slumps heavily onto her back; he tilts to the right, and drops, his arm draped across her calves. Bella kicks him aside, shimmies into a crouch. She blinks and blinks and finally looks up. Focuses on the shape looming over the fallen man.

Aunt Claudette, with shadows and lamplight dancing across her white nightgown, which is now spotted with a spray of wet red blossoms. In her shaking hand, a poker from the fireplace dangles between slackened fingers. The women stare at each without a word. Eventually, Bella heaves herself forward and checks for the pulse in Augustin's throat. It is slow, sluggish. She knows it won't be long before it stops, unless something is done.

She snatches her hand back, wipes it and wipes it on her torn skirt, turns to her Aunt for a cue.

Claudette is not as tall as Bella, nor as fit. She is *thin*, a bed-bound woman coddled to within an inch of her life. She stands there, swaying a little, her expression flicking between fear, hope, disbelief. Her glazed eyes meet Bella's and again her fingers tighten. She hefts the poker— as Bella gathers her wits and leaps up. She is at the casement in a few steps, out it in one bound and scampering down the tree like a squirrel.

As she hares into the woods, she can hear her name being called. In a small part of her mind—the same part that tells her a fluttering rag is a witch-skin, that interprets voices on the air—she *knows* it's not a cry of panic or condemnation; there is no tone of threat or accusation. In that same small part of her mind, she knows she should go back and help her not-aunt. *What if he wakes? She'll be alone. . . .* But Bella is running, feet barely touch the ground. Running away from Augustin, from danger. Running to Tancred and safety. Without magic, her stride goes *thud, thud, thud* in time with her beating heart, and soon she is almost at the fairy hill—*he must still be there*—soon almost in Tancred's arms. On the path, she slows, tries to control her panting, the shaking and shuddering her body is committing without her say-so. Bella walks now, quickly, quietly and as she rounds the stand of trees that hid them both not even an hour ago, she sees Tancred's arms are otherwise engaged.

"Thanks for clearing those nasty old bird-skins."

"Couldn't have my best lady suffering the creeps, now could I?"

"I *am* your best, aren't I?"

Naked and gleaming, a girl with white, white hair and smooth bronze skin laughs, riding Bella's lover as if he's a steed, bouncing and writhing much as Bella was not so long—now, forever—ago.

The Widow Paris's front door is never locked—only the sorriest fool would enter there without permission—and Bella knows where all the fixings are, the ones she requires. In her pocket the pilfered piece of witch-skin weighs heavy; she pulls it out, lays it on the countertop.

She places the heavy basalt mortar and pestle beside it, then begins. Collecting and adding ingredients, grinding and stirring them as she goes, making sure the mix is properly combined. There are scarlet rose petals, hyacinth oil, powdered mint leaves and rosemary, dried lavender, a tiny dash of the gold dust the Widow Paris is always so miserly with, a crush of indigo, a smear of marigold, two pansy petals and then half a spoon of imported honey. She spits into the mess and whisks it about, hard and fast, then takes a knife, a small thing, fit for peeling fruit, and pulls it across her right palm. From the shallow cut drips fat jewels of blood to seal the deal—for all dark magic, all curses, all dreadful things dearly wished for, cost something personal. Bella needs no recipe for this potion; *this* alchemy comes from the deepest knowledge of heart and hurt.

Soon the paste is thick and dark and red, with a sheen that only hatred can give. So, they want each other, Tancred and Eugenia? They want to be together? Bella will give them what they want. She pours in a flacon of rainwater, takes the shreds of witch-skin and adds them to the admixture, bubbling of its own accord. The thin membranes float into the pestle and disintegrate as soon as they hit the liquid. Without hesitation, Bella whispers over it, feeling heat rise off the surface. "Here's my wish for you both: to love an ideal of each other without reason, to see an eidolon never a soul. Let your wings be clipped, let your love be a cage, let it trap you both forever." She murmurs their names across the brew so the spell will *know* them, so there can be no mistake, no misdirections. So the enchantment will hook its claws into the fabric of their lives and never let them go. *Happily ever after.*

When the spell leaves her Bella feels exhilarated and empty, as if a part of her soul has darkened in payment for this wicked wish, for this vengeance. The air seems thick and time still—until the front door creaks and Eugie's entrance echoes along the corridor. Hastily, Bella decants the potion into a small vial, stoppers it and slips it into her apron pocket. She runs a hand through her hair and waits to hear Eugie pass by the workroom. *So, what? I'm to sneak out?* Bella snorts. *Why should I creep around?* She opens the door and steps out into the hallway.

Halfway up the stairs, Eugenia spins around. "What are you doing here?"

But before Bella can answer, there is a crash and a thump upstairs, coming from the direction of the widow's room. Both girls race towards the sound.

"*Mémé!*" Eugenia's cry is heart-wrenching, or would be if Bella hadn't seen what she'd seen earlier. If her heart hadn't hardened.

The Widow Paris is half-on, half-off the bed, the linens caught up around her waist and legs, a knitted shawl 'round her shoulders despite the heat. While they watch, she slides fully to the floor with a thud. Her nightdress is open at the collar, the thin cotton clinging. Curls frizz out of her sleeping-bonnet, sticking to her ashen face, some tipped with droplets of cold sweat. High arched eyebrows, not much more than a few wisps on a shrivelled brow, frame lashless lids, closed on sunken eyes. Until she moans, Bella thinks she's already dead.

Death rattles the old woman's lungs as she blinks awake, her gaze unfocused, searching. "*Mémé,*" Eugie wails, rushing to her great-grandmother's side, hugging her close.

"Get away, child. You're smothering me."

"But we've got to get you on up into bed—"

The Widow Paris waves the girl quiet. "Let me be. We all start low, Eugenia. Ashes to ashes, dust to dust, dirt to dirt—no matter what heights you reach in life, in the end it's all the same. Back to beginnings. I'm just saving y'all the trouble of hauling my old shell down off the bed. *No*, I said." Eugenia's tugging her by the armpits, forcing her upright. She gets the woman into a seated position, then kneels, clings to her hand. The lady extricates her fingers, pushes the girl further away.

"Just let me be. Save your fussing for after I'm gone; I've no use for it." She coughs, long and sloppy, and Bella thinks, this time, the tide of her life must surely have ebbed for good.

"You in pain, Miz M?" she asks, mouse-quiet, coming close enough, but no closer.

"I'd expect more from you, Isabella Beaufort," the widow replies. "Sure you can *guess* what state I'm in." The widow blinks, and this time her eyes stay shut.

Her lips go slack and a puff of rancid meat air escapes them. Bella finds herself crouched beside Eugie, inhaling that stale gust. Finds her head resting on the old woman's scarecrow shoulder, ear pressed to her chest. Finds herself counting the seconds between heartbeats, tracing symbols across the desiccated breast, grasping at words, at spells to keep the faltering thing ticking.

"Take care of this house, Eugenia," the Widow Paris mumbles at last, eyes searching, unfixed. "I may crumble, but there's sure as hell no reason it has to follow me into the earth."

"Don't say that, *mémé*. We'll get Doc Coffey down here, you'll be just fine, we'll—"

"Hush, now. Mind my house, child, that's all I ask. You do that for me?"

Eugie whimpers, tears coursing down her round cheeks, and nods.

"Good girl," the widow says, before turning to Bella. "Now, you." Marie folds her fingers around Bella's palm. She feels sharp angles, a cold glassy surface, a rough sphere with many facets.

"You," says the old woman, "*you* mind my business. You keep it going, my girl. You keep it going."

Bella opens her hand—there is the stone, the single biggest she will ever see. A white diamond the size of a child's heart.

"I will," Bella promises. "I am."

There is no moment of silence to honour the dead.

"She gave it to you! You! You're nobody! You're nothing. You're not even family." Eugenia's face boils crimson, and she's making a sound like a kettle left on the heat too long.

"Yet here we are, Eugie. Together with the one person who loved us both," says Bella smoothly. "Close as family."

Eugie weeps until she hiccups, hiccups until Bella thinks the girl might be sick in her own lap. She pours a glass of water from the bedside table and tips one, two, three drops from the vial into it— Eugie is too distracted to notice. The red liquid quickly disperses, tinting the clear fluid with only the slightest shade of pink. She hands it to Eugenia, who takes it without thanks, and gulps it down, down. All of it.

Bella smiles.

It will take. Oh, yes. It will sit inside her, stirring, gestating, ready to come to life the moment she sees Tancred. And when she does, the spell will uncurl, rise up and take hold. She'll be ruined in soulless love— there'll be nothing but obsession. The only tremors Eugenia will feel, the only excitement, the only fireworks, are the ones she casts with magic. It will be like eating, but never feeling full. She'll get nothing from Tancred, empty paragon of lies. And Tancred? Greedy, beautiful Tancred will take anything from Bella's hand, anything at all. He need only take this last thing. And he will.

While Eugenia sobs on the floor, Bella crosses to the window and looks out between the sheers. In the street below is the lady's maid Evangeline, gazing up at the house. Bella raises her hand, guessing, *knowing* she is safe. Aunt Claudette would not have sent Evangeline to *arrest* her; if that were the case, there would be constables roaming about by now. But there is nothing unusual on the road, in the fields. No-one but the servant.

Bella lets the curtains fall shut. Closing her eyes, she turns and perches on the sill. Runs her palms across her tattered apron, her twisted, torn skirt. *Eugie never even commented on it*, she muses, then blocks out all thoughts of the girl, all thoughts but the ones thrilling through the air. Quiet, she listens. Listens to the present, feels the truth of it in her belly. Her aunt's voice, not so feeble as it once was, explaining to Doc Coffey how Augustin has had a terrible accident, how he has fallen down the stairs. Listens to the doctor, who never liked the man, declare it's an open-and-shut case, no need to examine the wounds on his head. Listens to the night, replayed in her mind, and knows she will go back to that uncle-less house. She will tend to Claudette, who may not need her as much, in that uncle-less house, but Bella knows she'll want her there anyway. To keep an eye on her. To ensure her silence.

As she exhales, Bella senses the future, hears it through the other girl's wailing, hears the beat of what's to come, the pulse. Knowing Eugenia will ache for Tancred though he is hers, and Tancred yearn for Eugenia, both fighting for more, neither getting enough, everyone getting what they deserve. And she, Bella Beaufort, will be there to see it all. To watch how the battle unfolds.

a spell for scrying mirror gremlins

PETER CHIYKOWSKI

Find a bird
crushed by a car or window
and sprinkle water on it daily
until it grows to the size of a
grudge. Hang it
on a string around your neck.

Turn off the lights in your bathroom
and utter your own name
once for each time
you have sinned against
expectation. Open the steaming tap
and let the glass
glaze until you see the dark spirits
that have been stretching you out
in front of yourself
like a dog's tired tongue.
Watch them wear you, puff
your belly, chew your hair,
stuff sacs of venom
under your eyes.

In a low whisper, tell yourself
*this is the work of inhuman forces,
of elves, of dead birds
and albatrosses.* Repeat
until you believe it, until your face
sours like a bruise
under the mirror's hard skin.

the book of judgement

HELEN MARSHALL

Let us say that she was sitting at needlework when he came for her; that her fingers were still deft, that they moved without a stumble as the thread tucked in and out; or perhaps it is better if she were at the pianoforte, playing, and she *did* stumble, her fingers slipping on a jarring note. It might have been something by Handel or Haydn or Dibdin or Samuel Webbe; or, were she venturing further afield, she might have attempted Corelli or Cramer. But, no, despite what they say, *I* know better, and she had no especial taste for the pianoforte; she did not care for it though all the world said she did; *I* know she did not, I *know* it.

And so it could not have been that she was at the pianoforte when the stranger came, but let us *say* she was, let us not unsettle the sensibilities of those who claim intimate knowledge of her practices, let us say she was there, bent just so, rapt in the rhythm of Handel, then, (for I admit *I* am partial to Handel even if Jane was not) and let it be a jest between us against my detractors if it were not as I have described it exactly.

When the stranger entered, he may have startled her, so that the "March" in *Judas Maccabeus* was insensibly altered, and her chin might have nodded up at the unexpected sound of the door, and perhaps a slight gasp even escaped her lips when she saw him; this Hun invading the centre of her quiet domesticity. Some might describe him as tall, and that would be a perfectly adequate description; he *was* tall. But to say that is not to capture the sense of magnitude he brought with him, the grandeur. I have been told that some hear a rushing noise like a cataract when they first look upon him, the sound of pounding blood, and it may be this that she heard, her heartbeat accompanying the forever-marred Handel. I cannot say. And to say he was handsome, again, might be seen as somehow a lessening, and such falsehoods, such tendencies toward understatement are inappropriate in a chronicle such as this, which requires the strictest veracity in all things; his hair was soft as lamb's wool, curled gently over his forehead; black, most likely; he had dark, piercing eyes, possessed of intelligence and keenness, and sensuous lips of the kind true lovers, or lawyers, possess. Perhaps, she had some subtle premonition when she first saw him; perhaps she heard a note like a bell, tolling, as some saints do. But there was almost certainly something; *that*, at least, is not in question.

And so her pen might have fallen from nerveless fingers, *yes*, it was a pen after all, and so it was the writing desk at which she sat and not the pianoforte. And he will have said to her, "Fear not, madam, that I should disturb you at this late hour, for I have come with tidings." And she will have been shocked, but that stubborn grace to which she was born will have steeled her resolve, and she will have said, "Indeed, sir." And he will have said, "You are to die." And she will have said, "That is known. For is it not that every woman on God's earth is appointed an hour of death?" And he, with a terrible smile, though not terribly meant, of course, but frightening, nonetheless, to a mortal, will have said, "Yes, Miss Austen. That is so."

Since the beginning of Time, there has existed in Heaven a perfect record of all deeds, an accounting of each man and woman upon which they will be judged, a great Book written with words of gold, watched over by Saint Peter, the holiest and most trusted of the Apostles. All this I revealed to the astonished Miss Austen, her face flushed to a beautiful pink, like the first blossom of a rose; all this I revealed and something more: that I, myself, had been chosen as the Author of that Book. Certainly, she was wonderstruck that such a task had been entrusted to one so beautiful and terrible, though, of course, not willingly terrible, never willingly terrible to her. Certainly, she will have felt as if her story were perfectly safe, that each notation should accord perfectly with how it had been performed in History, that the accounting should be true and her immortal soul safe.

And I assured her, eagerly, that this was so; that there had never been a keener observer of her manners than I; that none had been so attuned to her every thought, the reveries, the little meanderings of her brain, than the one who stood before her. And she might have nodded, just a little, but at this point I will have noticed that the wonderment she felt, the jarring to her soul had jarred her hand as well, and a thin pool of ink might have been gathering on the pages before her. Gallantly, I might have said something to draw attention to this, "Madam, the ink is running." And she will have said, "Why should ink matter when an Angel of the Lord stands before me?" and I will have said, "Because it is all that matters. Was not the universe brought into being with a Word?" And she will have said, "Yes, perhaps." And I will have laughed gently, "Then you must attend to words, to your little creations, lest some force of evil enter into the world." Perhaps this was not a very kind joke.

The other angels had little in the way of poetic sensibility; they were wise, yes, and terrible, certainly that, but none of them, at their hearts, were aesthetes. They were messengers, servants, builders, killers even—you might say that there was a certain creative flair in, for example, that little episode with Lot's wife, but you have to realize that even Azrael was a little embarrassed about it, he didn't know what had come over him, and the others, they wouldn't trust him with anything apocalyptic for centuries. You see, they wanted wisdom; they wanted terror; but poetry, that was a thing for mortals, that was a way of imagining the world not how it was but how it *could* be; and as the world was exactly how God had ordered it in his Infinite Wisdom and Infinite Knowledge, it was, therefore, Infinitely Perfect. Why sadness, you might ask? Why death? Why pillars of salt and punishment? Why manna in the wilderness and the twelve plagues of Egypt and the forbidden fruit if not for the sheer *poetry* of it? I asked Azrael once, but he only looked at me with those eyes that had seen the passing of eons, that had basked in the radiance of a most perfect love and had delivered thousands upon thousands of mortals from one world to the next—eyes that did not want questions, only thousands put to the sword, not even a fiery sword, just a simple iron sword with two sides honed for cutting down mortals like wheat—and he said, "I don't *know* why I did it, mate. I don't."

Jane did not like jokes. That was very clear to me; she might have, in youth, enjoyed the odd frivolity, but in old age her mind had hardened into a shell around her frail body, and she did not smile.

"Am I to die, then?" she will have said, and I will have said, "Yes. I have said as much."

"But when?" she will have asked me. "When?"

But I could not tell her, I could not tell. To do so would make me anathema, and besides, I was not there as a messenger, nor as a servant, nor even as a killer—I was there to record. And it would be then that I heard a knock at the door, and in will have come a great clod of a man wearing his bulk upon him as if it were an expensive suit, tailored to fit, a plain-looking man, aggressive in conversation and almost completely tactless, with a quite unappealing stutter. And he will have said, "You have r-r-r-ruined the Handel." Stricken, she will have apologized though I am sure she did not wish to. "Indeed," he will have said, "again please." And he will have left the room as abruptly as he had entered.

"Mister Harris Bigg-Wither," I will have stated, and even then words were written, somewhere, in shining gold on pages white as snow. *A great clod of a man . . .*

"My husband."

"I know."

"He proposed after his time in Oxford."

"I know."

"Marriage might offer many practical advantages. A permanent home for Cassandra, assistance for my brothers in their careers . . ."

"I know, Miss Austen," I might have whispered, and, somewhere, the words *many practical advantages . . .*

"Do not call me that."

God, it is said, sees all things at once; for Him there is no such thing as Time, for indeed, He exists outside of Time and for Him all things are immediate, all things perpetual. God has no understanding of narrative; how can He? For narrative is the pleasing arrangement of one incident after another, the compelling build of drama and the proper, appropriate resolution when all things have occurred, as they must, in a certain order.

In Heaven, it is said, there sits the Book of Judgement and each mortal is recorded there so that upon the day of death, Saint Peter might open the book and find ascribed there a full recounting of their deeds. But it is not said, that albeit the words are of the finest gold and they shine like the light of Heaven itself, albeit the parchment is of the finest white vellum, as smooth as newborn flesh, as white as newfallen snow, when one reads from the Book of Judgement it is a fast and simple thing: *Missus Clara Crawford lived a good life and is deserving of reward;* or *Mister Timothy Branton was good for many years but fell under the influence of evil friends.*

And I read from the Book and I examined the lives of those I had been sent to watch over, and each of them seemed like such a tiny thing, so tiny, and I would turn the page and ask, "But where are they, the little loves and betrayals, the tests and mishaps and abandonments and reversals?" and Peter, with an infinitely loving look, with the weight of ages sitting upon his poor, beetled brow, would say, "Just leave it, already. We don't have time for plot."

Miss Austen played very nicely this second time, and the G major was sweet and pleasing to the ear, her transition to the "Duet" flawless. I said nothing. I simply watched her at the pianoforte, watched the elegant curve of her neck bowing toward the keys, the litheness of her fingers, the way her eyes would close for a moment as she played and then flutter open furiously. She was a beautiful woman, this Miss Austen, or as she preferred, Missus Bigg-Wither, and as one who has seen the many specimens of Creation, I can say with some authority that here was a remarkable creature, here was a creature of virtue and kindness, deserving in every way of the especial attention of one such as myself.

When the piece came to an end, she sat for a moment, utterly composed, and I thought she would speak but she did not, not immediately, she listened as if to some phantom music of her own; but that was not it, it was not some inner symphony she attended to, no, but the creak of the house, the sound of footsteps in the hall. There was none. She relaxed.

"Are you here to haunt me?"

"No," I said, "This is not one of your Gothic tales, with wild-haired men and buried secrets."

"I do not have time for stories."

"No," I said. "Not any longer."

"Why do you look at me like that?"

"Like what?" I replied, startled.

"As if you were a child, and I a much sought after sweet that had suddenly turned sour in your mouth."

I regarded her in silence for a time; her body shuddered with the effort of playing, and I found myself listening too, for the sound of footsteps, for the sound of something beside her breath coming in and out of her lungs in ragged little bursts. There was light streaming in from an open window and it touched her hair, burnished it to gold.

"I think you are very beautiful," I said.

"You must not say such things."

"But I am bound to truth in all things." *She was very beautiful. . . .*

"I am not," Miss Austen replied, and she turned her head so that the light slid off her hair, touched her lips, her eyes. "Truth is a not a thing for a woman, or novelists, to be concerned with; it is only the appearance of truth that touches us, for a thing feigned becomes true enough given only sufficient time and inclination for the masquerade."

"It is different for an angel."

"Yes," she said softly. "I would very much like to imagine it is."

Let us say, now, that her husband, Mister Bigg-Wither, never entered the room; let us say that we sat, the two of us listening, for some time, and we heard only birdsong or, perhaps, the pianoforte, but no footsteps in the hall.

At the beginning of the War—and even I do not remember, good record-keeper, good servant that I am, which it was—Azrael was thrilled.

"It will be good to see action again," he said, "just to try my hand at it again. A sword is an easy thing to lose touch with, a sword requires practice, effort, and I," he confessed, "have not done much of either." Azrael went to the Peninsula where the French were massacring the British and the British were massacring the French, and as I visited Miss Austen, so did he watch the course of the War creep across those other lands; when I saw him, he was gleaming, resplendent, and there was a thrill to his voice when he spoke, as if the crack of cannons had infused him with a thunderous rapture. Azrael was happy with the simple tasks of warfare.

"Let them do as they will," he would say to us, "it's all the same. French. English. Not a Joan of Arc to look out for among them, not a vision to dispense with. Just mind the cavalry and keep out the way. Easy work." He smiled then, happy to have something to do, happy to be of service. But the next time he didn't bother with bringing his sword. "All muskets now, isn't it? Not like the old days. Muskets and cannons. Good things, cannons, I'm not complaining, but it's all a bit imprecise, isn't it? They just fire and, hey, maybe it'll hit, maybe it won't. But never let it be said that I'm complaining, I like a good war, a war is a good thing."

But he looked sad, somehow, and after that he confided to me, "I don't know what I'm doing there. I just don't know. There aren't any orders. I just watch, now, it's all just watching. I don't know what it's supposed to mean. Shouldn't I be trying to inspire them? Shouldn't one side have a moral right over the other?"

"It means that history is advancing, and Creation is more infinitely complex than we can possibly imagine," I said.

"I stride about the battlefield," he said, "and I watch the cannons go off, and the charge, and then I sort through the dead, and when I come across one, someone writes down his name and puts a little tick beside the box. And they respect me, the ones from Records, they absolutely respect me, you can see it in their eyes. But all they want to know is did that one manage to hit anything? Because if he did, that's it then, isn't it? The little bastards know which box to tick."

When Jane's beauty left her, she still had the pianoforte, and her skill at it was extreme, sublime. Her fingers were precise if arthritic; and when she played it was as if a tremor rippled through me, as if she were revealing some hidden part of the divine plan, some especial function of grace that I had never been privy to. And I would listen to her, sometimes, and we would speak, sometimes.

"I do not understand why you have come," she would say to me.

"It is my purpose to discover your secrets, that I might see the truth of you and write it in Heaven."

"There is no truth to me that you have not seen," she would say, "for I have no pretensions to that sort of elegance which consists in tormenting a respectable man, and as such I have laid bare for you whatever you ask."

"Ah," I would exclaim, "what I search for is the parts of yourself that you do not yet, and may never, understand; for that is where the true character of a woman is written, not in what she knows she can reveal and does however willingly, but in what she is unaware of, even in herself."

"Then you assume I do not know myself."

"No mortal can."

"And yet I have made a study of it, these long, lonely years, a perfect study so that I could paint a likeness of myself for your Book that, I have no doubt, would be suitable to your purposes."

"What would you say?"

"That I am a woman."

"That would not be enough."

"It was enough for Eve," she would say, "and it is enough for my husband."

"It is not enough for you."

It is said that in Heaven there is an order to things, and we angels understand it perfectly, that we lack the requisite means to question, those of us who stayed, that is, who did not fall in the War. And so I did not question when Azrael came to me, no longer resplendent, the crack of cannon fire gone from his voice.

"They've taken me off Warfare," he said, and his voice was melodious and sad. "They say that I do not understand the New Order, that I am a cog in a perfectly ordered machine but, perhaps, it is the wrong machine, not the machine of Warfare. I don't even know what that means," he confessed, "but one of them, one of the dying ones, asked for a sign. And so I appeared to him, I let him see that God's love was infinite and that he was safe, and that flesh was just a little thing, just a very little thing, and he had a place in the cosmic order. That God was merciful.

"Did you know that they have a Book? And in that Book are the names of the angels—everyone one of us? And it says, *Azrael—a good servant for many years*. For many years, what does that mean? Am I not eternal? Am I not free of flesh and beyond the scope of Time? *For many years*. And one of them found me. He said to me, 'Azrael, you are made to serve.' And I was. I am. I live to serve, service is the very truth of what I am, that's what I told him. 'Good,' the little bugger said."

Jane never lost her beauty; let it not be said by anyone that she lost her beauty, for Beauty is an eternal thing, like Truth, and there can be no changing it once it is possessed.

And I said this to Azrael, as he stood by me, I said, "Is she not beautiful, is she not possessed of some higher substance? Does she not deserve something more than that clod of a husband? What a noble mind, what a keen observer of the human condition, what a record-keeper of all that transpires in the hearts of those who surround her."

And he said, "I was made to serve just like you. This is what they have asked of me, it's not cannons, it's not thunder and death, but it's what they asked me to do."

"Let me speak with her."

Let us say that she was sitting at her desk when he came for her; let it not have been the pianoforte where she had laboured, for hours, for the love of a husband who did not love her in return. Let us say that there was no husband. Let us say that she was only passably good at the pianoforte, and that she had, instead, a keen fascination with words, with writing out the hearts of men and women upon the page. Let us call her, not Missus Bigg-Wither, as she herself might have done, but Miss Austen, alone, yes, but beautiful and keen-witted and happy.

Perhaps she would have heard a tolling of a bell, as some do, and she would have turned to see a stranger standing before her, tall, resplendent, with hair as soft as lamb's wool. Perhaps there would have been a rushing noise in her ears, the sound of a great cataract, more deafening, perhaps, than the crack of a cannon.

And he will have said to her, "Fear not, madam, that I should disturb you at this late hour, for I have come with tidings."

And she will have been shocked, but that stubborn grace to which she was born will have steeled her resolve, and she will have said, "Indeed, sir." And he will have said, "You are to die." And she will have said, "That is known. For is it not that every woman on God's earth is appointed an hour of death?" And he, with a terrible smile, though not terribly meant, of course, but frightening, nonetheless, to a mortal, will have said, "Yes, Miss Austen. That is so."

Afterwards, I would say to Azrael, "Why pillars of salt and punishment? Why manna in the wilderness and the twelve plagues of Egypt? Why sadness? Why death?"

And he would shrug, looking uncomfortable. "I don't know, mate."

They say, in Heaven, that there is a Book, and in it are written all the names of the universe, that an accounting can be made of each. They say that beside the name of Azrael it is written, *He was a good servant.* And I know it to be true. And there will be another name, Harris Bigg-Wither, and there will be a very brief account, and there will be another name, Jane Austen, and it will say, *She was very beautiful and died too early. Let her fondness for words have never stinted, let her books last for generations, let them be written as truth in the hearts and souls of the generations to come; let her never have feared the footsteps on the hall, let her have known much love, let her have disliked the pianoforte.* I do not know if it is a kindness, these things I have written. But it *is* a record. Of a sort.

They say, in Heaven, that Time is infinite and all things happen at once, that there is no order to events; that there is no such thing as music for all notes sound together and the listener cannot differentiate; music is temporal; music is of the flesh; it is mortal. In Heaven, they say, there is no grand sweeping narrative, for God stands outside the possibility of such things; that He sees all things, the loves, the triumphs, the betrayals and reversals in a single moment, an eternity that renders as chaos for his servants what is perfect order for him. They say that His forgiveness is absolute, his His love is absolute, His observance is absolute. They say this, my many detractors. Let it be a jest between us; let it be the first betrayal; let it be a mark, spilled ink, in that perfect chronicle of His that I should believe otherwise, that I should doubt, that this doubt should run through to the very depths of me.

In Heaven, there is a book, and in that book, there is a name: *Lucifer, called Lightbearer, a good servant, once, turned rebel.*

the audit

SUSIE MOLONEY

Poor Janet lay in bed listening to the alarm, trying to ignore it and knowing it would never, ever go away. In the first few blinks of waking up she had nudged at Les, curled up on his side beside her. When he slept on his side, he didn't snore as badly. She nudged him and felt his body roll with the force of it, but otherwise, gave no other response. She was about to speak *Les get up time for work* when she remembered that Les wasn't working these days and then the day ahead washed over her and her stomach tightened and any thoughts of sleeping in or not getting up were lost in churning waves of stomach acid and tightened shoulders.

I'm being audited.

The alarm kept up its tinny shriek, a cross between bells and a rattling aluminium door. It sounded just like one of those wind-up alarm clocks of the sort that she remembered in her parent's room from when she was a kid, but it wasn't. It was a plug in. The wind-up clocks wound down eventually, and after a minute of the ringing, you could go back to sleep. If you could stand a minute. In January you could; when the floor was cold and the car had to run a full fifteen minutes before you could drive it without stalling, and if the coffee had to be made and if you forgot to make your lunch for work before going to bed, you could stand it. Probably you could stand two minutes of ringing if it meant not putting your bare feet on to the cold January floor. The plug in alarm didn't run down. It rang until the little button was pushed. It was Les' mom's old alarm clock. She gave it to them when Jan complained about Les not getting up for work. The clock was procured like magic, practically out of a hat. Les's work record embarrassed his mom. They fought about it all the time. When he wasn't working, they avoided his mom's place.

Les-than-a-man. That was what Jan's mom called him.

It was all the way across the room. To shut it off, you had to get out of bed. You couldn't even crawl to the end of the bed and reach out to the dresser and shut it off. He'd done that too many times. They started to put it on the chair in the corner. Something about the chair made it sound louder too. *It's the acoustics*, Les-than-a-man had said, grinning. *Makes the chair vibrate with it.*

Janet didn't know if that was true, but it did seem louder.

"Shut off the fucking alarm," Les mumbled from under the blanket. Jan was already half-way out of bed by then, so she didn't say anything back. The bedroom was freezing. They all but shut the heat off at night *save a little dough*, Les said. Les-than-a-man.

It was 5:30. She had five hours to get her shit together before her meeting with the government accountant. She was being audited.

I'm being audited. Jan thought it to herself as she pushed in the little button on the back of Les's mom's alarm clock in hopes that the words would lose some of their power, the power they had held over her for the last two weeks, but in spite of the two weeks that she had to get used to the idea, it all still made her stomach tight and sore and her head ache.

I'm just a dumb waitress, she thought. *I'm a big nobody. What do they care what I have?* She'd said this and more to everyone who would listen for the last two weeks, until Les-than-a-man told her to can it. She scuffled a foot under the end of the bed fishing for her slippers and found one and put it on. She got down on all fours to find the other one. Les had pulled it off her in a stupid gesture (it was supposed to be romantic or something but it had just been *stoopid*) last night when he wanted to have sex. She told him she wasn't in the mood, but he said *I'll make you in the mood* and then what was she supposed to do? But her slipper had gone flying.

He always did the wrong thing at the wrong time. Like mornings, when he slept instead of going to work.

The house was cold enough that she wrapped her robe around her middle tight and hugged her arms to her middle. She slipped out of the bedroom and closed the door behind her. The first thing she did was turn the heat up. No way was she doing bullshit paper work in a cold house. Then she made coffee. Strong.

It was still dark out when she went down into the basement and started hauling boxes of receipts upstairs. She brought the first two up and even just the sight of them, with their box tops folded in on each other in a pinwheel felt so overwhelming that she decided to start with just the two of them and then work her way up to the other box, still in the basement, and then the assorted bags and folders with the other papers in them.

The boxes were from the liquor store, from when they moved. One was a Captain Morgan's Rum box and the other a Canadian Club. Scratched out with black marker was the notation "kitchen" in her handwriting. Written under that was "tax shit," in Les's handwriting. *Ha ha*, she thought, Les-than-a-man. That's what it was, though. Shit.

The coffee maker gurgled as though there wasn't a care in the world that couldn't be taken care of by Maxwell House in the Morning, but it filled the kitchen with such a warm and homey smell, that Janet thought she might cry. It reminded her—the dark, the coffee smell, the tight stomach—of when she was in school. Her dad would get up and make coffee *come on girls* and then call her and her sister to breakfast. Her mom worked a night shift at a bakery and she slept while the three of them ate and mumbled quietly at the table before school and work. Jan hadn't done well in school, mornings before she went filled her with a familiar, comfortable sort of dread, based more on the tedium of the long day ahead than any real fear. It wasn't she was worried about failing a test, or a grade or getting a bad mark on a paper. She didn't do well, and wasn't expected to by either her parents or teachers. Sometimes it just worked that way. She left after tenth grade, not exactly with her parent's blessings, but with a basic understanding that neither she nor school were doing each other any favours. She went right to work at a diner on Rail Road, making $3.25 an hour. She'd been a waitress ever since. And she was a damn good one. She even liked it. Her parent's had her sister to be proud of. Betty had gone all the way through school and then, in a move that was incomprehensible to Jan, went on to more school. She was a medical secretary now, and worked at one of the hospitals in the city. She was married with two kids. Her husband was a mechanic. He made good money too.

But no tips, was their joke together. Not very funny, considering it was the tips that got her into this mess.

I could just kill Terri Pringle.

Janet had been waitressing for ten years. Never once had she claimed any tips. Not once. Ten years, ten tax reports filed, not once had anyone said fuck all about tips. Then she was talking to a new waitress, Terri Pringle, who said, in passing one day, that you had to claim your tips on your income tax.

"They'll come after you, if you don't," she'd said. Terri worked part-time. She was a student at the community college and she had said the whole thing with such confidence that it shook Janet up.

Tentatively she had said to Terri, "I've never claimed my tips." She'd tried to say it with as much mustered confidence as the younger, student-y Terri, but hadn't managed as well.

"My dad's an accountant," she said. "They'll come after you for that." Then the shift had changed and everybody went home. Terri didn't even work there long.

Jan had asked around after that. She asked the other waitresses and they would sigh and the debate would start, but most of them said they never claimed their tips. One girl said they automatically assume tips on top of your wages. "Ten per cent," she said. "Look over your last year's return. Where it says: undeclared income?' Look there. They'll have added ten per cent."

They hadn't. Her mother and dad said not to worry about it. "You get it done at the H and R Block, don't you?" She did.

"They do it for you there." But her mom had looked a little frowny over the whole thing *you don't want to do anything to get into trouble*, she'd said later, when they were alone.

Don't be such a putz, Les-than-a-man said. "Declaring your tips would be like when we borrow ten bucks from my mom and then declaring it as income." He laughed at the very thought and then watched TV. He reminded her, though, when they were going to the H and R Block to get their taxes done. *Don't be a putz*, he'd said, and he shook his finger at her and raised his eyebrows in a perfect imitation of his mother when she said to him, *You get a job now, you hear? Don't be a bum like your father.*

In the end, she declared her tips. Or at least, a rough estimate of them. The H and R man had raised his eyebrows, too, and Jan had trouble deciding whether that was because she was claiming them, or because the number was so low, or too high. Her face had reddened and she felt like she'd been caught in a lie, but of course she had no real way of knowing if she was lying or not because Terri Pringle—*I could kill Terri Pringle*—hadn't even mentioned declaring tips until nearly October. Jan had guessed based on what she made from around November-mid when she decided inside her head to play it right to the end of the year. She thought she was safe in her guess because people tipped more around the holidays, and she counted them.

She poured coffee into her bunny mug and got down on her hands and knees on the floor in front of the first box. She cracked it open, not knowing even what year she was about to see, let alone whether or not it would be her stuff or his. Les had a business on the side sometimes, fixing bikes. His stuff was mixed in with hers, but he only claimed the money he made working extra for his buddy Tom, who had a bike shop, because Tom declared it.

The box was filled to the top with little pieces of paper. A musty smell came from the box, like old books at a garage sale. A couple of little pieces fluttered up and settled back down, like fall leaves when you swipe by them on your bike on the way to school. Thinking about school set her off again. She wanted a Tums, but she'd eaten the last of them the night before.

Gee-zus.

Her and Les were both savers of paper. Paper had some kind of authoritarian hold over her feral self. Paper made her feel more feral than human, or certainly sub-human in some way. Especially white paper. Around very white paper with lines and numbers or words on it, she felt stained and dusty and smudgy. The lines, even and black or blue, the careful tally of numbers in a row, the dots matching up with each other, they seemed like representatives of some kind of legal authority. She also felt this way about soldiers and policemen, doctors and dentists; pieces of paper felt like they could boss her, regardless of what was written on them. Could as easy be a receipt from the drugstore for tampax as a subpoena, didn't matter. Coloured paper wasn't so bad. She kept the pizza flyers and the two-for-one deals that came from the carpet cleaning people, and ads offering her fifteen per cent off her next oil change, with a sort of grown-up sigh, and filed them in a pile on the table beside the front door. Anything that came in a white envelope (especially a white envelope with a little window on the front) went reverently over to the desk in the corner, where she paid bills. She even kept the newsletters sent by her member of parliament, just in case. You never knew. Someone might ask. Something.

You never knew.

She didn't claim much on her income tax. She claimed panty hose and her uniforms, of course. And shoes, but they were the special (ugly) orthopaedic shoes that she had to wear because of her bunions—an occupational hazard of working on your feet for ten years. In a few years she imagined she would have to have some sort of an operation on varicose veins. Annie had it done last year after she nearly couldn't walk for the pain. The operation fixed her up pretty good, she said, but by the end of the year—*when Terri Pringle left never to return—I could kill Terri Pringle*—new ones were troubling her.

She claimed gas mileage whenever she had to work extra at a catering job that her mother sometimes got her through the bakery. Mostly Bridge Lady teas and things, but once a Sweet Sixteen party. That had been quite a bash. Not only had it been catered, but the whole place had been professionally decorated by one of those balloon joints. They turned the No. 16 Legion Hall into a pink cloud, with a real balloon waterfall in the corner. Not just streamers, either, but yards and yards of pink fabric had been draped over walls and tables and the whole thing had been just beautiful, although a little hard on the eyes after an hour or so. Most of the teenagers took off after the presents were opened, but that was okay because the mothers and aunts and old ladies had stayed for hours, wanting only more tea and the waitresses weren't too taxed on their feet and were paid for the whole day. Her mom and the others had made tiny little cakes—twelve kinds—the sort that were just a bite and sickly sweet after the first couple, but lovely to look at. Just perfect. They were tipped as a group and shared after those events. She wondered if the others had claimed the tips on their income tax.

Janet started going through the receipts, one by one, noticing that while her whole body felt sick and tired, and shaky, it was only her hands where it showed.

Sometime over the next two hours, Les woke up and ambled into the kitchen and poured himself a cup of coffee. Janet, engrossed in 1996 fuel receipts didn't even look up. In fact, didn't realize he was up at all until he kicked and scattered a pile of health-relateds (Les's filling, but paid for by her, ergo *her* health-related receipt, plus two massages and a visit to the chiropractor, all from 1998) receipts when he opened the fridge door to get the milk. They went flying towards the free-standing cabinet where she kept her baking stuff and tupperware.

"*Don't*," she shrieked, shocking them both. She bent over double from her position, sitting on the floor surrounded by boxes and pieces of paper (almost all of them white), and fished out two receipts that had slipped under the cabinet. "This took me *hours*," she said.

"*Sor-reee*," he said, and muttered something about someone being a little cranky under his breath. He settled in on the living room sofa, out of Janet's line of vision, but she heard him open the paper.

She felt mildly guilty for snapping at him when he'd just woken up—Les was not a morning person—and so called to him in the living room, "How come you're up so early?"

He grunted. She waited for his answer, and realized the grunt was going to be all she got, and so bent back over her receipts, searching for something, anything, over the last six years that would save her ass.

"Dear Mrs. Lancaster," the letter has started. Right away, reading it, before she even opened the envelope in fact, she knew it was bad news. The long, thin, pristine white envelope was addressed to her and her alone, the erroneous "Mrs." making it somehow worse. The corner was stamped with a government of Canada logo and no return address. Under the logo was "Department of Revenue," and her stomach had tightened.

She had come home after her shift smelling like French fries and mud pie and wanting nothing more in the whole wide world (ever again) than to take her shoes off and sit on the couch. Les's truck hadn't been in the drive and that had given her a little lift. The house would be empty and quiet. She didn't even wonder where he was, didn't give it a thought (although hoping in the same breath that he was out looking for work and knowing that it was more likely he was playing pool at the legion or else was at his mother's cadging twenty bucks). She grabbed the mail not even looking at it and threw it on the table. The letter from the government skittered out, sliding across the Formica with its weight.

"Dear Mrs. Lancaster," it began. "A review of your 2000 tax remittance noted that you filed $362.96 in income under 'other source.'

"Your explanation of the additional income was for gratuities received through your employment at the Happy Diner where you are listed as 'serving personnel.' A sequential review of tax information filed for the years 1996-1999 indicated that while during those years you were also employed by the Happy Diner as serving personnel, no gratuities were claimed for those years.

"You are therefore required to appear at your nearest tax office on or before February 13, 2001 with records indicating this discrepancy in an independent audit. Please call the number at the bottom of this page to make an appointment with your auditor, no later than ten days after the receipt of this letter."

It was signed by a secretary for a director at Revenue Canada (Auditor's Department!) whose name was Mr. Peter Norris. Peter

Norris. She'd never heard of him, never would meet him, but she had a vague feeling from then on that he had her file on his desk ready to be stamped, "Guilty," the implications of which could only be dreamed about, in a nightmare fashion.

She'd left the letter lying around for a couple of days, never once forgetting about it for even a moment. That had been a Friday. Saturday night her and Les had gone out for a couple of beers with their friends Gord and Paula and Janet had drank more than a couple of beers, uncharacteristically, pissing Les off because it meant he had to drive them home and he'd had a warning four years earlier for drinking and driving. "They'll cut my ass off, I get caught," he'd said, petulantly, more than a little in his cups himself. She'd laughed at that. "They won't *cut your ass off*. They'll take away your license," she'd said, matter-of-factly. "Cut your ass off. What does that even mean?" She could get snarky like this only when she was a little drunk.

"Same thing," Les said. She fell asleep in the car and *even then*, didn't stop thinking about the audit.

She finally told Les about it that Sunday, when he was trying to watch football and nursing a hangover with a beer. "Get yourself a lawyer," was what he said.

She told her mom and dad that same day, walking over to their place right around supper time, needing just a little comfort food and maybe a bit of advice. What she thought she really wanted was to hear her dad tell her it was all right and then to tell her to bring her stuff over to him and he would take care of it. Maybe call her Princess, like when she was little.

"Just get your things together and explain to the government that you didn't know you had to declare your tips and that you're very sorry and you won't do it again," her mother told her. She made beef casserole with shell noodles. It tasted like grade five and homework, because of how she felt.

"You never should have declared them in the first place," her dad said, from his chair in the living room, where he was watching the game and switching over to Matlock, between quarters.

On the following Monday, Abby at work said, "You get yourself a good accountant and let them do the work."

She got herself Ramona Jacobson, who *tsk-tsk-ed* and *oh my-ed* everything, called her *Lancaster* and charged by the hour and talked really fast. The woman wore those half-glasses that old people wore, even though she didn't look more than ten years older than Janet, and sometimes she peered at her over them as though Janet were some sort of alien creature worth a second study.

Ramona Jacobson scared her almost as much as the audit, but at least she was on her side.

The phone rang at eight-thirty just about knocking Janet out of her slippers. Her eyes were stinging from being open so long and her fingers were black and coated with ink. It rang twice before she realized Les wasn't going to pick it up and she got up off the floor, very careful not to disturb any of the fifteen piles of varying years and subject matter (unfortunately in no particular order) that were distributed around the floor in the kitchen.

Les was still reading the paper. He shifted without looking at her, his bulk moving slowly over the vinyl seats of the sofa, so that air escaped from one of them making a hissing sound, like a fart.

She grabbed the phone on the fourth ring.

"Hello?" she said, like a question.

"Lancaster, I just wanted to remind you to bring all the **co-malgamated T-7s**. And while I got you, don't forget the **super-annuated** close forms. Even the ones for your spouse." Ramona Jacobson spoke *very* fast on the phone, breathing it all into Janet's ear like sitting too close to a speaker for too long.

"Huh?" she said. "Bring the what?"

"That's right. And the T-6s, too. From the legion work. Gotta go. If you need anything, I'm in a meeting for the next hour and then you can get me on my cell. You have that number?"

"I don't know."

"It's—" and then at the speed of light she rattled off what seemed to be an account number at the world's largest bank.

"Um thanks," Janet said.

"You can get me on it until 11. *Shit!* I have your **Geswins**! Well, that's all right. What time's the appointment?"

"Um—"

"1:30, right. Hmmm. Forgot about that. Anyway, I'll meet you there. If you need me, you can still get me after the hour. Gotta go, I'm late, good luck!" And she hung up.

Janet hung on to the phone, desperation creeping over her face more quickly as she realized that Ramona Jacobson had hung up before she had a chance to ask what **co-malgamites** were. And the **super-annuated** thing? Had she said that? **Malgamites**, or something. What was that? Something else too. She hung up before Jan had a chance to ask—

What everything is.

She hung up and stared at the phone as if it was going to ring again. It didn't.

"Who was that?" Les said from the couch.

"The accountant," she said, bewildered.

"Oh yeah, when's that thing?" He turned a page of the newspaper with such slowness, such snapping of newsprint, such rolling of fat that she wanted to turn and scratch him to pieces as though making him bleed and scream would somehow release the rising pulse of terror inside her.

"1:30," she said. The only thing she knew.

"Well, you're in for it. Shouldn't have claimed them in the first place," he said, then he chuckled. And he folded the paper over, smoothing the pages down against the coffee table. Jan went back into the kitchen, glancing up at the clock. It was 8:35. She had three hours left before she had to get in the shower and get dressed and down to the auditor.

There was a fourth box in the kitchen when she re-entered. It was perched on the edge of the vinyl chair that was covered with brown flowers, a cast off from her mom's place. Their old kitchen suite. The kitchen chairs of her youth. If you got close enough they smelled like her sister and mashed potatoes.

On the side of the box was written, "taxes 1997." She thought she had been through all the 97s. Her heart sank, and yet lifted at the same time, as though in this new box might be the answer, the legendary, mythical piece of paper that would lead to the path that keep her out of prison. The Holy Trail.

Ignoring the rest of the receipts in the box she'd last opened ("tax crap 98 or 96"), she went right to the new box and pulled open the flaps. Little pieces of paper fluttered up. She grabbed one closest to the top.

"Windlemiers," it said at the top. She frowned. Windlemiers? She shook her head. There were a series of code numbers at the top. Then a lonely figure. "$267.95." Two more figures followed, the only two she could puzzle out. The itemized taxes: Provincial and federal. *Okay that's good.* Janet nodded encouragingly to herself. *Taxes, right, good; that was what she was looking for, right?* Under the taxes was the total and then another series of codes. A figure that might have been the date seemed absent. She puzzled over the first series of codes, in case that was it, and then the one at the bottom. Nothing seemed remotely date-related. She tried to think of what on earth might cost $267.95 all at once and could come up with nothing but a car repair. They rarely had $267.95 (or even just $267.00) all at once to pay something. Not after pay day, anyway.

She nodded to herself. Car repair. That would be good. She could say it was car repair to get to a Legion job. There was no date. Her heart pumped a little harder with the lie. (Not that it was *necessarily* a lie, it could be true, how did she know? *How on earth* was she supposed to *know?*)

She dropped it with haphazard abandon in the vicinity of the pile supposedly of "car repair." The year no longer seemed to matter. She could hear the clock ticking in her belly.

The phone rang again about twenty minutes later and it was for Les. Jan had just cut her finger, a paper cut, and it stung. She stuck it in her mouth and sucked, the pain exquisite and small. Through that, she heard him mumbling into the phone, listening with only half an ear (he wasn't currently cheating as far as she knew, and he wasn't actively seeking employment and so it would only be some bum friend or other and therefore was not very interesting. Then he called from the living room.

"Hey Lancaster!" he called (he had taken to calling her that when she told him about the accountant calling her that; he thought it was funny). "Call-waiting for you." She stumbled into the living room, her eyes unable to see great distances after all their small work.

She looked at him questioningly. He shrugged.

"But get off, cause I have Beaner on the other line." A bum friend.

She took the phone and the man on the other end was talking before it even got to her ear.

"—confirming your 1:30 P.M. appointment. You understand that you're expected." Her mind snapped awkwardly on the moment and gave her all her reference material out of panic.

"Yes, I understand. I will be there. I am meeting my accountant," she said, hoping the last bit came out with some authority.

"Good, good," he said, and then paused with horrible time-stealing importance and affability. "So many people just try to avoid the inevitable by not showing up, you understand. It's not that I believe you won't be here—I'm not saying anything at all about you personally, it's just that many people try to avoid the inevitable," he said. It seemed to Jan that he had just spoken in a loop, saying every word with such deliberation that the time it took excluded the others and so he repeated them, endlessly.

"Yes," she said, because she couldn't think of anything else.

"And you'll be sure to bring your **liabostities**?" he asked.

"Yes?" she said firmly, having no idea what he was talking about. *The accountant will take care of it,* she heard her father's voice in her head. And Abby's. And her mother's. Even Les might have said something like that right after sex. Maybe.

"Good, good," he said again, his voice on a loop. She nodded into the phone, eyes glazed over, looking towards the sunburst clock over the dresser they kept in the living room to keep their CDs in. There were sweaters in the bottom drawers. "Yes," she repeated, because he seemed to need something more.

"Good, good, then," he said. It was almost 9:30. "At 1:30 A.M., then," he finally finished, as though it were an affair or something pleasant. His voice was *affable,* something she'd only read about and that filled her with suspicion. He hung up and she handed the phone back to Les.

"Thanks for taking so long," he said, sarcastically. She went back into the kitchen.

Three more boxes were in the kitchen when she came in.

One was beside the stove, and written in big, bold black letters, all capitals was, "Existentials, 1999." The other two were half-hidden under the table, but she saw them, even as they tried to wiggle closer under. The box she had been working on was only just started, but she tore into the new one with a fierce sort of will. The kitchen was littered with paper, her comings and goings had scattered some of the neat stacks until they were literally piles. *You get piles from sitting on cold cement in your pyjamas,* she thought wildly; her mother used to threaten that.

Ripping open the new box she stared blankly at a receipt that appeared to have no dollar figure. The date was 99, though, as the box had promised. For this, she was eternally grateful. *June 16, 1999. Thank you, Jesus, I am absolved of sin in the blood of the receipt. Thank Jesus.*

Jesu anumi ablo.

What would Jesus do?

"Jesus wouldn't have claimed them in the first place," Les said from the door. "I'm Picking up Beaner and we're getting that starter for the pickup," he said vaguely. "I might stop over at mom's after," he said. She didn't look up. He picked his way around the piles of paper and said nothing about them.

Good bye. Maybe she only thought it.

Ramona Jacobson called back at ten. "Don't forget the **willimusteers and the mono-magnisiums. Also the Pat-Rilancers; they're with the S-2 forms. Okay?** Gotta run. You know you didn't bring them to the last meeting and that was your choice, Lancaster. Oh! For god's sake, jiggle things around and make sure there's at least a thousand bucks in your mainstream, eh? Get me on the cell, 873dog95-24eat at sam's30." And she hung up.

Janet cut her finger, a paper cut, on the pad of note paper by the phone. She sucked at it.

There were six more boxes, all unopened when she walked back into the kitchen. She stared at them with a baleful, exhausted sort of defiance. They were marked only randomly, some had the routine, black felt marker scrawled across, others didn't. They were marked, "Hornets, 98." "Case Histories, 1996." And worse, "Receipts and Recipes for Disaster, 1998."

In one she found a bird's nest.

Her grade ten orienteering report.

A bill of sale for a car she'd never owned.

A copy of the *Desiderata* on pink paper, decorated with filigrees on the edges.

A receipt for fourteen pairs of panty hose (taupe) in size 7.

"Go placidly among the noise and haste—" she recited, remembered from a vague and unmemorable adolescence.

Sometime after four that day, Les and Beaner walked into the house and heard the phone ringing. They'd picked up the starter for the truck and then dropped by Les's mom's place. She'd given him twenty bucks after a hard ride. *You get a job, Lester. Get a haircut, Lester. You're living in sin, Lester.*

He and Beaner had laughed at this at the Kegger on Main, Les a little less hardier than Beaner, whose mother was dead and in her grave fifteen years.

"You gotta tape that, Mom, put it on a loop so I can play it back later, like a motivational thing, you know," Les had said to his mom. They'd repeated this bon mot up until their fourth beer when they got into sports with more of a vengeance.

"Janet," Les screamed when he walked in. The phone rang. "Let the machine get it," he said to Beaner. "Old lady's not home. Must be working," he said to Beaner.

"Wanna beer?"

"Does the Pope shit in the woods?" Beaner answered. This struck Les as hilarious.

In the living room the machine picked up the phone. A woman's voice screamed fast, into it. "Lancaster! Lancaster! Lancaster!" The boys ignored it.

Beaner followed Les into the kitchen. The fridge was blocked by an enormous pile of paper, literally blocked. Everywhere in the room was paper. It reached as high as the counter.

"What the *hell*?" Beaner gasped.

Les tried to get the fridge door open and couldn't. He looked around at the mess, a mess he sure-as-shit wasn't cleaning up.

"She had some tax thing. Guess she didn't get it cleaned up. She'll do it later," he said, but his mouth was dry. It was more paper than he'd ever seen, ever. He brought a hand up to shield his eyes, the sunlight, filtering in the west window was shining off the endless white, nearly blinding him. "Fuck," he said, equally vaguely, utterly unsure as to what to do. The paper presented a problem.

"Holy *shit*!" Beaner said. "What the hell is that?"

Les looked at his buddy and then followed his gaze to a spot on the floor where the mountain dipped nearly to linoleum. Pinky-brown flesh showed against the blinding white. A slender wrist and hand.

Without a word, Les stepped one giant step around the mound nearest the fridge and crouched, piles of paper reaching right to his crotch, a necessary lunge that pulled his groin muscle.

He picked up the hand, gingerly, like he might a mouse. "Cold," he said, but not without feeling. "Better call someone," he added, his voice cracking. Beaner didn't move.

There were tiny scratches all over the arm, little nicks in otherwise white, smooth flesh.

"What are those marks?" Beaner said.

"Looks like paper cuts," Les said, nodding. One summer Les had worked at a heating and ventilating company in the city. Mostly he had stuffed pink insulation into walls and then covered them up. He stuck his hand through the mounds of paper, along the route of the arm that he'd just felt, curious.

The body itself was warm.

"Body's warm," he said. He looked over his shoulder at Beaner's pale, sick face.

"Paper's a good insulator," he said.

sixteen colours

DAVID LIVINGSTONE CLINK

On a parallel Earth, much like ours, there are only sixteen colours. There is no tomato, candy-apple, or fire engine red. There is just red. When you say green, purple, maroon, aqua, or ivory, they know what you mean. The sun is yellow, snow is white, the sky is blue, the night is black, bottled water is clear, pumpkins are orange. There are no "shades of grey" for them. As a people they don't understand our need for shades of colour. The biggest difference between us and them, however, is that they have a million shades of meaning in how they relate to each other, their feelings far richer and more varied on their world than in ours. A nervous glance means the end of a relationship, a wink the heart learning to beat again. On any given day you can witness two people tearing each other's clothes off under a tree that has a brown trunk and leaf-green leaves, a woman slapping a man clean across the face on the grey of a nearby parking lot, and someone stepping off a ledge, falling six stories to the pink carnations below. They kill each other in jealous rages, commit suicide by the thousand, and write great poems. They don't know how to hold back. How could they?

the old boys club

GEOFF GANDER

Mr. Jonathan Lichtmann
1607 Mortimer Avenue
Unit 1404B
Toronto ON M5W 1E4

June 17, 2010

Dear Jonathan,

I am pleased to inform you that your application to Pickman College has been accepted, following a rigorous review by our selection committee. I have every expectation that you will excel at our school. I am sure your family is very proud of you.

An information package will be mailed to you in the coming weeks, which should answer most, if not all, of your questions concerning life at the College, our curriculum, and other matters.

Many influential men in business, government, and academia spent their formative years at Pickman College; you will be in distinguished company. I look forward to meeting you in September.

Sincerely,

Edwin J. Marsh,

Headmaster

FROM: Headmaster@pickman.on.ca
TO: judie.lichtmann@fergusonmassey.com
DATE: Sept 15 2010 11:23
SUBJ: Your recent email

Dear Ms. Lichtmann,

Thank you for your recent email. It is a pleasure dealing with parents who care so much about the well-being of their children.

Jonathan is adjusting as well to life at Pickman as can be expected for a young man who has never been away from home before. He has been in no trouble to speak of, so there is no need to worry on that account.

We are well aware of the difficulties Jonathan faced in his previous school. Unlike the beleaguered public education system, our resources are considerable. Our boys are generally a studious lot, but on the rare occasions where problem behaviours arise, we are always able to address them well before they get out of hand. By the time you see him at our Hallowe'en Festival, I am sure you will note many positive changes.

Sincerely,

Edwin Marsh

P.S. Based on the recommendation of Mr. Phipps, our physical education instructor, Jonathan will be placed in our special outdoor education program, which combines our regular academic program with an added weekend wilderness component. As a young man from a heavily urbanized environment, he will benefit immensely. There will be no extra cost to you.

FROM: Headmaster@pickman.on.ca
TO: judie.lichtmann@fergusonmassey.com
DATE: Oct 21 2010 15:43
SUBJ: RE: course readings

Dear Ms. Lichtmann,

Thank you for the kind note praising the work of our instructors. I take personal pride in guiding boys like Jonathan—who were ill-served by the public system—in achieving their potential. I am confident he will be in the top third of his class by the end of the year.

In answer to your question, Pickman College goes far beyond the core curriculum as mandated by the Ministry of Education. We feel that young minds are further broadened when they explore key literary and philosophical concepts through non-traditional works. That is why our fourth-year course in Political Theory, for example, looks at the role of the state through the lenses of Hobbes, Rousseau, and Marx, as well as more recondite thinkers.

Bearing that in mind, I can assure you that *The King in Yellow* is a real literary work, if a lesser-known one, as are *The Rending of Reality* and the *Livre d'Ivon*, and that Jonathan will benefit greatly from having read them in addition to works by Shakespeare and modern writers and poets.

Sincerely,

Edwin Marsh

FROM: Headmaster@pickman.on.ca
TO: judie.lichtmann@fergusonmassey.com
DATE: Nov 1 2010 16:59
SUBJ: Response to your call

Dear Ms. Lichtmann,

I have just listened to your telephone message. I appreciate your candour.

First off, I assure you that the staff at Pickman College meant no disrespect to any holiday traditions, and we certainly do not force any particular religious viewpoint on our students. Since its founding in 1805 by United Empire Loyalists from the former Massachusetts colony, the College has striven to distance itself from divisive religious and political debates. For this very reason, the founding Trustees established traditions that were unique to the school, and not associated with any established faith. Those traditions have been built up by successive generations of students and teachers over the ensuing 200-plus years, to the extent that there are many elements of our celebrations that might seem odd to outsiders. If you look at schools such as Oxford, Cambridge, or even your local Upper Canada College, you will find similar strong traditions.

The Hallowe'en Festival you attended should be considered part theatrical retelling of the founding of the College, and part male bonding. No one was harmed during the production, and I believe the boys can be forgiven a few outbursts of exuberance, given how much time they spent practising their roles. Jonathan seemed to be in high spirits, as well he should, given that the role of the Altar Bearer is normally given to a second or third year student. A number of parents came up to me afterwards to compliment his wonderful performance.

You should know that the older boys are coming to accept Jonathan, despite his having been an outsider at the beginning of term. His enthusiasm for our traditions will go a long way towards building deep friendships with the other boys.

Sincerely,

Edwin Marsh

FROM: Headmaster@pickman.on.ca
TO: judie.lichtmann@fergusonmassey.com
DATE: Dec 21 2010 13:02
SUBJ: RE: Jons acting strange

Dear Ms. Lichtmann,

As always, it is a pleasure to hear from you. It is good to know that Jonathan made it home for the holidays in advance of the winter storm.

While I am happy to note that you approve of the changes in Jonathan's dress and deportment, I feel a little explanation is in order. As mentioned in the information package that was sent to you this summer, Pickman College is a private school in the classic tradition— we emphasize physical and mental growth, as well as discipline, professionalism and a respect for tradition that can indeed come off as conformity. Our program is strict, but those who persevere often go on to achieve singular greatness in their fields. Wearing a jacket and tie, even when outside of class, has become second nature to your son.

I must also remind you that, with a student body of less than 300 living on a campus more than 50 kilometres away from any major urban centre, our college is largely a self-contained world. This home visit is Jonathan's first time away from his adoptive community in more than three months, and you should not be surprised if he wants to spend a little time by himself for the first day or two.

I am afraid I have no answer to your question about the disappearance of the birthmark on Jonathan's left arm. I consulted our physician, who examines every student upon admission to the College, and he has no record of there ever having been such a mark.

Best wishes for the holiday season,

Edwin Marsh

FROM: Headmaster@pickman.on.ca
TO: judie.lichtmann@fergusonmassey.com
DATE: Jan 2 2011 08:45
SUBJ: FWD: Ms L please see these pics

Ms. Lichtmann,

Thank you for notifying me of this latest development. I gave it my full attention immediately.

I care not to speculate as to why young Mr. Pirzada would claim he saw Jonathan torturing a homeless man to death in the park on New Year's Eve. The camera phone pictures attached are impenetrably blurry and frankly could be of anything. I suggest that you weigh this outlandish claim against the observed behaviour of the mature young man your son is rapidly becoming.

I understand that Jonathan and Mr. Pirzada were once close. But, despite their having some shared minor entanglements with the law, it is clear from your son's file that he was anything but a budding criminal. Whatever the cause of Mr. Pirzada's accusations—I hesitate to suggest envy—they are clearly fabrications.

In closing, thank you for bringing this to my attention.

Sincerely,

Edwin Marsh

FROM: Headmaster@pickman.on.ca
TO: judie.lichtmann@fergusonmassey.com
DATE: Jan 22 2011 11:48
SUBJ: RE: The book of eibon

Dear Ms. Lichtmann,

Thank you for sharing with me your research on the Book of Eibon. I can see now where Jonathan gets his resourcefulness.

In response to your direct question, there is nothing diabolical about the literature our students read, and the *Book of Eibon* is most definitely not a work of witchcraft. The early 20th-century source you consulted is, unfortunately, based on a rather bad 16th-century translation by Michael Stewart of the original 14th-century French. Stewart's translation was written at a time when anything that even remotely questioned official church doctrine was branded as heresy, and thus he left a good deal out—and I suspect he added material reflecting his prejudices. The author of your book, an obscure writer with no notable academic credentials, was therefore using shoddy source material. The College is fortunate enough to have a digitized copy of the original manuscript, and Jonathan's instructor is fluent in Middle French.

As for your general comments about our school and its teachings, I can only reiterate what I told you when you last raised this matter. Our school's only official doctrine is to help our pupils cast aside their veils of ignorance, and behold the true world so that they can prosper in it. In fact, several Pickman alumni who went on to prominence by way of various Ivy League universities have been quite taken by Jonathan on recent visits to the campus. They have expressed interest in helping him gain admission to these schools, and perhaps even membership in the most exclusive social clubs therein, when the time comes. You are of course welcome to withdraw your son from Pickman College at any time, but I hope you will carefully consider the impact that decision would have on Jonathan's future opportunities.

Cordially,

Edwin Marsh

P.S. I let Jonathan know about the recent death of Mr. Pirzada. While he was saddened by his former friend's passing, he accepted it with maturity, and said he understood how a life lived so recklessly could only end in tragedy. I spared him the details, as recounted so tastelessly by the *Toronto Star*. I hope the police find the wild animal soon.

FROM: Headmaster@pickman.on.ca
TO: judie.lichtmann@fergusonmassey.com
DATE: Mar 29 2011 23:20
SUBJ: [blank]

Ms. Lichtmann,

I must admit to being taken aback by the tone of your email.

First, as I have explained to you several times, Pickman College is not tied to any church, and we do not push any particular religious doctrine on our students. If we promote any viewpoint at all, it is one of encouraging curiosity about the world, and ensuring our students become what they are meant to be. This Mark Tilsley who contacted you is very likely the same man I expelled in 1987 for selling answers to the final exams. I have since visited his website and would suggest you consider what his motives might be for spreading such fanciful lies.

We have provided a supportive learning environment in which Jonathan is flourishing as never before, as you well know. That he seems different to you in appearance, mannerisms and speech is because he has lived away from home for seven months, surrounded by people from outside of his traditional peer group, and is being challenged daily to grow in new ways. I would suspect the prolonged separation from your son has cast these changes into sharp relief.

Finally, your son was most certainly not "abducted" during March Break; he elected to remain at the College. Our information package clearly states that students may undertake special directed studies in the spring and fall. You gave your consent when you signed your son's registration forms.

I have little to say in response to your remarks about what allegedly happened during your attempt to visit the College, unannounced, on the night of February 23rd. The sky was clear and the driveway was well-lit. In that context, it is difficult to believe that you saw "a black rippling thing the size of an elephant" crouching by the main gates. Such a thing would have left enormous tracks, which would have excited a great deal of local interest.

Based on the foregoing, and the general character of our recent interactions, it would be best if we discussed matters in person. I believe there have been many misunderstandings. If, after our discussion, you still feel the same way, you may withdraw Jonathan at no penalty, and I will prepare a letter of recommendation for him.

Please let me know if this is agreeable to you.

Sincerely,

Edwin Marsh

FROM: Headmaster@pickman.on.ca
TO: judie.lichtmann@fergusonmassey.com
DATE: Apr 6 2011 10:08
SUBJ: RE: Thank you

Dear Ms. Lichtmann,

Thank you for the kind note. It was delightful meeting with you over lunch in our Faculty Dining Room, despite the unfortunate accident. I am happy that we were able to clear the air.

Now that we come to see eye-to-eye regarding Jonathan's education, I am pleased to tell you more about the planned field trip this summer. As I mentioned to you, Jonathan has been selected to accompany our anthropology instructor to New England, where he will assist in retrieving and cataloguing artefacts for eventual display in our library. He will take the Second Oath while he is there, and the temple will benefit from a fresh bloodline. The College will, of course, cover all of his expenses while he is away. Please ensure that Jonathan's passport is in order. It would be a shame if he were to miss out on an opportunity like this.

I fully expect Jonathan will surpass all of our expectations, and he will almost certainly be in good enough health to return to his studies in September.

In closing, I am passing along our college physician's recommendation that you rest as much as possible. He said that the headaches and dizzy spells will fade quickly, and advised that you should not be alarmed about any memory loss. I trust you will be feeling better soon.

Sincerely,

Edwin Marsh

P.S. I am inclined to agree with you that Mr. Tilsley's death was unfortunate, but not unexpected. Given the quality and content of his writings, one must wonder about his mental state, and the kind of audience he attracted. Nevertheless, the reporter exercised poor judgment in speculating how Mr. Tilsley's "twisted and mummified" remains could have been stuffed into his twelve-inch wide chimney. I must write to the *Toronto Star* in protest; young minds should not be exposed to such sensationalism.

fin de siècle

GEMMA FILES

He had very little interest in life, and was full of crepuscular dreams, religious images, sickness, and suffering; but he hid those deep-seated wounds beneath an elegant exterior. . . . The walls of his soul were so thin that a strange light shone through them that was not of this world.

—Camille Mauclair

1909, Bruges, Belgium. The studio is mapped in flat, watery light, which seeps, unchecked, through warped glass windows to silver the ceiling, the walls, the floor. Gustave Knauff can barely gather enough strength to draw the blinds, or open them farther. His head is already full of absinthe-hangover, that toothache want and pull which settles a puke-green filter over everything within reach. Fumes rise from an open paint box. In front of him, the latest canvas sulks, unfinished.

In the corner, meanwhile, his family's dreadful guardian angel goes on with "her" endless card-game: Shuffling them, laying them, turning them back up, red and black, and red-black-red. Gustave tries his best not to look her way as she does so—in fact, ever—but the noise they make (soft, papery, repetitious) is intoxicating, very nearly unbearable. It calls to him, a degenerate gambler's siren-song, made somehow even more naturally seductive in juxtaposition with the angel's supremely unnatural pictogram rush of no-voice, laid lightly overtop—

Come, Dame Knauff's seventh son, can we not be friends just once more, before I take my leave? Sit down, let me deal you in. Drink deep. Win back your life.

"I won't," he says, out loud.

Ah, then. You must suit yourself, I suppose.

The angel sits erect, posture perfect, gloved right hand neatly folded while her bare left hand skims restlessly back and forth

Though illusory, her bottle-green dress strikes the faultless height of fashion, perfectly *a la mode.* Her veil, which hangs opaque from hat-brim to breast, is just a shade or so lighter—slightly iridescent, with poisonous blue tints to it; the same ones which inform a corpse-fly's back, or a peacock-feather's fringe.

Our very own Peacock Angel, Gustave thinks. But no—his mother would frown to hear him make such a blasphemous comparison. This phantom is only a kissing cousin of that particular principality, a mere forerunner of the true Angel to come. The nails on her bare hand are hooked and black, like cormorant's beaks; they carve slight scratches on the cards' faces wherever they touch, barely perceptible ghost-weals. And though he was raised almost from babyhood knowing her name, adding it always to his backwards midnight prayers, he has yet, even now, to see her naked face. . . .

(Not, to be sure, that he has ever actually wanted to.)

Ma'ashith, once an archangel of punishment, who announces the deaths of children; Ma'ashith, "sister" to Af, to Kesef, to Hemah, to Meshabber—to wrath and destruction, human mortality, animal cruelty. Who prefers always to appear in female form, though (like all her kind) she exists far beyond the boundaries of what Gustave and his ilk would call either sex, or pity.

An excerpt from *Strange Provenance: Lost Works of the Fin de Siècle,* by Ellin Pataky-Hemsworth (2002, Millipede Press, Connaught Trust Legacy Library copy):

One of the most mysterious figures of late Decadence must surely be Gustave Knauff, who left behind little except a tantalizing series of lacunae. We have no clear idea where or when he was born, where he studied, or even what he looked like (though some sources hold that the faceless, blurred background figure sitting next to a veiled woman playing solitaire in the unfinished piece "Au Café Brumaire," by Jan Toorop protégé Degouve de Nuncques, might—possibly—have been meant to be him). Even Knauff's sold works, all few and far between, seem to have met similarly obscure fates. We are left, instead, with reactions to the paintings rather than the paintings themselves, as here—

Saw also the third panel from Knauff's "Hymnes de Paon," finally complete, before it was removed from the exhibition at Rouen, after great public outcry . . . a morbid and dreadful picture painted in hues of luminous decay, most of it various cold shades of lilac tinged with moonlit white, with a little lettuce-green mixed with milk for sheen. I would give much never to have seen it at all, particularly so because in spite of the revulsion this painting aroused in me when I stood in front of it, I cannot help feeling a certain attraction to it—sick, strange, and growing with each passing day—now that I am safely far away.

—J.K. Huysmans, 1903

By collating such "rave reviews," we confirm that Knauff's most infamous—and thus sorely-missed—work was undeniably the legendary "Black Annunciation" (1907?). According to Odilon Rédon, who devoted a page of his unpublished memoirs to the painting, "[t]his joyful and polluting blasphemy performs the most holy service of all unholy creations, placing the logic of the visible firmly at the service of the invisible. I saw it only once, and it has informed my dreams ever since . . ."

In 1869, the angel tells him, not looking up from her spread, *three children were playing in a meadow near Alton, in Hampshire, when a local clerk approached them—a young man of great respectability, though his father was a known maniac, and he himself was subject to depressive fits.*

"Don't speak to me, angel. I beg you."

But she does not seem to hear him. Simply deals another card, this one's face is all black, with no visible design on it at all—how his heart clutches, to see it so!—and goes on:

This clerk gave the children a ha'penny each, and asked one of them—a little girl—to walk with him in the woods nearby. This she agreed to, gladly. Then, after some time had passed, the girl's mother began to worry; she sent her husband to town to gather young men, for a search. And later, much later, at the edge of yet another field . . .

Gustave has heard this story before, many times; he shuts his eyes and shakes his head, as if to clear it. But feels absinthe-hunger drive a metaphorical spike deep through the orbit of one eye at the same instant, clean and pure as new grass: dig it deep, twist it, corkscrew-crooked. Leave it there to sting.

"Did you hear what I said?" he forces himself to ask, angrily.

The angel's arms are discreetly fringed with oblong feathers, pasteboard-stiff; she lets them rise and fall at once, a body-long shrug, with much the same thrum and patter of her game. Because: *Yes, they could simply be cards*, Gustave thinks, absently, his eyes starting to burn. *Plucked and played, then replaced without me seeing it; simple sleight of hand. Like Houdini. Nothing so very worship-worthy at all . . .*

Oh, certainly, the angel replies, for all he has not spoken aloud. *But perhaps I do not even address you—have you never considered that? Perhaps I talk merely for my own pleasure, because the sound of my own voice amuses me.*

"Then I won't listen," Gustave says, and busies himself by rummaging in his paint box. At the moment, the canvas is a shapeless morass of purple and violet, with only a wash of black here and there, taming the chaos enough to suggest vague shapes: houses, boats, a stairway leading downward. A few odd dabs of acid Indian yellow to suggest gaslights flickering from the nearest bridge-side, while potentially fatal smears of Emerald Green (a deadly poison) show where the river's current surfaces, undertow drag and all. As Rodenbach puts it: *The pale water, which goes away along paths of silence . . .*

The angel shrugs again, a literary avalanche. *The detail we are never allowed to hear of, in any case*, she continues, conversationally, *is exactly what this young man did with the one thing he took from her body, after he had torn the rest of it apart and left it scattered across the grass like the Aztec moon-goddess Coyotlaxqui—limb from limb, a last shred of sinew letting one plump leg gape wide, to show the red hole between. This item, slack and hairless, he put in a box tied with satin ribbons, originally meant for chocolates, and kept under his bed.* Turning over a new card, with a delicate flick: *Until it began to smell, that is.*

Gustave's hand trembles, still reaching for the green. "You will not make me think of such things!"

I doubt I could make you do anything, Knauff's son. Yet you do think of them, nevertheless. You are thinking of them now.

Gustave shivers. Outside, the waters of *Bruges-la-Morte* flow by, pulling drowned prostitutes from the river's scummy bottom— Rodenbach's dead city, the new Ys, criss-crossed by canals and abandoned to its fate. He came here two years ago, to escape everything . . . but mainly his family, their cultish ways, their insane and secret schemes, their inevitable vengeance for the slights he had already given them. Or a rustling footstep and a flash of green behind him in the dark, as she grew ever closer.

He knows now that the final stage of his journey began three weeks earlier, when—while blunting cadmium red with a dilution of lampblack—he thought he smelled something burning, and glanced up just in time to catch the mirror above his wash-stand gaping open like a lidless silver eye. But it was not until he came home late the next morning, reeking of sweat and aniseed, that he knew his mother's immaterial spies must have truly found him at last; not until the landlord called out cheerfully to him as he went by, in both of Bruges' official languages:

"*Gut' tag, m'sieu.* Did she find you yet, your friend?"

"I beg your pardon?"

"*Ton jolie copine la,* in her veil, *bien sûr—eine Engel-frau, mein herr!* Or so my daughter tells me. She saw her coming up the back stairs, all *en verte,* like the Green Fairy herself." A sly wink: "And we all know how devotedly you favour the Fairy, *Herr* Knauff. . . ."

When he climbed up the narrow stairs, he could see the landlord's daughter sitting in the window above him, combing her hair (blonde, limp, in ringlets) and grinning a gap-toothed smile, with her skirt hiked to the knees. He thought her to be ten or eleven years of age, baby-fat and chestless, though her dresses looked to be cut-down versions of ones the landlord's long-dead wife might once have worn, thus tending to gape immodestly. He remembered then how he had once heard her announce to playfellows that when she was older, she would go far away to model for artists like the mysterious *Herr* Knauff—perhaps to Paris, that wickedest of places, where she would pose without her underthings and be paid with jewels and sweets. . . .

And inside he had found the angel, waiting for him. Saying only, mildly: *That girl likes you a great deal, Dame Knauff's son. There are many ways you could take advantage of her affections, if you chose to.*

Three weeks ago, only that. He could have run farther, he supposes, given the inclination—or the money.

Yet here he is, still. And she, his angel.

On the low wooden table at which the angel sits, her latest run of cards is plucked up, tucked away. Another appears to take its place, almost immediately—seven pasteboard faces blinking up at him, black-red-black, red, black. Her claw-nails now make a noise like picks scraping across salt, leaving visible tears in their wake.

Immediately, Gustave feels that red impulse he now seems to spend so much of his waking life fighting, rise in him like fumes, lightening his head. His stomach swims, and he has to brace against the easel for support, making it creak beneath his weight. The desire for absinthe is a fist to his face, a broken stick in his throat.

Oh God, my family's most ancient enemy, please tell me quickly, before she does: How will this all end?

From *Strange Provenance*, Pataky-Hemsworth:

Supposedly even more disturbing than Leon Frederic's "Le Torrent" (part of his own triptych, entitled "Tout est Mort"), which shows an entire mountain valley choked with dead, naked children splayed in pedophile-pornographic poses, what Knauff's "Annunciation" appears to have been blaspheming against was both the Gospel story of the Slaughter of the Innocents—the massacre of a whole generation of Jewish infants, ordered slain by King Herod because they were born on the same day as Jesus Christ, in order to make sure none of them would become a Messiah powerful enough to displace or punish him—and the Annunciation itself . . . the exact moment when the Archangel Gabriel told the Virgin Mary that she had been chosen to bear God's son.

From Rédon's further description of the "Annunciation."

A sort of semi-monastic diablerie in a landscape inhabited by flowing, undulating, vomitory spectres, like a tidal wave of leeches. The whole background looks shrouded in gauze. The foreground is occupied by a heap of dead children, some of whose throats are still being ritualistically cut by figures in copes and cassocks; these ecclesiastical executioners seem half-lapidified, weighed down by gold and jewels, both sacred and profane. . . In the middle, enthroned on a chair made from bones, sits an equally childish figure—the Virgin—whose flower-soft eyes roll back in apparent rapture as she listens to the figure whispering poison into her ear, a veiled hermaphrodite in a bottle-green robe, caught in the act of placing a winged mantle made from peacock feathers onto the Virgin's shoulders. A horrible halo, black and crackling with arcane energies, connects them both. . . .

Regard the Virgin. Is there, in Art, anything more beautiful and terrible than her visage, especially were it to have been copied from life? Beneath the horizontal immobility of the long eyebrows, under languid Hindu lids, her gaze is laden with dreams and death. The mouth is tinged with just a hint of blood . . . she is silent, rigid, both despoiler and despoiled. Her white eucharistic flesh, framed by plaited viper tresses, is marked with an irreparable kiss. Her folded hands cup her own belly, delicately heralding a spectacle of the future . . . surely some unborn monster, perhaps even that Beast foretold, which cannot possibly be allowed to come to term. . . .

A month ago, he can still recall taking his usual Sunday meal in the Café Brumaire, happy and productive. He sat next to two younger painters and listened to them argue about Wilde and Moreau, about whether the chimera or the Sphynx was the more fitting mascot for the age. Fleur was there, holding his hand tightly imprisoned in her lap and smiling into his eyes, like the willing whore she was; he let her thighs' warmth seep steadily through his glove, knowing well she wore nothing beneath her skirt but garters. Delirious with both absinthe and possibility, the former already paid for, the latter seemingly boundless.

But I was there, too, even then, the angel says, *though you could not see me. I have always been there. Your family and I have made a covenant. They serve the one I wait for, and I serve them, while waiting.*

"That has nothing to do with me, any of it!" Gustave protests, racked with nausea. "It never did!"

A skirl, a further flutter, a flurry of cards and feathers, table and chair abandoned—and abruptly, awfully, he feels the train of Ma'ashith Punisher-angel's ghostly skirts brush up against his trembling legs, from waist to ankle and back once more. She is near enough for him to taste her breath, if she had any.

Ah, but your mother thinks so. You have disappointed her so gravely, Knauff's son—telling Melek-i-Taus' secrets in paint, however obliquely. Selling them for gallery fees, an hour's drunken friendship, a review in La Plume.

Oh, and now she is even closer yet, that cormorant-clawed hand spreading a fresh half-deck of cards before his wavering eyes, flipped open and shut quick as a courtesan's fan: red and black and red, black-red-black. *She will wear black the rest of her life for you.*

"But she sent you to me, nevertheless."

Mmm. And I go where I am bidden, as ever. We have no free will, my kind and I . . . not since Eden, or before. That was His gift to you, and yours. How do you enjoy it?

A simple question. Yet one to which Gustave, like most human beings, has no easy answer.

Your family bound me to them with false promises, Knauff's son, the angel observes, *like all humans. Yet as it is in the nature of angels to serve, no matter who, I do not count myself so terribly sinned against. I will have my freedom, eventually.*

He throws up his hands; impossible to appeal to "her," he knows—and yet he finds himself doing so nevertheless, words tumbling from his mouth like sharp stones. "Orders aside, why haunt *me*, even so? I, who alone of all of them, sympathize with your plight . . . you know it, *have* known it, since my childhood. It is only *they* who wish to change the world, for better or worse, in . . . that other angel's . . . name. I have no stake in it."

Oh, and they will. They are changing it already. You, too.

Have you truly not noticed?

Gustave's eyes blur, sting, the green-hangover filter abruptly irising deeper, darker, to touch everything around him with muck. Upstairs, through the ceiling, he can hear his landlord's daughter blundering joyfully around, stomping like a little goat: she is not a *lady*, after all, and probably glad enough for it. Not yet old enough to have to restrain herself.

Perhaps she will be coming down here soon, that girl, the angel says. *To see you. The way the young shepherdess in Italy went to watch her cousin at work in the barn, only to be found the next day with her mouth full of earth, her intestines torn out and trailing in the dirt. Or the way that bell-ringer from Boston invited a five-year-old up to his attic, on the pretext of showing her his pigeons, and instead beat her to death with a bat—beat her so badly, so completely, that when her own mother was shown the body later on, she could not positively identify her remains. . . .*

But: "I'm not like that," Gustave spits back, his mouth full of bile. "I only—dream. Paint. I've never . . . done anything . . . more than that."

As yet, no.

Feet on the stairs, girlish, tripping. Gustave claws for the wall again, upsetting his paint stand. Finds the smeary palette knife suddenly poised within gripping range, its handle toward his guilty, palsied hand.

Ah, but perhaps, if you only drink the last of your Green Fairy I will go away, Knauff's son, like any other morning-after hallucination. Or . . . perhaps not.

The girl is right outside now, separated from him only by a thin layer of wood and metal; she skips from step to step, singing some sort of counting-out rhyme in French (or German). He bites his tongue at the very sound of it, grinding until he tastes blood.

Why fight? the angel asks, in his ear, her no-voice thin as a murmuring dream of bees. *I know you, all of you, caught as you are in time's net like dead fish rotting, drunk on your own decay. You love only what you destroy, because you can destroy it—but do you really dream you are the worst this century will have to offer? Are you so arrogant?*

By the way her voice has faded, it would seem that the landlord's daughter has finally reached the landing. Gustave can only pray she stays there, frozen in much the same way he now finds himself unable to move, straining for whatever the angel's next words might be in the intimately gathering gloom—

Listen, Knauff's son: Here is what will happen, with or without your mother's plans to blame for it. First, in five years' time, there will be war . . . but not one of those many, tiny wars you and your friends worry over—this will be different, epic, startling. A true horror to behold. Fire will gush from the sky; lead will fall like rain; the muddy ground will be honeycombed with buried bombs, with trenches full of gas and disease. A war, as all of you will say, to end all wars—until the next one comes.

More shuddering, more fluttering; sharp-edged, crisp enough to cut. Down in the front hall, the landlord's daughter pauses, possibly having forgotten something. She turns on her heel, turns back, to mount the rickety stairs once more. Gustave presses palms to ears in order to block out the sound, but finds this only makes the angel's voice ring more hollowly in the hissing cavern of his skull—damnably reasonable, utterly unstoppable.

And then, then . . . just as He once spoke the Word and sent Gabriel Archangel to turn Sodom and Gomorrah into salt, so your kind will crack the atom like an egg, turning two more cities into glass. Nothing will be left behind but shadow and ash, factories run on rag and bone, a long and wasting invisible death that poisons the soil and sky, great holes full of corpses. Men and women of every age and station will die there together, families and strangers alike, thieves and saints and yet more Sodomites too, of any and all descriptions. . . .

"And children?"

Oh yes, and children, always. Children, more than any others. I have seen it so for centuries, ever since He sent me to lay my hand on Pharaoh's first-born's sleeping head.

From *Strange Provenance*, Pataky-Hemsworth:

According to part of a letter found plastered into the wall of Knauff's former room (possibly dated 1908, or perhaps '09), the "Annunciation" was sold to a private buyer that same year, which explains how it escaped the Bruges fire. In the missive, Knauff goes on to decode his painting's various symbological features as a gesture of "educative good-will" towards "a loyal supporter and enthusiast"—this unnamed purchaser?

Knauff identifies the sexless figure in green as "that same angel who culled Egypt's firstborn," now Fallen into acting as a sort of herald or guardian for the "Virgin"; the peacock-feather cloak it offers her reveals the involvement of Melek-i-Taus, notorious Peacock Angel of the Yezidic Goetists, who may be using her womb—or whatever comes out of it—to birth "himself" back into the material world. In other words, what Knauff seems to have at some point belonged to . . . and obviously later betrayed, thus probably leading to his death . . . was yet one more end-of-the-century cult with a distinctly familial slant, a birthing-pit for potential Anti-Christs.

And now, of course, there is a knock at the door—hesitant but soon repeated, growing ever stronger. Gustave looks down to see his knuckles already white around the palette-knife's handle, while (looking up again) he finds the canvas he's worked so hard on is less a soothing canal landscape than a black forest made from bones and meat, a place of slaughter just aching for some wayward red-caped maiden to amble, foolish-fearless, down any of its overhung paths.

Believe me, Knauff's son: All this will come to pass, whether or not the Peacock Angel comes home at last. But you, if you wish, my little Gustave—

(hapless Goetist, self-made traitor, born too soon for doctors Jung and Freud, too late for the Inquisition's tender mercies. You werewolf's heart wrapped in a man's slick skin, all canines and eye-whites, your quivering limbs kept irrigated by terror and desire alike)

—you need not live to see it.

The inquiring cry comes, long expected, in a voice innocent of all but the most cat-killing curiosity: "*Herr* Knauff? *Herr* Knauff, are you there?"

But no, he knows it now: he will not answer, after all. Thank any god but the one his mother worships. . . .

It is surprisingly easy for him to turn the knife upward, even to make that last, imperative slash, paint burning in his wound like cleansing fire: Chemicals, poisons, beauty. The sole real surprise is how little it seems to hurt, and how long the fall to the floor seems to take.

He stays conscious just long enough to see the door open, the landlord gape down at him, before he finally dies choking on his own blood, with an oddly gentle smile on his red-soaked lips.

The girl's scream goes straight up to Heaven like an ill-shot arrow, missing its target entirely; she will live and die unaware of her own close escape from what the Germans are only now learning to call *lustmord*, sent to Buchenwald instead after sheltering Jews in her father's basement, while he himself takes a far more merciful bullet to the back of the head, as he tries to tear her from an SS officer's arms.

And neither of them, in the end, is fast (or attentive) enough to see the angel Ma'ashith vanish, her task complete—blinking from existence in a spray of red-black cards which rise, fall, then hit the floor and scatter once again, eddying away as nothing more than dust.

From *Strange Provenance*, Pataky-Hemsworth:

The brief, intense fire which destroyed Knauff's Bruges studio around Easter of 1909 only adds to his mystery; in addition to consuming the remainder of his unsold works, the one body found therein was so fire-damaged as to make identification largely speculative—the accelerant-effect of the studio's paints and turpentine is blamed for this. Though the rest of the pension survived, the entire roof had to be replaced and lowered, essentially wiping all trace of Knauff from the city in which he had lived the last years of his incredibly ill-documented life.

While many scholars posit that Knauff might have painted under a pseudonym (the name sounds suspiciously close to "Knopff," after all), or even been a "house name" used by a coalition of like-minded artists trying to break into the last wave of the Decadent scene, my own research suggests it is far more likely he was related to the family behind Knauff's of Switzerland, an international trading house founded by a Crusader who returned from the Holy Land having already married a woman "of singular beauty and sinister antecedents" who claimed she—along with the rest of her family—had already converted to Christianity when the Swiss delegation arrived.

(In fact, a quick survey of those few remaining photos of the Swiss Knauffs prior to their 1946 emigration to Canada reveals that the female members of their line all seem to bear a striking resemblance to Rédon's favourite blasphemous anti-Mary—most strikingly in the case of Mara Knauff, the company's main stockholder since her 1939 *debut*, and great-grandmother of the current crop.

(There are even rumours of a very early Kodak colour-process memorial photo taken three years after her marriage which shows her posing with a stillborn twin boy in either arm, attended by a slim young nurse or nanny dressed all in green, her face discreetly averted from Mrs. Knauff's grief, a small and similarly-coloured veil further obscuring her shadowed features.

(An odd further detail: Cards, surely inappropriate in such circumstances, are laid out on a nearby table.)

Slowly and surely a belief is growing in the bankruptcy of Nature which promises to become the sinister faith of the twentieth century.

—Paul Bourget

since breaking through the ice

DOMINIK PARISIEN

I have seen them bend a man in an impossible way
and pull him down a fishing hole; wrapped
my hands, too cold to hold, around my neck
and dreamt of drowning under white skies;
discovered a mark like a crow's wings
around my left calf;
scoured the shore in spring for blue-black
bodies I pray wash up but never do;
walked on water as though it were frozen,
tried diving in only to hit a rippling surface;
yearned for the day the ice breaks under me
again, so I may go home to them.

the pack
MATT MOORE

DOCUMENT 1: COMMUNIQUÉ
SENDER: Dr. C.-L. Ibarro, Medical Director, Advanced Soldier Enhancement and Survival Program (ASESP)
RECIPIENTS: Brigadier General Douglas Stern, Advanced Weapon Systems Research, Development and Engineering Center (AWSRDEC) / Clark Bernshaw, Assistant Deputy Under Secretary of Defense

I have completed assessments of the six surviving members of the ASESP.

The nanites now constitute between 2% and 3% of the men's body weight. This represents an unanticipated 300-fold increase from initial dosage.

There is another complication. Each man was injected with a unique nanite model. Each man now hosts an identical hybrid model which appears to be the result of cross-contamination and replication.

I cannot explain the periods of prolonged silence reported among the program's survivors.

I cannot predict what other side-effects may occur.

I will repeat that I warned that field testing could result in unexpected consequences.

I recommend the nanites be removed immediately.

DOCUMENT 2: COMMUNIQUÉ
SENDER: Brig. Gen. Stern, AWSRDEC
RECIPIENT: ADUSecDef Bernshaw

Sir —

Dr. Ibarro was unable to remove the nanites. She is unsure how to proceed.

I'm worried by these men, who took on the nickname "The Pack" during their training. The few times I've talked to Sergeant Calabrese, it's like he's looking right through me.

I haven't heard one laugh, seen one smile, get mad. When they're together, they'll go hours without saying a word. It's eerie. Makes me wonder how far Dr. Ibarro went with having those things play with their brains.

The only outsider they retain any respect for seems to be Colonel Holding. If it wasn't for him, I don't think they'd follow chain of command. I have increased Holding's security clearance. We will need him fully informed on the nature of the program if we are to have any hope of working with these men further.

Honestly, I think something happened to them in the desert.

— Doug

DOCUMENT 3: COMMUNIQUÉ
SENDER: ADUSecDef Bernshaw
RECIPIENT: Brig. Gen. Stern

Doug: I know you opposed early discussions of extreme ASESP termination measures, but I ask you to look to the safety of your command and the American people. Consider the changed behaviour of these men and the capabilities this program was designed to instill. I have come to believe they could pose a significant danger.

The men volunteered. They were aware of the risks. It seems Dr. Ibarro's technology did not undergo a thorough shakedown on their last mission; perhaps a more dangerous mission is called for.

DOCUMENT 4: TRANSCRIPT
(Audio file on cell phone recovered from ADUSecDef Bernshaw's basement. The voice has been confirmed as Sergeant Calabrese.)

CALABRESE: Good, you're awake. Didn't mean to hit you so hard, but couldn't have you screaming like that. It could draw attention in this nice Arlington suburb.

Stop struggling, Under Secretary. The straps are too tight. No one is coming to save you. Your bodyguards? Dead.

You know who we are, right?

BERNSHAW: Sergeant Calabrese. From—

CALABRESE: Good. Now, you're going to tell us what the hell you did to us. Then, how to fix it. And I'm recording this in case anything happens to us.

BERNSHAW: Let me make a phone call. We can sort this out—

[SOUNDS OF A STRUGGLE; MUFFLED VOICE]

CALABRESE: No. No calls. Going to tell someone where we are? We'd just kill them, too.

[SEVERAL SECONDS OF SILENCE]

CALABRESE (cont'd): My friends say to kill you. But you're going to understand, Under Secretary. What we've been through. What we've become.

Colonel Holding had three hundred volunteers that first day. Three hundred guys willing to put their lives on the line. We didn't even know the risks. "Become better, stronger soldiers," they told us. Win these damned wars and get our boys back home. And after guys got screened out or flunked out, you had ten of us. We put up with injections and drinking crap that looked and smelled like motor oil past its prime.

Some quick shakedown missions. Then the big one. Dropped deep behind enemy lines to hit a supply depot. We pulled it off, then waited for an evac chopper that never came. Heard about the double agent, the chopper getting shot down, in debrief. All we knew then was that we had strict radio silence orders and a fifty-klick march through hell.

We reported minimal enemy contact. But that's bullshit. We got hit on the third day.

Small arms fire and mortars. We'd been holed up, catching some sleep. Had some of our gear off. Shrapnel cut Bailey across the middle, guts spilling out. Screaming, thrashing. I held him down and Gündersen got a pressure bandage on. Over Bailey's screaming, Gündersen said he felt something moving. I told him to shut up and dug for a fentanyl tab in my kit. But Gündersen lifted the bandage.

The rip in Bailey's skin looked like scorched, ragged lips pulled back over a mouth of blood-smeared meat. But the bleeding had stopped. And I thought I was seeing things, but the organs were shifting, putting themselves back where they belonged. Should've shit my pants. Or puked. Or something. Instead, I put the tab in Bailey's mouth, calm as can be. Knocked him out a few seconds later. The organs kept moving. Then two feet of ripped-up bowel got shoved out of the wound. And I'll be damned if the skin didn't pull together on its own.

Next second, a mortar threw me into a rock, head first. I didn't have my helmet on. Just remember the sound of my skull breaking.

When I came to, the enemy had broken off. Gündersen was down. Caught five rounds in the chest.

Five rounds I saw get pushed back out of the entry wounds.

The next day, the three of us were up like nothing had happened. We knew the program would make us tough, but this? I felt like nothing could stop Bailey, Gündersen and me. We were tight. And I don't mean because we'd been through the shit together. We acted as one. Like we knew what each other was thinking.

Two days later, an RPG took Nawaz's arm and half of Pratt's face. And then they were Pack, too.

Soon we all were.

But we lost people. Whatever you did can't fix an artillery shell taking your head off.

Or Danielson. Cut in half by an IED. Chest level. Could see the bottom of his lungs inflating. Still alive, dragging himself through the sand and rocks, begging for us to kill him. But we couldn't do it. Knew we had to, but couldn't. He finally offed himself.

Ever lose anyone close, Under Secretary? A parent? A child, maybe? That's nothing. Imagine your happiest memories torn away. A healthy tooth ripped out of your jaw. A ragged, bloody wound that will never heal.

And then those things we did to the locals. Soldier, revolutionary, counter-revolutionary. Even civilians. Cutting them, beating them, killing one while another watched.

It wasn't payback. It just needed to be done. We needed the intelligence: enemy size and location, passable routes, places where we could get food and water.

I figured we were getting frosty.

But the truth is, I could murder a hundred infants with my bare hands. To protect the Pack. You bastard, what did you do to us?

Damn it, a good soldier needs to know when to stop.

So after three weeks, six of us walked out of that desert. All Pack. Even Depardieu, who hadn't been hit. And with Lieutenant Carter dead, I was its leader.

We lied to Holding during the debriefing, of course. Didn't tell him we'd survived shit that should have killed us. He's a good officer, but we lied to his face. Figured if we didn't, you might start poking and prodding us. Maybe split us up.

And we couldn't handle that.

Wasn't a surprise when Colonel Holding told us we had a new mission. More dangerous than the first. We knew a suicide mission when we heard it.

So we tied Holding like we got you tied. Worked him over. Following orders, he said. Came down through a General, but started near the top. You.

Don't know why we let Holding live.

So we got off the base. Quick, clean. When six men work as one there's not much we can't do. But our pictures were all over the news within hours. So we cut up our faces. Used hammers on our jaw and cheek bones. Just enough to not be recognized. It healed, of course, so we'd do it again.

Day after day.

Think about the pain, Under Secretary.

Think.

About.

It.

Now do you get it? We didn't volunteer for this. To be dead inside. You made us, so you're going to fix it. Turn us back into the men—the soldiers—we used . . .

One of my friends has found something. He's . . .

Who's . . . ?

[SILENCE]

This is you.

[SILENCE]

You're Pack.

[SILENCE]

[To Recorder] Colonel Holding: If you're looking for us, we're going back to the desert. Call off the search. We're not a threat. We understand now that we can never go back to our lives. But we can make peace.

DOCUMENT 5: COMMUNIQUÉ
SENDER: Col. R.C. Holding
RECIPIENT: Brig. Gen. Stern
Sir. Thank you for forwarding me that transcript. I've found their trail. Ramstein, then Blackjack Air Base. Looks like transport was authorized by ADUSecDef Bernshaw himself. It seems the Pack took him with them.

I'm healed up and ready to go. Arthur Neech can assume command while I'm gone.

DOCUMENT 6: COMMUNIQUÉ
SENDER: Dr. Ibarro
RECIPIENT: Brig. Gen. Stern

I have reviewed Colonel Holding's medical files from the exam following his interrogation by Sergeant Calabrese.

He has nanites in his blood at levels comparable to those in the program. I believe he is now a member of the Pack. This would explain his rapid recovery.

I believe the transmission vector is simple exposure. Hospital conditions allow containment, but outside those the nanites might spread. I believe that when a serious wound is inflicted, the nanites replicate at an accelerated rate to repair the wound. Anyone so exposed will be Pack.

I have also reviewed the audio file from Under Secretary Bernshaw's basement.

We must first assume Under Secretary Bernshaw has become infected given the head injury inflicted by Sergeant Calabrese that rendered Bernshaw unconscious.

I also believe Sergeant Calabrese's reported lack of emotion is caused by the nanites' modifications to the amygdala. The modifications' original purpose to reduce stress reactions caused by critical injuries has become amplified. Members of the Pack may be incapable of emotional reactions or attachments, similar to psychopaths. They do, however, possess a strong bond with one another.

I am further beginning to suspect the shared hybrid model allows some form of wordless communications. The recording and Colonel Holding's reports include moments of prolonged silence. Each nanite model communicates using a unique wireless network. This hybrid model would have a single network. This network may allow the only emotional attachment these men can feel. Further study will be required.

I recommend Colonel Holding be found and detained immediately.

DOCUMENT 7: COMMUNIQUÉ
SENDER: Brig. Gen. D. Stern
RECIPIENT: Maj. A. Neech, Officer Commanding (Acting), ASESP

Arthur —

We tracked Holding to Forward Air Base Blackjack, but lost him. We've got reports he headed into the desert. We think he's going to join Calabrese and the Pack. Fighting is down in that sector, so I want you to find Holding, Under Secretary Bernshaw and all surviving members of ASESP. Neutralize them. Ibarro thinks killing the host will cause the nanites to shut down.

We've got to contain this, Arthur. There's no way to know what'll happen if this gets out of hand.

— General Stern

DOCUMENT 8: COMMUNIQUÉ
SENDER: Lt. Col. A. Neech
RECIPIENT: Brig. Gen. D. Stern

General Stern: This will be the last communiqué you'll receive from me.

Despite daily patrols these last few weeks, there's no sign of Bernshaw, Holding, Dr. Ibarro or any other member of the Pack.

We've had no enemy contact, either. In fact, there's been no fighting across eighteen sectors for five weeks.

It must be the Pack. They're spreading. These heartless killers are spreading peace. Just by their presence. Just by being here.

But desertion rates have passed 35%. Men are wandering off from patrols or in the middle of the night. Somehow the Pack has breached our walls, the infection spreading.

I imagine the deserters are feeling the pull of the Pack the way Holding must have, despite being tortured by them. The way Calabrese must have, realizing some of the people he'd tortured had become Pack and he'd left them behind.

They can't stand being away from those like them. To feel like you belong instead of the slow stripping of anger and joy and fear. To be at peace.

And General, I want it, too. Dear God, I don't think I can fight it anymore.

invocabulary

GEMMA FILES

The small shall become great, the crooked become great, and though blind, I shall see.

—Desumiis Luge.

At this very moment, what I'm avoiding most of all
is laying a curse on you.
I've thought about it, a lot, and really,
it's far too much trouble
for far too little reward. So I sit here
smiling pleasantly,
avoiding carving your name with my fingernail
into a sheet of soft lead, then melting it
over a fire. On no account
will I drip wax into water and see
which of the resultant
lumps looks most like your face, then
drive pins into the places
where your eyes should be. Neither will I bury
your cat alive in a cemetery at midnight,
or weave your hair into a nest for birds
to fuck and shit in. None of that.
The worst part of my own forbearance is how you
frankly don't even seem to notice how much effort
it takes for me to avoid making
my thoughts real, killing you long-distance,

sending black words down into your blood to bloom
like microbes. Nevertheless, I refuse
to spit into your food, to lick your spoons,
to show my vagina in your shaving mirror, in hopes
that its reflection will strike you blind. To take
photos of you while you sleep, then burn them.
You can't make me, no matter what you do,
or don't.

i was a teenage minotaur

A.G. PASQUELLA

At the mall a lady offers me a free sample of zit cream and I'm about to be all sarcastic, like "Look, lady—I've got a giant bull's head. No one's going to notice a few zits."

But there's something about the way she's smiling at me, not a plastic fantastic artificial airbrushed smile like all the ladies on the magazines, that draws me up short and makes me smile back at her (have you ever seen a bull smile? It took me years of practice to get my lips to curl just right) and yeah, I know she's been trained in the fine art of zit cream sales but either she's the best actress in the world or she's the nicest person in the world and either way my heart just melts. Zits or no zits, suddenly I know this year is going to be different.

"You're sure you want to do this?" my mom asks, piling my plate with spaghetti and drenching it with sauce, just the way I like it.

"I'm sure," I say, thrusting out my jaw all determined-like. I would never say so because I don't want to break Ma's heart but the sauce is a little bland.

"Last time we didn't have much luck."

I rummage through the cupboards, searching for spice. "Yeah, but that was elementary school. This is different. This is high school."

As the years grind by the memories recede. It's like it all happened to some other person, not me. Your body's cells change completely every seven years (or so I've read) so really it's true. I wasn't me, I was someone else, I was Li'l Minotaur peering through the slats in our fence as the other kids tumbled from the school bus and ran laughing through the streets. Li'l Homeschooled Minotaur begged and pleaded to go to school with all the other kids until finally his parents relented and he rushed for the front doors so excited, untied shoelace thwapping on the school house steps, oversized Superman backpack stuffed piñata-full with binders and pencils and paper and pens. Inside the school, kids screeched to a halt. One washed-out little blonde girl's lower lip trembled before she burst into big terrified sobs. A little brown-haired tousle-headed boy in a red and white striped shirt turned tail and booted it down the hallway while an older kid, a hall monitor, boomed after him with the voice of grade six authority: "No running!" Then the hall monitor turned and spotted Li'l Minotaur and he, too, shrieked and took off running.

Special assembly, man, that shit was embarrassing. Some well-meaning teacher with a droopy moustache and a winter landscape on his fuzzy sweater got up in front of the entire school to talk about how 'everyone is different and differences are what makes us beautiful' and even at the time I knew that was all jibber-jabber and jive. I felt more ugly than ever, trying to shrink down small so my horns would be swallowed up by the wooden auditorium seats.

After assembly I was hauled off to the guidance counsellor who said, "Now, Mitch, this is just a precaution, I'm sure your parents discussed this with you at home" and then he stuck corks on my horns—corks!— and my face burned hot beneath my fur. Then I slunk back down the hallway tugging on the straps of my too-big Superman backpack with corks on my horns and yeah, I must've looked ridiculous because some loudmouthed asshole stared at me as I shuffled past and then burst out braying hardy donkey guffaws.

But that was then.

Dad looks over the top of his newspaper. "And you're sure this is what you want?"

"Man, why do you guys keep asking me that?" I know he means well but all this touchy-feely-new-age-what-about-his-feelings crap is really grinding me down. I've been homeschooled for years and it's time for a change. It's been almost a decade of Dad's voice droning on and on about Napoleon this and right angle that and tomorrow we're going to go on a field trip to the Natural History Museum—Won't that be fun? Yeah, that'll be fun all right, except the last time we were there two security guards followed us into the stuffed bird room, past the dead ducks and the giant albatross dangling from the ceiling and now and then they would whisper to each other and I couldn't shake the feeling they were wondering how I had escaped my cage.

THE BEST CANADIAN SPECULATIVE WRITING

Those guards didn't know me and these high school kids don't know me. I could be anyone. I'll always be a Minotaur but now I have the chance to be the best damn Minotaur I can be. A Hippy Minotaur. A Gourmet Pizza Chef Minotaur. A Badass Secret Agent Kung-Fu Minotaur. A Tap-Dancing Disco Priest Minotaur. Whatever.

It's the first day of high school and I'm strutting down the hallways rockin' some brand-new threads: white jacket with the sleeves rolled up, turquoise T-shirt, acid-washed blue jeans, high-top sneakers with graffiti-style airbrushing that I did myself in the backyard.

"Is that dude a Minotaur?"
"For real! And did you see those shoes?"

And so it begins. The taunts and jeers and jibes, ripped ketchup packets on my chair, ink sprayed from snapped pens, punched in the stomach almost as an afterthought as a bully walks by. If I don't fight back, it's open season on Minotaurs. If I fight and some kid gets gored, I'll be hunted with torches and pitchforks and driven into the sea.

I shuffle toward the cafeteria, deflated like a dollar store balloon. I don't know why I thought this time would be different. In the cafeteria a guy from my Social Studies class—Bill? No, Dave—clanks down his tray and sits down beside me.
Dave leans back, all leather jacket cool. "Why are you eating alone?"
"I don't know if you've noticed, but I have a giant bull's head."
Dave slurps milk. "So?"
"What do you mean, 'so'?"
Dave shrugs. "Everyone's got something."
The cafeteria is a cauldron of hormones and hairspray. All eyes are on me. "It's my jacket, isn't it?"
Dave smiles. "Dude, you could be wearing a garbage bag splattered with rat blood and it wouldn't make a lick of difference."
He's wrong. We humans—and yes, I am human, thanks for asking— are visual animals. The small details add up to the big picture. Good grooming is important. Before every special occasion I brush my fur and wax my horns.
Dave says something else but I don't hear him. Walking towards us, hair flowing, is a beautiful girl in ripped denim. Her jacket is a patchwork riot scrawled all over with pen and paint.

"This is my girlfriend, Jenna. This is—"

"Mitch. I'm, uh, I'm a Minotaur."

She has the biggest brown eyes I've ever seen. She smiles and shakes my hand. Her hand is warm, so warm.

She smells like cinnamon.

Have I ever dated? Yeah, right. Oh, I'm sure there's some freaks out there into the whole barnyard thing but let's get serious.

There was that one girl, Andrea, back at the homeschool Halloween party. She was drinking and running her hand along the muscles in my arm. She pulled me into the pantry and looked up at me with half-lidded eyes. "Take off that mask and kiss me."

I hate Halloween.

I'd be lying if I said I've never thought about plastic surgery. I know what you're thinking—Oh, but Mitch! How could you turn your back on your proud Minotaur heritage? To which I reply, What heritage? Mom and Dad aren't Minotaurs. I'm the only Minotaur I know. What do you think, some focus group is going to call me up to get a handle on the valuable teenage Minotaur demographic?—Say, Mitch, what did you think of that movie Titanic? It sucked.

Once I tried hitch-hiking to this plastic surgeon I had seen advertised on the back of a bus. I thought Mom would be happy. My mom never says so but I can tell she's—what? Not ashamed of me, exactly—maybe embarrassed in front of the bridge-club-braggers. My little Susie is a hang-gliding marathon-running PhD Rocket Scientist from Yale. My boy Mitch is, uh . . . a Minotaur.

She caught me four blocks from our house. Instead of being happy she looked so sad.

"Get in the car, Mitch. Now."

I got in the car (cracked vinyl seats, stuffy air smelling slightly like spearmint) and we drove home in silence.

It's a full moon tonight. Dave and Jenna smoke pot in the playground, lying atop a wooden pirate ship-style climbing structure, looking up at the stars.

"What if you're not really a Minotaur?"

"Oh, I'm a Minotaur, all right."

"What if this is like some Matrix-style False Reality?"

"You mean, what if I've got a body with a human head tucked away in a Sci-Fi tube somewhere and this Minotaur body is just my avatar?"

"Man, you're really hung up on this whole Minotaur thing." Dave sits up and takes a drag on the joint. "So you've got a bull's head. Big whoop."

"There's more to it than that. Minotaurs are legendary."

"THE Minotaur was legendary. A legendary loser. Didn't he get his head chopped off?"

"Well, yeah, but—"

"You've never even been to Crete. Am I right? You're no maze monster."

"If you want to get technical, it was a labyrinth, not a maze."

"You mean that David Bowie movie with all the puppets?"

I look over Dave's shoulder. In the parking lot, two black pick-up trucks circle like wolves.

Truck doors slam. At my side Dave remains cool, nonchalantly propped against the wooden wall of the pirate ship.

Four bros with beers stride into the playground. "Hey, Jackass! What's with the Halloween mask?"

And here we go. I give that one a 2.5 out of 10. Not very clever or original and believe me, I've heard 'em all.

Shit People Say to Minotaurs

> Do you use, like, human toilets?
> *Snaps Red Towel* Toro, Toro!
> Do you eat people food?
> Do you eat people?
> So, you must be pretty good at mazes, huh?
> Do you fuck cows?

Dave leaps down from the ship. His face is twisted and vicious. "If you want him, you have to go through me."

Here's the part in the playbook that calls for more puffed-up posturing and then fisticuffs but instead the bros stomp back to their trucks and rev away.

Dave, normal again, saunters back to the pirate ship and lights another joint.

223

In the morning Mom and Dad knock on my door and peek into my room. "Mitch? May we come in?"

"It's a free country."

"Mitch, we're concerned about these new friends of yours."

"I thought you wanted me to make friends. Remember the homeschool girls?"

In order to stave off social isolation, all of us homeschooled kids got corralled together once a month. We'd emerge blinking into the light to stand awkwardly in the corner of parks and unfamiliar homes. Because our moms were friends I was always forced to mingle with these two sisters. They liked to play dress-up and dangle Christmas ornaments from my horns. It wasn't all bad, though. In the summertime they had a homemade Slip 'n Slide made from a black plastic tarp and a garden hose (initial hose-blast hot, standing water summer-baked inside) and that shit was tons of fun.

Dad stares at me over the tops of his bifocals. "You've changed, son."

"Nope." I tap my horns. "Still a Minotaur."

That night I walk back to the park. It's deserted except for Jenna, looking lonely on the swings.

"What's up?"

"Same old, same old." Jenna looks away. "Waiting for Dave."

"Have you and Dave been dating long?"

"Seems like forever." Jenna's hair blows backwards. She pushes a few stray brown strands away from her face. "Do you ever think about the future?"

I tell her that I think about it a lot. Where will I be in ten, twenty, thirty years? A crazy recluse on the hill, bull-fur growing grey by a crackling fire? Or will I be quivering on a cliff-edge surrounded by torch-waving villagers? Deep down I know it's not going to end well.

Jenna dangles from the swing and drags the toe of her Doc Martens through the dirt. "You don't really think that."

I shrug. "Why not? It's not all fun and games being a Minotaur."

Jenna scowls, suddenly fierce. "You think you're the only one with problems?"

She leaps from the swing and storms away.

I stand there like an idiot and then I run after her.

In the parking lot a black Camaro rolls past me and I get ready for the inevitable splattering of soda but then the driver's side window rolls down and there's Dave grinning behind the wheel. "What's shaking?"

I point to Jenna's retreating back. "Jenna—"

"I'll handle it."

Dave guns the engine and rolls out. I watch him go and think, maybe I should buy a leather jacket.

That night I have that dream again. The one with the villagers and the pitchforks. My head on a wall. Caged behind bars. Shot 'by mistake' in the forest. I'm so tired of being afraid.

The next day at school Coach calls me down to his office.

"You must be the Minotaur."

"What gave me away?"

Coach ignores my sass and I grin because I can guess what's coming.

"Mitch, have you ever seen the movie *Teen Wolf*? And to a lesser extent, *Teen Wolf Too*?"

Oh hell yes. I can see me now, strutting down the hallway in my varsity jacket, cheerleaders with short flapping skirts running toward me, Jenna smiling as I push them aside and take her in my arms.

Coach keeps talking. "I know things are different. You're a Minotaur, not a Werewolf. We're talkin' football, not basketball. Middleton has a strong football tradition. We were district champs back in 1972. Remember?"

"I was negative ten."

"Anyway, Mitch, we want to rename the team. The Middleton Minotaurs! How does that grab you?"

I grin. That grabs me just fine. "One problem, Coach. It might be tough getting a helmet my size."

"What?"

"You know, my horns. We'll have to keep 'em under wraps."

Coach shakes his head. "No, no. You won't be playing." Coach points over to the corner where two halves of a ratty bull costume lean against the cinder block wall. "You like it? I got it second hand from the Brownstown Bulls. The assistant coaches and I think, uh, it'll make the fans feel more comfortable." Coach pats my shoulder. "Don't worry. You can be the head."

"I don't want to be the head."

Coach frowns. "You want to be the butt? Frankly, Mitch, that doesn't make a whole lot of sense."

"I don't want to be the butt, either."

When I was a kid I dreamed about going to Chicago. Somehow I'd get there—hitchhiking, winning a free flight, climbing aboard a billionaire's private railcar—and then I'd become the mascot for the Chicago Bulls and Michael Jordan and I would ride around in the Chicago Bulls bus solving mysteries.

Really, what other jobs are out there for a teenage Minotaur? Or for that matter, a middle-aged Minotaur? Minotaur middle management. An ol' paunchy Minotaur waddlin' after the morning paper before heaving himself into the front seat of his second-hand Toyota with a custom-built 'sun roof' so he has someplace to cram his fat bald head.

What else? Door to door salesman. No, that's out. You look through your peephole and see a giant man with a bull's head—are you going to open your door? No.

Restaurant spokesperson. I've thought about it a lot. Basically I'd go into a partnership with a dude who owned a barbecue joint. Then I'd stand out front to meet the people and be all like, Hey man, this BBQ is pretty good, and they'd be like, Well all right, let's eat! But really that's just me being a different kind of mascot and anyway Pop says the restaurant business is tough. Four out of every five fail in the first year, or something like that. I think it's because being in the restaurant business is seen as glamorous. Four out of every five MRI clinics don't fail because people don't up and open an MRI clinic on a romantic whim. Oh, Richard! Let's open our own MRI Clinic like the one we saw in Tuscany!

What else? Scary rodeo clown. Carnival freak. Undercover work's out. I'm not exactly incognito. The dealers would catch wise pretty damn quick—Yo, don't sell to the Minotaur.

Coach smiles. "So what do you say?"

"I'll think about it."

That Friday, Jenna and Dave and I go camping. On our way out of town, we pass grey-faced men outside the soup kitchen, weeds struggling up through sidewalk cracks. What would it be like to be mayor of this town? Come for the drag racing, stay for the meth. Prostitutes? Shuttered factories? Empty warehouses with busted-out windows? Hey, we've got 'em!

We roll into the campsite. Bonfire and beer, orange and red sparks rising into the night. Dave rummages through the cooler, pulls out three beers and then drinks them.

"What's eating you, Mitch?"

"Coach wants me to be a mascot."

"Oh yeah?"

"He says it could really help lift the town's spirits."

"What did you say?"

"I haven't decided yet."

Jenna snorts. "It's going to take a lot more than some stupid football game to save this town."

I follow Jenna down to the water.

"Are you okay?"

"Dave and I broke up."

"I'm sorry."

"It happens."

"I'm still sorry."

Jenna goes off to gather more firewood. Dave and I watch her go.

"She likes you, man."

"Yeah, right. 'Beauty and the Beast.'"

"She doesn't care about that." Dave smiles wryly. "She dated me, didn't she?"

Jenna returns and sits down beside me. Dave passes out, legs tucked beneath his oversized sweatshirt like he's ten years old.

We watch the moonlight bounce off the surface of the lake.

Jenna stands up. "Let's go swimming."

"I didn't bring my suit."

Jenna smiles. "Neither did I."

Sand crunches beneath our feet. Skin and sand and waves and wind. Why live in fear? Sure, I could end up a mounted head on a plaque in an oak panelled living room that smells like stale cigars. Or I could be a half-assed mascot for some crappy small town football team. Or I could own my own factory, glistening bottles of Minotaur

Brand Hot Sauce rolling down the production line, crowds of happy workers heading off to cash their paycheques. Hell, anything could happen.

She smiles as she swims, cutting through moonlight.

weep for day

INDRAPRAMIT DAS

I was eight years old the first time I saw a real, living Nightmare. My parents took my brother and I on a trip from the City-of-Long-Shadows to the hills at Evening's edge, where one of my father's clients had a manse. Father was a railway contractor. He hired out labour and resources to the privateers extending the frontiers of civilization towards the frozen wilderness of the dark Behind-the-Sun. Aptly, we took a train up to the foothills of the great Penumbral Mountains.

It was the first time my brother and I had been on a train, though we'd seen them tumble through the city with their cacophonic engines, cumulous tails of smoke and steam billowing like blood over the rooftops when the red light of our sun caught them. It was also the first time we had been anywhere close to Night—Behind-the-Sun—where the Nightmares lived. Just a decade before we took that trip, it would have been impossible to go as far into Evening as we were doing with such casual comfort and ease.

Father had prodded the new glass of the train windows, pointing to the power-lines crisscrossing the sky in tandem with the gleaming lines of metal railroads silvering the hazy landscape of progress. He sat between my brother Velag and I, our heads propped against the bulk of his belly, which bulged against his rough crimson waistcoat. I clutched that coat and breathed in the sweet smell of chemlis gall that hung over him. Mother watched with a smile as she peeled indigos for us with her fingers, laying them in the lap of her skirt.

"Look at that. We've got no more reason to be afraid of the dark, do we, my tykes?" said Father, his belly humming with the sound of his booming voice.

Dutifully, Velag and I agreed there wasn't.

"Why not?" he asked us, expectant.

"Because of the Industrialization, which brings the light of Day to the darkness of Night," we chimed, a line learned both in school and home (inaccurate, as we'd never set foot in Night itself). Father laughed. I always slowed down on the word 'industrialization,' which caused Velag and I to say it at different times. He was just over a year older than me, though.

"And what is your father, children?" Mother asked.

"A knight of Industry and Technology, bringer of light under Church and Monarchy."

I didn't like reciting that part, because it had more than one long "y" word, and felt like a struggle to say. Father *was* actually a knight, though not a knight-errant for a while. He had been too big by then to fit into a suit of plate-armour or heft a heavy sword around, and knights had stopped doing that for many years anyway. The Industrialization had swiftly made the pageantry of adventure obsolete.

Father wheezed as we reminded him of his knighthood, as if ashamed. He put his hammy hands in our hair and rubbed. I winced through it, as usual, because he always forgot about the pins in my long hair, something my brother didn't have to worry about. Mother gave us the peeled indigos, her hands perfumed with the citrus. She was the one who taught me how to place the pins in my hair, both of us in front of the mirror looking like different sized versions of each other.

I looked out the windows of our cabin, fascinated by how everything outside slowly became bluer and darker as we moved away from the City-of-Long-Shadows, which lies between the two hemispheres of Day and Night. Condensation crawled across the corners of the double-glazed panes as the train took us further east. Being a studious girl even at that age, I deduced from school lessons that the air outside was becoming rapidly colder as we neared Night's hemisphere, which has never seen a single ray of our sun and is theorized to be entirely frozen. The train, of course, was kept warm by the same steam and machinery that powered its tireless wheels and kept its lamps and twinkling chandeliers aglow.

"Are you excited to see the Nightmare? It was one of the first to be captured and tamed. The gentleman we're visiting is very proud to be its captor," said Father.

"Yes!" screamed Velag. "Does it still have teeth? And claws?" he asked, his eyes wide.

"I would think so," Father nodded.

"Is it going to be in chains?"

"I hope so, Velag. Otherwise it might get loose and—" he paused for dramatic effect. I froze in fear. Velag looked eagerly at him. "Eat you both up!" he bellowed, tickling us with his huge hands. It took all my willpower not to scream. I looked at Velag's delighted expression to keep me calm, reminding myself that these were just Father's hands jabbing my sides.

"Careful!" Mother said sharply, to my relief. "They'll get the fruit all over." The indigo segments were still in our laps, on the napkins Mother had handed to us. Father stopped tickling us, still grinning.

"Do you remember what they look like?" Velag asked, as if trying to see how many questions he could ask in as little time as possible. He had asked this one before, of course. Father had fought Nightmares, and even killed some, when he was a knight-errant.

"We never really saw them, son," said Father. He touched the window. "Out there, it's so cold you can barely feel your own fingers, even in armour."

We could see the impenetrable walls of the forests pass us by—shaggy, snarled mare-pines, their leaves black as coals and branches supposedly twisted into knots by the Nightmares to tangle the path of intruders. The high, hoary tops of the trees shimmered ever so slightly in the scarce light sneaking over the horizon, which they sucked in so hungrily. The moon was brighter here than in the City, but at its jagged crescent, a broken gemstone behind the scudding clouds. We were still in Evening, but had encroached onto the Nightmares' outer territories, marked by the forests that extended to the foothills. After the foothills, there was no more forest, because there was no more light. Inside our cabin, under bright electric lamps, sitting on velvet-lined bunks, it was hard to believe that we were actually in the land of Nightmares. I wondered if they were in the trees right now, watching our windows as we looked out.

"It's hard to see them, or anything, when you're that cold, and," Father breathed deeply, gazing at the windows. "They're very hard to see." It made me uneasy, hearing him say the same thing over and over. We were passing the very forests he travelled through as a knight-errant, escorting pioneers.

"Father's told you about this many times, dear," Mother interjected, peering at Father with worried eyes. I watched. Father smiled at her and shook his head.

"That's alright, I like telling my little tykes about my adventures. I guess you'll see what a Nightmare looks like tomorrow, eh? Out in the open. Are you excited?" he asked, perhaps forgetting that he'd already asked. Velag shouted in the affirmative again.

Father looked down at me, raising his bushy eyebrows. "What about you, Valyzia?"

I nodded and smiled.

I wasn't excited. Truth be told, I didn't want to see it at all. The idea of capturing and keeping a Nightmare seemed somehow disrespectful in my heart, though I didn't know the word then. It made me feel weak and confused, because I was and always had been so afraid of them, and had been taught to be.

I wondered if Velag had noticed that Father had once again refused to actually describe a Nightmare. Even in his most excitable retellings of his brushes with them, he never described them as more than walking shadows. There was a grainy sepia-toned photograph of him during his younger vigils as a knight-errant above the mantle of our living-room fireplace. It showed him mounted on a horse, dressed in his plate-armour and fur-lined surcoat, raising his longsword to the skies (the blade was cropped from the picture by its white border). Clutched in his other plated hand was something that looked like a blot of black, as if the chemicals of the photograph had congealed into a spot, attracted by some mystery or heat. The shape appeared to bleed back into the black background.

It was, I had been told, the head of a Nightmare Father had slain. It was too dark a thing to be properly caught by whatever early photographic engine had captured his victory. The blot had no distinguishing features apart from two vague points emerging from the rest of it, like horns or ears. That head earned him a large part of the fortune he later used to start up his contracting business. We never saw it, because Nightmares' heads and bodies were burned or gibbeted by knights-errant, who didn't want to bring them into the City for fear of attracting their horde. The photograph had been a source of dizzying pride for my young self, because it meant that my father was one of the bravest people I knew. At other times, it just made me wonder why he couldn't describe something he had once beheaded, and held in his hand as a trophy.

My indigo finished, Mother took the napkin and wiped my hands with it. My brother still picked at his. A waiter brought us a silver platter filled with sugar-dusted pastries, their centres soft with warm fudge and grünberry jam. We'd already finished off supper, brought under silver domes that gushed steam when the waiters raised them with their white-gloved hands, revealing chopped fungus, meat dumplings, sour cream and fermented salad. Mother told Velag to finish the indigo before he touched the pastries. Father ate them with as much gusto as I did. I watched him lick his powdered fingers, that had once held the severed head of a Nightmare.

When it was time for respite, the cabin lights were shut off and the ones in the corridor were dimmed. I was relieved my parents left the curtains of the windows open as we retired, because I didn't want it to be completely dark. It was dim enough outside that we could fall asleep. It felt unusual to go to bed with windows uncovered for once.

I couldn't help imagine, as I was wont to do, that as our train moved through Evening's forested fringes, the Nightmares would find a way to get on board. I wondered if they were already on the train. But the presence of my family, all softly snoring in their bunks (Velag above me, my parents opposite us); the periodic, soothing flash of way-station lights passing by outside; the sigh of the sliding doors at the end of the carriage opening and closing as porters, waiters, and passengers moved through the corridors; the sweet smell of the fresh sheets and pillow on my bunk—these things lulled me into a sleep free of bad dreams, despite my fear of seeing the creature we'd named bad dreams after, face-to-face, the next vigil.

When I was six I stopped sleeping in my parents' room, and started sleeping in the same room as my brother. At the time of this change, I was abnormally scared of the dark (and consider, reader, that this was a time when fear of the dark was as normal and acceptable as the fear of falling from a great height). So scared that I couldn't fall sleep after the maids came around and closed our sleep-shutters and drew the curtains, to block out the western light for respite.

The heavy clatter of the wooden slats being closed every respite's eve was like a note of foreboding for me. I hunkered under the blankets, rigid with anxiety as the maids filed out of the room with their lanterns drawing wild shadows on the walls. Then the last maid would close the door, and our room would be swallowed up by those shadows.

In the chill darkness that followed, I would listen to the clicking of Nightmares' claws as they walked up and down the corridors of our shuttered house. Our parents had often told me that it was just rats in the walls and ceiling, but I refused to believe it. Every respite I would imagine one of the Nightmare intruders slinking into our room, listening to its breathing as it came closer to my bed and pounced on me, not being able to scream as it sat on my chest and ran its reeking claws through my hair, winding it into knots around its long fingers and laughing softly.

Enduring the silence for what seemed like hours, I would begin to wail and cry until Velag threw pillows at me and Mother came to my side to shush me with her kisses. To solve the problem, my parents tried keeping the sleep-shutters open through the hours of respite, and moved my brother to a room on the windowless east-facing side of the house when he complained. Unfortunately, we require the very dark we fear to fall asleep. The persistent burning line of the horizon beyond the windows, while a comforting sight, left me wide awake for most of respite.

In the end Velag and I were reunited and the shutters closed once more, because Father demanded that I not be coddled when my brother had learned to sleep alone so bravely. I often heard my parents arguing about this, since Mother thought it was madness to try and force me not to be afraid. Most of my friends from school hadn't and wouldn't sleep without their parents until they were at least eleven or twelve. Father was adamant, demanding that we learn to be strong and brave in case the Nightmares ever found a way to overrun the city.

It's a strange thing, to be made to feel guilty for learning too well something that was ingrained in us from the moment we were born. Now nightmare is just a word, and it's unusual to even think that the race that we gave that name might still be alive somewhere in the world. When Velag and I were growing up, Nightmares were the enemy.

Our grandparents told us about them, as did our parents, as did our teachers, as did every book and textbook we had ever come across. Stories of a time when guns hadn't been invented, when knights-errant roved the frigid forest paths beyond the City-of-Long-Shadows to prove their manhood and loyalty to the Monarchy and its Solar Church, and to extend the borders of the city and find new resources. A time coming to a close when I was born, even as the expansion continued onward faster than ever.

I remember my school class-teacher drawing the curtains and holding a candle to a wooden globe of our planet to show us how the sun made Night and Day. She took a piece of chalk and tapped where the candlelight turned to shadow on the globe. "That's us," she said, and moved the chalk over to the shadowed side. "That's them," she said.

Nightmares have defined who we are since we crawled out of the hot lakes at the edge of fiery Day, and wrapped the steaming bloody skins of slaughtered animals around us to walk upright, east into the cooler marches of our world's Evening. We stopped at the alien darkness we had never seen before, not just because of the terrible cold that clung to the air the further we walked, but because of what we met at Evening's end.

A race of walking shadows, circling our firelight with glittering eyes, felling our explorers with barbed spears and arrows, snatching our dead as we fled from their ambushes. Silently, these unseen, lethal guardians of Night's bitter frontier told us we could go no further. But we couldn't go back towards Day, where the very air seems to burn under the sun's perpetual gaze.

So we built our villages where sun's light still lingers and the shadows are longest before they dissolve into Evening. Our villages grew into towns, and our towns grew into the City-of-Long-Shadows, and our City grew along the Penumbra until it reached the Seas-of-Storms to the north and the impassable crags of World's-Rim (named long before we knew this to be false) to the south. For all of history, we looked behind our shoulders at the gloaming of the eastern horizon, where the Nightmares watched our progress.

So the story went, told over and over.

We named bad dreams after them because we thought Nightmares were their source, that they sent spies into the city to infect our minds and keep us afraid of the dark, their domain. According to folklore, these spies could be glimpsed upon waking abruptly. Indeed, I'd seen them crouching malevolently in the corner of the bedroom, wreathed in the shadows that were their home, slinking away with impossible speed once I looked at them.

There are no Nightmares left alive anywhere near the City-of-Long-Shadows, but we still have bad dreams and we still see their spies sometimes when we wake. Some say they are spirits of their race, or survivors. I'm not convinced. Even though we have killed all the Nightmares, our own half-dreaming minds continue to populate our bedrooms with their ghosts, so we may remember their legacy.

To date, none of our City's buildings have windows or doors on their east-facing walls.

And so the train took us to the end of our civilization. There are many things I remember about Weep-for-Day, though in some respects those memories feel predictably like the shreds of a disturbing dream. Back then it was just an outpost, not a hill-station town like it is now. The most obvious thing to remember is how it sleeted or snowed all the time. I know now that it's caused by moist convective winds in the atmosphere carrying the warmth of the sun from Day to Night, their loads of fat clouds scraping up against the mountains of the Penumbra for all eternity and washing the foothills in their frozen burden. But to my young self, the constant crying of that bruised sky was just another mystery in the world, a sorcery perpetrated by the Nightmares.

I remember, of course, how dark it was. How the people of the outpost carried bobbing lanterns and acrid magenta flares that flamed even against the perpetual wind and precipitation. How everyone outside (including us) had to wear goggles and thick protective suits lined with the fur of animals to keep the numbing cold of outer Evening out. I had never seen such darkness outdoors, and it felt like being asleep while walking. To think that beyond the mountains lay an absence of light even deeper was unbelievable.

I remember the tall poles that marked turns in the curving main road, linked by the ever-present electric and telegraph wires that made such an outpost possible. The bright gold-and-red pennants of the Monarchy fluttered from those poles, dulled by lack of light. They all showed a sun that was no longer visible from there.

I remember the solar shrines—little huts by the road, with small windows that lit up every few hours as chimes rang out over the windy outpost. Through the doors you could see the altars inside; each with an electric globe, its filament flooded with enough voltage to make it look like a hot ball of fire. For a minute these shrines would burn with their tiny artificial suns, and the goggled and suited inhabitants of Weep-for-Day would huddle around them like giant flies, their shadows wavering lines on the streaks of light cast out on the muddy snow or ice. They would pray on their knees, some reaching out to rub the faded ivory crescents of sunwyrm fangs on the altars.

Beyond the road and the slanted wet roofs of Weep-for-Day, there was so little light that the slope of the hill was barely visible. The forested plain beyond was nothing but a black void that ended in the faint glow of the horizon—the last weak embers in a soot-black fireplace just doused with water.

I couldn't see our City-of-Long-Shadows, which filled me with an irrational anxiety that it was gone forever, that if we took the train back we would find the whole world filled with darkness and only Night waiting on the other side.

But these details are less than relevant. That trip changed me and changed the course of my life not because I saw what places beyond the City-of-Long-Shadows looked like, though seeing such no doubt planted the seeds of some future grit in me. It changed me because I, with my family by my side, witnessed a living Nightmare, as we were promised.

The creature was a prisoner of Vorin Tylvur, who was at the time the Consul of Weep-for-Day, a knight like Father, and an appointed privateer and mining coordinator of the Penumbral territories. Of course, he is now well remembered for his study of Nightmares in captivity, and his campaigns to expand the Monarchy's territories into Evening. The manse we stayed in was where he and his wife lived, governing the affairs of the outpost and coordinating expansion and exploration.

I do not remember much of our hosts, except that they were adults in the way all adults who aren't parents are, to little children. They were kind enough to me. I couldn't comprehend the nature of condescension at that age, but I did find the cooing manner of most adults who talked to me boring, and they were no different. Though I'm grateful for their hospitality to my family, I cannot, in retrospect, look upon them with much returned kindness.

They showed us the imprisoned Nightmare on the second vigil of our stay. It was in the deepest recesses of the manse, which was more an oversized, glorified bunker on the hill of Weep-for-Day than anything else. We went down into a dank, dim corridor in the chilly heart of that mound of crustal rock to see the prisoner.

"I call it Shadow. A little nickname," Sir Tylvur said with a toothy smile, his huge moustache hanging from his nostrils like the dead wings of some poor misbegotten bird trapped in his head. He proved himself right then to have not only a startling lack of imagination for a man of his intelligence and inquisitiveness, but also a grotesquely inappropriate sense of levity.

It would be dramatic and untruthful to say that my fear of darkness receded the moment I set eyes on the creature. But something changed in me. There, looking at this hunched and shivering thing under the smoky blaze of the flares its armoured gaolers held to reveal it to its captor's guests, I saw that a phantom flayed was just another animal.

Sir Tylvur had made sure that its light-absorbent skin would not hinder our viewing of the captured enemy. There is no doubt that I feared it, even though its skin was stripped from its back to reveal its glistening red muscles, even though it was clearly broken and defeated. But my mutable young mind understood then, looking into its shining black eyes—the only visible feature in the empty dark of its face—that it knew terror just as I or any human did. The Nightmare was scared. It was a heavy epiphany for a child to bear, and I vomited on the glass observation wall of its cramped holding cell.

Velag didn't make fun of me. He shrank into Mother's arms, trying to back away from the humanoid silhouette scrabbling against the glass to escape the light it so feared; a void-like cut-out in reality but for that livid wet wound on its back revealing it to be as real as us. It couldn't, or would not, scream or vocalize in any way. Instead, we just heard the squeal of its spider-like hands splayed on the glass, claws raking the surface.

I looked at Father, standing rigid and pale, hands clutched into tight fists by his sides. The same fists that held up the severed head of one of this creature's race in triumph so many years ago. Just as in the photograph, there were the horn-like protrusions from its head, though I still couldn't tell what they were. I looked at Mother who, despite the horrific vision in front of us, despite her son clinging to her waist, reached down in concern to wipe the vomit from my mouth and chin with bare fingers, her gloves crumpled in her other hand.

As Sir Tylvur wondered what to do about his spattered glass wall, he decided to blame the Nightmare for my reaction and rapped hard on the cell with the hilt of his sheathed ceremonial sword. He barked at the prisoner, wanting to frighten it away from the glass, I suppose. The only recognisable word in between his grunts was "Shadow." But as he called it by that undignified, silly nickname, the thing stopped its frantic scrabbling. Startled, Sir Tylvur stepped back. The two armoured gaolers stepped back as well, flares wavering in the gloom of the cell. I still don't know why the Nightmare stopped thrashing, and I never will know for sure. But at that moment I thought it recognised the nickname its captor had given it, and recognised that it was being displayed like a trophy. Perhaps it wanted to retain some measure of its pride.

The flarelight flickered on its eyes, which grew brighter as moisture gathered on them. It was clearly in pain from the light. I saw that it was as tall as a human, though it looked smaller because of how crouched into itself it was. It cast a shadow like any other animal, and that shadow looked like its paler twin, dancing behind its back. Chains rasped on the wet cell floor, shackled to its limbs. The illuminated wound on its back wept pus, but the rest of it remained that sucking, indescribable black that hurt the human eye.

Except something in its face. It looked at us, and out of that darkness came a glittering of wet obsidian teeth as unseen lips peeled back. I will never forget that invisible smile, whether it was a grimace of pain or a taunting leer.

"Kill it," Velag whispered. And that was when Mother took both our hands tight in hers, and pulled us away from the cell. She marched us down that dank corridor, leaving the two former knights-errant, Father and Sir Tylvur, staring into that glimmering cell at the spectre of their past.

That night, in the tiny room we'd been given as our quarters, I asked Velag if the Nightmare had scared him.

"Why should it scare me," he said, face pale in the dim glow of the small heating furnace in the corner of the chamber. "It's in chains."

"You just looked scared. It's okay to be scared. I was too. But I think it was as well."

"Shut up. You don't know what you're saying. I'm going to sleep," he said, and turned away from me, his cot groaning. The furnace hissed and ticked.

"I think papa was scared also. He didn't want to see a Nightmare again," I said to Velag's back.

That was when my brother pounced off his cot and on top of me. I was too shocked to scream. My ingrained submission to his power as an elder male authority figure took over. I gave no resistance. Sitting on my small body, Velag took my blanket and shoved it into my mouth. Then, he snatched my pillow and held it over my face. Choking on the taste of musty cloth, I realised I couldn't breathe. I believed that my brother was about to kill me then. I truly believed it. I could feel the pressure of his hands through the pillow, and they were at that moment the hands of something inhuman. I was more terrified then than I'd ever been in my entire short life, plagued though I'd always been by fear.

He held the pillow over my head for no more than four seconds, probably less. When he raised it off my face and pulled the blanket out of my mouth he looked as shaken as I was. His eyes were wet with tears, but in a second his face was twisted in a grimace.

"Never call papa a coward. Never call papa a coward. Papa was never afraid. Do you hear me? You never had to sleep alone in the dark, you don't know. I'm going to grow up and be like papa and kill them. I'll kill them," he hissed the words into my face like a litany. I started crying, unable and probably too scared to tell him I hadn't called Father a coward. I could still barely breathe, so flooded was I with my own tears, so drunk on the air he had denied me. Velag went back to his cot and wrapped himself in his blanket, breathing heavily.

As I shuddered with stifled sobs, I decided that I would never tell my parents about this, that I would never have Velag punished for this violence. I didn't forgive him, not even close, but that is what I decided.

I was seventeen the last time I saw Velag. I went to visit him at the Royal Military Academy's boarding school. He had been there for four years already. We saw him every few moons when he came back to the City proper to visit. But I wanted to see the campus for myself. It was a lovely train ride, just a few hours from the central districts of the City-of-Long-Shadows to the scattered hamlets beyond it.

It was warmer and brighter out where the Academy was. The campus was beautiful, sown with pruned but still wild looking trees and plants that only grew further out towards Day, their leaves a lighter shade of blue and their flowers huge, craning to the west on thick stems. The sun still peered safely behind the edge of the world, but its gaze was bright enough to wash the stately buildings of the boarding school with a fiery golden-red light, sparkling in the waxy leaves of vines winding their way around the arched windows. On every ornate, varnished door was a garish propaganda poster of the Dark Lord of Nightmares, with his cowled cloak of shadows and black sword, being struck down by our soldiers' bayoneted guns.

I sat with Velag in a cupola in the visitors' garden, which was on a gentle bluff. In the fields adjacent, his fellow student-soldiers played tackleball, their rowdy calls and whistles ringing through the air. We could see heavy banks of glowing, sunlit storm-clouds to the west where the atmosphere boiled and churned in the heat of Day, beyond miles of shimmering swamp-forests and lakes. To the east, a faint moon hung over the campus, but no stars were visible so close to Day.

Velag looked so different from the last time I saw him. His pimples were vanishing, the sallow softness of adolescence melting away to reveal the man he was to become. The military uniform, so forbidding in red and black, suited his tall form. He looked smart and handsome in it. It hurt me to see him shackled in it, but I could see that he wore it with great pride.

He held my hand and asked about my life back home, about my plans to apply to the College of Archaeology at the University of St. Kataretz. He asked about our parents. He told me how gorgeous and grown-up I looked in my dress, and said he was proud of me for becoming a "prodigy." I talked to him with a heavy ache in my chest, because I knew with such certainty that we hardly knew each other, and would get no chance to any time soon, as he would be dispatched to the frontlines of Penumbral Conquest.

As if reading my thoughts, his cheek twitched with what I thought was guilt, and he looked at the stormy horizon. Perhaps he was remembering the night on which he told me he would grow up and kill Nightmares like Father—a promise he was keeping. He squeezed my hand.

"I'll be alright, Val. Don't you worry."

I gave him a rueful smile. "It's not too late. You can opt to become a civilian after graduation and come study with me at St. Kataretz. Ma and papa would think no less of you. You could do physics again, you loved it before. We can get an apartment in Pemluth Halls, share the cost. The University's right in the middle of the City, we'd have so much fun together."

"I can't. You know that. I want this for myself. I want to be a soldier, and a knight."

"Being a knight isn't the same thing as it was in papa's time. He was independent, a privateer. Things have changed. You'll be a part of the military. Knighthoods belong to them now and they're stingy with them. They mostly give them to soldiers who are wounded or dead, Velag."

"I'm in military school, by the saints, I know what a knighthood is or isn't. Please don't be melodramatic. You're an intelligent girl."

"What's that got to do with anything?"

"I'm going. I have more faith in my abilities than you do."

"I have plenty of faith in you. But the Nightmares are angry now, Velag. We're wiping them out. They're scared and angry. They're coming out in waves up in the hills. More of our soldiers are dying than ever before. How can I not worry?"

His jaw knotted, he glared down at our intertwined hands. His grip was limp now. "Don't start with your theories about the benevolence of Nightmares. I don't want to hear it. They're not scared, they *are* fear, and we'll wipe them off the planet if need be so that you and everybody else can live without that fear."

241

"I'm quite happy with my life, thank you. I'd rather you be alive for ma and papa and me than have the terrible horde of the Nightmares gone forever."

He bit his lip and tightened his hand around mine again. "I know, little sister. You're sweet to worry so. But the Monarchy needs me. I'll be fine. I promise."

And that was the end of the discussion as far as he was concerned. I knew there was no point pushing him further, because it would upset him. This was his life, after all. The one he had chosen. I had no right to belittle it. I didn't want to return to the City on bad terms with him. We made what little small talk was left to make, and then we stood and kissed each other on the cheek, and I hugged him tight and watched him walk away.

What good are such promises as the one he made on our final farewell, even if one means them with all of one's heart? He was dispatched right after his graduation a few moons later, without even a ceremony because it was wartime. After six moons of excited letters from the frontlines at the Penumbral Mountains, he died with a Nightmare's spear in his chest, during a battle that earned the Monarchy yet another victory against the horde of darkness. Compared to the thousands of Nightmares slaughtered during the battle with our guns and cannons, the Monarchy's casualties were small. And yet, my parents lost their son, and I my brother.

In death, they did give Velag the knighthood he fought so hard for. Never have I hated myself so much for being right.

When Velag was being helped out of Mother by doctors in the City, my father had been escorting pioneers in the foothills. I see him in his armour, the smell of heated steel and cold sweat cloying under his helm, almost blind because of the visor, sword in one hand, knotted reins and a flaming torch in the other, his mount about to bolt. A new metal coal-chamber filled with glowing embers strapped to his back to keep the suit warm, making his armour creak and pop as it heated up, keeping him off-balance with its weight and hissing vents but holding the freezing cold back a little. Specks of frozen water flying through the torch-lit air like dust, biting his eyes through the visor. His fingers numb in his gloves, despite the suit. The familiar glitter of inhuman eyes beyond the torchlight, nothing to go by but reflections of fire on his foes, who are invisible in the shadows, slinking alongside the caravan like bulges in the darkness. The only thing between the

Nightmares and the pioneers with their mounts and carriages weighed down by machinery and thick coils of wire and cable that will bring the light of civilization to these wilds, is him and his contingent.

How long must that journey have been to him? How long till he returned alive to see his wife and new son Velag in a warm hospital room, under the glow of a brand new electric light?

By the time I was born, armourers had invented portable guns and integrated hollow cables in the suit lining to carry ember-heated water around armour, keeping it warmer and enabling mercenaries and knights-errant to go deeper into Evening. The pioneers followed, bringing their technology to the very tops of the foothills, infested with Nightmares. That was when Father stopped going, lest he never return. They had new tools, but the war had intensified. He had a son and daughter to think of, and a wife who wanted him home.

When I watched Velag's funeral pyre blaze against the light of the west on Barrow-of-Bones cremation hill, I wondered if the sparks sent up into the sky by his burning body would turn to stardust in the ether and migrate to the sun to extend its life, or whether this was his final and utter dissolution. The chanting priest from the Solar Church seemed to have no doubts on the matter. Standing there, surrounded by the fossilized stone ribs of Zhurgeith, last of the sunwyrms and heraldic angel of the Monarchy and Church (who also call it Dragon), I found myself truly unsure about what death brings for maybe the first time in my life, though I'd long practised the cynicism that was becoming customary of my generation.

I thought with some trepidation about the possibility that if the Church was right, the dust of Velag's life might be consigned to the eternal dark of cosmic limbo instead of finding a place in the sun, because of what he'd done to me as a child. Because I'd never forgiven him, even though I told myself I had.

How our world changes.

The sun is a great sphere of burning gas, ash eventually falls down, and my dead brother remains in the universe because my family and I remember him, just as I remember my childhood, my life, the Nightmares we lived in fear of, the angel Dragon whose host was wiped out by a solar flare before we could ever witness it.

Outside, the wind howls so loud that I can easily imagine it is the sound of trumpets from a frozen city, peopled by the horde of darkness.

Even behind the insulated metal doors and heated tunnels of the cave bunkers that make up After-Day border camp, I can see my breath and need two thick coats to keep warm. My fingers are like icicles as I write. I would die very quickly if exposed to the atmosphere outside. And yet, here I am, in the land of Nightmares.

Somewhere beyond these Penumbral Mountains, which we crossed in an airtight train, is the City-of-Long-Shadows. I have never been so far from it. Few people have. We are most indebted to those who mapped the shortest route through the mountains, built the rails through the lowest valleys, blasted new tunnels, laid the foundations for After-Day. But no one has gone beyond this point. We—I and the rest of the expeditionary team from St. Kataretz—will be the first to venture into Night. It will be a dangerous endeavour, but I have faith in us, in the brave men and women who have accompanied me here.

My dear Velag, how would you have reacted to see these beautiful caves I sit in now, to see the secret culture of your enemy? I am surrounded by what can only be called their art, the lantern-light making pale tapestries of the rock walls on which Nightmares through the millennia scratched to life the dawn of their time, the history that followed, and its end, heralded by our arrival into their world.

In this history we are the enemy, bringing the terror of blinding fire into Evening, bringing the advanced weapons that caused their genocide. On these walls we are drawn in pale white dyes, bioluminescent in the dark, a swarm of smeared light advancing on the Nightmares' striking, jagged-angled representations of themselves, drawn in black dyes mixed from blood and minerals.

In this history Nightmares were alive when the last of the sunwyrms flew into Evening to scourge the land for prey. Whether this is truth or myth we don't know, but it might mean that Nightmares were around long before us. It might explain their adaptation to the darkness of outer Evening—their light-absorbent skin ancient camouflage to hide from sunwyrms under cover of the forests of Evening. We came into Evening with our fire (which they show sunwyrms breathing) and pale skins, our banners showing Dragon and the sun, and we were like a vengeful race of ghosts come to kill on behalf of those disappeared angels of Day, whom they worshipped to the end—perhaps praying for our retreat.

In halls arched by the ribcages and spines of ancient sunwyrm skeletons I have seen burial chambers; the bones of Nightmares and their children (whom we called imps because we didn't like to think of our enemy having young) piled high. Our bones lie here too, not so different from theirs. Tooth-marks show that they ate their dead, probably because of the scarcity of food in the fragile ecosystem of Evening. It is no wonder then that they ate our dead too—as we feared. It was not out of evil, but need.

We have so much yet to learn.

Perhaps it would have given you some measure of peace, Velag, to know that the Nightmares didn't want to destroy us, only to drive us back from their home. Perhaps not.

Ilydrin tells me it is time for us to head out. She is a member of our expedition—a biologist—and my partner. To hide the simple truth of our affection seems here, amidst the empty city of a race we destroyed, an obscenity. Confronted by the vast, killing beauty of our planet's second half, the stagnant moralities of our city-state appear a trifle. I adore Ilydrin, and I am glad she is here with me.

One team will stay here while ours heads out into Night. Ilydrin and I took a walk outside to test our Night-shells—armoured environmental suits to protect us from the lethal cold. We trod down from the caves of After-Day and into the unknown beyond, breath blurring our glass faceplates, our head-lamps cutting broad swathes through the snow-swarmed dark. We saw nothing ahead but an endless plain of ice—perhaps a frozen sea.

No spectral spires, no black banners of Night, no horde of Nightmares waiting to attack, no Dark Lord in his distant obsidian palace (an image Ilydrin and I righteously tore down many times in the form of those Army posters, during our early College vigils). We held each others' gloved hands and returned to Camp, sweating in our cramped shells, heavy boots crunching on the snow. I thought of you, Father, bravely venturing into bitter Evening to support your family. I thought of you, Brother, nobly marching against the horde for your Monarchy. I thought of you, Mother, courageously carrying your first child alone in that empty house before it became *our* home. I thought of you, Shadow—broken, tortured prisoner, baring your teeth to your captors in silence.

Out there, I was shaking—nervous, excited, queasy. I wasn't afraid.

I have Father's old photograph with the Nightmare's head (he took it down from above the mantelpiece after Velag died). I have a photograph of Mother, Father, Velag and I all dressed up before our trip to Weep-for-Day. And finally, a smiling portrait of Velag in uniform before he left for the Academy, his many pimples invisible because of the monochrome softness of the image. I keep these photographs with me, in the pockets of my overcoat, and take them out sometimes when I write.

So it begins. I write from the claustrophobic confines of the Night-Crawler, a steam-powered vehicle our friends at the College of Engineering designed (our accompanying professors named it with them, no doubt while drunk in a bar on University-Street). It is our moving camp. We'll sleep and eat and take shelter in it, and explore further and longer—at least a few vigils, we hope. If its engines fail, we'll have to hike back in our shells and hope for the best. The portholes are frosted over, but the team is keeping warm by stoking the furnace and singing. Ilydrin comes and tells me, her lips against my hair: "Val. Stop writing and join us." I tell her I will, in a minute. She smiles and walks back to the rest, her face flushed and soot-damp from the open furnace. I live for these moments.

I will lay down this pen now. A minute.

I don't know what we'll find out here. Maybe we *will* find the Dark Lord and his gathered horde of Nightmares. But at this point, even the military doesn't believe that, or they would have opposed the funding for this expedition or tried to hijack it.

Ilydrin says there's unlikely to be life so deep into Night—even Nightmares didn't venture beyond the mountains, despite our preconceptions. But she admits we've been wrong before. Many times. What matters is that we are somewhere new. Somewhere other than the City-of-Long-Shadows and the Penumbral territories, so marked by our history of fear. We need to see the rest of this world, to meet its other inhabitants—if there are others—with curiosity, not apprehension. And I know we will, eventually. This is our first, small step. I wish you were here with me to see it, Velag. You were but a child on this planet.

We might die here. It won't be because we ventured into evil. It will be because we sought new knowledge. And in that, I have no regrets, even if I'm dead when this is read. A new age is coming. Let this humble account be a preface to it.

what i learned at genie school

JOCKO BENOIT

That most people want pretty much
the same thing, except more of it
than the other guy has.

That when all the adepts impose
their favourite lunches on the cafeteria
everyone still complains about the food.

That the number three inspires so much
anticipation and even more dread.

That grammar is important, but so is
moral syntax and a fluency in consequences.

That each genie has infinite power
and infinite imagination but is
a slave in a wisher's market.

That when you live in a lamp your memory
of the outside is of breezes, clouds, and
scents that are not your own.

That you don't choose when your lamp
is rubbed or who does the rubbing.

That two thousand wishes would not be enough
to teach the short shelf life of the new.

That the genie union never gets collective
bargaining or better working conditions
and learns the first lessons of fatalism.

That centuries of service and ingratitude
make a genie want to give someone
exactly what they wish for.

That even the kindest wish hurts someone.

That most of the time you will sit in a dark
place lamenting your untapped potential.

aces

IAN ROGERS

Soelle got kicked out of school for killing one of her classmates.

They couldn't prove she actually did it, which was why she received an expulsion instead of a murder charge, but there was no doubt among the faculty that she was responsible.

Soelle told me she didn't care if they kicked her out or put her in jail. She just wanted her tarot cards back.

At dinner that night I asked her if she wanted to talk about it. Our parents should have been the ones dealing with this, but we hadn't seen them in four years.

"Talk about what?" Soelle snapped. "Tara Denton is such a baby. I read her cards wrong on purpose. She wasn't really going to die!"

"But she *did* die," I pointed out.

"Yeah, because she ran in front of a bus."

"So you did predict her death."

Soelle tilted her head to the side and gave me a long-suffering look, as if she was the older sibling and I was the younger. "We all predict our own deaths, Tobias."

"Nice. Where did you get that?"

She frowned. "*Ghost Whisperer*?"

"Why don't you tell me what actually happened."

Soelle blew a strand of her straggly blonde hair off her forehead and dropped her fork on the plate with a loud clink. She was going to be sixteen in August, but she still had the mannerisms of a young child. Most people grow up; Soelle was growing inward.

"It was Algebra and I was so bored I could die. I was feeling fidgety so I took out my tarot deck and started shuffling it, practising some of those fancy shuffles you taught me. I started snapping cards down on my desk—maybe a bit too loudly, I admit—and Tara, she was sitting beside me, started giving me these dirty looks. I shot one right back at her and asked if she wanted to play. Do you know what she said to me? She said, 'I don't gamble.' Like she had never seen a tarot deck before. What a zero. Anyway, Mrs. O'Reilly put some big complicated problem on the blackboard and said she had to step out for a few minutes. I heard she's a drunk, so I figured she was heading off to the boiler room to get juiced. Robbie Moore said he saw her in the parking lot one time and—"

"*Soelle.*"

"So the teacher left and I turned to Tara. She was kind of pissing me off at that point. I snapped down a few more cards, some of the trumps, and I said, 'Do these look like *playing* cards to you, sistah?' I was expecting Tara to say something smart, but she surprised me; she actually picked up the cards, one at a time, and looked at them. She asked me what they were, and I figured, what the hell, and I started explaining what tarot is. We weren't bonding or anything—I was still thinking she was a twit—but she seemed seriously interested. I could tell because she looked kind of scared. She probably heard some the rumours about me that are always floating around. . . ."

I nodded. "Go on."

"So I asked Tara if she wanted me to give her a reading. I told her she had to ask me to do it or else it wouldn't work. I don't think that's true—in fact I'm pretty sure it isn't—but it sounded kind of occult, sort of vampirish, and she seemed to eat it up. By then a few of the other kids had gathered around us, and Tara must've known it was too late to back out. So she started acting smarmy, telling me to play her cards and read her future, or am I too scared. I didn't like that. First she says 'play' her cards, right after I told her they weren't playing cards, and she says it in this joking tone, not for my benefit, or even hers, but because we had an audience. Then, to top it all off, she asks me if I'm scared, which I found doubly insulting since she was the one who was actually afraid. But then I figured out what the problem really was. What *her* problem was." Soelle paused for a moment, possibly to take a breath, more likely for effect. "I realized she wasn't scared *enough*."

"So that's what you did?" I said. "You scared her?"

"I don't care if people disrespect me. They can say whatever they want about me. They can write it on the bathroom walls—they could write it in neon on the front of the school, for all I care. But tarot isn't something to be laughed at. The cards don't like it. They told me so."

"Uh-huh. So what happened?"

"I dealt out her spread. Then I sat there for a while staring at her cards, looking like I was concentrating really hard on them. I knew the longer I took the more agitated Tara would get. So I started her reading—her *joke* reading, I might add. It wasn't real. I made it up. I just wanted to take her down a peg, and in front of all the jerks she was trying so hard to impress. I put on this serious expression and shook my head, telling her I didn't like what I saw. I began asking these medical questions, like if there was a history of heart problems in her family, is her father a smoker, stuff like that. Tara started getting freaked out. I had her cards laid out facedown, and I was flipping them over one at a time. The first card I turned over slowly and smoothly, barely making a sound, but each one after that I started snapping them louder and louder. When I flipped the last one—a card I slipped to the top of the deck on purpose without Tara noticing—it sounded like a gunshot, and Tara actually jumped in her seat. She was really scared, Toby. That last card was Death, which, as any self-respecting tarot reader will tell you, doesn't actually mean death but change."

"I would say death is a fairly big change."

Soelle's shoulders twitched in a small shrug. She was tall for her age and tended to slouch, which gave her the appearance of someone expressing perpetual indifference.

"Tara wanted to know if I was making it up. I told her I wouldn't do something like that. I told her that the cards would turn back on me if I read them incorrectly. I'm pretty sure that's bull, too, but it didn't matter much because Tara wasn't listening anyway. She stood up and started flapping her arms like she had to pee or something. She was breathing really fast and looking all around the room. She looked at me with these big saucer eyes and asked how she was going to die. Then I realized why she was looking all around like that. She was seeing death everywhere. I told her I didn't know how she was going to die, that the cards weren't that specific. Maybe she'd slip in the shower and break her neck. Or maybe she'd get kidnapped and chopped into little pieces."

"Or get hit by a bus," I added.

Soelle shrugged again. "Or that."

"Then what happened?"

"Some of the others were trying to calm her down. They tried to get her to sit back in her chair, but she pushed them away. She started saying something really fast. I didn't understand all of it, but I think she was worried that one of the chair legs was going to break and she was going to fall backwards and fracture her skull. She started moving down the aisle toward the door, turning around and around. She bumped into Jack Horton, who was just coming back from sharpening his pencil, and she started screaming at him, accusing him of trying to kill her. She was absolute loony tunes. She started spinning around pointing at the chalkboard, the globe, even Blinky the classroom iguana—screaming about death, death everywhere. Then she ran out of the room. Nobody followed her, but some of the others went over to the windows. A few moments later we saw her come running out of the school and into the street. The buses were just arriving and"—Soelle drove her fist into her palm—"el smacko."

"You sound real broken up about it."

"Tara Denton wasn't my friend. She was some twit I sat next to in Algebra who believed too much in tarot. I didn't like her, but I didn't kill her."

"And yet you got kicked out of school."

"They've been waiting to do that for a long time," Soelle said, with a noticeable lack of resentment. "Ever since the school mascot drowned himself."

"Right," I said. "Because he thought he was a real shark."

Soelle shrugged. "That's the rumour."

"Seems to be a lot of rumours at that high school," I mentioned. "Most of them about you. Would it kill you to make some friends?"

"I don't need friends. Just my brother."

She gave me her NutraSweet grin: full of artificial sweetness.

I remember the day when I became an adult.

It was four years ago. I was eighteen and Soelle was eleven. I'd just graduated from high school. My student co-op at the paper mill had turned into a full-time job. I drove a forklift. The hours were long, the work monotonous, but it was union and the pay was decent. I wondered if it was possible to do this kind of mindless labour for the next thirty or forty years without developing some sort of psychotic disorder. I was thinking about getting my own place and finding a girl to take back to it.

One day I came home from work and found Soelle sitting on the porch swing. She was drinking an Orange Crush and reading one of her Anne of Green Gables books.

"Mom and Dad are gone," she said.

"What do you mean they're gone?"

"They're gone." She took a sip of her drink. "I went out walking this morning, and when I came back they were gone."

I looked over at my car sitting in the driveway, parked behind my parents' station wagon. "Where did they go?"

"I don't know," Soelle said. "I thought they went visiting, but they haven't come back."

"Well that's it, then. They've just gone over to the Mullens' or the Heaths'. They'll be back."

Soelle lowered her book and gave me a patronizing look. "Mom and Dad haven't gone visiting in years, Toby. Where have *you* been?"

I was beginning to wonder that myself. I felt like I had been away much longer than seven hours. More like seven years.

I left Soelle on the porch and checked the house from top to bottom. There was no sign of our parents. No sign that they had suddenly packed up and left, but no sign that they had been dragged out of the house by force, either. No sign of anything at all. It was like they had been ghosts haunting the place rather than flesh and blood people who had once lived here. My memories of them felt hazy already.

I didn't feel scared or frantic. I felt angry. I didn't know why I felt that way, and that made me angrier. Where they hell could they have gone? Why would they leave me alone with Soelle?

I called the police and they searched the house. They talked to the neighbours. They asked for phone numbers of our other relatives, but we didn't have anyone we were close to.

The police came to the same conclusion I had reached hours earlier: that our parents had left the house seemingly of their own volition, but with absolutely no evidence of having done so. Their belongings hadn't been disturbed or removed and their luggage was still stacked in the crawl space. The neighbours didn't recall seeing them leave the house, nor did they report seeing any unusual people in the area.

Time passed. Days turned into weeks, and I kept waiting for a social worker from the Children's Aid Society to come and take us away. Soelle and I would be placed in a province-run care facility until adequate foster homes could be found. They would try and keep us together, but there were no guarantees. We would eventually be passed off to different families. Over the next few years Soelle and I would exchange birthday cards, Christmas presents, the occasional letter, but eventually we'd drift apart until we finally forget we even had a brother or sister. It was stuff shitty made-for-TV melodramas are made of.

But it didn't happen. The social worker never showed up. I thought maybe Soelle and I had slipped through the cracks, as so many kids are supposed to do, if you believe the news magazine shows. The truth was much simpler.

They didn't come because I was eighteen and working. The mortgage was already paid off, and I was bringing in enough to cover the bills and keep us fed. I had grown up without realizing it. I was an adult.

Soelle had a reputation as an unusual child even before she started school.

My earliest memory of an "incident," which was what our parents called the strange things that happened in Soelle's presence, occurred when Soelle was two years old and I was nine. We were in the back yard, Soelle playing in her turtle kiddie pool, me sitting on the swing set that I was already too big for. I was bored out of my skull. I had been tasked with keeping an eye on Soelle and making sure she didn't drown herself in fourteen inches of water.

Something caught my attention in the farmer's field that our property backed onto. I don't recall what it was. A deer, maybe. I wandered over to check it out, and when I came back, no more than two minutes later, the turtle pool was gone.

The pool wasn't very big, but it was a painfully bright lime green that stood out on our parched yellow lawn like a radioactive spotlight. Still, it took me a moment to realize it was gone. Part of that was because Soelle was still right where I had left her, blonde hair in a ponytail, decked out in her My Little Pony bathing suit, and sitting in the spot where the pool had been only a moment ago.

"Soelle," I said, "where's the pool?"

"It's gone!" She was crying and slapping at the ground, which was turning muddy from the hose that was still spraying out water.

"Where did it go?"

I was thinking some kid must have come into our yard and taken it.

"It went away!" There were tears on her face. I remember that because she wasn't the kind of kid who cried very often. She raised her hands, the hose still gripped in one of them, and sent a spray of water into the air.

I actually looked up then, half-expecting to see a green turtle-shaped pool floating in the sky over my head.

Of course there was nothing there when I looked.

But I saw plenty of other strange things over the years since then.

After Soelle got kicked out of school, she started disappearing most nights. I'd be walking past her door on my way to bed and, more often than not, her room would be empty, the bedsheets neat and undisturbed. She was always back in the morning, acting as though she hadn't left, and although I questioned her about it at first, she always gave me the same reply: "I was just out walking."

After a couple of weeks of this, I started going out looking for her. Silver Falls isn't a very big town, but it still took me a few nights to find her, walking barefoot along the banks of the Black Creek, near the Cross Street bridge. She was wearing her nightgown, and looked like an oversized child.

"What are you doing down there?" I called from the bridge railing.

"Oh, I'm just looking around," she said, her arms held out to either side, walking along the water's edge, one foot stepping in front of the other like she was walking on a tightrope.

"What are you looking for?" I spoke in a low, harsh whisper. I didn't know why I bothered. We were on the edge of town, almost into the woods, and there were no houses nearby. Even if there were, no one would have thought anything of it. Not if they knew it was Soelle.

She giggled and disappeared under the bridge. I swore under my breath and went around to where the embankment slanted down to the creek bed. Soelle was staring up at the underside of the bridge. I tried to see what she was looking at, but it was too dark.

"I asked what you're doing out here. Don't you know it's after midnight?"

Soelle shrugged. "I'm looking for dead bodies."

I wasn't sure I heard her right. The creek was very loud under the bridge.

"Did you say dead bodies?"

Soelle gave a small nod, still staring upward. "I watched a TV show about police psychics. The kind used to track down dead bodies. They said most bodies are found in the vicinity of water. Lakes, rivers, ponds. I got to thinking about it and realized I've never seen a dead body before."

"And that's a bad thing?"

"Sure. I don't like the idea of not experiencing all that life has to offer."

"So you decided to go out in the middle of the night and look for dead bodies."

"Yes."

"Anyone in particular?"

"No. Anybody will do." She giggled. "Any *body* will do."

I hesitated, picking my words carefully. "You realize how messed up that sounds?"

Soelle turned and looked at me, and I felt a momentary pang of terror. Then her brow creased in puzzlement. She was looking at something above my head. I looked up and saw something hovering there: a small white rectangle. "What . . ."

Soelle touched my arm, startling me. She was standing right in front of me now. "Give me a boost."

I hunched over and laced my fingers together. She slipped her foot into the cup formed by my hands and I hoisted her up gently. I tried to crane my head back, but it was all I could do to keep from dumping us both into the creek. I looked over at the dark water churning by. There was something strange about it; something I hadn't noticed earlier. I couldn't be sure—it was too dark—but I thought it was flowing in the wrong direction.

"Got it!" Soelle said. I lowered her to the ground. She was holding the white rectangle in her hand, flipping it back and forth between her fingers. "Now *this* is exciting," she said.

It was a playing card.

The ace of hearts.

A few weeks after that, I came home to find Soelle in the front yard holding a leash. She was dragging it back and forth across the lawn like she was walking an invisible dog. I came over and saw there was a collar on the end of the leash. It was red with the words my favourite pet embroidered on it.

"Dare I ask?"

Soelle smiled. "I went down to the store to get a chocolate milk, and the guy behind the counter called me a witch."

"He said that," I said, sceptically, "right out of the blue?"

"Well . . ." Soelle hesitated. "I asked him if he had seen any aces lately."

"Any aces."

"Like the one I found under the bridge. I'm looking for the rest of them. I thought he might've seen one of them around. That's when he started looking at me funny. He said he recognized me and that people were talking about me."

"So what else is new?"

"They've always talked, but no one's ever called me a witch before."

"And what, you're worried they're going to burn you at the stake?"

"No, of course not. The guy in the store did say he'd call the cops if I didn't leave, though. He was a real *ace*-hole. But it got me thinking, what if he did call the cops? How would the poh-lease deal with a witch?"

"I think they shoot them on sight," I told her, "but they use silver bullets."

"That's for werewolves, you nerd."

"What does it matter? You're not a witch. People in town, they're just . . ."

"Yes?"

"They don't know what to make of you."

"Maybe I am a witch."

"You're still young. You can be whatever you want."

Soelle shrugged. "Maybe I want to be a witch."

"A witch who looks for aces. Sounds like a wise career choice."

"Thank you."

"It still doesn't explain the leash."

"Oh, this." She held it up like she didn't even know it was in her hand. "This is for my familiar. I figure if I'm gonna be a witch, I'd better start acting the part."

"You're already acting the part," I said. "That's why people think you're a witch."

Soelle nodded thoughtfully. "Toush."

"That's touché, you nerd."

Soelle started dragging the leash with her everywhere she went. This went on for about two weeks, and then one day I noticed her without it.

"Give up on the familiar?" I inquired.

"No," she said, smiling brightly. "I already found one."

"Oh?"

"He's been living with us for the last week, as if you didn't notice."

"I'm afraid I didn't."

Soelle turned her head to the side, as if hearing something I could not. "Oh," she said. "You can't see him. Only I can."

"What happened to the leash?"

"He doesn't like wearing the leash. He said it was degrading to his person."

"He actually said that? Degrading to his person?"

"Yes. The Haxanpaxan is quite sophisticated. He's going to help me find the rest of my aces."

"The Haxanpaxan?" I said. "What's that, a zebra or something?"

"It's a name." Soelle rolled her eyes at me. "And I wouldn't make jokes about it. The Haxanpaxan doesn't have a sense of humour."

"Sounds like he's a lot of fun at a party."

Soelle glared at me. "I'd watch that."

Ahh, the Haxanpaxan. How he made our lives so very interesting.

"Soelle, I told you to turn off the TV if you're not watching it."

"The Haxanpaxan's watching it."

"The Haxanpaxan is watching *Canada's Next Top Model*?"

"He likes it. He says the models remind him of himself."

"Soelle, did you leave the back door open?"

"The Haxanpaxan did. He went outside to do his business."

"Well, can you tell him to close it when he's done?"

"You don't *tell* the Haxanpaxan to do anything."

"Can you ask him, then? Pretty please, with sugar on top?"

"Toby, do you remember what I said about being funny?"

"Soelle, do you know anything about the Conroys' minivan getting smashed up last night?"

"I'm afraid not, Toby. But on a side note: the Haxanpaxan doesn't like minivans. And he doesn't like the colour lime green. He finds it offensive to the senses."

"Uh-huh. The back door was open again all night."

"The Haxanpaxan was out."

"Doing his business?"

"No, silly. He was looking for aces."

On an unseasonably warm Saturday in March, I was outside on the porch swing reading the paper when Soelle came skipping up the cobblestone path.

"Hard day at the office?" I asked.

"Look what we found."

She was bouncing around and waving something in her hand. It took me a moment to figure out what it was: a playing card. The ace of clubs.

"The Haxanpaxan was the one who found it, actually. He's very smart."

"Where did you find it?"

"Mrs. Ferguson's birdbath."

"Mrs. Ferguson?" I pictured an old woman who lived alone with her pet Rottweiler. An animal she could've thrown a saddle on and ridden around town. "You went into her back yard?"

"Duh. That's where her birdbath is."

"What about Kramer? Wasn't he outside?"

Soelle flashed me a wicked grin. "Oh, he was there all right. But one look from the Haxanpaxan and his fur turned completely white."

"Uh-huh."

"Yep. Then he ran around the side of the house and we went over and got the card."

"Aces."

"That's right." She winked at me and skipped up the porch steps and went inside. I was picking up my paper when I heard the porch steps creak. The front door swung open on its own, then closed again.

Just the wind, I thought.

Soelle called me from a pay phone and told me I had to come over to Mrs. O'Reilly's house.

"Who?" I asked, groggily. I had been asleep. I looked over at the clock radio and saw it was half past two in the morning. "Do you know what time it is?"

"It's not important. You need to get over here now."

"Who's Mrs. O'Reilly?"

"My Algebra teacher. Duh!"

Soelle gave me the address, but the house turned out to be easy to find. It was the one on fire.

A pair of fire engines were parked out front, blocking off the street. Firefighters ran hither and yon, dragging heavy canvas hoses. A group of rubberneckers stood off to one side. Soelle was among them.

"What the hell's going on?" I asked her in a low voice so the others wouldn't hear.

"I didn't do it," Soelle said immediately. "The Haxanpaxan did."

"There *is* no Haxanpaxan."

"The Haxanpaxan doesn't like it when—"

I grabbed her roughly by the arm. "Stop it, Soelle. This is serious."

"You're telling me."

She nodded at the house. The firefighters had stopped running and were staring at it, too.

The flames were green.

"So you're saying you didn't burn down your Algebra teacher's house because she was the one who confiscated your deck of tarot cards and got you expelled."

"Ex."

"What?"

"She was my ex-Algebra teacher. I feel the need to have that stated for the record."

"The record? You're not on trial, Soelle."

"Really? You could've fooled me."

"You said the Haxanpaxan did it."

"That's right."

"But there is no Haxanpaxan."

"I wish you would stop saying that. It makes him very angry."

"Was the Haxanpaxan angry at Mrs. O'Reilly?"

"No. I guess you could say he was angry on my behalf."

"And that's why he burned down her house."

"I don't control the Haxanpaxan, Toby. He knew I was upset, and I guess he just took it out on her."

"Well, that's just . . . just . . ."

"Aces?"

"No, Soelle, it isn't aces. It's the exact opposite of aces."

I got a phone call from the guy who owned the convenience store. He said Soelle was loitering around outside, and if I didn't come down and collect her, he was going to call the police. I realized this was the guy who started all the witch talk. He sounded terrified. As I got in the car and drove over, I wondered how he got our phone number.

Soelle wasn't there when I pulled into the strip mall. I parked and went around back to where the dumpsters were. I found her writing on the brick wall with a piece of pink chalk. She was drawing squares, one next to the other, one stacked on top of another.

"What the hell are you doing?"

"What does it look like?"

"It looks like you're tagging the back of the store."

"Tagging? Oh, Toby, you're so street." She snickered and kept on drawing. "And it's not graffiti. It'll wash off in the rain."

"Then what are you doing?"

"Testing a theory," she said vaguely.

She drew one final square, then walked back to where I was standing. She handed me the piece of chalk and walked further back, toward the screen of trees between the plaza and the lake. She stopped on the grassy verge, turned around, and suddenly ran full-tilt at the wall. I started to call out, but she sped past me, arms pumping, brow furrowed in concentration.

At the last moment, she leaped into the air, throwing her legs out in front of her like a long-jumper, and landed on the wall.

And stuck to it.

She stood frozen there, in a half-crouch, on the wall. Then, slowly, she began to stand up straight . . . or rather, sideways. She was standing in the middle of the first square she had drawn. She hesitated a moment, then hopped sideways and landed on the next one. I tilted my head, trying to watch her, but it was disorienting. It was one thing to see her defying gravity by sticking to the wall, but it was quite another to watch her hop up and down in a sidelong fashion. It was like watching someone walking up the crazy stairs in an M.C. Escher print.

It wasn't until Soelle reached the final square and turned around and hopped back that I realized what she was doing.

Playing hopscotch.

Things quieted down a bit after that.

Soelle didn't do anything too weird, and there were no unusual occurrences in town. It was a textbook Silver Falls summer: hot, quiet, and uneventful.

September arrived and the kids went back to school. October came and the leaves started changing colour. Everything was still quiet. I started to think maybe it was just a phase Soelle had gone through. Like puberty or something. I thought about getting her back into school, or at least helping to get her high-school equivalency. On the one hand I was surprised I hadn't received a summons from juvenile court. On the other it was just another example of how removed Soelle was from everyday life.

I had asked Soelle what she wanted to do with her life, and she told me her first priority was to find those last two aces. I told Soelle we'd have to work on that, but until then maybe she'd like to help me rake the leaves.

I told her to get started while I went down to the hardware store to buy some paper leaf bags. As I was coming out of the store, I happened to look across the street at the people lounging around in Orchard Park. They were all looking up at the sky. I went over to see what was going on. I tried to follow their collective stare, but I couldn't see anything. Then I saw it, something small and dark floating high above the trees. It looked like a black balloon. Everyone was talking in low, excited voices, some of them pointing. An old man holding a bag of bread crumbs he had been using to feed the pigeons was shaking his head and saying, "It ain't right. No sir, it ain't right at all."

Whatever it was, it started to come down closer to the ground. It bounced back up, then came down again, lower this time, and I could make out what it was.

Soelle.

She was wearing a black dress and black shoes (part of her witch's wardrobe, I assumed). As I watched her descend lower, one of the shoes slipped off her foot and fell into the park fountain with a splash.

"Heads up!" she called down in a giggling voice.

"Soelle!" I shouted. "Come down from there!"

I felt absurd saying those words. Like I was only asking her to come down off the roof.

"Are you kidding?" she hollered back. "Do you know how long it took me to get up here? I've been working on this for weeks!"

"Get down right *now*!"

"Don't be such a drag." She swung around in a lazy turn and started coming down lower. She brushed the top of one of the tall elms and called out: "Oh, wow!"

"Be careful!"

She came floating down to the ground, looking like a gothy version of Mary Poppins (*sans* umbrella). The people in the park ran away, some of them screaming.

"This can only end well," I said, watching them scatter.

Soelle waved a dismissive hand. "They're just jealous," she said. "Forget them. Look what I found at the top of that tree!"

She passed it to me.

The ace of spades.

The van showed up the day after the levitation incident.

I knew something was coming. There was a tension in the air, the kind that reminded me of the wet-battery smell before a powerful thunderstorm.

I was in Soelle's room changing her sheets. Not that there was any sign she actually slept in her bed those days. I was just going through the motions of a normal life. I was putting on the pillowcases and staring at the spider that built a web outside Soelle's window every spring. The web it had made this year was bizarre to say the least. It was all over the place, for one. It was coming apart in places and in others the webbing had been spun into strange, almost geometric shapes.

I was watching the spider running madly back and forth when the van pulled up: a white van with no markings on it except a plus sign on the side. Sort of like the Red Cross only black.

A man and a woman got out, both dressed conservatively—the man in a dark suit, the woman in a skirt and jacket ensemble. They looked like Jehovah's Witnesses. The man was carrying a briefcase, but I didn't think there were copies of *The Watchtower* inside.

I reached the front door just as they were knocking on it.

"Hello," the man said. "My name is Waldo Rand. This is my partner, Leah." He motioned to the woman behind him without taking his eyes off me. "May we speak with you?"

"About what?"

"You have a sister." It wasn't a question. "May we see her?"

I turned my head and looked into the living room. Soelle was sitting on the floor amid a drift of our father's old *National Geographics*.

"What for?" she asked gruffly.

"This won't take very long," Waldo assured me. "And it won't hurt," he added to Soelle, who didn't look convinced. "Just have a seat here." He gestured to the table in the dining room. Reluctantly Soelle came over and took a seat across from Waldo. His partner, Leah, stood in the doorway, one hand resting on her hip, fingers tapping against a bulge under her jacket.

"Do you have a lot of friends, Soelle?"

Soelle stared at him for a moment before answering. "No. I don't need any."

"Not even an imaginary one? Someone only you can see? Do you have one of those?"

"Yesss," Soelle said slowly.

"Is he or she in this room right now?"

Soelle made an effort of looking all around her, then she shook her head.

"She's burning hot," Leah mentioned in a strangely casual voice.

Waldo took out a folded piece of paper, unfolded it, and put it down with a pen in front of Soelle. "Can you draw me a picture of him?"

Soelle stared at the paper, then raised her eyes up to Waldo.

"The Haxanpaxan doesn't like to be drawn, does he?" he said.

Soelle shook her head.

"Have you ever played with tarot cards?"

"You don't *play* with tarot cards."

"I've never seen anyone shift like this before," Leah said in a low, awe-filled voice. She raised one of her hands toward Soelle, fingers wavering slowly back and forth. "I'm surprised she's even visible."

"*Leah*," Waldo said curtly. He turned back to Soelle. "Have you ever *used* tarot cards before?"

"Yes."

"A girl died," I mentioned.

"I didn't kill her! She ran in front of a bus."

Waldo held up a calming hand. "It's okay. We're not here about that."

"Then why are you here?" Soelle snapped.

"We just have one more question." Waldo cleared his throat. "Have you ever played . . . Have you ever used a Ouija board?"

"No," she said emphatically.

Waldo let out a deep breath. He wiped his brow and looked over his shoulder at his partner. She crossed her arms and leaned back against the wall. "Thank God for small favours," she said.

Waldo stood up and led me into the kitchen.

"May I call you Tobias?"

I nodded.

"Tobias, your sister is . . ."

"Please don't say special."

"I was going to say dangerous."

"That's awfully . . . frank."

Waldo frowned. "I'm afraid I don't know any other way to be."

"It's okay," I told him. "It's just unexpected. I've become sort of used to—"

"Covering up for your sister?" Waldo finished. "Making excuses for her? We know, Tobias. We know all about it."

"What do you mean by that?"

"Soelle is having an adverse effect on reality. She's out of phase.

She's not supposed to be here. I'm sure you've noticed some unusual phenomena while in her presence. People and animals acting strangely, unusual weather, apports . . ."

"Apports?"

"Objects that appear seemingly out of thin air."

"What kinds of objects?"

Waldo gestured vaguely.

"Like playing cards?" I suggested.

"Sure," Waldo said. "Small objects usually."

"Soelle's been finding playing cards—aces, specifically—around town. She's become intent on finding them."

"Aces?" Leah said, coming up behind us.

"Yes," I said. "She found one under a bridge. Another in a tree—a tree that she was levitating over at the time."

"Levitation." Leah's gaze drifted away for a moment, then came back in force, boring into me. "Has she found them all?"

"No. She's found three of them so far."

Leah turned to Waldo and said, "We need to move quickly."

Waldo cleared his throat and turned to face me.

"Tobias, we have a man in our employ. A psychic. He has the ability to see the future in his dreams. He lives in one of our most remote stations, in Lhasa. That's in Tibet. The Roof of the World, they call it. We have him there because the high elevation causes people to dream in extremely vivid detail. It makes his ability that much more potent."

"What does this have to do with Soelle?"

"This man," Waldo said, "he's been dreaming of her. In those dreams, Soelle destroys the planet."

"She's not supposed to be here," Leah muttered.

"Where is she supposed to be?" I said. "Tibet?"

Waldo shook his head. "It's not important. All you need to know is that she can't stay here." He reached out and gave my shoulder a firm but comforting squeeze.

"Tobias, your sister needs to come with us."

Soelle didn't put up a fight. In fact, she wanted to go.

"I have to widen my search," she said. "You understand."

"Sure," I said. You could have filled a barn with all the things I didn't understand at this point.

I offered to help pack her stuff, but Leah said it wasn't necessary.

"We'll get her new clothes," she assured me. "We'll take care of her."

Waldo shook my hand and thanked me. I didn't know for what, but I said "You're welcome" anyway. Then they stepped outside to let me say good-bye to Soelle.

"Take care of the Haxanpaxan for me," she said.

"He's not going with you?"

"Leah says there's only room for me."

"Too bad."

"Yeah, but at least neither of you will be lonely."

I nodded. "Be good, Soelle."

She gave me her NutraSweet grin. "I'll try." Then she did something she hadn't done since she was little: she kissed me on the cheek.

Then she was gone.

I watched the van drive away. The plus sign on the side was gone. In its place were three wavy lines. I didn't know what that meant.

One more thing to add to the list.

After a while I went upstairs. As I was passing Soelle's room, the door slammed shut. I tried to open it, but it wouldn't budge.

The door still doesn't open, and I haven't been in her room since.

No one ever questioned Soelle's disappearance. I never called the police, and no one ever came around asking about her. I think it was more than just the town being glad she was gone. Maybe she really didn't belong here.

I heard from her only once. I got a letter. It was postmarked from a town in Mexico, some place I couldn't even pronounce. It contained two items. One was a colour photograph of a Mayan pyramid. On the back she had written: *I found it, Toby. It was here all along.*

The other item was a playing card.

The ace of diamonds.

no poisoned comb
AMAL EL-MOHTAR

For Caitlyn Paxson and Jessica P. Wick

A story in the teeth of time
will shift its outlined shape, be chewed
to more palatable stuff.
Thus death; thus cold demands
for a hot hot heart,
for slivers to simmer in warm plum wine
on winter nights.

Nonsense.

They say I told him to bring me her heart,
but I didn't.

It is a fact well known
that the fashion for wearing hearts on sleeves
has passed. Young girls today,
with their soft looks, their sharp lashes,
wear their hearts as cunning hooks
in their cheeks—that supple flesh
so like to apples, so red, so white,
smelling of fall and summer both,
of sweet between the teeth.

My huntsman hungered.
So did his knife.
Do you eat the red cheeks,
I said to him that day,
and I will eat the core.

I cored her. Oh
her looks might've hooked
the hearts of mirrors, of suitors
in dozened dimes, but my huntsman
hooked her looks, carved sweet slices,
blooded the snow of her face, and I
gave her the gift of a fabled room
whose walls were mirrors.
The tale is wrong. Their way
is kinder, I confess.

But mine is fair.

what a picture doesn't say
CHRISTOPHER WILLARD

BOB BEZERHKO

A man who lies about his name and carries a varnished cane will never babysit my future kids. I see him from a distance. He dances poorly this Bob Bezerhko. He shimmies like he can go from zero to vermouth in a second. Framing him are two perhaps-strippers if the dank boas are a clue to intent. Alligator Skin and the Rubber Woman sit nearby, mentioned only because they are not pictured.

I wander past the sideshow stage and linger at the crude canvas tarps. Animals, humans, all are frozen. Jolly ripe depictions of a past that separated oddities, freaks—whoa, diversity, and political correctness hiding around here? How to look? How to resist?

DUCKS WITH 4 WINGS! ALIVE!

Duck Wins Fast Flier Record? Or. Glued on Flappers from a Dead Relative? Too depressing. True story: In a room while waiting to have my prostate palpitated I read in *Chinese Cooking for Exeprets*, and this is a quote, "If peopel can manufacture ducks wiht for wings then restaranteres very happ men."

HALF BEAR, HALF MONKEY! ALIVE!

I'm thinking marmoset or red panda. Next.

MIDGET HORSES, ALIVE!

Last week after Eight Belles broke its front legs at the Kentucky Derby a thought popped into my head, "What about the midget horses?" Here they are, Alive! On the painted canvas a beefy man, whose head comes out of his chest, grasps the manes of two tiny horses. The Strong Man's legs are too short. What kind of stunt-legged-depicting Michelangelo did this art?

FOUR-LEGGED DUCKS. ALIVE!

What is it with this Alive! thing? What is this four appendage fetish? City dwellers will never pay to see mutant livestock. We can't even wrap our head around the fact hotdogs come from pig or weasel, or wherever they come from. I suspect such bizarre animals shock norms central to central states. "Okay, listen up kids, this is your principal speaking. We've just heard that the Iowa State Fair has a Rhode Island Red with a hair lip, Alive! Busses are waiting out front."

MIDGET BULL! ALIVE!

Probably a good thing, but I can't figure out why. Minute steaks? I'll have the half ounce T-bone please.

MINIATURE STALLION. ALIVE!

I already saw the poster for the midget bull. Skip.

KNIFE THROWER!

Bob Bezerhko proves no patter is so mundane that yelling won't help. "Step right up, all and one, gents and dames, boys and girls, washed and unwashed. Five gets you a back row seat. Shudder as he flings blades of razor sharp steel at our half-naked Hilda. All this while blindfolded!" I'm sure the painter means the knife thrower and not the audience.

"See Fat Boy, the world's darling weighing in at a delicate 856 pounds. Ask him what he eats in a day! Try to lift him!"

THE MERMAID

So they captured the mermaid. She doesn't appear too upset. Her marlin tail displays rings of blue, violet, and dill pickle green. Blonde seaweed hair covers her breasts. She's such a prude when out of water. Play a game? Old man and the sea? Oh yes, she ain't that little either.

KNIFE THROWER REDUX

Buff, Italian. Protruding rump and head jutting from his shoulders, again. Here's a trick you artists, if you really can't paint necks, just omit them. Or, could be he just hated tall people? The thrower holds his arm in the air, ready, counterbalanced by purple bell-bottoms. Across the painting Hilda strains against her ties in a flesh-coloured bikini that must have fooled hundreds. The knife thrower wears the expression of intense concentration, Hilda the expression of skipped portrait classes. Twenty or so stilettos describe her sleek outline. At least as many more are plugged like duckpins into a table near the thrower. Three Medieval axes suggest drunken fun back in the trailer.

OLGA AND HELGA HELM

Two-headed baby or one-bodied babies? Where does one get such grammatical advice? Helm from the Norse *hjalm* for rudder or the old English *helan*. Thus the sentence: "The two-headed baby scudded aimlessly across the map much like a ship without a helm." Note the incredibly witty play on the name! A fabulously painted nurse who looks even more fabulous in her hospital green operating garb hands off Olga/Helga to the eager mother who looks fabulous too in her stunning Spring ensemble of hospital green. She seems to have somehow forgotten that less than few minutes ago she pushed a two-headed monstrosity through a less than apt birth canal. In the corner of the painting are the words, "Frighteningly Factual Facsimile."

IMAGINARIUM 2013

PAUL AND PAULA

Half man, half woman. Psychologists posit there are now five genders: man, woman, man born as woman, woman born as man, and transgendered. Paul and Paula make six don't they? What a romantic stroll they take on the moonlit pier. How their loving narcissism beckons, how they demonstrate the ultimate gesture of self-love. Is s/he onanist, this man and manna?

POPEYE, THE MAN WITH THE ELASTIC EYEBALLS

Dropped the ball here. They could have written Al-EYE-ve! Ping pong anyone? He's not sneaking a peek at the mermaid is he? Can he see that the turned down corners of his mouth suggest he may not be as awed as we are?

TATTOOED WOMAN

Teen revolt mixed with Potemkin village. Yawn.

EEKA ALIVE!

Eeka, the wild teeth-gnashing woman of every man's dreams. Eeka the nasty half-clad with an insatiable appetite, wink. Eeka in leopard bikini with matching tail has lazy eyes. Don't be fooled. No man survives Eeka the black widow of the human world. From the tropical unnamed paradise it is Eeka the captured, Eeka Alive! Eeka in all her Tongan toplessness. Eeka feasts upon an arm ripped from a fallen maiden who was more than likely warned many times not to go out alone at night looking for that elusive nutmeg oil. Eeka grinds her teeth against the elbow. How can she not know where the meat is? The dripping blood is as red as the areolas on her large breasts. Then it hits me she could have played the tobacconist in Fellini's *Amarcord*. Eeka, oh sweet deadly Eeka! And it hits me, I sure would like one of those sausage on a roll with fried onion things.

HOO LA LA ALIVE!

The dichotomous sibling of Eeka sways from the happy side of the Pacific basin. She walks tall on black strapped heels and she offers, with flapping hands, a simple lei. But, I ask, does her smiling demeanour make her any less pigfaced? A rolled scroll lies behind her, upon which must be inscribed many secrets such as the Siren song that lured Captain Cook to his death and just why Hot Pockets® has so many fans.

LEGLESS WOMAN!

Her name is Julie Klepterschurrer although if asked she will deny her stint in the Stuchenhier prison. She debuted at Coney Island where she used to lie on stage and describe how she lost her legs in a waterskiing accident. She married Mr. Lift It who picked up cement blocks with a hook through his nipples. She's advertised too, I'd like to point out.

SIDE SHOW, ALIVE!

I push five bucks into the hand of Bob Bezerhko who now pushes tickets. Inside the tent the lights dim as I survey a gum-covered bench. Fat Boy trundles out. Years ago he would have been called Harry's Beef Trust.

"If you're wondering what I weigh, I weigh 856 pounds, not a pound less an not a pound more." His voice resonates like turkeys fighting in a kettle drum. "Ask me a question." I mentally calculate how many of the spectators will equal his weight.

"Go ahead," Fat Boy says.

Bob Bezerhko suddenly speaks over a microphone, "Get your fill of Fat Boy because he's already gotten his fill of dinner."

"Ask me any questions you want like what I et for breakfast," says Fat Boy who then answers before anyone asks. "Okay I'll tell ya what I et for breakfast. I et two dozen eggs, extra large, and a loaf a bread an butter, two pounds of bacon, an I drunk a gallon a whole milk, an a gallon a orange juice, an for dessert I et ten pancakes, and a pile a sausages."

He pauses, "Oh yeah, an a espresso."

"Okay, ask me another question," he says. "What did I et for lunch?

Okay I'll tell ya I et a loaf a bread an a pound a bologna an a tub a mustard an five dozen cans a beef ravioli an I drunk a gallon a whole milk an I et a package a Oreo cookies, an a whole punkin pie an a half with whip cream."

Fat Boy thinks for a moment and adds, "Oh, an a espresso."

A farmer next to me tugs his overalls in an American Gothic moment and says, "Is that just your gut or do you have a double hernia?" A woman answers, "Gonads the size of Rhode Island."

"Ask me what I et for Dinner," Fat Boy continues. "Okay I'll tell ya what I et for dinner. I had me one of them bar-be-ques and I et two packs a hot dogs an two packs a hot dog rolls and a couple a pounds a hamburger an a bag a hamburger rolls and a bag of vin'gar chips an a jar of sweet pickles an a gallon a whole milk an for dessert I et a tub a vanilla ice cream an a jar a butterscotch sauce." Then fat boy stares at us for a long time and we stare back.

"What about the espresso?" someone asks.

"Not at night. Too much coffee gives me the shits."

Then we can pay an extra buck to see Rubber Woman squeezed into a tiny box and another buck to see Alligator Skin who sits behind a screen and then a man comes out with a cardboard box that contains broken glass and a lightbulb, which he proceeds to crack and chew.

BOB BEZERHKO

I corner him as I'm leaving the tent. "Cheap show ya got here," I say.

"No refunds," he states flatly.

"Advertising the legless woman and then leaving us empty-handed. You have her on a banner out front."

"Yeah well a picture says a thousand things, don't it," says Bob. "One of them things it don't say is how she ran away with that asshole who ran Tahiti Boat." And then he throws me a look that lies somewhere between a punch in the Adam's apple and a bald-faced lie.

the last islander

MATTHEW JOHNSON

Saufatu stood neck-deep in the water, watching the dawn arrive over the great empty ocean to the east. He raised the coconut shard in his right hand to his mouth and nibbled on the flesh, enjoying the mixture of sweet and salty flavors, then quickly glanced over his shoulder at the shore. He knew before looking that there would be no-one there: even Funafuti, the biggest of the Eight Islands, was nearly always empty except on Independence Day. Here on Niulakiti, the first of the islands to sink, he had never seen another soul.

He turned back to the sea, took another bite of his coconut and frowned. Something was out there. He squinted, trying to make out the dark smudge perhaps a half kilometre out towards the horizon. It looked like someone swimming, or rather thrashing at the surface; suddenly he remembered what he had put out there, realized what was happening, and pushed himself out into the waves.

It had been a long time since he had been swimming, but a childhood spent in the sea had inscribed his muscles with the necessary motions. He inhaled and exhaled salt spray with each stroke, getting nearer and nearer to the man—for he could now see that it was a man, dark-haired and tanned but unmistakeably white—who was struggling for his life. The snout and fin of the grey reef shark, rising and falling from the water as it fought to draw the man down, completed the picture.

"Bop it on the snout!" Saufatu called as he got closer, hoping the man spoke English.

The man, who to this point had not yet noticed him, looked his way and tilted his head.

"Bop it on the snout!" Saufatu shouted again. He slowed to tread water for a moment, raised his left hand out of the water and smacked it against his nose twice.

The man turned back to the shark, which was working to fasten its jaws on his leg, and tapped it gingerly. A moment later he smacked it harder, and the shark turned its head away; another hit and it thrashed its head from side to side, snapped its jaws on empty air and dove under the surface.

Saufatu reached the man a few minutes later, closing his mouth to avoid inhaling the bloody water. The man looked pale, but surprisingly composed given what he had just been through. He put his right arm around Saufatu's shoulder and kicked his legs weakly.

"Not that way," Saufatu said, shaking his head. "Past here it's all algorithmic. Just let me pull you."

The man nodded and then coughed, spitting out seawater. "Thanks," he said.

Saufatu said nothing, concentrating on his strokes as he drew the man back to shore. He helped the man out onto the beach, watching him carefully to make sure he did not have any more water in his lungs, and then leaned him against a tree. Saufatu picked up his clothes from where he had left them, and the jug of toddy he had left there as well. He went back to the man, handed him the jug, and set to work tearing up his shirt into bandages for the wounds on the man's leg. Luckily they were not deep, and had already been cleaned by the seawater; he was unlikely to carry them with him when he left.

The man took a swig of toddy, and then another. "Thanks again," the man said. "I'm Craig, by the way. Craig Kettner."

"Saufatu Pelesala," Saufatu said. He glanced out at the sea. "We don't get many visitors here."

"I can see that," Craig said, "what with the welcoming committee and all. You really should put a sign up or something, warn people before they go swimming."

"It's only instanced in that spot," Saufatu said. "People know not to go there unless they want to experience it."

Craig frowned. "Why would they want to?"

"It's a memory. That's where it happened." He gestured out towards the sea. "Or so I'm told. Apisai Lotoala, he was one of the last people to grow up here—he was attacked by a shark right out there, so that's where I put the memory."

"And that's how he got out of it? By hitting the shark on the nose?"

Saufatu shrugged. "That's what he always said. All I know is, I've seen the scars."

Craig nodded slowly. "So—what is this place, anyway?"

"You came here. Didn't you know where you were going?"

He shook his head. "I just picked it by random, pretty much. I look for . . . low-traffic sites. Mostly places that are basically empty, or abandoned. I didn't expect anybody else to be here, to be honest with you."

"Neither did I."

"So—what is this place? Why are you encoding instanced shark attacks?"

"This is my home," Saufatu said. "The Eight Islands were very very low, too low when the waters rose. So my family was given the salanga of taking a record of them, as best we could."

Craig looked along the beach from left to right, his head nodding slightly. "And it's all like this, full immersive dreaming?"

Saufatu shook his head. "We were able to record some of the other islands immersively, but this one is mostly 2-D. I was able to convert some of it, like this beach, but the algorithms are expensive."

"What did you use?" Craig asked, crouching down and running his hand over the white, fine-grained sand appraisingly.

"Extrapolator 7," Saufatu said. "Price was an issue," he added, shrugging slightly.

"What about the shark attack? How did you record that?"

"I build the instanced events myself based on stories people tell me, or records in the old newspapers."

"Why?" Craig broke into a grin, held up a hand. "Sorry, I don't mean to be rude."

"We do it to remember," Saufatu said. "So there would be a record of our home."

Craig looked up and down the beach. "So where is everybody?"

"They have their own lives," Saufatu said. "They know it is here, and they tell me their stories to help build it."

"And who pays for it? This must all take up a lot of headspace."

Saufatu sighed. "There is some money. A fund—we had a lucky name, when they handed out the Web addresses, that other people wanted to buy. Of course most of it went to resettle our people, but there is enough left to do a little, for a little while."

Craig nodded. "Listen, I run this—it's like a guide, to interesting places in the Web, places my scouts and I find that not too many people know about. I think people would be really interested in a place like this."

"I don't know," Saufatu said. "We never had many tourists, even when we were above water."

"But that's just it. This place is *real*, you know, not just another dream with the same old tricks. If people were coming here you could maybe get funding from UNESCO, or the WikiHistory Foundation. Not just to keep the place going but make it better—emotion-encode the events, get custom algorithms." He took a breath, shook his head. "Listen, just think about it. If you decide you're interested, let me know."

Craig held out his right hand, and after a moment Saufatu took it: Craig's PID crossed the handshake, to be logged in Saufatu's terminal. Then Craig gave a small wave, and turned to walk back to the entry portal at the edge of the beach; Saufatu waited until he had gone, and then woke up.

Losi was already gone when Saufatu emerged from his room, so he boiled a kipper, cut it out of the plastic and put it on his plate next to a half-can of pulaka. They had been close when she had been younger—mother-uncles and sister-nieces typically were, compared to the more formal relationships between parents and children and the taboo on cousins mixing—but since she had entered her teens she spent nearly all her time in her room or out of the house.

When he went outside he saw that she had left the truck. That was good for him, since it meant he didn't have to face the long bus ride from Waitakere down to his shift at the Auckland airport, but he couldn't help wondering who she had caught a ride with. He sent her a text, offering to pick her up when his shift was done, then got into the truck.

Traffic was worse than usual that morning, spreading out from downtown as far as the Mangere Bridge. It was still faster than the bus, though, and he had time for a coffee-and-toddy with a gang of the other Islanders before his shift started. There were maybe a dozen of them who worked at the airport, though the precise numbers shifted fairly often. Mostly they talked about nothing—work and fishing and the kilikiti matches—and sometimes, when Saufatu closed his eyes, he almost felt the water around him, like they were all standing hip-deep in the Funafala lagoon.

They all finished their coffee before it began to get cold and queued up at the security check. Saufatu's heart sank when he saw a new officer at the security kiosk, and he moved ahead of the others. When he got to the kiosk he took out his DP card and held it out.

The security guard, a ruddy-faced man in his twenties with buzz-cut hair, squinted at the card. Finally he shook his head. "Refugee card's not ID," he said.

"I'm not a refugee, it's a displaced persons card," Saufatu said. He jerked his head to indicate the row of islanders behind him. "We all have them."

The guard frowned. "I have to call this in," he said. He picked up his phone and dialled it carefully, keeping a close watch on Saufatu as he whispered urgently to whoever was at the other end of the line.

Saufatu sighed. It was like this every time someone new came on at the security desk. There were more Islanders living in Auckland than anywhere else in the world, but they were still just a drop in a tremendous bucket: the city was home to thousands of migrants from all across the Pacific, all there for different reasons: guest workers on visas, refugees from the political violence on Tonga and Fiji, second- and third-generation residents and citizens, native Maori, and people like him, whom the UN had provisionally declared Displaced Persons.

Finally the guard put down his telephone and waved Saufatu through. The other islanders followed slowly, as the guard took each one's DP card and scrutinized it carefully before letting him pass. When they were all through Saufatu headed towards the baggage terminal, noticing when he saw the Arrivals board that he was fully ten minutes late for his shift—half an hour's pay gone thanks to the new man at the security desk. He kept his pace up all morning, so that by noon he was ahead of schedule and could take a few minutes to watch the planes take off.

That was how he had gotten into the business: as a boy he had watched the flights that landed and took off from Funafuti's airstrip every day, watching the planes get smaller and smaller until they looked like frigate birds. Even when he was grown and working at the tiny airport he would sometimes think about flying away on one, visiting all of the places he had seen in the travel magazines visitors left behind. When the time finally came for everyone to leave, though, the airstrip was under water and they all went on old freighters that stank like septic pits and crawled like snails across the ocean. Then, when his sister and brother-in-law had left Auckland to join the Extraterritorial Government in New York, he had stayed to carry out the family's salanga, gathering stories and memories from the expats to build the virtual islands. Only Losi, just ten at the time, had stayed with him: "The surfing sucks in New York," she had said.

She was surfing when he came to pick her up, off a beach in Maori Bay that was studded with black volcanic rock. The road ended at the beach, no parking lot, so he just set the parking brake and leaned out the door, watching as she rode her board into the oncoming breakers, a little bit differently each time—hitting the waves a bit higher or lower, cutting left or right once she was riding a swell. It didn't look much like fun to him, but perhaps the fun part had been earlier in the day. The sun was low on the horizon behind her, and as it turned to red Saufatu began to get a headache; finally he honked the truck's horn, twice, and a few minutes after that he could see her paddling her board back to shore.

Once Losi was out of the water she unzipped her wetsuit, peeled it off and rolled it into a messy ball. She stood on the beach in her black one-piece as a man with kneelength shorts and a ball cap came to meet her; she reached up to the back of her neck, detached the recording module from her 'jack and handed it to him. The man touched his pico to the module, downloading everything she had experienced that day so it could be cut up in bits, stripped to pure sensation and plugged into surfing dreams.

A blond-haired boy wearing a wetsuit that was unzipped to the waist came up and gave Losi a hug; she leaned close to say something to him, said goodbyes to all the other white boys crowded around them and then finally gave a wave to Saufatu and started towards the truck.

"Good day?" he asked as she climbed into the truck, shoving her crumpled wetsuit under her seat.

She shrugged. "Caught some good waves this morning."

Saufatu started the truck, shifted gears and worked at getting it turned around. He noticed a long scrape down her left shoulder. "Looks more like they caught you."

"I spent a little time up at the north end of the beach, getting knocked into the rocks."

"On purpose?"

"Someone's gotta do it."

"I didn't see that white boy doing it," he said, looking straight ahead.

She laughed. "Are you kidding? He got bashed twice as hard."

"If you say so." Saufatu was quiet for a few moments, watching for the turn back to the highway from Muriwai Road. "That reminds me, I met a fella last night who made me think of you—he was out swimming and ran into Apisai Lotoala's shark attack."

"What, a tourist?"

"Not exactly, I don't think. He said he goes looking for low-traffic places—his name was Craig Kemper, I think. Heard of him?"

She shook her head, then stopped. "Wait. Craig *Kettner*?"

"Yes. Yes, that's it."

"How can you not know who that is?" Losi asked. "What was he doing in the Islands, anyway?"

Saufatu shrugged. "He said people would like to visit them. Do a lot of people follow him?"

"Enough to crash your server," she said. "God, I can't believe you sometimes."

"Well, he asked to see the rest of the Islands—you can come if you want, show him yourself."

She nodded slowly—trying, he could tell, to stay cool. "All right," she said, and smiled.

There was a fatele that night, just a small one, in Donald Tuatu's back yard. Saufatu went over after supper, filled a plastic coconut-half from the bowl of toddy and inched around the periphery of the party. There were no singers, just an old boom box, but a few teenage boys were dancing out the lyrics, two from one side of their "village" squaring off against three from the other.

Saufatu spotted Apisai Lotoala sitting nearby, filled up another coconut half and headed towards him. He was a big man, still powerfully built despite his age, and the old folding chair he was sitting on buckled beneath him. He was wearing shorts and a short-sleeved shirt and the scars on his leg shone white in the moonlight.

"Here," Saufatu said, carefully handing him the coconut shell. "You looked dry."

Apisai drained the shell he was holding, set it on the ground and took Saufatu's. "Ta," he said, and tipped it back.

"Fella ran into your shark last night."

"Oh? What'd he do that for?"

Saufatu shook his head. "Didn't know it was there. He's not an Islander—American, I think."

"He get out all right?"

"Sure. I told him to bop it on the nose, just like you did." Saufatu took a drink of his toddy. "Look, I may be getting a chance to upgrade the Islands some. I'm going to need you to help me fill in Niulakiti."

Apisai shook his head. "I told you everything I can remember. I wasn't there long, you know—off on a freighter at sixteen, like all my mates. Ask me about that, I could talk all day."

"Saufatu!" Apisai's wife Margaret had spotted them talking and now came over. She was almost as tall as he was and wore a flower-print dress that fell in straight lines from her shoulders to her ankles. "Saufatu, where is that niece of yours? I haven't seen her in years, it feels like."

"She turned in early," Saufatu said. He tapped the back of his neck. "She surfs—records how it feels, they sell it to the dreamcasters. A whole day of it tires her out."

"But how is she going to meet a boy?" Margaret asked. "You know the ones her age, they're all getting jobs, in the city or on the ships." She turned to her husband. "She's so busy, we're going to have to find her someone nice. Can you think of anyone?"

"Leave me out of this," Apisai said.

"She's coming with me to the Islands tomorrow night," Saufatu said. "You can come too, if you like. I mean, you can come anytime—it's all for you."

"Oh, Saufatu, I don't know how you have the energy for those dreams," Margaret said. "You must have it very easy at the airport. I have to be up at five to go and clean my houses."

Saufatu turned to Apisai, who had been retired for nearly a decade now. "Well?"

Apisai shrugged and took another drink of his toddy.

Before going to bed Saufatu sent Kettner a text, suggesting they meet again the next night. He disabled the real-time lock and then went from island to island, planning the tour he would give to Kettner and Losi.

To his surprise, Losi was still there when he got up: even more surprising she was in the kitchen, boiling a bag of kippers and heating a bowl of pulaka in the microwave. "Good morning," she said, putting a plate and fork down as he sat at the table.

"Good morning."

If Losi noticed his bemusement, she showed no sign of it; instead she pulled the bag out of the boiling water with tongs, cut it open and slid the reddish fish onto his plate, getting to the microwave just as it began to beep. "How was your night?" she asked.

"Fine," Saufatu said. He flaked off a piece of kipper with his fork and chewed it slowly. "Fine. Thank you.'"

She spooned a pile of hot pulaka onto his plate. "Have you heard from Craig Kettner?"

Saufatu shook his head. "Not in the night. I haven't checked my texts this morning, though." He took another bite of the salty fish, chewed it thoughtfully. "Do you need a ride this morning?"

"Are you sure you have time?"

He nodded. "Sure. Just let me finish up and let's go."

"Sure." She smiled, then turned to put the empty bowl of pulaka in the sink. "Do you have time to check your texts first?"

Luckily she was recording at Karekare Beach that day, a bit nearer to home than where he had picked her up the day before; luckier still the regular security guard was back on duty and waved him right through, so that he was only twenty minutes late and short an hour's pay. He checked his texts before starting work and found one from Kettner, agreeing to meet him on the Islands that night (though of course it would be morning for Kettner, if he lived in America.) After that the day went quickly, his mind barely registering the bags he moved from plane to carousel as he rehearsed the tour he had planned.

When his shift was done he picked Losi up from the beach, smiled at the way her eyes lit up when he told her about the text from Kettner; she was nearly bouncing in her seat the whole ride home, and throughout supper she pressed him for details on his first meeting with Kettner. Finally it was time to hook up their dreamlinks and go to sleep; after the usual moment of wild dreaming the REM regulator kicked in and they both found themselves on the pink sand at the tip of Funafala, the narrowest inhabited island in the Funafuti group, where they could see both the lagoon and the western islands and east to the open sea. It was also home to the village where he had grown up, and most of the landscape was drawn from his own childhood memories: thick stands of coconut trees, huts with thatched or sheet-metal roofs; and the wrecks of small boats that he and his friends had used as forts and playhouses. Kettner was already there, looking at a pair of small wooden boats, with outboard motors and canvas soft tops, that had been pulled up onto the beach.

Saufatu waved to him, took Losi by the hand and led her over to the boats. "Craig, thank you for coming. This is my sister-niece Losi—she does dream work, too."

"Really?" Kettner said. "What do you do?"

Losi shrugged dismissively. "I'm a recorder—we just do B-roll, you know, generic surfing stuff, but Brian—that's the guy I work with—

he's an indie dreamcaster. Whenever we have enough time and money we record some more."

Kettner nodded appraisingly. "That's great. Why don't you give me your demo reel, I'll check it out."

"Cool," Losi said, smiling. "Yeah, I will, cool." She held out a hand, and after a moment Kettner reached out to shake it.

"Do you mind if I take some recordings?" Kettner asked. "Just samples, to show people what I'm talking about."

"I can do it," Losi said. "If that's all right with you, Uncle."

Saufatu nodded quickly. "Yes, all right."

Before he had finished speaking she was in the water, making a long and shallow dive out towards the wrecks in the distance. Kettner watched for a few moments as she crested the low waves, then turned to Saufatu. "So what am I seeing here?"

"This is where I grew up," Saufatu said. "It's the southernmost island of the biggest atoll. All the islands in this group ring around Te Namo—that's the lagoon, there—the swimming's good here, on both sides, and there's reef snorkelling too."

"Your niece mentioned surfing?"

Saufatu shook his head. "We never did that here. Losi, she grew up in Auckland—her dad worked for the consulate there—and those kiwis are mad for it. You get bigger waves on the sea side of the western islands, but we always stayed in the lagoon where it's safe."

"Safe?"

"Well, except for the sharks."

For the rest of the night Saufatu led Losi and Kettner around the islands—carefully avoiding Fogafale, where paved roads and cement houses spread out from the airstrip to fill every inch of the island in a thick sprawl; though he had recorded it accurately, he suspected it was not the side of the Islands that Kettner thought his followers would want to see. Instead he took them up to the five small islands in the Conservation Area on the western side of Te Namo, where there were good-quality instanced interactions with green turtles and fairy terns. The World Wildlife Fund had financed the recording of these atolls, which was why they had more detail and interactive features than the inhabited islands. Only Tepuka Savilivi, the sixth and smallest island, had had to be reconstructed from tourist photos and satellite maps; it had been swamped before the recording began, the first of the islands to sink entirely.

Everywhere they went Losi recorded samples—diving in the warm, shallow water of the lagoon, climbing trees to cut down coconuts and peering close at terns that hovered curiously in front of her, hanging in the air just inches from her face before flitting away into the trees. Saufatu ended the tour in Nanumea, where they could see the wrecks of small ships just offshore from the village and, out towards the horizon, the rusting hull of the *John Williams*.

"That's a US Navy cargo ship—the Japanese sank it in the war," Saufatu said.

"Can we go out there?" Kettner asked.

"To the ones near shore, yes, but not the big one," Saufatu said. He threw a look at Losi. "It's still there, though, just a little bit further under water. Someone could go out there and record it, if we had the money."

"This is really remarkable," Kettner said. "I can't believe nobody knows about it."

"Nobody knew about the Islands before they sank," Losi snorted.

"I never tried to publicize it," Saufatu said. "It's really just meant— for our people, you know. But if you think that this can bring some money in—make it so more of us can be involved in upgrading it . . ."

Kettner shrugged. "I can't promise that, but I do think a lot of people will be interested in seeing this. So much of what's out there is so fake, you know? But this really lets you feel what it was like to live here." He held up a hand. "I won't do anything unless you're sure you're okay with it, though. This is your baby."

Saufatu looked over at Losi, then nodded. "Yes," he said. "Go ahead."

"Great—I can do a preview reel from the stuff Losi captured, and I'll let you know when the piece is going to run," Kettner said. "You might want to rent more server space."

Losi spent most of the next day locked in her room, carefully culling the footage she had recorded—Saufatu told her that Kettner would surely edit it himself, but she said she wanted him to be picking between good, better and best—only emerging more than an hour after he came home from the airport to eat a reheated bowl of mackerel and breadfruit and then crash in dreamless sleep.

Saufatu had hesitated to tell other Islanders about this business with Kettner, unsure what they would think about a bunch of foreigners coming to the Islands, but when he saw Kettner's "preview reel" he knew he had to share it—proud of the work he had done in conserving the Islands, of course, but also of Losi's work in capturing it. The footage had not been stripped and sliced, unlike her usual work, so that it captured not just what she had experienced but how she had felt about it as well. It had all been as new for her as it had been for Kettner, and her joy in swimming, climbing and exploring was clear— not to mention her evident pleasure at showing off. He forwarded the preview to everyone on his mailing list, along with an invitation to join them when Kettner did his show two nights later.

The next day was Saturday, Saufatu's day off, and he suggested to Losi that they go out to the beach together. They had not done this in a long time, not since she tired of the calm and shallow water he preferred, but she gathered up the towels and picnic gear and brought them to the truck—stopping, he noticed, every few minutes to check her texts.

She was silent most of the way out, distracted, and he didn't push her to talk; the truth was that he felt much the same way, thinking about how things might change for the Islands. They spent all morning in the water, swimming and bodysurfing on the gentle waves, then lay out their lunch and tucked into their sandwiches.

"I'm glad your friends could spare you," he said, looking out at the clear sky and whitecapped sea.

Losi shrugged. "They're going to have to get used to it," she said. "All the stuff I do for Brian is stripped and sliced, so he can replace me easily enough if he has to."

"Would it be nice, doing work that has a bit more meaning to it?" Saufatu asked. "More of *you* in it?"

She shrugged, then nodded, and looked away; they finished their lunch in silence and then went back into the water, swimming against the waves until they were tired enough to be sure they would sleep.

Losi spent the whole trip back leaning out the window, her right knee bouncing and her left hand tapping the seat. Before he had even turned off the engine she was out of the truck and running to the door of the house.

Saufatu set the parking brake and drew the keys out the ignition. He was just climbing out of the truck when he heard her shouting from inside; he ran to the house, not bothering to lock the truck, and met her at the door. "What's going on?" he asked.

"It's Craig," she said. "He just texted me. He wants me to be one of his scouts."

"What?"

"I mean, I knew he liked my footage when he didn't strip it, but I wasn't sure—you know, I mean, *every*body wants to scout for him—"

"But—" Saufatu frowned. "What about the Islands?"

Losi frowned too, cocking her head. "What about them?"

"I thought—Kettner said he thought we could get funding to finish the Islands, upgrade them. I thought you could help me with that."

"I'm—I'm sorry, Uncle," she said. "I just can't pass this up. This is—I'll never get a better chance. And it's work I can do from here, I won't be moving—not right away, anyway."

"And what will I tell your father? What will he say when he hears you're just giving up on your duty?"

"He'll probably be glad I won't waste my life, building some crazy fantasyland nobody but you cares about," Losi said. She glared at him for another second, her jaw set, then turned and ran back into the house.

Saufatu stood for a long moment, shaking his head slowly, then turned at a noise behind him. Apisai Lotoala was standing in front of his house, looking uncomfortable. "Everything all right?" he asked.

"I'm sorry you had to hear that."

Apisai shrugged. "I have a son, you know. They're all the same at that age."

"No, it's—it's more than that. She was never interested before, in any of it, and then when she wanted to come see the Islands I thought . . ."

"Nobody's interested in home, not at that age. None of us could wait to leave the Islands." Apisai shrugged. "Maybe it would have been different if we'd known we could never go home, but I don't expect so."

"But you can," Saufatu said. "Come tomorrow night, you'll see. And we're going to make it even better, it'll be just like being there."

"I know what that's like," Apisai said, then held up a hand before Saufatu could respond. "Fine, fine—I'll be there."

Losi's door was shut when Saufatu went inside, and his hand hovered over it, ready to knock; after a long moment he took a breath and let it drop to his side. What could he say to her? He had thought she didn't care because she had grown up here, had never known the Islands, but he had to face the fact that none of the ones who had grown up there cared either. He sat down at the kitchen table and started to write a text to Kettner, to get him to cancel his visit: it felt like a fraud now, absurd to think that a virtual reconstruction could give someone any sense of what it was like to be an Islander. For the tourists, it would be nothing more than another fantasyland, like Losi had said; for the Islanders it was just a dusty photo album.

Saufatu's hand hesitated over his pico's airboard; after a moment he waved it back and forth to cancel the message, then picked up the pico and took it to his room. He hooked his 'jack up to the dreamlink and then forced himself to go to sleep and get to work.

Saufatu walked down the Niulakiti beach to the shore, dodging tourists as they ran back and forth across the sand. He had seen them all over the Eight Islands, walking along the beaches, watching the fearless birds, swimming out to the wrecks—everything that had been in Kettner's preview reel.

Apisai Lotoala was at the shore, standing just ankle-deep in the water and surrounded by a knot of Islanders who were all chatting together, drinking toddy from plastic milk jugs and casting occasional glances out to sea. So far as the Islanders were concerned, this was no more meaningful than a backyard fatele; Apisai waved to him as he neared but Saufatu just nodded back, not feeling any need to be humoured.

He spotted Kettner and Losi about a half-mile out, near where the shark attack was instanced: he thought he recognized the blond boy who had been surfing with Losi out there as well. He waved, and Kettner and Losi began to make their way back to shore.

"What did I tell you?" Kettner said as he walked out of the water. Losi followed a few steps behind, her eyes lowered. "They love it."

"It's very gratifying," Saufatu said.

Kettner laughed. "I'm glad you think so," he said, and shook his head.

Losi tapped Kettner on the arm. "Listen," she said, "I'm going to go, okay? Text me."

"No, wait," Saufatu said. He took a step past Kettner, looked her in the eye. "Just stay, a little longer. Please."

"Uncle—"

Suddenly there was a noise, a deep note like someone blowing on a conch shell. A ship had appeared out on the water—or rather dozens of instances of the same ship, a battered old freighter that hauled itself slowly towards every shore of the Eight Islands.

A moment later and tourists and Islanders alike were aboard the ship, packed tight on the decks or else peering out of the portholes below. From there they could see the deep-water wharf at the north end of Fogafale and beyond to the narrow streets and concrete buildings where most of the Islands' people had lived for the last fifty years.

There was no water on the ground; this was no sunken city, no drowned Atlantis—only an island that had become too low and too salty to be inhabitable, just one more of the thousands of lifeless atolls that dotted the Pacific.

Kettner was at his elbow. "This is what it was like, isn't it?" he asked. "When you left."

Saufatu nodded. He saw Apisai Lotoala leaning out over the rail, his head turning in wide arcs from side to side and his eyes gleaming with tears. Of course his people hadn't needed the simulated Islands: every one of them already had an unchanged memory of their home the way it used to be. What they had not had, until now, was a chance to say goodbye.

The ship's horn blew again, two sharp blasts, and it began to move away from the wharf. Saufatu turned to see Losi standing behind him. "I'm sorry, Uncle," she said.

"Don't be. You were right."

"But you're not—sinking it? Everything you did?"

"No," Saufatu said. "It'll still be here, for people to see what it was like before—or to help people remember. But this will be the only way to leave."

"Listen," she said, "I could help out for awhile, if you like. I'm sure Kettner would understand."

He shook his head. "Do you know, when our people left Tonga and Samoa they thought everywhere in the ocean had been settled? But they set out again into the open sea, just to see what was out there." He took a deep breath. "Go with Kettner. See what's out there."

She nodded, and they both turned back to look over the side. The wharf and the islands beyond it were moving away in accelerated time, shrinking and then finally fading from view, lost in the trackless ocean.

the best canadian speculative writing

IMAGINARIUM
2013

honourable mentions

Files, Gemma. "Gabbeh," *World Fantasy Convention Souvenir Book*

Forest, Susan. "7:54," *On Spec*, Summer 2012

Forest, Susan. "Killing the Cat," *Immunity to Strange Tales*

Gavin, Richard. "The Word-Made Flesh," *At Fear's Altar*

Gavin, Richard. "Annexation," *Cthulhu 2012*

Gavin, Richard. "Darksome Leaves," *At Fear's Altar*

Ghaznavi, Yaqoob. "Kin," *Poet to Poet*

Goldberg, Kim. "Codex Exterminarius," *Igniting the Green Fuse: Four Canadian Women Poets*

Hannett, Lisa L. & Slatter, Angela. "Of the Demon and the Drum," *Midnight & Moonshine*

Hannett, Lisa L. & Slatter, Angela. "Burning Seaweed from Salt," *Midnight & Moonshine*

Hannett, Lisa L. & Slatter, Angela. "Prohibition Blues," *Damnation and Dames*

Hannett, Lisa L. & Slatter, Angela. "The Red Wedding," *Midnight & Moonshine*

Hoffman, Ada. "Mama's Sword," *Blood Iris 2012*

Hoffman, Ada. "Sage and Coco," *Kazka Press, Volume 2, Issue 2*

Janz, Kristin. "Clear Skies in Pixieland," *Nine: A Journal of Imaginative Fiction, Issue 1*

Johanson, Karl. "The Airlock Scene," *Here Be Monsters 7: Tongues and Teeth*

Johnson, Matthew. "The Afflicted," *Fantasy & Science Fiction Magazine*

Kelly, Michael. "October Dreams," *Supernatural Tales #22*

Kelly, Michael. "The White-Face at Dawn," *A Season in Carcosa*

Kennedy, J.Y.T. "Fingernails," *Danse Macabre: Close Encounters with the Reaper*

Keyes, David. "The House of Sleep," *I Do So Worry for All Those Lost at Sea*

Keyes, David. "Lost at Sea," *I Do So Worry for All Those Lost at Sea*

King, Barry. "Pythia," *The Colored Lens, Issue 3*

Künsken, Derek. "The Way of the Needle," *Asimov's Science Fiction*, March 2012

Lalumière, Claude. "The Secondary 4 Class of Prettygood Park High School," *Ride the Moon*

Lalumière, Claude. "The Ministry of Sacred Affairs," *Here Be Monsters 7: Tongues and Teeth*

Larson, Rich. "Like Any Other Star," *AE: The Canadian Science Fiction Review*

Larson, Rich. "Strings," *Here Be Monsters 7: Tongues and Teeth*

Laycraft, Adria. "The Agreement," *James Gunn's Ad Astra*

Macleod, Selene. "Home," *December Dead Dreamers Vol. 2*

Marshall, Helen. "Dead White Men," *Hair Side, Flesh Side*

Marshall, Helen. "In the High Places of the World," *Hair Side, Flesh Side*

Marshall, Helen. "The Mouth, Open," *Hair Side, Flesh Side*

Marshall, Helen. "No Ghosts in London," *Hair Side, Flesh Side*

Marshall, Helen. "Sanditon," *Hair Side, Flesh Side*

Marshall, Helen. "This Feeling of Flying," *Hair Side, Flesh Side*

Marshall, Helen. "Leda's Daughter," *Abyss & Apex, Issue #41*

Matheson, Michael. "Rebirth," *Aoife's Kiss, Issue #41*

Matheson, Michael. "White Noise," *Lovecraft eZine, Issue #10*

Meikle, William. "Growth," *Nature (Futures) #488*

Meikle, William. "The Mill Dance," *Dark Melodies*

Meikle, William. "Out of the Black," *Fading Light*

Merriam, Joanne. "The Candy Aisle," *Journal of Unlikely Entomology,*
    Issue #4

Moore, Matt. "But It's Not the End," *Undead Tales 2*

Moore, Matt. "Delta Pi," *Torn Realities*

Moreland, Sean. "Unrah, Late of Old Vegas," *The Peter F. Yacht Club*

Moreno-Garcia, Silvia. "The Performance," *Journal of Unlikely Entomology,*
    Issue #3

Morin, Hugues. "i-Robot," *Solaris 184* (trans. Sheryl Curtis)

Parisien, Dominik "A Mask Is Not a Face," *Goblin Fruit*, Summer 2012

Parisien, Dominik "In His Eighty-Second Year," *Stone Telling 7*

Parisien, Dominik "My Dead Hands Lover, I'm Leaving You,"
    Through the Gate 1

Perron, Kristene. "Lucky Me," *Denizens of the Dark*

Pflug, Ursula. "Casteroides," *Stone Telling 8*

Pflug-Back, Kelly Rose. "Hepatomancy," *These Burning Streets*

Pi, Tony. "The Miscible Imp," *When the Villain Comes Home*

Pi, Tony. "Remains of the Witch," *Orson Scott Card's InterGalactic*
    Medicine Show #26

Pi, Tony. "Susumu Must Fold," *Daily Science Fiction*

Rayner, Mark A. "Nude Clanking Down a Staircase,"
    Pirate Therapy and Other Cures

Rayner, Mark A. "The Wonderful Thing About Tautologies,"
    Pirate Therapy and Other Cures

Reynolds, Tim. "Dragons in Suburbia,"
    Mytherium: Tales of Mythical and Magical Creatures

Richildis, Ranylt. "Long After the Greeks," *Postscripts to Darkness II*

Ridler, Jason S. "Rikidōzan and the San Diego Swerve Job,"
    FriendsMerrilContest.com
Roberts, Angela. "A Song for Death," *Danse Macabre:*
    Close Encounters with the Reaper
Rogers, Ian. "Autumnology," *Every House Is Haunted*
Rogers, Ian. "The Cat," *Every House Is Haunted*
Rogers, Ian. "Deleted Scenes," *Every House Is Haunted*
Rogers, Ian. "The House on Ashley Avenue," *Every House Is Haunted*
Rogers, Ian. "Hunger," *Every House Is Haunted*
Rogers, Ian. "Midnight Blonde," *Supernatural Tales #22*
Rowe, Michael. "Loon Voices Calling in the Distance,"
    World Fantasy Convention Souvenir Book
Schnarr, J.W. "Anna's Jar of Hurts," *Things Falling Apart*
Schnarr, J.W. "Dorothy of Kansas," *Things Falling Apart*
Schnarr, J.W. "The Matchstick Man," *Things Falling Apart*
Schnarr, J.W. & Sunseri, John. "Sunlight & Shadows," *Things Falling Apart*
Senese, Rebecca M. "Moon Dream," *Ride the Moon*
Smith, Douglas. "The Walker of the Shifting Borderland,"
    On Spec, Fall 2012
Smith, Julian Mortimer. "The Mugger's Hymn,"
    AE: The Canadian Science Fiction Review
Soulban, Lucien. "The Four Horsemen Reunion Tour: An Apocumentary,"
    Blood Lite III: Aftertaste
Stanton, Steve. "Saturday Night in Saskatchewan," *Perihelion Science*
    Fiction Magazine, October 2012
Steiner, Tarquin. "Cobbled," *Here Be Monsters 7: Tongues and Teeth*
Storey, Mags. "Being Cherry Red," *Fearsome Fables*
Strantzas, Simon. "Swallow," *Slices of Flesh*
Sutherland, Joel A. "Fade," *Cemetery Dance Magazine*, Issue 67
Sutherland, Joel A. "Blood-Red Greens," *Blood Lite III: Aftertaste*
Wise, A.C. "The Book of Little Deaths," *Jabberwocky 14*
Youers, Rio. "The Happy Bird and Other Tales," *21st Century Dead*

copyright acknowledgements

about the editors

SANDRA KASTURI is a writer, editor, book reviewer and the co-publisher of World Fantasy Award-nominated ChiZine Publications and co-creator of the children's animated series, *Sinister Horde*. Sandra's work has won several prizes for writing, including the Whittaker Prize and first prize in *ARC Poetry Magazine*'s 10th Annual Poem of the Year Contest. Her book reviews have appeared in *The Globe & Mail*, *The National Post* and *The Toronto Star*. She has written three poetry chapbooks and has edited the poetry anthology, *The Stars As Seen from this Particular Angle of Night*. She is the author of two poetry collections, *The Animal Bridegroom* (2007), which featured an introduction from Neil Gaiman, and *Come Late to the Love of Birds* (2012), both from Tightrope Books. Sandra's fiction and poetry has appeared in various magazines and anthologies, including *Prairie Fire*; *CV2*; *On Spec*; *Taddle Creek*; various *Tesseracts* anthologies, *2001: A Science Fiction Poetry Anthology*; *Northern Frights 4*; *Girls Who Bite Back: Witches, Slayers, Mutants and Freaks*; *Shadows & Tall Trees*; *Evolve*; *Evolve 2*; *Chilling Tales*; and *Chilling Tales Two*. She is fond of Manhattans without the cherry, and Michael Fassbender, who can have a cherry or not, as he likes.

SAMANTHA BEIKO has worked in the Canadian publishing industry for the past three years in various capacities, first in marketing and publicity, and now in editorial and layout design. She has had the opportunity to acquire and edit some remarkable books, and is thrilled to have been able to edit *Imaginarium 2013: The Best Canadian Speculative Writing*, with Sandra Kasturi. Samantha is also an emerging author, and her first book, a YA fantasy novel called *The Lake and the Library*, came out with ECW Press in Spring 2013. She currently resides in Winnipeg, Manitoba, and is working to broaden the speculative fiction community there through her writing and publishing work.

CHIZINEPUB.COM

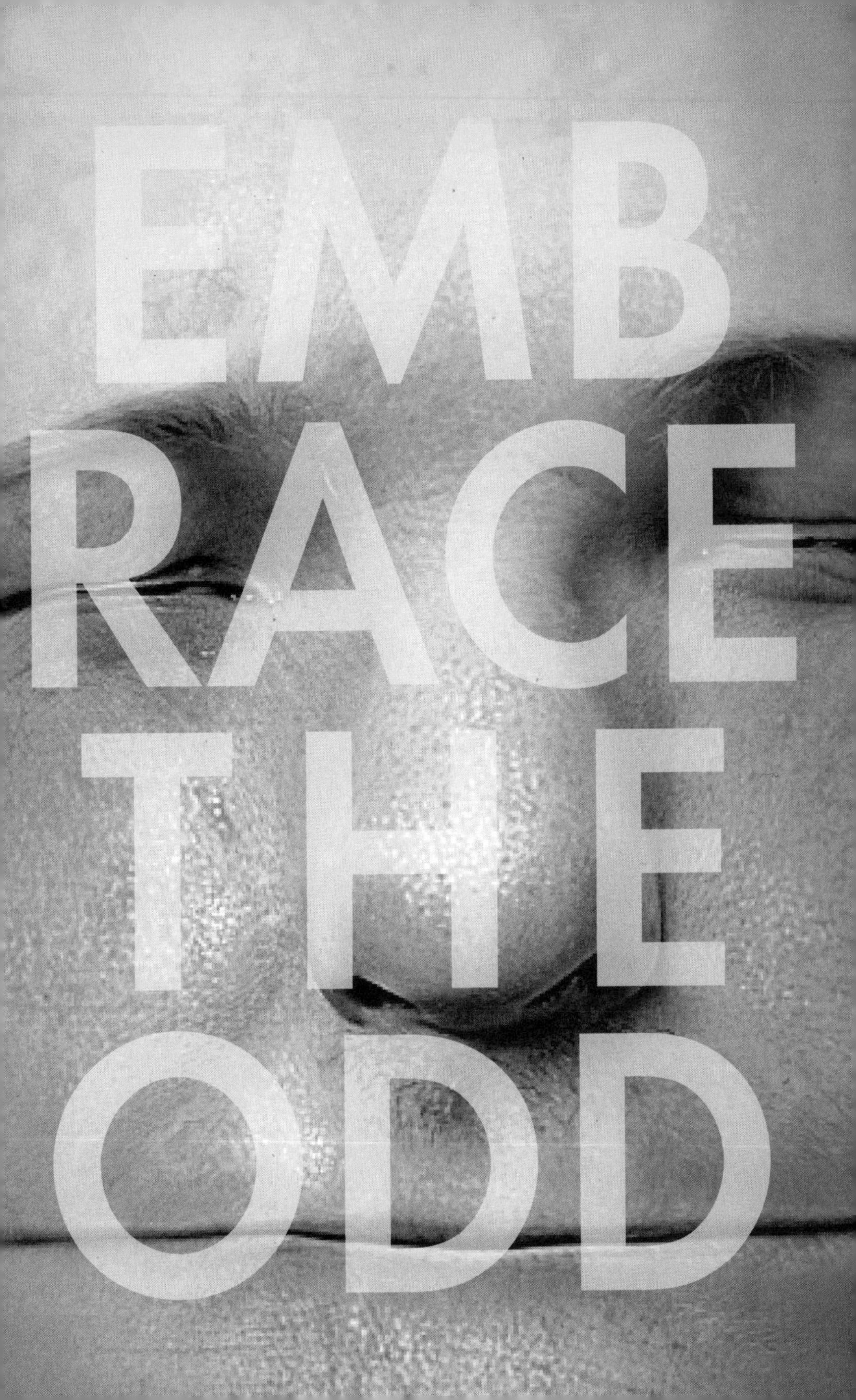
EMB
RACE
THE
ODD

THE INNER CITY
KAREN HEULER

Anything is possible: people breed dogs with humans to create a servant class; beneath one great city lies another city, running it surreptitiously; an employee finds that her hair has been stolen by someone intent on getting her job; strange fish fall from trees and birds talk too much; a boy tries to figure out what he can get when the Rapture leaves good stuff behind. Everything is familiar; everything is different. Behind it all, is there some strange kind of design or merely just the chance to adapt? In Karen Heuler's stories, characters cope with the strange without thinking it's strange, sometimes invested in what's going on, sometimes trapped by it, but always finding their own way in.

AVAILABLE NOW
978-1-927469-33-0

GOLDENLAND PAST DARK
CHANDLER KLANG SMITH

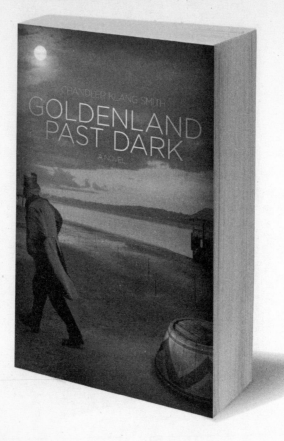

A hostile stranger is hunting Dr. Show's ramshackle travelling circus across 1960s America. His target: the ringmaster himself. The troupe's unravelling hopes fall on their latest and most promising recruit, Webern Bell, a sixteen-year-old hunchbacked midget devoted obsessively to perfecting the surreal clown performances that come to him in his dreams. But as they travel through a landscape of abandoned amusement parks and rural ghost towns, Webern's bizarre past starts to pursue him, as well.

AVAILABLE NOW
978-1-927469-35-4

ZOMBIE VERSUS FAIRY FEATURING ALBINOS
JAMES MARSHALL

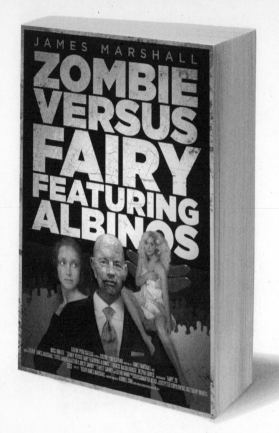

In a PERFECT world where everyone DESTROYS everything and eats HUMAN FLESH, one ZOMBIE has had enough: BUCK BURGER. When he rebels at the natural DISORDER, his marriage starts DETERIORATING and a doctor prescribes him an ANTI-DEPRESSANT. Buck meets a beautiful GREEN-HAIRED pharmacist fairy named FAIRY_26 and quickly becomes a pawn in a COLD WAR between zombies and SUPERNATURAL CREATURES. Does sixteen-year-old SPIRITUAL LEADER and pirate GUY BOY MAN make an appearance? Of course! Are there MIND-CONTROLLING ALBINOS? Obviously! Is there hot ZOMBIE-ON-FAIRY action? Maybe! WHY AREN'T YOU READING THIS YET?

AVAILABLE NOW
978-1-77148-141-0

THE MONA LISA SACRIFICE
BOOK ONE OF THE BOOK OF CROSS
PETER ROMAN

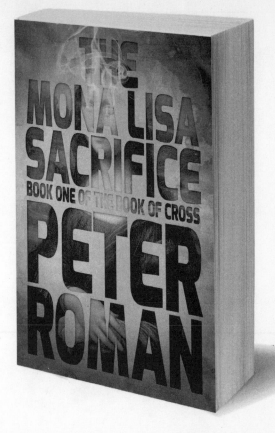

For thousands of years, Cross has wandered the earth, a mortal soul trapped in the undying body left behind by Christ. But now he must play the part of reluctant hero, as an angel comes to him for help finding the Mona Lisa—the real Mona Lisa that inspired the painting. Cross's quest takes him into a secret world within our own, populated by characters just as strange and wondrous as he is. He's haunted by memories of Penelope, the only woman he truly loved, and he wants to avenge her death at the hands of his ancient enemy, Judas. The angel promises to deliver Judas to Cross, but nothing is ever what it seems, and when a group of renegade angels looking for a new holy war show up, things truly go to hell.

AVAILABLE NOW
978-1-77148-145-8

THE 'GEISTERS
DAVID NICKLE

When Ann LeSage was a little girl, she had an invisible friend—a poltergeist, that spoke to her with flying knives and howling winds. She called it the Insect. And with a little professional help, she contained it. But the nightmare never truly ended. As Ann grew from girl into young woman, the Insect grew with her, becoming a thing of murder. Now, as she embarks on a new life married to successful young lawyer Michael Voors, Ann believes that she finally has the Insect under control. But there are others vying to take that control away from her. They may not know exactly what they're dealing with, but they know they want it. They are the 'Geisters. And in pursuing their own perverse dream, they risk spawning the most terrible nightmare of all.

AVAILABLE NOW
978-1-77148-143-4

CELESTIAL INVENTORIES
STEVE RASNIC TEM

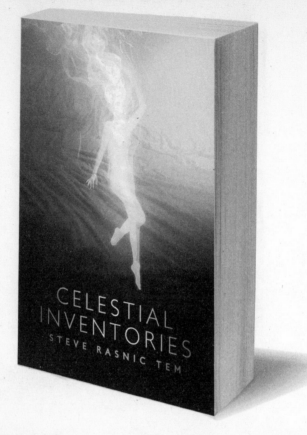

Celestial Inventories features twenty-two stories collected from rare chapbooks, anthologies, and obscure magazines, along with a new story written specifically for this volume. All represent the slipstream segment of Steve Rasnic Tem's large body of tales: imaginative, difficult-to-pigeonhole works of the fantastic crossing conventional boundaries between science fiction, fantasy, horror, literary fiction, bizarro, magic realism, and the new weird. Several of these stories have previously appeared in Best of the Year compilations and have been the recipients of major F & SF nominations and awards.

AVAILABLE AUGUST 2013
978-1-77148-165-6

TELL MY SORROWS TO THE STONES
CHRISTOPHER GOLDEN

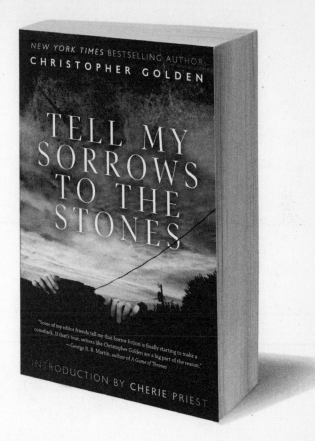

A circus clown willing to give anything to be funny. A spectral gunslinger who must teach a young boy to defend the ones he loves. A lonely widower making a farewell tour of the places that meant the world to his late wife. A faded Hollywood actress out to deprive her ex-husband of his prize possession. A grieving mother who will wait by the railroad tracks for a ghostly train that always has room for one more. A young West Virginia miner whose only hope of survival is a bedtime story. These are just some of the characters to be found in *Tell My Sorrows to the Stones*.

AVAILABLE AUGUST 2013
978-1-77148-153-3

THE DELPHI ROOM
MELIA McCLURE

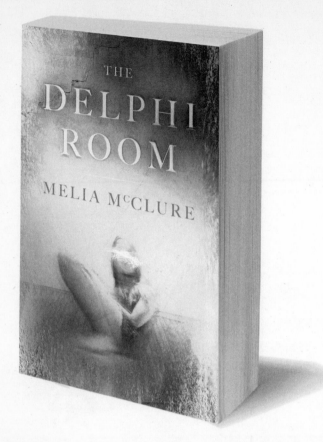

Is it possible to find love after you've died and gone to Hell? For oddball misfits Velvet and Brinkley, the answer just might be yes. After Velvet hangs herself and winds up trapped in a bedroom she believes is Hell, she comes in contact with Brinkley, the man trapped next door. Through mirrors that hang in each of their rooms, these disturbed cinemaphiles watch the past of the other unfold—the dark past that has led to their present circumstances. As their bond grows and they struggle to figure out the tragic puzzles of their lives and deaths, Velvet and Brinkley are in for more surprises. By turns quirky, harrowing, funny and surreal, *The Delphi Room* explores the nature of reality and the possibilities of love.

AVAILABLE SEPTEMBER 2013
978-1-77148-185-4

MORE FROM CHIZINE

HORROR STORY AND OTHER HORROR STORIES ROBERT BOYCZUK [978-0-9809410-3-6]

NEXUS: ASCENSION ROBERT BOYCZUK [978-0-9813746-8-0]

THE BOOK OF THOMAS: HEAVEN ROBERT BOYCZUK [978-1-927469-27-9]

PEOPLE LIVE STILL IN CASHTOWN CORNERS TONY BURGESS [978-1-926851-05-1]

THE STEEL SERAGLIO MIKE CAREY, LINDA CAREY & LOUISE CAREY [978-1-926851-53-2]

SARAH COURT CRAIG DAVIDSON [978-1-926851-00-6]

A BOOK OF TONGUES GEMMA FILES [978-0-9812978-6-6]

A ROPE OF THORNS GEMMA FILES [978-1-926851-14-3]

A TREE OF BONES GEMMA FILES [978-1-926851-57-0]

ISLES OF THE FORSAKEN CAROLYN IVES GILMAN [978-1-926851-36-5]

ISON OF THE ISLES CAROLYN IVES GILMAN [978-1-926851-56-3]

FILARIA BRENT HAYWARD [978-0-9809410-1-2]

THE FECUND'S MELANCHOLY DAUGHTER BRENT HAYWARD [978-1-926851-13-6]

IMAGINARIUM 2012: THE BEST CANADIAN SPECULATIVE WRITING
EDITED BY SANDRA KASTURI & HALLI VILLEGAS [978-1-926851-67-9]

CHASING THE DRAGON NICHOLAS KAUFMANN [978-0-9812978-4-2]

OBJECTS OF WORSHIP CLAUDE LALUMIÈRE [978-0-9812978-2-8]

THE DOOR TO LOST PAGES CLAUDE LALUMIÈRE [978-1-926851-12-9]

THE THIEF OF BROKEN TOYS TIM LEBBON [978-0-9812978-9-7]

KATJA FROM THE PUNK BAND SIMON LOGAN [978-0-9812978-7-3]

BULLETTIME NICK MAMATAS [978-1-926851-71-6]

SHOEBOX TRAIN WRECK JOHN MANTOOTH [978-1-926851-54-9]

HAIR SIDE, FLESH SIDE HELEN MARSHALL [978-1-927469-24-8]

NINJA VERSUS PIRATE FEATURING ZOMBIES JAMES MARSHALL [978-1-926851-58-7]

PICKING UP THE GHOST TONE MILAZZO [978-1-926851-35-8]

BEARDED WOMEN TERESA MILBRODT [978-1-926851-46-4]

NAPIER'S BONES DERRYL MURPHY [978-1-926851-09-9]

CHIZINEPUB.COM CZP

"IF YOUR TASTE IN FICTION RUNS TO THE DISTURBING, DARK, AND AT LEAST PARTIALLY WEIRD, CHANCES ARE YOU'VE HEARD OF CHIZINE PUBLICATIONS—CZP—A YOUNG IMPRINT THAT IS NONETHELESS PRODUCING STARTLINGLY BEAUTIFUL BOOKS OF STARKLY, DARKLY LITERARY QUALITY."

—DAVID MIDDLETON, JANUARY MAGAZINE

ALSO AVAILABLE FROM CHIZINE PUBLICATIONS

Live from Death Row

MUMIA ABU-JAMAL

Introduction by JOHN EDGAR WIDEMAN

PREFACE BY THE AUTHOR